REALM OF DRAGONS

FIGHT FOR THE CROWN

L.C. Conn

Between the Lines Publishing
410 Caribou Trail
Lutsen, MN 55612
btwnthelines.com

First Published: April 2021

ISBN: 978-1-950502-39-4 (paperback)

Library of Congress Control Number: 2021936429

Liminal Books is an imprint of Between the Lines Publishing.
The Liminal Books name and logo are trademarks of Between the Lines Publishing.

REALM OF DRAGONS

FIGHT FOR THE CROWN

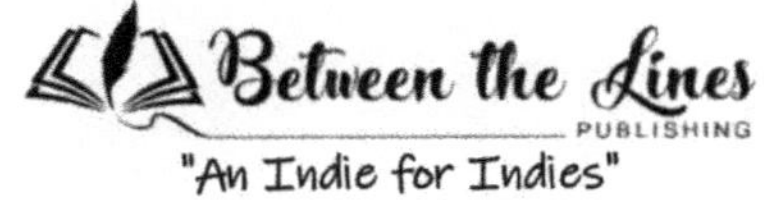
Between the Lines
PUBLISHING
"An Indie for Indies"

Other Books by L.C. Conn

This book is dedicated to the memory of R.E. Fisher.
A fellow author and friend who created the most
magical world I had ever read.
I miss our conversations my friend.

Betrayal

Thick, bright orange hair, threaded through with daisies and buttercups, danced merrily out behind the little girl as she skipped up the stone stairs. Her tunic and leggings were grass-stained and smeared with mud from her brief moment of play. Scampering up from behind, on oversized and clumsy feet with his tongue hanging out the side of his mouth, came a russet and black striped puppy, a recent birthday present from her father. Running through the large open doors, she raced down the long and wide hall, the soles of her shoes slapping loudly on polished marble floors. Teagan was late, and she hoped her father would not be angry.

Skidding on the floor, she turned to climb the large white and gold staircase. Her own breath puffing as much as the puppy that followed in her wake. Reaching the top, she could see the doors to the balcony were already open and the straight back of her father as he stood looking out on a clear blue sky. He turned at the sound of her steps and bent down, his arms thrown wide and a smile on his face. She rushed into those arms and he picked her up.

"Papa, I'm sorry," she cried out breathlessly.

"You're just in time, my Teagan." He turned with her in his arms, and they looked over the lake-filled valley that spread out below them.

Teagan heard the noise before she saw the Riders and their magnificent mounts. The rush of their wings as they powered through the air was a soft whooshing sound, but the cry from their gaping and teeth-filled mouths was loud. It echoed off the steep mountain sides of the lake valley, and she watched in awe as the Riders passed them. Their green leather armor gleamed in the summer sunshine as they bent over the necks of the dragons they rode. As they passed the balcony she was on, they each raised an arm in salute to her father, the General of Riders. Teagan's heart swelled with pride for her father. All too soon they had passed and were moving out for their mission.

"Papa, when I grow up, I want to be a Rider," she exclaimed to him.

"My daughter? Just a common Rider? I think not." He placed her on the ground in front of him, stood at attention and saluted her. "No, my daughter will one day be the greatest of Generals."

He took her hand gently in his own large one and they walked back inside the citadel. The puppy followed dutifully behind, stopping to sniff at the plinths that lined the corridor, each holding a bust of a past General of Riders. They were just nearing the head of the stairs when they heard a platoon of soldiers coming up. Their burnished helmets gleamed in the light that filtered through the large windows as they ascended higher with their spears all straight and tall and their swords strapped to their sides. Their booted feet sounded loud in unison as they approached the General and his daughter.

"General Loinsigh," the man in front said as they came to a halt in front of the pair. His armor was highly decorated with a golden inlay in great swirls.

"Is there something you wished to see me about, Domnall?" her father said, still holding her hand tightly.

"You are to come with me Sir; you are wanted by the King," Domnall said loudly. "Don't make a fuss in front of your daughter, Tharain, go with dignity and face the accusations about to be laid at your feet," Domnall added quietly to him.

Teagan looked up at her father and saw him straighten himself to his full height. He looked down at her and gave her a small grim smile.

"You have to be brave today, Teagan. Show me that you have the spirit to become your dream," he said, and he moved around the assembled soldiers and headed down the stairs with her hand firmly clasped in his.

Teagan turned her head to watch the soldiers turn and follow them down, then she caught sight of her little puppy.

"Bili come," she called to him in a small, frightened voice. The puppy looked down the stairs and hesitated before he began to bound down after her.

Her little feet had to hurry to keep up with her father's long strides as he made his way to the throne room. A narrow red carpet ran the length of the long room. It had a high ceiling and many banners hung off the upper balcony that was supported by thick, white marbled columns. The carpet led to the throne, which sat on a dais, and perched on the red cushions of the most ordinary looking chair was a man. A plain circle of beaten gold sat on his brow; his clothing was so simple that if he had been walking down the street no one would presume he was anything but an ordinary man. His dark hair was pulled back and tied with a cord at the nape of his neck.

At his feet and to the side sat a chest and beside that chest on his knees was a man in a dark leather jacket. His blond head was bowed, his hands were tied behind his back, and two more of the soldiers that followed Teagan and her father were standing over him.

Tharain stopped in front of his ruler and bowed deeply to him. He did not let go of his daughter's hand and he stood again, straight, as he faced his king. From a side door, two more men arrived, both in the uniform of high-ranking Riders. Walking a step behind, two boys followed them in. One was in the garb of a common Rider and the other an apprentice. Neither of the men looked at Tharain or his daughter as they stopped, and all four bowed to the throne.

Teagan looked at the younger men and the apprentice winked at her. He had smiling eyes and his hands were clasped behind his back as they turned from her and back to what was going on before them.

"My Lord King Urmond," Tharain addressed the man on the throne.

"General Loinsigh, is it true? For, I cannot understand how one of my highest-ranking advisors can be accused of such a crime. Tell me that this man lies, and I will punish him for it and continue the search for the true criminal," King Urmond said, his voice gentle.

"I have never lied to my King and I will not start now," replied Tharain and his large hand trembled slightly around his young daughter's smaller one.

The King hung his head for a moment and then pushed himself out of the chair. Slowly he descended the short steps down to stand in front of Tharain. "Why, my friend? Tell me why?"

"I would appreciate it, my King, if we could not discuss this matter in front of my daughter." There was a catch in his voice and the King looked down at the little girl. He crouched and his hand went out to scratch at her puppy's ears.

"Teagan, will you take your dog outside for a moment? I think he would enjoy exploring the formal garden." King Urmond had kind caring eyes and he had always had a kind word to say whenever they had met. He stood and looked around him. "Muniath, will you please escort this young lady into the garden with her puppy? We will send someone when the matter is over."

"It would be my honor, Your Highness," the young man with the smiling eyes said coming to attention and bowing.

"Go with the boy, Teagan. You'll be safe with him," her father reassured her as he held out her hand to the young man.

Her hand was transferred over and soon she was led out the same door as the four had entered by, her puppy bounding along at her side. As they stepped through the door Teagan looked back at her father and saw him fall to his knees, his head bowed in front of the King.

Outside the sun shone warmly on the small walled garden that was at the side of the throne room. His hand held hers firmly as he led her to a seat, then bent down and picked her up, depositing her onto the white marble bench. Muniath turned from her looking back into the hall, trying to see what was going on inside.

"What's happening?" Teagan asked him quietly and he turned back to her.

"Something very serious, my lady," he told her and came to sit at her side. The puppy was sniffing around the bushes and flowers and came running back to them, his soft ears flapping. "What's your puppy's name?" he asked her.

"Bili. My father gave him to me for my birthday," she told him.

"A good sensible name for a dog. When was your birthday?" he asked just to be talking of something.

"It was two weeks ago." Teagan looked at the young man who she could see did not want to act as her babysitter.

Muniath's hair was dark and pulled back in the style appropriate for an Apprentice Rider, the same style as the King wore. His eyes were equally as dark and there was a twinkle to them that made her want to smile. He was tall and thin, but younger than she thought he was. His white shirt was carefully tailored, and the green leather jerkin was tight fitting over his frame. His dark woolen leggings that were common for Riders to wear, were tucked into the high-topped soft leather boots. He carried no weapons at his belt, but his wrists were covered in tough leather cuffs, buckled with common steel, which would change as he rose in the ranks.

"Happy birthday, My Lady, if it is not too late to say it." Muniath smiled down at her. "How old are you?"

"Thank you, and I'm nine. What did Papa do?" she asked him.

"I don't think you should worry about that my lady."

"But I am worrying about it. Why did he fall to his knees like he was a criminal?" Teagan had seen enough of court in her short life to know what a penitent looked like.

"Your father stands accused of stealing something very precious to our lands," Muniath told her hesitantly.

"My Papa is not a thief!" Teagan protested loudly, leaping from the bench. "My Papa is the General of Riders."

"Yes, he is, Lady Teagan. And it is because of his rank that makes the crime he committed even worse." Muniath kept his voice low and calm.

"What is he accused of stealing?" she demanded.

"Dragon eggs, my lady."

Teagan stared at him for a moment. Even at her tender age she knew this was a great crime. Dragons were precious in their lands, they depended on them to keep their borders safe, and she knew that the bond a Rider had with his or her dragon was absolute. From the moment the creature hatched from the egg the Rider was the first contact the small creature had.

"No, he would not. I don't believe you." She turned to run back to the hall and to her father, desperate to find the truth of the matter.

"My Lady." Muniath reached out and caught her arm in his hand and held it firmly, stopping her running to Tharain.

"Let me go!" she called.

"My Lady, you cannot interrupt the King and his court. It would not help matters with your father."

"But he will be killed, that crime is punishable by death." Her eyes were wide with fright and stinging as tears started to spring from them. She remembered that fact from her lessons.

"I am sure our King is just and will pass a fair judgement on your father. You need to be calm and act like a true lady of the court would, for the sake of your father."

The tenderness in his voice calmed her and his arms enfolded her as the tears spilled from under her lashes. Muniath sat on the bench and pulled Teagan up onto his lap and held her close, her head buried into his shoulder as she cried in fright and worry for her father.

"Lady Teagan is wanted inside, Muniath," a voice spoke close to them.

Muniath pulled her away and set Teagan down on her feet but kept a hold on both of her arms. He looked at her and gently wiped the tears away from her face.

"You are a lady of the court and you must act like it now. Be strong and be brave for your father," he said kindly, then took up her hand and led her back inside behind the other young man who looked very much like him.

The King was once more on his throne and her father was standing before him. The guard that had escorted them into the throne room was no longer behind him but stationed at the door waiting. Teagan let go of Muniath's hand and walked with her head held high towards her father and looked up into his face. Tharain did not look down at his daughter, guilt and shame covered him like a cloak.

"General Tharain Loinsigh, you are stripped of all rank, titles, lands, and you no longer have a place at this court. You know what the punishment is for this crime, but I will not leave an innocent child an orphan. Tharain you are hereby banished from these lands, and from this world. By way of portal, you will be sent to your exile, along with what you can carry, and your daughter will go with you. This is my judgement and my ruling," King Urmond declared in a clear and loud voice. "General Domnall Gerarailt, escort Tharain and his daughter to their quarters and allow them to pack. I would take care of what you choose Tharain, with the world you will be spending your days on."

Tharain nodded and turned, not even waiting for Teagan to follow, or taking her hand. She trotted after her father, the words of the King still rolling through her mind. Her father was safe, he would not be killed. But they had to leave their home; the only home she had known; the place where her mother had died.

The doors to their quarters were guarded by two of the Foot Soldiers. Their spears were crossed before them and they stood at ease. As soon as Domnall neared, they snapped to attention, their shields held before them and they stepped out of the way. Tharain opened the door and waited for Teagan to enter after him, then closed it as soon as she was through. He walked past her and sat in his chair by the fire, beckoning her over to him. Teagan ran to him and threw her arms around his neck.

"I am sorry my girl, so very sorry." He sobbed as he held her. "I have been so very stupid."

"Why Papa? Why did you do it?" she asked him.

"Muniath told you then. It's just as well he did." He disentangled her arms from him and held her face. "I have a problem with gambling and since your good mother died, it has got away from me. I stole the eggs to pay a debt, instead of going to our King and seeking help, and now you have been brought down by my foolishness. Can you forgive me, Teagan? Will you forgive me?"

"Where are we to go, Papa?" she asked quietly, frightened by how he was acting.

"A world that is vastly different to ours. They do not know our way of life and dragons are only a myth to them. They lost their great beasts long ago." He placed her back on the floor and stood. Tharain took in a deep breath and unclasped his uniform. "Go pack a small bag of clothes. Nothing fancy and the stout pair of boots I got you to hike in."

Teagan did as she was told and soon was changed into a plain shirt and leggings. The boots her father had requested were firmly on her feet and she held onto the strap of her bag, which was slung across her chest. She was just stepping out of her room when there came a polite knock on the door, and it opened without her father granting permission.

Domnall stood with his hand resting on the pommel of his sword strapped to his side. "Are you ready, Tharain?" he asked with a note of sadness in his voice.

"We are ready," her father answered him, and he looked to his daughter, holding out his hand for her to take.

Rushing to his side she took it and smiled up at him. "As long as we are together Papa I don't care where we go." Teagan said bravely, remembering the words Muniath had told her.

Tharain nodded to his daughter and gave her hand a squeeze and then turned to face the doorway. "Lead the way, Domnall."

They were marched with a squadron of Riders in front, and Foot in the back. Among the Riders was Muniath. As they joined the procession, he glanced at Teagan and gave her a small smile, then turned back to the front. The walk was long as they traversed the halls of the palace and then as the procession moved through the long corridors of the citadel. Teagan did not see anyone else for the whole of the journey. Normally the halls and rooms were buzzing with people going about the business of keeping the kingdom running smoothly, but now it was empty and deserted.

A pair of Riders stood blocking their way, standing at ease, their long sabers resting point down on the floor and their hands clasped the pommels. They stayed at ease until another man arrived. He was the same age as her father, and she recognized him from the throne room. His dark hair was cut short, and he came to stand in front of Tharain.

"My General," he greeted him solemnly and with great respect.

"Not anymore, Galanan. You are General now," Tharain said sadly but taking the man's offered forearm.

"You are still my General until the moment you step through that portal," Galanan told him stoically.

"Then you best give the order to open the gates. We still have a long way to go, and I want to get Teagan somewhere safe before night falls on that world."

Galanan stepped away from the formed-up troops and stood at the head of the column. "Open the gates," he called out in a loud and powerful voice.

The two Riders still standing at attention, moved as one to open the large double doors and stand aside for the Riders to enter. As Tharain and Teagan moved through, she became aware of the Foot soldiers and General Domnall stopping on the threshold behind them, then remembered only Riders were allowed into the Hall of Secrets.

Turning now to the front she looked down the dimly lit passage. On either side large mirrors were hung on the walls, each adorned with a different dragon motif. The style of dragon denoted where they originally came from and there were so many different types. Elongated water wyrms, short stocky cave dwellers, and of course the large dart-like air gliders. She turned her head as she looked at the many silvery surfaces and dark frames, fascinated by them.

Waiting for the procession further down the hall stood the King and the other man who had been in the Throne room. As they approached, the Riders stepped to the side and stood at attention to their denounced general. Tharain stepped up to his King, Teagan's hand still firmly in his, and bowed his head then went to his knee.

"My Lord King Urmond," he said.

"You know that this punishment must be proclaimed throughout the land. It grieves me so much to see you laid so low by your own hand. Tharain. Rise and face me," the King spoke gently.

"I shall carry my shame for the rest of my life, my Lord King," Tharain promised.

"Try to live out the rest of your life with honor and dignity. You have the beautiful Teagan to look after. Do not let your vices get the better of you, cousin," the King said and then embraced Tharain. When he let him go, Urmond knelt before Teagan. "And you, my little cousin, look after your father, he is going to need you more than ever to lean on. Be strong and maybe one day we will see you at court once more. I have a gift for you, little one." He reached into his cloak and pulled out a necklace. Hanging from an intricately woven chain was a pendant of the finest silver, worked into the symbol of their land. An ornate sword with two dragons entwined around it, and an oval emerald set in the cross of the sword. "Keep it safe, Teagan. You may need it one day to come back to us," the King told her.

"Thank you, my Lord King," her voice was small as he placed it over her head.

The King was replaced by the other man now. He moved forward and grasped Tharain's forearm just as Galanan had. "It has been a great honor, General, to serve under you."

"The honor should have been mine, but I wasted it Taran. Don't make the same mistake I made," he advised the man and he stepped away.

Behind them they heard the grouped Riders move suddenly, their sabers raised up and pointing over their heads. Tharain turned to take their salute one last time. "The General," they cried out as one and then returned to their attention posture.

"We must go now, Teagan," Tharain said to her as he hefted his bag higher onto his shoulder and took her hand once more. They turned to face the large mirror and Tharain pulled her along.

Teagan's breath caught in her throat, and her heart began to thump faster inside her chest as they neared the mirror. She could feel her father's hand tighten around her small one, and her feet began to slow as he pulled her closer. She did not want to go near the portal and she did not want to leave her home. Tharain kept walking forward towards the silver surface and he reached out a hand first. She watched it pass through and ripples were left in its wake, like the surface of a very still pond. His hand was followed by his body, the other hand still clasped hers tightly, almost hurting her. Teagan turned one last time and looked at the gathered men and women in the dim hall, she saw their faces, grimly looking back at her and the last glimpse of her home was the solemn face of Muniath, his eyes no longer sparkling, as she passed through the portal.

Theft

The caves were dark and dry, and the entrance was surrounded by lush trees and ferns. One side was barred off with a walkway and by the other a small stream passed merrily to rush down the steep drop off and into the valley below. The cavern sat high up on the side of the mountain, just under the top and large openings along the walkway showed the star strewn sky above which gave little light without the moons to shine the way.

Two pairs of soft soled shoes crept over the barrier, the leather that made up the coverings just as soft as the tunics the two men wore. Their shirts were black and so were their wool leggings. One man stood taller; his almost shaved head showed the stubbly growth that should have been cleaned off days ago. Light blue eyes darted around the area, searching out the guards and night patrol he knew should be there. Beside him was a younger man, just out of boyhood, and his apprentice. It was an arrangement that would last for another seven years and the only way the boy could get out of the arrangement, was to either be passed on to another master or die. The younger man was furtive and jumpy at the thought of their task. It was the first time he was to come up against the beast that they sought.

Keeping to the deep shadows of the cave and away from the sporadic torches that lined the walkway they moved deeper into the system of caverns. A large opening gaped dark and wide, and the bald man strode on past it, as if he belonged there, while the younger dashed with quick steps, trying to keep quiet. He clutched a satchel bag to himself tightly, his breath coming in fast and shallow gasps.

"Do try to be quiet, Loxa," the older man said softly, with a hint of menace and boredom.

"Sorry, Master." The boy followed along, trying to emulate his master, Scetis No Name, dubbed as such as no one knew who or where he was from.

More openings passed them, inside a few sounds could be heard. Soft talking of men from some, and others a sighing sound, like material being swished across a floor. A rumble came from the last one, a bellow quickly followed along with a belch of flames that momentarily lit up the rock that sounded the beast.

In that moment of brief light from the flame Scetis saw his prey. A great golden and red dragon curled in on itself and in an agitated state. A man stood to one side of the great beast, carefully watching it.

"It's alright girl, you're just about done. Just one more to come now, Screamer," the man said gently. Scetis could see he was not as calm as his voice was trying to sound. He was on edge and knew this was not the Dragon Master or even a Dragon Warden.

The only reason he had even thought of trying to do what he was there for was because the Dragon Master was dead, and the current Dragon Warden was in disgrace. He had been suspended and banished for a time from court and the Cave of Dragons. With the men that were left in charge, Scetis knew they would become lax in the absence of true authority. Scetis stepped in through the entry to the cavern and walked up behind the man. Earlier in the evening, before they had made the long climb up to the caverns, he had taken a serum to enhance his night vision. The concoction he had carefully created for just this moment was made up of crushed vaccinium and biloba berries, along with the oils extracted from the small white Euphrasia flowers, and other less palatable parts of a small, rare animal. The serum was now taking full effect and the Rider did not see him coming.

A hand reached up and grasped around the Rider's neck, while the other was placed over his mouth and nose to muffle any sound he made. With a quick twist Scetis broke his neck with ease and let the man drop where he had been standing. Another bellow from the dragon was loud in their ears and Loxa came running up to his master.

"Go fetch the eggs, there's a good boy," Scetis told him calmly.

"Me? You want me to go near that thing?" Panic was rising in Loxa's voice as he stared wide eyed at the large creature.

"Who else, unless you would like to finish your apprenticeship now?" It was a common question Scetis used when Loxa's lack of enthusiasm for something that they were doing annoyed him enough. "Move along, it will be morning soon and I want to be gone from this place long before it has been discovered we have been here."

Loxa took a hesitant step towards Screamer, who let out another belching flame ball. The large dragon was moving, its long thin body undulating, and its shimmering gold wings held high up in the ceiling of the cavern. He eyed up its gaping maw, filled with razor sharp teeth as he stepped closer and closer to it. The body moved revealing the nest where she was laying her eggs as she prepared to birth another. Quickly Loxa ran and picked up the two eggs that sat on the straw, turned, and fled while the dragon was preoccupied with the next birth.

Handing over the two precious eggs to Scetis, Loxa knew better not to expect praise from his master. Instead, he shuffled the bag that was slung across his body around to the front and held it open for Scetis to carefully deposit them in.

Scetis looked at each egg. Alternating bands of gold and red lay on one, while the other shone a brilliant emerald green in the semi-darkness. Carefully and quickly, he placed them in the bag that his apprentice held open, and then turned without another word to the entry. He was not willing to wait for the third egg, two would more than suffice for this order.

If Loxa had seemed nervous going in, he was now terrified of heading out. Scetis did not blame him. To be found in possession of the prohibited items would place both of their necks firmly on the executioners chopping block. It had happened in his lifetime; he had remembered the last Trader of Mystical Medicine who was caught with dragon eggs. His punishment of losing his head should have given Scetis enough warning to stay away this time. But he was aware of his own abilities and strengths, and felt he was the only one to successfully be able to fulfill the order. In addition, it had been hinted as to who the originator of the order was.

Scetis reached out a hand and pushed Loxa up against the rough stone of the cavern, well into the dark reaches of the shadows. Further ahead footsteps could be heard and the light from a lone bobbing torch could be seen coming towards them on the walkway. Loxa held his breath and waited for the Rider to pass them, his eyes fixed firmly ahead of him and not expecting any strangers or trouble, yawning as he went.

As soon as the man had passed, Scetis pulled on Loxa's arm to get him moving again and then quickened his step. They made their way out of the caverns by the same way they had entered, bypassing the barrier at the entrance of the caverns, and taking a long unused steeper path down the mountain. Reaching almost halfway down they came across their hidden climbing ropes and lashed themselves once more into them. While the steps that were embedded in the side of the mountain and the path they were on both led down to the citadel below, their ropes would take them straight to the bottom of the valley and to their horses that were tethered waiting for them. The pair would be able to ride for cover before the sun came up and be well away from the citadel, palace, and town that surrounded it before any alarm was given.

The heels of soft leather boots clicked loudly on the hard-polished surface of the marble floors. The cloak Captain Venicones Magaoidh wore billowed and swung out behind him as he rushed to the General's office. His dark hair was cut short and neat against his head, and his dark eyes looked serious and determined as he neared the open doors. He could already see the General behind his desk, looking at the paperwork in front of him. Carefully he stepped up to the door and waited to be permitted entry.

The older man looked up, his hair greying at the sides and great bags were evident under his eyes, showing the lack of sleep he had had in the last couple of days. He nodded his assent and the younger man walked into the office and stood at attention in front of him.

"General Magaoidh," he greeted him.

"Captain Magaoidh. Sit, have you had anything to eat or drink before you came to see me and report?" the General asked, waving him into the chair at his side.

"No Sir, I have not, I came straight from the back of my ride. We have not been able to ascertain as to where the miscreant is hiding. We have interrogated the school and the mastery arms of the Convocation of Mystical Medicine and they tell us that there is no one missing from their ranks. The Regulator also inferred we should look into our own ranks again," he spat the last statement.

"It was one man who did this and the only reason to take such a precious thing is for medicinal uses. What is a lay person to do with a dragon?" Galanan slapped his hand hard down onto the surface of his desk.

"If I could make a suggestion, General?" the Captain offered.

"Anything, at the moment I would have the men out looking under each and every rock."

"If I could suggest just one name, we know of someone who could do this job of finding the egg and returning to us."

The General looked at the Captain hard and sat back in his seat.

"I mean, Father, he is the only one in our generation to have the skills to hunt it down and the man who took it. You know I'm right."

"But Venicones, he is in disgrace. I couldn't get him back into the ranks and not make it look like a slight to our Lord King," Galanan shook his head.

"But Sir, Muniath…"

"He may be your brother and my son, but what he did was beyond forgivable. It was all I could do to keep the King from banishing him permanently."

"What if it were done without the King knowing, or even if I asked him to help without your knowledge?"

"But you are making me aware of it now, Son. I could not in all good conscience allow you to do so. I forbid you to do it." Galanan gave a great sigh and then looked significantly at his son. "You have been on the go since this all began. I think you need to have a rest and recuperate. Don't you have time owed to you?"

"I do, Father." Venicones nodded his head.

"Why don't you take some time to visit Meara? Every time I step foot in her tavern to visit with Taran she asks after you. Take the next couple of days off. I insist on it." He winked at his son.

"I will. Thank you, Father." Venicones stood and stretched out a hand to his father, who grasped his wrist.

As the young man was heading out of the door the General called to him, "And tell Mun to get his act together."

Later that afternoon Venicones opened the door to a tavern. This was not one of the seedier inns in the town where the lower ranks spent their days off drinking and whoring. This was a nice establishment that catered to a more gentile clientele. The floors were scrubbed each morning, the windows clean, and the food was delicious and wholesome. Scattered at various tables sat lords and ladies of the court discussing politics and events of the day. There was no fighting allowed in this tavern, except with words, yet even a raised voice was enough to have a patron politely asked to leave.

Venicones walked to the bar and rang the small bell that was sitting there. From out of the back a woman with tight, curly blond hair and a curvy figure came hurrying to wait on her customer. Her large blue eyes grew even larger when she saw who it was and raced around the bar to hug the man.

"What are you doing here? You don't normally visit my tavern?" she asked, giving him a mischievous and teasing grin as he pulled away.

"Well Meara, I think you know why I'm here. I'm looking for my errant brother," he said seriously as he kissed her cheek.

"Yes, he's still here. I have him in one of the back bedrooms upstairs, so he won't disturb any of my other customers. Follow me," she said and led the way to the staircase in the corner.

From out of her pocket, she produced a key and they stopped at the very end of a corridor which had many doors leading from it. Slipping the key into the lock she turned it and opened the door, then stepped back from the smell that came hurtling out and assaulting their noses.

"Oh, good lord!" Venicones declared placing a hand over his nose and mouth. "How long has he been like this?"

"Since he emerged last, I would say it's been a good two weeks this time. I'm pleased you've finally come to claim him. He may be like a brother to me, but he's using up a room I could hire out, not to mention eating and drinking me out of business. But to shift him you're going to need help. Did you bring anyone?" Meara asked, taking the bold step to move into the room in order to open the window and let in much needed fresh air.

The crumpled lump on the bed moved and groaned slightly as Meara tore open the curtains letting the sunlight spill into the room for the first time since he had taken up residence.

"I didn't bring anyone. I didn't think he would be still so far gone. I thought he might have drunk himself sober by now."

"Fuck off!" a dark voice muttered from the depths of the now grimy looking pillow.

"Charming, I'm sure. You have never talked to me that way before, Muniath. I'll go get Pa to help you." She started to head out of the door.

"Meara don't. I don't want to put the burden on Taran. Not with his injury and all," he called out and she stopped.

"Wick then, he's strong enough now. I'll go fetch him, all he'll be doing is getting the old stories from Pa and not much else." She smiled at Venicones. "Don't be too hard on him Ven, he's been through a great deal in the last few months. It's not his fault," she said tenderly.

"I know it isn't, but he was the one who acted out and only has himself to blame for that. The King is still not happy with him."

"I'll be right back." Meara smiled and headed out of the room.

Venicones turned back to the crumpled and knotted covers on the bed and nudged the shoulder of his younger brother.

"I said, fuck off," the voice growled once more from the pillow it was muffled by.

"Get up Mun, there's a job to be done." Venicones pushed him again.

"I'm not working remember, I've been banished." The form moved on the bed and rolled over. Muniath's eyelids pried themselves apart and were bloodshot from too much drink. He scratched himself and his mouth smacked as he tried to get rid of the dryness that seemed like he had been suckling on a duster.

"You've not been banished, only put on leave until you sort yourself out. This is rather important. I need you clean and sober before I tell you my news."

"What news?" Muniath groaned and sat up while he rubbed at the dark stubble of many days' growth on his chin.

"It can wait. I'm not going to tell you only to see you go off unprepared and insensible."

"Must be big, so why aren't the Riders and Foot not dealing with it?" He picked up a shirt that was grey with dirt, sniffed it, then slid it over his head.

"Get washed and have something in your stomach that isn't liquid for a change and then we'll talk."

"You wanted me, Uncle Ven?" A boy of about fifteen walked into the room and stopped dead in his tracks. "Oh, yuck Uncle Mun, you stink." He held his nose and wafted the stench of the room with his other hand.

"Yes, I did, Wick. Go down and make sure the baths are nice and hot for Mun to get into and then ask your mother for a hot meal of oats. When that's done, I want you to go to our parent's house and get a clean set of clothes for your uncle here."

Wick was already backing out of the door. "Sure thing. Great, it'll be me who has to clean this room." He walked down the corridor still muttering under his breath.

"He's a good kid," Muniath said trying to stand, but wobbled and sat down heavily again on the bed.

"He is and it's about time he was apprenticed. He has the same talent as his father, and you," Venicones told him.

"I know, he keeps asking me when he thinks I am sober enough."

"Well then take him on. You're the only one left who can train him and you're the best in our generation, and according to the council the best there has ever been."

"It's too hard at the moment." He wiped his hand across his face to hide the grimace of pain that he knew would be showing, and through his long dark matted hair.

"It's going to have to be soon. Otherwise, the talent will wane, and he'll lose it." Venicones then struck out with the flat of his hand at the head of his brother.

"Ow! What the hell was that for?" Muniath rubbed the spot he had just been clouted.

"That's for being an absolute pain to everyone who loves you. For taking yourself off and not letting us help you through it," he said savagely.

"You don't understand what it's like."

"No, I don't. I can't even begin to imagine what it feels like to not only lose dragons you are bonded with, but also your mentor. None of us know what you went through up on that mountain. But I'm your brother. I see the worry in both our parents' eyes. I see them concerned that you might drink yourself to death. I see our father floundering at work, because the man he is supposed to depend on is off getting himself suspended and carousing night after night."

"Alright. I get the message." Muniath stood and held onto his brother's shoulder for support. "I'm sorry. I'll apologize to Mother and to Father when I see them. Now help me down to the baths, because I am going to throw up if I have to smell myself for much longer." He gave his brother a crooked grin.

A better groomed, sweeter smelling, and awake Muniath was soon sitting at the inn's kitchen table, eating his fill of porridge. Meara walked over and placed a mug down in front of him.

"Milk as ordered," she said and sat down beside Venicones, opposite Muniath.

"That reminds me, Mea. Here. This should just about cover all his expenses." Venicones held out a gold coin for her and when she wouldn't take it, he placed it on the table in front of her.

"He's family and you look after family," she said, refusing to take it.

"Just take it, Mea, he'll only give it to Taran to give to you later," Muniath told her between mouthfuls.

Slowly she slipped it from the table and into her pocket. "It's nice to talk to you sober for a change, Mun."

"So, brother of mine, what's this news you come looking for me to impart?" he asked Venicones grandly.

"Two eggs have been stolen," his brother whispered, looking around at the door which led to the inn's bar nearby.

The spoon stopped halfway to Muniath's mouth and then headed slowly back to the bowl.

"Which dragon?" he asked hesitantly.

"Screamer."

"I take it that this news is not generally known?"

"No, it's not," Venicones confirmed for him.

"Mea, I know you can be trusted with this and Venicones has probably asked you already about strangers."

"He has indeed, Mun, and I know to keep my mouth shut, I am my father's daughter," she said proudly.

"I thank you dear foster-sister for your care and attention over the last few weeks. But I think it might be time for me to return to the real world." He pushed himself up off his chair and gently and quietly pushed the chair back under the table.

"You're most welcome, and I'll take you in next time you find yourself in the same situation. Either one of you. Give my love to your parents please." Venicones hugged her and then Muniath took his place, holding her close for a long time, then kissing her cheek.

"Mother wants to see you first, Mun," Venicones warned him.

"Right then," Muniath said, releasing his foster-sister. "Let's get the visit over with the main dragon first. Then I'll face Father." He took a deep breath and headed for the door.

Escape

Scetis reigned in his horse at the top of the rise before the road followed the slope down to where it met the border crossing over the river below. Already he could see that changes had been ordered and a large black dragon now lay in front of the guard house, its enormous horned head resting on its front claws and its wings wrapped around it. Soldiers of the Foot were placed across the entry to the bridge, their burnished shields gleaming in the afternoon sunshine as they checked the credentials of all travelers heading out of the Realm.

For the last couple of days, the pair had been hiding and eluding the great flying dragons and their Riders. They had changed their appearance and clothing in a bid to show that they were common travelers. Scetis' most favored leather jacket had been buried in order to keep their identities a secret. There was no need for an ordinary person to be wearing the garb of a Trader in Mystical Medicine.

Their only other escape route from The Realm of Dragons was two days' travel down the fast-flowing and cold river that was before them. The kingdom was well guarded and secluded from the world, hemmed-in all around by large imposing mountains, all capped with thick snow year-round. The road before them was just as mountainous but was the only pass that was easily navigable for travelers in and out. The deep river gorge that carved its way out of The Realm ended in an extremely large and spectacular waterfall.

"Well, that is going to be a problem," Scetis said as he wheeled his horse around and headed back the way they had come. Scetis guided Loxa away from the well-used road and into a thicket of trees and shrubs.

"We'll camp here tonight. Make the fire only a small one, Loxa, we don't want to be seen from the road." Loxa, already in the process of doing just as Scetis commanded, rolled his eyes and bit his tongue as he dug a small pit in the soft dirt in which to make the fire.

"Surely, Master, we should just dump the eggs and get back home." He finally raised the idea that had formed shortly after it had become apparent to him that they were not worth the risk.

"And waste all that time and effort harvesting them. Not to mention the handsome advance that has already been paid for the things. No, we will get them home. I know a way, but it will be dangerous, and you are going to have to do exactly as I tell you," Scetis told him.

Loxa sighed and got on with his chores. The meal was a necessarily small one, as their supplies were running low, and the fire was quickly extinguished as soon as it was cooked. The night would be another long, dark, and cold one and he got out his blankets to get ready for it.

"Pass me the bag, Loxa," Scetis asked him, and the boy did as he was told.

Scetis reached in his hand and pulled out one of the eggs and looked at it.

Loxa could see their colors were luminescent, glowing softly in the darkness. The gold and red sitting like a jewel in the palm of his hand. They were not as big as some would have thought for such a big creature. The eggs were large by any other standard, but smaller than the egg of a rokh, the giant eagle that inhabited his once mountainous home, which Loxa had only seen once. The shell was smooth to the touch, not like the scaled versions he had imagined from the stories told by his grandmother.

His master's eyes glinted in the blue and green moons that hung heavy in the sky. Scetis placed the egg back into the bag gently and withdrew its sibling. The green, which had appeared as a dark emerald when they had snatched it from its mother, now appeared a deeper shade, almost black. This color change in the shell obviously worried Scetis.

"It must take after its sire, for the other is a match to the mother. Pass me one of your shirts, Loxa, I think this one needs a little bit more warmth," Scetis demanded.

Reluctantly he pulled a shirt out of his bag and handed it to Scetis, who wrapped it gently around the sickly egg then tucked it safely back into the bag.

"I'll look after them from now on. Get some sleep, tomorrow is going to be dangerous, and I need you awake and fully aware."

"Where is he?" a harsh woman's voice called out at the entrance to the house.

Muniath looked up from his window seat and over to his brother, who was now standing and waiting for their mother to enter.

The door opened quickly, and Captain Aideen Magaoidh strode into the room. Their mother was second in command to the General of the Foot Domnall Gerarailt. Closely following her was her assistant, and Muniath and Venicone's sister, Ide. Both women wore the uniform well and proudly. Aideen stood tall, her chestnut-colored hair cut short and only showing a small sign of age. She was still stripping off her gloves, while Ide helped to unbuckle her sword, before taking care of her own.

Aideen's green eyes scoured the room and finally landed on her wayward son. She shook her head and walked up to where he still sat.

"Are you done then? Should we welcome you home, or do you still want to fight and drink some more?" she asked him coldly.

Muniath stood, and although his mother was tall, he was still a head taller than her. "I am done, Mother. I've heard the news and I've come to do what I must."

"Welcome back then." Her eyes softened and her arms embraced her youngest child. She held him tightly and then pulled away. "Have you seen your father yet?"

"Not yet, I was told to see you first," he said, resuming his seat as she moved away from him, he watched Ide finish unclasping her cloak. "How are you, Ide?" he asked, looking at her sideways, waiting for her words and knowing he deserved them.

"You and I shall speak later, when I can say what I want without Mother pulling me up on charges." Ide scowled at him.

"Don't be silly, Ide, I wouldn't bring you up on charges on anything you would have to say to Mun, warranted or not. And besides, what is said in this house does not fall under military rule," Aideen said with a wicked smile.

"Has Orcades recovered from his injuries?" Muniath asked Ide.

"He has, and you can apologize to him tonight. He's coming to dinner," Ide told him, now starting to take her own sword off.

"I'll make sure that I do," he said leaning back and looking out of the window at the view over the lake at the bottom of the valley.

"How is Mea?" Aideen now spoke to Venicones.

"She is well and sends her love. I've been talking to Mun about taking Wick on as an apprentice. He needs to begin soon."

"How old is he now?" Aideen asked settling herself into a chair.

"He's almost sixteen."

"Yes, well and truly time. He'll lose the ability soon if he's not introduced to the dragons."

"There would be no need for him to be anywhere near them if things had turned out differently," Muniath muttered.

"What was that Muniath?" Aideen asked.

"Nothing. When is supper? I think I'll go for a walk before Father comes home." He stood and started to make his way to the door.

"Mun, don't stray from the path. Supper will be at the usual time. Make sure you are back for it," she said, taking his hand as he passed her. He looked down at her and gave her hand a squeeze before going on his way.

He heard them still talking as he left but could not comprehend what it was they said. His feet took him out of the house that sat on the shores of the lake, far below the towering spires and fortifications of the Citadel and the town of Hunndaidh. It sat like a brilliant white gem in the dying light of the sun. Mun looked away and turned to take the path along the shores.

The cobblestones had been laid in the long distant past and the path meandered its way beside the lake. Within the gaps and cracks, grass and other plants grew in brilliant shades of green against the dark stone, some with iridescent colored flowers. Along the slight rise on the side lay a grassy bank with daisies and buttercups. Large rocks protruded from the ground at various intervals, and he sought out his favorite spot.

A particularly large rock pushed its way out of the lush grass and moss. Its almost flat top sloped back towards the mountain and it was a lighter shade than the others. Muniath had often found that it was perfect for sitting on and contemplating the world. Growing from the back of the rock, with roots that spread out, searching for any crack that they could sink down into was a tree, a Dragon Blood tree. The long, flax-like needles spread out over the top, looking like the spines and horns of a dragon, while underneath the exposed blood red colored branches twisted and wove themselves through each other, while the trunk grew straight, wide, and strong. Muniath pulled himself up onto the rock and placed his back against the trunk, seeking out the shelter it gave.

Muniath did not realize that he had fallen asleep, until a wet nose touched his cheek and he woke with a start. A russet and black striped dog with its tongue lolling out of its mouth and breath that stunk of its last meal stood beside him, his tail wagging madly making his whole-body shake.

"Bili, get back here," a voice rang out from around the bend.

The dog looked back over its shoulder and then back to Muniath. He then sat and waited for his owner. From around the bend a man with dark hair, pulled back and tied at the nape of his neck, hurriedly walked with a stick in his hand and he stopped short when he saw Muniath.

Muniath recognized him and leapt to his feet, bowing deeply to King Urmond, who walked on to stand in front of him.

"I see you are back," the king spoke to him.

"I am, My Lord King," Muniath said standing up straight again.

"Have you apologized to my nephew yet?" he asked as he went to sit on the rock Muniath had just stood from.

"Not yet, I'm seeing Orcades at dinner tonight."

"Make sure you do. I do understand why you did it Muniath, and we are in sore need of your skills just now. Is that why you're back, did your father call for you?" he asked shrewdly.

"No, my brother found me and dragged me out of the hell I had put myself in. He told me the news."

"As soon as you have apologized, you can come back to your full status once more. Screamer's eggs must be returned."

"Eggs? I thought there was only one taken." Muniath spoke quickly with some shock.

"No, two were taken. It looks like she was in the middle of birthing her third when the thief, or thieves stole them."

"That would be the easiest time, she would've been so preoccupied with the birth that nothing else would have been noticed."

"We lost a good man as well. His neck was snapped." King Urmond looked at Muniath.

"Who was it?"

"Vist." Urmond watched for signs that the madness that had taken Muniath would once more descend.

"All that experience lost, what a waste." The younger man's eyebrows knitted together.

"Yes, it is. It should have been you there at the birth, I think that's why they decided to act. They must have known that you were out of the way."

"I am sorry, My Lord King." Muniath knelt quickly in front of Urmond.

"That is neither here nor there, you needed time to grieve, you had not only just lost your Master, and three dragons, but also Cara, a Rider who I think you were close with. A hard task for anyone to overcome." Urmond reached out and scratched the ear of the dog at his side. "My nephew was an ass for saying what he did to you at that time. But striking, not only a higher-ranking officer, but a prince of the court was something I could not overlook, Muniath. I have spoken strongly to Orcades and explained where he went wrong—although I don't think he took it on. Please be the bigger man and not react to anything he might say tonight."

"I won't and thank you."

"Yes, well you are needed now more than ever. It's times like these that I miss Tharain. My cousin would have found the thief by now and strung him up for good measure. I don't mean any disrespect to your father, he does a very good job, but Tharain was like you. He had the gift of understanding dragons, if only a fraction of what you have."

"I was there when you banished him and his daughter." Muniath's eyes went to the dog.

"Yes, this was Teagan's pup, I couldn't face sending it to the kennels to be brought up with the other hounds. She was such a little ray of sunshine in our court." Urmond gave a sigh and smile. "Maybe one day she'll find her way back to us."

"Is that possible? The world they went to has no return portal anymore." Muniath approached Urmond and scratched the silky ears of the dog.

"It's possible. Do you remember the pendant I gave her before they went through?"

"I do. It was the crest of our realm."

"It is also a key. It will locate the point of entry into the world and help summon a temporary portal. But she will have to want to come back to us, that is if she even remembers our world. She was very young when they left." He sounded sad at it.

"Nine. She had just had her birthday before they left."

"She did. I remember now, Orlagh oversaw the making of her cake." Urmond chuckled as he remembered.

"Your daughter is a very talented Rider," Muniath said.

"She is unhappy everyone still calls her Princess." He laughed now. "She just wishes to be one of the people."

"But she never can, I'm surprised that you let her train to become a Rider, with her being your only heir."

"I would have preferred she trained in the Court of Diplomacy in preparation of her taking over when I die, but she so wanted to be a Rider. She loves the glamour of it, the excitement. I can't say I blame her. When I am on the back of Screamer it's the most thrilling and freeing time I have," Urmond said with a smile.

"It's something those who have never ridden cannot understand. Nor the bond we have with our mounts," Muniath said sadly.

"No, that is a special bond indeed." Urmond stood and Bili leapt down from the rock with him and went to sniff around the boulder. "Can you pass on a message to your mother for me, Muniath?"

"It would be my honor."

"Can you tell her that I am inviting myself to this dinner tonight." Then he saw the brief dark look Muniath had. "Not because I fear you might do something stupid to my nephew, only I fear that my nephew might do or say something stupid at the meal. Your brother and father would then feel obligated to step in on your behalf to defend your honor, and it would also cause a rift between you and your sister. I need your family intact and in place at their posts."

"I will inform my mother of your intended visit, My Lord King." He bowed to Urmond.

"Right. Well, I'll see you in an hour or so. Welcome back Muniath, with you in your rightful place I know that Screamer's eggs will be found safe and returned to her." Urmond then turned and headed back the way he had come down the path. "Bili, come."

The rusty and black striped dog lifted his head from the hole in the bank he had been sniffing at and his tail began to wag enthusiastically. Urmond gave a shrill whistle and the dog barked, then bounded forward after the retreating back of his master.

Muniath watched them go then turned to the now dark waters of the lake, the wind had dropped, and the surface was glassy and reflected the mountains on the other side like a mirror. A call from above echoed against the almost sheer sides of the mountains as they climbed up into the still blue sky. It came again and he now saw the large black dragon that it had come from. His wings were spread wide, and he could see the membrane rippling as the air passed underneath them. They beat a couple of times before the dragon used them to help turn to get to the caverns at the top of the mountain that were the home to the Riders mounts.

Returning to the path, he retraced his steps to his family home. The sun was well and truly set as he climbed the steps to enter the large house. As he stepped into the large entry hall, he caught one of the many servants in his parents' employ and asked him to inform Aideen of the King's impending visit for dinner and then went to change himself.

Sitting back in his chair, Muniath held onto the goblet tightly in his hand, while the food on the plate in front of him went largely untouched. The only liquid it held was the clear and fresh water from the household spring. He looked across the table at the man his sister wanted to marry, the king's nephew, Orcades Braonáin. He was the only child of the King's sister and two years older than Muniath, with blond hair that was cut short at the back but was left a little longer on the top and front. He held himself regally and arrogantly. He was muscular, and Muniath knew he liked to work out to excess, even seeking out herbs and medicines to aid him in his quest to be larger than any other man in the ranks. Orcades knew his position and liked to remind everyone else of it as well.

Looking down to the head of the table where King Urmond sat joking with his father, he compared the King and his nephew. Where Urmond was self-effacing, humble, and fair, Orcades was belligerent, believed that rank was everything, and liked to make sure that every eye was on him. A couple of times Muniath could see his king react slightly to some condescending tone or comment his nephew made.

Ide was oblivious to all Orcades' mean and hurtful ways. Muniath could not understand what she saw in him and wondered again how she could think herself in love with the man. She deserved so much better, especially knowing how Orcades acted when Ide was not around and there were other ladies in the room. He bit down his anger that was threatening to spill once more and took a sip of his spring water, while eyeing up the carafes of wine that sat on the overly abundant table.

Venicones looked over to Muniath and caught his eye, he gave his younger brother a tight small smile of encouragement and then turned back to the conversation between their father and the king. Aideen was sitting beside Muniath and leaned over to him to speak quietly.

"You are doing well, son, just keep up the pretense while he is here, apologize, and then let the matter rest." Aideen sat back and started to speak once more to Ide.

Between mother and son, it was no secret that she detested Orcades and wished that Ide would get over the silly infatuation that she had for him. There were others at court and in the forces that Aideen preferred and deemed far more suitable matches for her daughter than the jumped up and pretentious nephew of the king. Aideen did not set store in climbing ladders socially by who you know and the advantages they could give. Instead, she valued hard work and loyalty as a means to someone making their way up the ranks in whatever profession they chose. She was a sensible woman who hoped she had passed on these ideals to her children, especially her daughter.

Urmond glanced down the table and saw Muniath regarding Orcades across the table. The set of his face determined that the meal was over, and he stood.

"Muniath, Orcades, I would have a word with you both. Galanan and Venicones would you join us? Ladies excuse us for a moment, we have unfinished Rider business to attend to." He bowed to them as Ide was about to stand and go with them.

Muniath placed his goblet back on the table and stood, dropping a kiss on his mother's head.

"Be sensible, son," she whispered as he left her side.

Following the king into Galanan's study the doors were closed after them and the king stood beside the large empty fireplace. Urmond looked significantly at Muniath.

"I wish to apologize, Prince Orcades, for my behavior, my words, and for striking you. It was inappropriate and I ask your forgiveness," Muniath said as he held out his hand to Orcades.

"I forgive your moment of weakness, Muniath," Orcades said as they clasped hands and shook. "Though to be so upset over the death of what really is just an overly large pet is rather foolish, don't you think?" he said jovially and looked around at the other men who were scowling at him.

"I think it was time you left this house, Orcades, before you say something that I will have to condemn. We have talked already about this, and your opinion on the matter—especially in this particular house—is probably not welcome," Urmond said grimly.

Orcades let Muniath's hand go and stood up straighter. He looked around at the brothers and their father and noticed for the first time their look of disapproval of him. Without a word he started for the door.

"Orcades," Urmond called to him just before he opened the door. "I think I will be talking to Domnall about giving you a posting away from the palace for a while. Somewhere remote and hard, probably somewhere where there are dragons as well. Your education in the matter you have such disdain for needs addressing. You are dismissed. I do not want to see you at court until it is time for you to take your leave for your new posting."

The door opened and Orcades left the house without even a word for his fiancé and her mother. The four men heard the front door slam shut after he had passed through it and Urmond turned to Muniath.

"Thank you for your apology, you handled yourself well, Muniath, under such duress and I in turn, apologize for my nephew," Urmond said.

"My Lord King, you do not need to apologize to me for his behavior. But I thank you." Muniath bowed to him.

"You are hereby reinstated to your full rank and I believe your father has a promotion for you. The crown is relying on you to retrieve what was stolen. Not only the crown, but I as a man, and one who is bonded to his dragon. Screamer wants her children back; she feels their loss keenly."

"I vow that we will find them, My Lord King. And we shall see justice done to those that have stolen the precious children of Screamer."

Search

The climb up the side of the mountain was a welcome one the next morning, and Muniath was pleased with himself for not succumbing to his inclination for a drink the night before. He had gone to his room after the king had left and found a full carafe of his favorite wine sitting on the table waiting for him. Carefully, he had sat down in the chair at the table and looked at it. He had picked it up and inspected the color, unstoppered the top and sniffed the bouquet that came from the contents, smiling at the quality of it. Then he took it to the window, opened it wide, and poured the contents out onto the ground far below.

The sleep Muniath had was restful and peaceful for a change. The nights of drinking until he forgot why he was drinking were gone. That pain, while still there and agonizing, was now managed and he looked up at the steps set into the side of the mountain, now eager to get on with not only his job, but his calling.

Muniath was the only one left of his generation to have what is called the gift. The gift of communing with dragons. He could sense their moods, their attitudes, and although not actually able to talk with the creatures, he caught glimpses of their minds and could keep them calm and train them to their fullest potential. The gift also came with something else, and that was the ability to track dragons, not just fully-grown ones such as the King's own bonded animal, Screamer, but their children that lay still in the eggs.

Reaching the top, he looked at the barrier to the Eyrie, the portal that let humans into the great caves that were home to the dragons. Studying it, he could see where the security could be increased and tightened and made a mental note to speak to his father about it when he reported to him later in the afternoon. The morning, though, was for the dragons.

The previous evening and in front of the king, Galanan had presented to his son the wrist cuffs adorned with silver buckles of a Captain of Riders. He now also, because of his gift, held the post of Master of Dragons and was responsible for every dragon that was in service to the king. While each dragon was bonded to its rider, and they had the day-to-day care of their mount, the Master of Dragons was in charge and the Riders would go to him for advice. He and any Warden under his command, were the ones they went to when their mounts were sick, injured, or not performing well.

The wrist cuffs were now firmly in place on his arms, and he adjusted the stiff leather before stepping through the barrier and into the semi darkness of the cave system. Up above, large holes showed the bright sky and the sun streamed through them in heavy beams, lighting up the path that led further into the mountain. The stream that ran to the entrance burbled away beside the wide walkway and he passed the dazzling display of the light playing on the water in his eagerness to see the dragons.

A bellow from further down sounded angry and denoted a dragon in pain. Muniath quickened his step and knew instinctively that the dragon in question was Screamer. He came to her cavern and entered, just as a belch of fire was released. He stopped at the entrance and waited for a moment while he sent out a calming and understanding thought to the large dragon, then set off softly and slowly as he neared her.

The great golden and red dragon raised her head, watching him come closer, a quieter and pleading sound came from her as she saw who was visiting. Screamer raised a large wing and moved her tail to show Muniath the lone egg that sat at her side, nestled in the bed of hay. It gleamed gold and green in the protective embrace of its mother.

"So, who is the sire this time, Screamer?" he asked her gently, his hand now raised and stroking the side of her large head. She almost seemed to coo at his touch and leaned into it. "Looks to me as if you have mated again with Raker. He has always been a good father to your children." Again, the dragon moaned. "I know, old girl, I promise I'll find your two lost children and bring them home. They'll be safe, and you can have whoever it was that took them." Muniath placed both hands on her head and touched his forehead against her. "Tell me what you saw that night, old girl. Did you see who it was?" Flashes of images were transferred to his mind, pictures flashing with bright orange fire and Vist who was leaning up against the wall while she gave birth. Two shadows moved further out towards the entrance before Vist dropped to the ground. Then it was all lost as she turned her attention to the birthing of her last egg.

The details were there and Muniath grasped at them. A shiny dark material had wrapped the taller of the two men, his shaven scalp picking up the dim light in the images. It was a Trader. There was no doubt about the style of the leather jacket. He pulled his mind from that of the dragon and gave her a tender kiss.

"Thank you, Screamer, for your help. You have given me enough to be going on with. Rest and keep this egg safe, it will soon be joined by its siblings."

Screamer looked at him through her reptilian eyes, which blinked. She moaned again softly from the depths of her long neck, and once more covered up her last remaining egg protectively.

When Muniath left Screamer's cavern, Venicones was waiting for him. The look on his younger brother's face said it all. He knew who was responsible.

"So, it was a Trader?" Venicones asked Muniath.

"Yes, and an apprentice I would say by the look of the other. When I get my hands on them —"

"You'll wait until father can bring them before the king," Venicones finished for him.

"I promised Screamer that she could have who was responsible."

"That is gruesome and old fashioned."

"What they did was cruel, and those eggs are in danger. I couldn't see their markings, but if one of them is a green then it needs warmth, more than one of the Gold and Red. Raker's kind are from a warm climate and if it is not properly cared for, it will die in the shell," Muniath said aggressively.

"You're not telling me anything I don't know, Mun." Venicones quickened his step to keep up with him. "Where are you going now, I thought you had to see Father?"

"I want to check on the rest of the mounts. I've been away for too long and even though I know the Riders have taken good care of them, I just want to make sure myself."

"Including my own?" Venicones asked, giving a half laugh.

"Everyone's," Muniath replied with a grin for his older brother and headed into the next cavern.

The next room was bright with torches dancing merrily on their metal sconces, which were pounded deep into the rock. The large red head of a dragon came out from underneath a wing and regarded the two men who had entered its space. It gave a series of clicks and then waited for them to approach it.

"Hello Scorcher. Has he been keeping you well?" Muniath asked as he lay a hand on the top of the large head with two twisted horns protruding from it. The scales on the enormous body were a burnished deep red and gleamed in the flickering light.

"Of course, I am, I remember my training," Venicones said defensively.

"He says that you don't give him enough meat. But he is always hungry and is overly large already. Don't worry, Ven, you're doing a fine job with him. He's beautiful. Have you thought of trying to mate him with Slasher? He and the gold would make amazing offspring."

"No, he seems to go all silly whenever Rain is around though." Ven said as he patted the neck of his mount.

"Rain is a blue. I don't know how that would work, I've never heard of anyone cross breeding a water and fire type. It would be interesting to find out though, maybe you should let him. Talk to Feth and see what her thoughts are, she knows her mount better than you."

They carried on for the rest of the morning visiting each of the twenty dragons that were in the caves. But there were so many more that were empty, waiting for an occupant. Muniath was not happy about this, they should have a full complement of fifty Riders with dragons in the caves alone, disregarding those that were currently positioned on the borders. Unfortunately, the females seemed to be breeding less and less.

"Once this business with Screamer's eggs is out of the way, I think we should go out and try and find some wild dragons. The numbers in this cavern at least seem to be diminishing at an alarming rate," Muniath said to his brother as they started to head to the entry.

As they neared the barriers Muniath started speaking his thoughts about changing the security with Venicones when a loud horn call pierced the air ahead of them. The two men stopped short and listened. The long note continued for some time and briefly halted before it sounded again. He looked at Venicones and the pair began to run. Quickly, and with no regard to their own safety, they started to descend the stairs back to the citadel, leaping two or three steps at a time and raced to the rear entrance, heading into the large building that dominated the side of the mountain, the focal point for the town below it.

Two Foot Soldiers stood guard at the entrance to the town below the citadel. The gates were wide open and the flow between the double metal-clad defensive doors was light on the mid-morning day. Above the porticus, the King's Crest stood out proudly and flags fluttered in the slight breeze on the top of the battlements. The soldiers looked not only young but bored with their posting. The youngest shifted his weight from one foot to the other, making a slight jingling sound with his armor.

Coming up the cobbled road that wound its way up the mountain two travelers trudged along. They looked like they had been on a long journey, footsore, and bedraggled in appearance. The eldest clutched a bag at his side and the youngest of the two seemed to be almost asleep as he walked. They approached the gates and a man stepped out from an alcove, barring their entrance to the town. His long cloak swirled around his legs and he had that sneering and officious look on his face that most bureaucrats seemed to wear.

"Morning travelers, your reason for entering Hunndaidh?" In his hands were a large book and quill.

"Visiting family, sir. This is unusual, I have never been confronted at the gates before." Scetis said, pulling himself up to his full height and adjusting the bag at his hip.

"There has been a general tightening of security. Your names and your professions please," the official demanded.

"We gave them at the border when we entered the Realm."

"And we need them now to confirm what you told my colleagues at the border."

The two soldiers became more alert at the tone of the official. Scetis flicked his blue eyes at the two and then smiled at the man.

"I meant no disrespect, sir, we are both tired from our journey and it has been a very long one for us. My name is Scetis, and this is my apprentice, Loxa. I am a Practitioner of Mystical Medicine. I have been summoned by an old uncle to help treat his gout," Scetis said with a little bow.

"I would see your credentials please, Scetis, and that of your apprentice." The official scribbled their details into the book.

Scetis nodded to Loxa when the young man looked at him. They both withdrew the medallions out of their shirts and held them out to be inspected. With a pudgy finger he took each one and peered down his large, oversized nose to inspect the ruins that spelled out their status. He gave them a curt nod and then handed them back.

"If you could open your bags for us, please," he said.

"Our bags? But they were searched at the border. Why do you wish to see what we have inside them?" Scetis demanded.

"A very serious theft has occurred, and we are trying to apprehend the culprits."

"What theft?"

"Dragon eggs, two of them from the King's own mount," the officious man said, his face going red as his anger rose.

"As we are entering the town, we would not have eggs on us, would we?" Scetis said calmly, recognizing this man could become difficult.

"Be that as it may, I have my orders from the King himself. No one is allowed in or out of Hunndaidh or the Citadel, without being searched. Especially of those from The Convocation of Mystical

Medicine." He pulled himself up to his full height, which was not very tall at all, as he only managed to make his large stomach protrude further before him.

With a sigh which he meant for this odious man to recognize as frustration, Scetis opened the satchel he had been clinging to. The little man peered inside the opening and found clothes, a couple of books, and a black case.

"What is inside that?" He pointed a pudgy finger at the case.

Scetis reached in and carefully opened the small leather case. Inside were vials of different liquids and powders, each with a small label attached and writing in a neat and careful hand declaring what each was.

"Medicines, sir," Scetis told him. "As I told you, I am here to treat an elderly uncle."

"Very good. And the other bag?" He looked to Scetis other side.

Scetis passed the black case to Loxa and opened it. Inside were bundles of food, and a small cooking pot, which was blackened, but clean.

"As you can see, good sir, our provisions for our journey here," Scetis said.

"And you boy, your bags, please." The man now turned his attention to Loxa.

"Yes, sir," Loxa replied and shrugged off the bag that was strapped to his back. This was larger than the two Scetis was carrying combined, and he held it out. "It's just our bedding, sir, and other items of clothing."

"Any weapons?" The man waved the bag away, there was a distinctive odor of soiled and unwashed items coming from it and his nose was wrinkling with distaste.

"No sir, we're medics, not soldiers. Our only sharp implements are those that we use in our profession, small knives and needles," Scetis informed him.

"Well, you seem to check out well enough. You may enter. Also, come see me at the citadel later, I have a need for your services."

"And your name, sir, so we have a way of finding you?" Scetis placed his bags back over his shoulders.

"I am Councilor Cruithne. Just ask at the main gate and they will find me."

"I would be delighted to come to your aid, Councilor Cruithne. But it will have to be after I have tended to my uncle. I will call on you tomorrow evening if you are free."

"That would be acceptable. And I hope your uncle recovers from his ailment." Cruithne inclined his head to Scetis and stepped out of his way.

"Thank you and see you tomorrow, Councilor." Scetis gave his own little nod to the official and then passed him with Loxa hurrying after his master while still struggling to get the large backpack over his shoulders.

The apprentice waited until they were well away from the entrance of the town before asking Scetis the question that had puzzled him. "Master, where did you put the—?" He refrained from saying the name as they were passed by a team of horses and cart.

"A man who is as pompous and pleased with his own importance is easily led. By my telling him that we are entering and therefore would not have the eggs, it made him lazy in his search. They are safe, and not for you to worry about for now."

"So, what now?" Loxa was looking around him at the town and its bustling people.

"Now, Loxa, we go to the citadel and try to gain entrance to the where we need to be." Scetis strode down the road, his face set and determined.

Inside the citadel both Foot and Rider troops were running to the call. The two long notes denoted an intruder had been seen inside the defensive walls. Venicones grabbed hold of a Rider and spun them around.

"Orlagh, what's going on?" he asked her.

"Captain." The king's daughter stood at attention and ready to report to her superior. "Two intruders, sir, both seen near the Hall of Secrets."

"Are you sure?" he asked her.

"I am, sir." Orlagh replied.

"Go tell your father, then fetch the General," he ordered her.

The princess ran off and Venicones led the way to the most secret of halls in the Citadel. They arrived and found the doors open wide and the two guards laid out on the ground, already their unconscious forms had been pulled out of the way and two others had taken their place.

"Report." Venicones demanded of them.

"Two individuals, Sir. They overpowered Deva and Tang and entered the hall; we were coming to relieve the guard and saw them. We rushed in, but one threw something at us. I recognized it as a dragon egg. We raced to make sure it did not land on the ground, while we were focused on the egg, the older of the men tossed something through one of the mirrors and they managed to escape us. We could not leave our posts and leave the hall unattended," he reported almost pleading their case for letting the men slip past them.

"Where's the egg?" Muniath asked coming forward now. His hopes were flaring.

"Here, sir. I've tried to keep it warm," the other guard said as he pulled the gold and red egg from under his tunic. Cradling it in both hands, he carefully handed it over to Muniath.

"It's Screamer's egg." Muniath said as he closely examined it. There were no cracks or damage he could see, and the colors were still bright and vibrant. It gave a little wiggle in his hand as the creature inside moved around. "What about the other egg?" He looked at them.

"This is the only one we saw, sir," the first guard told him.

"You said he threw something through a mirror?" Venicones asked him.

"Yes, it was something wrapped in a cloth."

"Did you see which mirror?"

"I did, sir," the second said. He turned and headed into the dimly lit hallway. Near the center, he stopped and pointed to a mirror.

"Are you sure it was this one?" Muniath demanded.

"Yes sir, I made sure it was this one," the Rider told him.

"Go back to your post. As soon as the General gets here send him down." Muniath dismissed the man, and he went back to his post.

"You know where this goes," Venicones said to him.

"I do, and there is no getting back. The portal was destroyed on that side." Muniath stood staring at the dark frame and the carved dragon that curled around it.

"What the hell went on here?" Galanan called from the entrance and the two brothers turned to face their father. At his side was the king, and closely following behind, Orlagh.

Venicones stepped in front of his brother and began to give his report to Galanan and King Urmond. Their expressions both changed, and they studied the mirror that they stood beside.

"There is no hope then," King Urmond lamented. "The dragon is lost to us. It will not survive if it is out in the open."

"My King, the sire of Screamer's children, was Raker again. He is a warm climate dragon, if the egg were more his then it could survive if the land is temperate." Muniath stepped forward as he spoke. "Please, let me go and find out if there is any hope for it."

"Muniath, you are now Master of Dragons, I cannot spare you, nor risk you not coming back. You know which world this mirror leads to?"

"I do, my King."

"There is no one else who can replace you, there is no apprentice yet for your skill. We still have two eggs."

"But not nearly enough, each egg is precious now. Our mounts are diminishing, we need every new generation. We are already at the point where we have more Riders than mounts."

"I am aware of the situation and it worries us. Your last mission—" Urmond saw the stricken look on Muniath's face at the failure which had led to his disgrace and spoke more gently to him. "Your last mission did not go as planned. The last Master of Dragons was rash, and we know it was not your fault. I would caution you to be more circumspect and think of the dragons we do have. If we were to lose you now, we would surely lose the dragons."

"My King, there is a boy in the town who we have identified as having the skill." Venicones spoke now and placed a hand on his brother's shoulder.

"Who is he? And why, Muniath, when you know that it is so important, have you not already taken him as an apprentice?"

"He is Taran's grandson, Wick. And I have not taken him on, because I have not had the time, my King."

"Then that is your most important task. I know the loss of this egg is great, but you must think of the Realm first and your duties to it. Sometimes we must make sacrifices we do not wish to make. Take this boy on and get on with your work. That, is an order."

"As my King wishes." Muniath bowed deeply to Urmond.

"These intruders, do we know where they went, did they go through the mirrors after the egg?" Galanan asked his sons.

"No, sir, they tossed the egg through the mirror and then used the other as a means for their escape. The alarm was raised at once and the gates to the town and citadel were closed immediately. They must be still in the citadel, and if not then in the town itself. We will hunt them down," Venicones told his father.

"Get on with it then. Princess Orlagh, I want to see General Gerarailt at once, go find him," Galanan gave the order.

"Yes, sir." the young Rider said and turned on her heel to race away.

"She hates being called that; you know that Galanan?" Urmond said with a grin.

"She is your daughter still, my King, and deserving of the title."

The two men were starting to head back to the entrance as they spoke, while Muniath was still looking at the mirror. He waited until they would be out of earshot before turning to his brother.

"There is a way back. The king told me that there is a key that will bring back those that really wish to."

"What are you talking about?"

"Do you remember when General Loinsigh and his daughter were banished?"

"Yes, of course I do."

"He gave the girl a necklace. That necklace is a key to a temporary portal that would bring the user back."

"No. You are not going in there. You don't even know if they are still alive, or where they would be. That world is vast and very different to our own. It could take your whole life to find them. Muniath, think about what King Urmond said. You have your duties and obligations here."

Venicones stepped up to his brother and placed an arm around his shoulder, then gently guided him out of the hall and away from the mirror he was still looking at. As they left the hall the two guards shut the doors and locked it. The older brother took the key from the slot and placed it in his pocket.

"No one is to go in there. I want the guard doubled from now on," he ordered.

"Yes Sir." They stood at attention and saluted their commanding officer.

Later that evening Muniath was still mulling over the problem with the lost egg and how he could retrieve it. The fate of the poor creature worried him as he made his way through the town while the shopkeepers were placing the shutters on their shop fronts, and the noise of music and laughter increased in the taverns. His feet found their way unerringly to the best of them and opened the door to the warm room.

A fire was merrily dancing in the grate and the smell of wonderful food assaulted his senses. He could almost taste the haunch that was cooking on the spit in the kitchen out back. Behind the bar, Meara was standing, chatting with a customer as she served him. She looked up and saw her foster-brother and the worry that creased his brow.

"Thank you, Cruithne, that's two coppers." She held out her hand to take the money from the short overweight man and then turned to Muniath.

"What's the matter now, Mun? You look like you have the weight of the world on your shoulders. You should be happy you're back where you should be," she said, and she wiped down the already clean and scrubbed bar.

"It's been a very interesting day Mae. I need to talk to you and to Taran, it's about Wick," he said as he tapped the bar.

"You want him as an apprentice." Her tone was flat.

"He has the skill, and no other child has been identified in the town who has it."

"Then search the Realm," she said defiantly.

"Mae, you know as well as I do that he needs to be trained, and soon."

"Hasn't this realm taken enough from my family? My husband, my mother, and my father who is now maimed and unfit for duty. Haven't we given enough service to the King?" Meara kept her voice down and low as her eyes scanned the room to make sure that they were not overheard by gossiping ears.

"Wick is sixteen. In another year or two he will lose the skill. Surely you cannot want him to just be an inn keeper for the rest of his life? You must want him to do so much more?"

"I want to keep him safe. Can you, in all honesty, promise me that he will be safe as an Apprentice Warden?"

"Can we go out the back and discuss this? Please, Mae, it is important."

Meara flashed hurt eyes at his request. "Give me a minute," she said, resigned to the fact they were going to have the conversation. She disappeared and soon Wick came through the door his mother had just disappeared through, wiping his hands on a white apron. For the first time in a long time, Muniath studied the young man who was his foster-nephew. He stood tall and proud, looking so much like his late father, with a brown hair and eyes that immediately brightened and smiled along with a wide grin when he saw Muniath.

"Uncle Mun, how are you?" Wick asked.

"I'm good thanks, Wick."

"Ma said to go through to the back."

"Thanks." Muniath started to head out the back and stopped turning back to the boy. "Do you enjoy working here, Wick, with your mother?"

"It's alright, you get to hear what's going on in the kingdom, and that. But it can be a bit boring. I'd prefer to be a Rider." The young boy grinned.

Muniath nodded and headed through the door.

In the kitchen, Taran was sitting at the table, a knife in hand as he cut up vegetables for the pot that sat in front of him, his damaged leg stretched out stiff to one side and the ragged scar still glowed slightly red down his face. He looked up from his work and spotted Muniath.

"Nice to see you sober, Mun." He laughed a little and gave him a wink.

"It is good to be sober, Taran." Muniath pulled up a chair and sat down.

"Mae will be back in a minute, but before she does, I will help you convince her to take Wick. The boy needs to go to his destiny, he can't be held back here in this place." He waived the knife indicating the neat and tidy kitchen.

"If it were up to me, Taran, Wick would remain safely here. But it's the King's orders."

"Then it's your duty to obey him. Mae will see that too when she calms down. She knows what her debt is to your family. Taking her in when I could not care for her."

"That is the past and my parents would have taken her in no matter what. She is your daughter, and you are my father's closest friend. But to ask, now, to take Wick from her, is not fair," Muniath told him quietly, aware that their conversation was probably being listened to by the subject of it.

"When the crown calls, it is all of our duty to obey and respond. I know you will look after him and not put him in danger, and he is to be a Dragon Warden, not a common Rider. He has the skill, and it must be used; you know this."

"But look what happened to you, to Nabarus," Muniath hissed Meara's late husband's name.

"You know being a Rider comes with certain risks. As Master of Dragons, you know there is every chance a dragon can turn on its Rider when injured. Nabarus saved my life that day, my mount was in mortal pain and he stepped in before Thunder could kill me."

"That is the reason I don't want my son anywhere near those creatures," Meara said stepping into the room.

"Mae, come, sit down and we will talk about it calmly," Taran told his daughter.

Sitting down she stared at Muniath. "So, convince me why I should allow my only child to be put into the service of the King, around animals that could kill him." Her tone was calm, but Muniath could hear the steel in it and remembered it well from growing up with her.

"As I said to Taran, if it were up to me, I wouldn't be here. But the King has ordered it and as one of his subjects—also Master of Dragons—I must obey. Mae he will be with me and you know I love him as a son. I promise you that I will do everything in my power and ability to keep the boy safe."

"Just because the King says, we all must obey. This is my boy, my son. He should have no right to be able to rip children from their mother's," she started to protest.

"No, I shouldn't have that right, Meara, but I do. And right now the Realm has a desperate need for your son's skills," a deep and soft voice spoke suddenly from the doorway.

The group at the table turned to find their king stepping out of the shadows and into the light of the kitchen. As always, he was dressed as one of his subjects, in hardwearing common leather pants, a white linen shirt and green vest, covered over by the hooded cloak which was the mainstay of the worker. Hovering behind him was Wick, who looked stunned at their visitor.

"My King, you do us honor by visiting us here," Taran said, heaving himself up from the table while wincing at the pain it gave him.

"Sit down, Taran, after all the faithful and honorable service you gave the crown, it is I who am honored," Urmond said as he pulled a chair out from under the scrubbed wooden table. He sat beside Meara and took up her hand. "Much has been taken from you and we thank you for all the sacrifice your family has given us. But you cannot deny that the boy has the skill necessary to become his destiny. He is the only one of his generation to have been identified with it and believe me, we have been looking for a long time. Since Muniath came to be an apprentice." Urmond looked at the Master of Dragons across the table.

"Sire, I do not wish to disobey your orders, and I know how important this is, but he is my only child," Meara said quietly and the pressure of the kings' hand over hers increased in comfort.

"My only child is a Rider, Meara, so I do know the pain of worrying about her safety around the Dragons. And remember he is not to be just a Rider, but eventually a Dragon Warden when he finishes his apprenticeship."

"Please, Ma, I can do it. I hear them every night in my dreams as they speak. I have to go, please Ma, let me go," Wick now said stepping up to his mother.

Meara sat quietly for a moment looking between her son and the King. She heaved a great sigh and closed her eyes for a moment. The decision was made already and out of her hands, her acceptance of that decision was all they were waiting for now.

"Alright. There is nothing I can do." Meara stood and withdrew her hand from Urmond. "My Lord King," she addressed him formally. "My son has the highly sought-after Dragon Sense; will you take him into your service as apprentice to the Master of Dragons? Will you protect and teach him all he needs to know to survive and thrive under your service?"

Urmond stood up and placed the chair carefully back under the table. He stepped back and then formally bowed to Meara.

"Meara, I do accept your son in our service and promise to protect and teach him all he should know. We are honored for the opportunity to have him work and care for our dragon mounts." He gave her a sad smile. "I know it is difficult for you to accept, Meara, and I thank you on behalf of our Realm."

Discovery

A white, four-wheel drive bumped along the dirt track, sending up plumes of dust behind it like a long tail as it headed deep into the native forest. The sound of the engine echoed against the large tree trunks and briefly interrupted the song of the birds high in their branches. The occupants were dressed alike in deep green colored shirts, khaki pants, and sturdy hiking boots. They moved with the vehicle as it rolled on the rutted ground, then came to a complete stop in front of one of the many barriers into the protected and fragile area. The front passenger door opened and a young woman with bright red hair jumped out to unlock and open the barrier, rushing after to close and secure the gate again once the vehicle had driven through. She ran to the door and jumped back in and the car carried on its way again.

"You can relax now, Teagan, that should be the last one," the driver said, giving her a grin.

"Thank goodness for that," she replied with an equal grin.

They drove further in until the track disappeared into a wall of green trees and ferns. The engine ticked loudly as it cooled, which sounded very alien in this environment, while the four people exited the car and started to pull backpacks from the back. The sound of the forest intruded into her awareness. The wind which sighed through the swaying treetops only seemed to add to the song of the birds, and all cancelling out the noise of the men she was with.

Teagan had just landed her dream job after finishing university, with the Department of Conservation. All through school and her studies she had volunteered with DOC, working hard, and enjoying the environment, and this was her first real assignment as a fully-fledged

DOC worker. She was looking forward to spending the next week in the forest.

A large fire had ripped through the back blocks of the state forest, caused by a lightning strike. It had been a dry summer so far and the forest, which was normally damp, had dried out, leaving the right amount of fuel for the fire. It was into this part of the forest that several precious and endangered Kiwi birds had been released into the wild only the year before. This was their purpose for being there. They needed to check on how much devastation the fire had visited on the area and if they could locate the seven birds that had been released.

Setting her pack on her back, Teagan followed the men into the cooler depths of the forest, heading into the hills, valleys, and mountains that made up the park. Their trek was long, and they reached the first of their homes for the next week late in the afternoon, a hut that held all the basics that they would need. A sturdy roof over their head, a potbelly stove that served as a heat source and cooking facilities, and a long drop out the back for those other needs.

Teagan chose her bed carefully, away from the men and dumped her pack on it, then pulled out her share of the food load, joining it with the others, before pulling out her sleeping bag and setting herself up. The two younger men, Phil and Mark, were loud and brash and gave each other grief over the smallest of things, laughing long and loud at their own jokes. Meanwhile Eric was like herself, getting on with the job at hand before settling down to rest for the evening.

An easy dinner of canned baked beans and toast over with, Eric opened and laid out a large map on the table and bent over it taking a closer look at the penned in markings he had made before leaving the office that morning. The three younger people came and joined him, with mugs of tea in their hands.

"This is the area we need to look at. It's rather large and spread out, so I think we should split into pairs and search the different sections that way," Eric said. Teagan had worked with him before while still a volunteer and liked the way he worked.

The other two men, Phil and Mark, were slightly older than herself, but not by much. They nodded and agreed with the assessment of Eric and she noticed that Phil looked her way.

"Right, Mark and Phil if you two take this first section, Teagan and I will take the second. Make sure you have your radios in working order and stick together. If you pick up any signals, radio in the position and make sure you take notes and photos," Eric ordered, and relief flooded Teagan at the realization that she would not be with either of the other two men.

The pair did not talk as they pushed through the forest the next day. The higher up into the hills they trekked the more their surroundings changed. The tree ferns and scrubby bushes which crowded underneath the dense canopy in the valleys gave way to larger trees, which spread out, leaving a dappled light to dance on the leaf strewn ground at their feet. Eric was in the lead, headphones encasing his ears as he listened carefully for the signal from the tracker on the Kiwi that had been released in the area they now searched. He swept the cone shaped device he held in his hand in gentle and slow arcs before him. The area was just on the fringe of where the fire had raged, and the first signal came in strong and loud as they neared it.

By the end of the day each team had traced the bird that they were searching for and found them in good health and doing well. They poured over the notes, writing up the reports that evening and looking at the photos they had taken of the damage they had seen of the burning.

For the next couple of days this was their life. They packed up and moved camp further into the forest. The hut they moved to had been affected by the fire. There was only a slight singeing of the hut, but the long drop was completely destroyed. While Eric and Teagan carried on with the search, Mark and Phil set about fixing the problem of the toilet facilities.

Around midday Teagan and Eric came to a stream. They sat and opened the day packs pulling out food for lunch.

"You know what I like about you, Teagan?" Eric asked jovially.

"What?" she replied as she bit into an apple.

"You don't seem to feel the need to fill in the silence of the forest with prattle."

"Prattle?" Teagan took another bite.

"Yeah, you know, like those other two, endlessly talking and joking." He bit into his sandwich.

"The forest isn't silent," she told him.

"No, it isn't. Tell me about yourself. We've worked together before, but I don't know anything about you."

"Nothing really to tell." She finished her apple and placed the core into a plastic bag, then took out an energy bar.

"Where are you from?"

"Here and there. We moved around a lot when I was young. Dad couldn't keep a job for long."

"What about your mum?"

"She died when I was a baby."

"What got you interested in this work?" He fished around in his pack looking for the apple he knew he packed in there that morning.

"I prefer the forest to cities and towns. I feel I can be me here. I don't interact well with people; they always take my quietness as being a bit standoffish."

"That is something I can understand." He finished his apple in a couple of bites, and they descended into silence once more, letting the forest speak around them. Once he had finished, he stood and made sure they didn't leave anything behind to mar the landscape.

"Shall we continue?" He placed the headphones back on his head and carried on, with Teagan following behind.

The devastation of the fire was all around them. The smell of the wet ash and charcoal from half-burnt trees invaded their senses. But already, signs of green were coming back in the form of grass and other plants pushing their delicate way through compacted ash. Teagan made sure she was careful where she placed her feet so as not to damage the new shoots as they descended into a steep valley. Somewhere around them Teagan could hear rushing water becoming louder and louder the lower they went.

"Careful in this valley, there is a cave system under our feet, and I don't know what kind of damage the fire may have caused the ground," Eric warned her and carried on sweeping the area for a signal.

The faint chirping signal came in shortly after he had spoken and Eric moved off in the direction it came from, with Teagan making her way gingerly behind him.

She stopped and waited for him to get a little further ahead as he swung the device, tracking the Kiwi they were searching for. A noise in the brittle undergrowth caught her attention. A dead fern shook, and a pair of dark eyes peered out at Teagan before they ducked back, and the creature scurried away from her.

Curious, she stepped closer to it and tried to see what it was. Something dark scurried away from her, it was too large to be a small skink, which was common all-over New Zealand, but looked more like the larger Tuatara. This puzzled Teagan as the native lizard could only be found now in the outer, pest-controlled islands.

Watching carefully, she followed the sounds and rustling plants that the animal was moving. It was quick and darted with fast movements. When she looked around for Eric, he was nowhere to be seen and she could not even hear where he may be in the forest.

A noise at her feet made her look down. The lizard stared up at her, making an almost purring sound. Its eyes were wide and dark, and it had another curious feature. Two protruding growths were on either side of its back, just behind the shoulders, that appeared to be skin flaps.

Teagan bent down carefully, not wanting to frighten the animal. The skin flaps moved and spread out. Her hand was just reaching out when she stopped in shock. They were wings.

The little creature let out a high-pitched growl at her and then darted away. Teagan was on the chase once more and rushed into the forest recklessly, forgetting Eric's warnings. Her foot suddenly landed on a pile of soft singed leaf matter and sank into it. It kept sinking and she found herself falling into nothing. The light left her and into darkness she sunk, it seemed like for a long time.

The ground when she finally landed was hard and it knocked the wind out of her. She lay gasping, the pain seeped through her, increasing as the shock wore off. Teagan lay still for quite some time until she caught her breath, and she could really look around where she was. A dim light filtered through several gaps in the ceiling and she could see the smooth sides of the cave. It was long and wide and at the end a waterfall fell from a stream up above and disappeared into the floor.

The radio at her hip crackled and she caught her name in amongst the static as she pulled it off and pressed the button.

"Eric?" she called out and her voice echoed around her. Again, the radio crackled, and she heard what sounded like 'are you?'

Gingerly she moved where she lay and was pleased to find no broken bones. She went to stand and found pain radiating out from her right ankle. Teagan grunted when she went to put more weight on it. Carefully she headed towards where there was more light shining down into the cave from above, a shaft of sunlight was strong and the mist of the waterfall muted it slightly, but the sound of the rushing water was louder and trying to hear the radio was more difficult.

"Hello, Eric are you there?" Teagan called loudly into the radio.

It crackled as she pulled her finger off the send button, and she almost cried when his voice came through loudly.

"Where are you?" She could hear the worry in his voice.

"I'm underground," she called out.

"Where?"

"Find the stream where it heads into the cave. I'm there."

"Be there soon. Don't move."

"I won't."

Teagan found a rock to sit on and collapsed onto it, pulling her backpack off her shoulders, and grabbing her water bottle out before dropping it down onto the ground at her feet. She took long gulps from the cold liquid and then sighed as she put the lid back on.

Observing her surroundings while she waited, Teagan saw where a slip had occurred, creating an opening beside the waterfall. It had also brought down with it trees and bushes, which clung on and continued to grow where they had fallen. They were untouched by the fire that had raged in the world above them, and the rocks and walls of the cavern were laced with a bright green moss.

A rustling inside her bag made her look down and saw it moving, something was inside it. Carefully she reached down and picked it up, placing it on her lap, hesitating for a moment, she opened the zip wider and peered inside. The same little purring sound she had heard earlier came from out of the canvas bag. Slowly she dipped into it with her hand and something small clasped onto her finger, a gummy mouth nipped at her and she tried to pull her hand away, but it held on tighter.

Instead of following her first instinct to throw the bag from her, Teagan relaxed, and her finger was soon let go, allowing a scaly and small horned head to rub against her hand. It was cold under her touch and shivered slightly, seeking out the warmth her body could impart.

The rope pulled tight and started to dig deep into her body as the tension grew. Slowly, Teagan began to be hauled up and out of the cave back into the light above. It jerked a little as the three men adjusted their grip to make the next haul. Her bag bumped against her hip and the strange creature moved inside, carefully she pulled it tighter to her. Again, the rope hauled her closer to the opening, some of the leaf litter and soil started to rain down on her as the movement dislodged it. Teagan closed her eyes tightly, not against the height—that had never frightened her—but from the particles that were settling on her head and body. As she neared the top Eric was there with his arm extended. Teagan lifted her own from where it gripped the rope to meet his, and he clasped her by the wrist to help her over the lip. Once over, she held tightly to the bag to her chest as she breathed deeply, while Eric checked her ankle and began to strap it.

"Phil, take her bag will you." Eric called out to one of the other men as they were coiling up the rope again.

"It's fine, I can still carry it," Teagan started to protest.

"How are you going to manage it? Don't be pig-headed."

"Pass it over, Teagan." Phil said as Eric began to strap her ankle and she gasped in pain. But her thoughts were on the creature.

A sling was soon fashioned with the rope and Teagan found herself in between Phil and Mark with her arms around their shoulders and sitting on the rope as they carried her back to the hut.

Inside they lay her on the bunk and Eric took a closer look at her injuries. A few scrapes and bruises, with the worst being her ankle. It was not broken, like she had first initially thought, but only sprained he declared, and strapped it up again. Mark and Phil got busy with preparing an early dinner and their talk soon turned to giving Eric an update on their progress with building a new out-house.

That night Teagan lay on her bunk and listened to the sounds of the forest outside, when she heard the distinct patter of feet inside, scurrying around. Tins were upturned and things gone through before a battery lantern flared into life. The noise stopped immediately.

"Bloody possums!" Eric muttered as he climbed out of his sleeping bag to investigate further.

Within the dancing shadows cast by his lantern something climbed on the bunk beside Teagan in the corner by her feet and crawled up the bed beside the wall. Two bright eyes sparkled at her as she came face to face with the little lizard. It clicked a couple of times at her and then started to bury itself in her sleeping bag. Its shining, dark green scales cool to her touch and it snuggled up with her. The vibrations from it was almost like a cat and Teagan looked around her to see if anyone else could hear the soft purring.

Eric stumbled around but couldn't find the offending animal or even where it may have come in. Giving up, he headed back to bed and switched the light off, plunging the hut back into darkness. There were no more disturbances that night.

In the morning, the men ate a quick breakfast, before all sagely advising Teagan to stay off her foot and to complete the written reports as they left for the final day of the survey. As soon as the door was shut the little creature came out of hiding from the depths of her sleeping bag. Its little head still partly covered, it stared at her and made the strange clicking sound.

"Hello," Teagan said softly to it, trying not to startle or scare it. The head came out further and she got her first proper look at the body. The scales were like jewels, gleaming and picking up the light, giving them a deep green, almost luminescent look. Its eyes were a deep black and showed no pupils. The spines down the center of its head were a lighter shade of the scales. But it was the wings that fascinated her the most.

As the lizard climbed out of the sleeping bag, it extended its wings and stretched. Spreading wide its little mouth, it showed the gummy interior. The noise it made was like the creature was trying to roar and she giggled a little.

"So, what are you?"

The wings started to flap, and a memory tugged in the deep reaches of her mind. Creatures which looked similar, flying past her while she was being held by her father. The flash came so quickly but stunned her so much that she had not seen the small lizard come up to where she sat. It climbed her leg and sat on her thigh, looking up at her with wide eyes.

The urge and need for food overtook Teagan, and she searched the table beside her. Picking up a piece of toast carefully she held it out to the small being.

"You can eat it," she encouraged. It sniffed the browned bread and took a tentative bite, then promptly spat it out. "Ok, so bread and toast are out." Teagan looked for something else to try. On one of the plates the men had failed to clean up before leaving, sat a small piece of sausage. Picking it up she held it out to the creature, and it was soon gobbled up.

"Okay, you're a meat eater."

The creature chirped again and then sneezed. A small puff of smoke exited its two small nostrils.

"Holy crap! You can't be. Are you a drag—?" she started. The creature looked up at her quizzically. "You are a dragon?" Teagan managed to get out.

The raft of memories came flooding back to her. Memories she thought were just vivid dreams or figments of her imagination. She remembered seeing the great creatures flying through the sky and wanting to be on the back of one of them. Remembered her father as a great general in charge of the Riders and how he had told her one day she would be a general. These memories she had suppressed and locked away to keep the hurt of being banished at bay. She had to concentrate on this world and keeping her father sane.

With a breath that was coming fast and sharp she stared at this creature.

"How did you get here?" Raising a finger, she stroked the small dragon's head. It purred again and leaned into her touch.

The awareness of heat all around her flashed in her mind and she slowly saw light through a chink of something. The gap widened and she poked her head through the gap and saw small flames dancing, accompanied with the roar of the body of the fire higher up. The warmth and the want of that warmth was great and so pleasing.

"You hatched in the fire. But how did your egg get here?"

Teagan's own memories with going through the portal when she and her father had been banished now rose to the surface.

"I understand now. You came through the portal, but why, is what I'm wondering. Why did they send you to this world?"

The small dragon looked past her face for a moment and then leapt from her thigh. Its wings were wide and flapping hard as it tried to gain the air. It landed back down with a thump and it was soon trying again, this time rising a little higher. The natural instincts of the creature were kicking in as it concentrated on flying.

"A little more, you can do it," Teagan encouraged it as she watched, fascinated by its efforts.

The tightly stretched membrane of the wings suddenly billowed out on the downstroke and it rose into the air, higher. The creature huffed and puffed audibly as it gained height. Its eyes focused fully on something in the rafters of the hut and she followed it as it reached the wooden beams. Scampering along, its long tail flicking out behind for balance, it raced along and caught something up in its mouth, chomping down on it, then swallowing.

"You can collect all the bugs you like, little one." She laughed at it as it looked down at her pleased with its efforts.

The small dragon spread its wings wide and launched itself off the beam to glide slowly down in wide lazy circles. It landed beside her on the bench seat and then crawled into her lap, curled itself up and promptly closed its eyes. Teagan stroked the little creature with wonder, and it began to purr again.

"What am I going to do with you now? We're leaving in the morning; I can't leave you out here to try and survive on your own. You'll have to come home with me. Dad should be able to help." Her thoughts tumbled from her lips and she tried to think her way through the problem of this little dragon.

"And what are we going to name you?" The dragon looked up at her with sleepy dark eyes and blinked a couple of times. It reminded Teagan of a movie she had seen.

"Gremlin."

The baby dragon clicked again at her, curled its head into its side flank and started to purr again as it fell asleep.

Illness

The water was swift and fast flowing. The splashes the pair made as they waded through the shallowest part sparkled in the late afternoon sunshine. Loxa stumbled over a rock and started to fall forward. Reaching out quickly, Scetis steadied him, his hand grasping onto the boy's shirt pulling it tightly.

"Be careful! You fall and what food we have left will be lost." He let the younger man go and carried on across the river. His feet squelching in his boots and the chill turning his toes numb as they carried on.

Scetis and Loxa had not stopped since they had been discovered in the Hall of Secrets. They had followed the banks of the river, fed from the large lake which filled the valley below the Citadel, hiding in amongst the trees and scrubby bushes that grew there.

Shortly before stepping into the water, they had spotted a farmhouse and outbuildings across the river. Smoke rose lazily from the stone chimney and they could see a farmer herding his flock into a pen for the night.

Scrambling up the bank, Scetis crouched down behind a bush to watch the farm once more. He parted the branches to get a better look, careful of where he placed his hands on the thorn laced wood.

"It's just about sundown. As soon as it gets dark, we'll go see what we can help ourselves to over there," Scetis told Loxa.

"Why can't we just knock on the door? They're farming folk, and usually generous with strangers who need help."

"The kind of help we need will not be given freely. They would have been warned about us and our descriptions spread widely over the land by now," he hissed at his apprentice. "No, we have to remain hidden."

"I had no idea that I would become a common thief and burglar when I became your apprentice," Loxa huffed as he moved the bag on his back from digging into his skin.

"We are Traders. Not Physicians. We go out and find the medicinal materials that the Physicians need," Scetis said calmly.

"But you know how to be a Physician, you have the credential on your medallion."

"Of course, I have the credential, I studied hard under my master to become a Physician, just as I did to also become an Apothecary. But Trading is something else. There is an excitement that treating patients can never come close to. You felt it the other night when you picked up those eggs, right under the nose of their mother." His eyes gleamed a little and Loxa edged back from him.

"I was petrified," Loxa told him with a shameful whisper.

Scetis studied the boy for a moment. "As soon as we get back to the Convocation, we'll set about finding you a more suitable calling and master." Scetis turned back to stare at the farmyard in the dying light. He could hear the boy moving about behind him and was fast losing patience. This apprentice had been forced upon him by the Regulator, after years of ignoring the hints that he should take one on by his various Masters.

Scetis glanced up at the deepening sky and soon the first stars of the night were gleaming brightly, and when he judged that it was dark enough, he stood and gently stretched out his limbs which had started to cramp after the cold water. His feet were still sodden, but he could ignore that. It was the weariness that was niggling away at his strength. He counted back in his mind and found that he would soon have to imbibe the concoction once more to keep him going.

Pushing his way through the brambles and low branched trees, he didn't wait for his apprentice to follow. It was expected that the boy should always be there nearby in case he was needed for something and to observe his master and learn. Scetis scanned the open ground around them, interspersed with fences of woven Betula branches, there was nothing around on the ground. He searched the sky, but there was nothing there either, no sound of birds fluttering still for their nightly perch or more importantly the sound of large wings beating through the air.

Moving quickly to the nearest fence, he crouched down behind it and shook his head when he heard the noise of Loxa following. Up and over the wicker worked structure, landing softly on the other side with hardly a thump escaping his feet. Only the soft squelch of water still trapped in his boots could be heard.

Across the open field he raced on cat-like feet, gaining the opposite fence line. Scetis stopped once more to wait for Loxa. Up ahead he could hear the flock of sheep penned up for the night, the odd bleat plaintively calling out into the gathering darkness. The heavy breathing of his apprentice soon clamored over the top and Scetis had to bite his tongue not to say something. So as not to tempt himself further he moved off again, making the side of the barn and pressed himself against it. Loxa was on his heels this time and Scetis went off to investigate further, motioning for the boy to stay put.

Noise from the house across the yard proclaimed the residents were all safely in for the night. Keeping the barn wall at his back he carefully kept going, searching for what he knew should be there, a cellar holding the stores of the farm ready for market. Rounding another corner, he found it. The steep stone steps that led down into the ground and under the barn. Not even waiting to see if he could open the door he carried on around the barn to where Loxa was waiting.

Carefully he watched his apprentice as he made his way forward on silent feet. As he stood at the boy's back, he could sense that Loxa had no idea that his master was behind him. Scetis' hand suddenly clamped over the boy's mouth and he felt Loxa go tense, but did not jump at the surprise, nor make a sound of alarm. There may be hope for him yet, Scetis thought to himself.

"They're all inside the house. The barn has a storeroom dug underneath and it is full of supplies. Follow me," Scetis whispered into his ear.

The hand was taken away and Loxa dutifully followed his master into the shadows, to the steps. Scetis made his way down into the darkness and found the door handle, carefully turning it. The door moved at his touch, squeaking a little as it opened wider. He retrieved the little box in his pocket which held his tinder and flint. With deft fingers in the dark, he struck a light and flames were soon gently burning in the tinder on a tray, giving them enough light to see through the deep blackness that had only a moment ago surrounded them.

The room was cool and was designed to be so during the hotter summer months. All four walls were lined with many shelves of rough-cut wood, each groaning under the weight of bags of grain, both milled and unmilled. There were jars stoppered and sealed with wax and many wheels of cheese, both large and small, stacked neatly. Large hams were hung from hooks buried deeply into the large beams overhead and swung slightly as Scetis made his way through them. Many more goods were packed in barrels in the corners and laid out in neat rows in the open floor. It had the distinct air that the farmer was just about to head to the market with his goods to sell.

Scetis began to take things off the shelves, only small amounts and only what they needed to get back to their own realm. He carefully sliced off a hunk of the ham and wrapped it in a waxed cloth he had found on one of the shelves. Loxa shrugged off the bag at his back and started to store the items away, while trying to ignore their shadows which danced in the light of the flame, sending up haunting images of themselves stealing from these good people who worked hard for what was there.

Their job soon done, the light was extinguished and Loxa was heading up the stairs following his master. Scetis stopped at the top and looked out of the doorway to see if anyone was about. A high peel of womanly laughter floated on the slight breeze from the house and the pair were on the move once more.

They soon found themselves back at the river, the rushing noise as the water tumbled over rocks filled the air, masking any sounds of the night. Scetis led on following the flow of the river down-stream and away from the farm holding. When the lights from the house could no longer be seen he pushed his way into a thicket and started to kick stones into the center.

"Make a fire, Loxa, and we'll eat." Scetis took off his own bags that crossed over his back and chest and sank to his knees.

The night's activities had taken a larger toll on him than he had first thought. He pulled one of the bags to him and opened the leather case he had shown to the officious councilor at the gates to the town. Scetis fumbled with the clasp for a moment and then pulled out a very thin and short flask. Delving back into the case he pulled out a silver tumbler, a little larger than a thimble and highly decorated. It gleamed in the fire that Loxa had just managed to get started.

Very carefully, Scetis put the flask and tumbler down beside the growing fire. He placed his hands out to the warmth for a moment, already the cold starting to creep and bite through his body. The effects of the long-ago poisoning were once more trying to kill him. While he futilely tried to warm himself, Loxa was pulling out the ham and cheese, carving off slices and handing them first to his Master. Scetis forced himself to eat, it would be the last food he would have for the next couple of days and knew he needed the strength it would give him. Once he was finished, he picked up the now warmed flask and tumbler, the heat from the metal objects radiated out into his skin.

Scetis held the silver tumbler between his fingers and slowly poured out the correct measure of the liquid from the flask. It was hard to see in the light of the small fire, but he stopped, took a deep breath and downed the honey-colored drink in one gulp. For a moment his breath stopped in his chest as it began to burn down to his stomach and spread out its increasing warmth to his outer limbs. He let out that breath in a long continuous stream and stoppered the flask. Stepping away from the fire he headed into the bushes, dug a small hole in the bank of the river before rinsing out the tumbler. Very carefully he buried the tumbler into the earth, placing a stone on top of the spot, before heading back to the fire and Loxa.

"What was that Master?" the young man asked him.

"Not for you, my apprentice. Do not go poking around with this flask, once you take this liquid you must have a small measure each month, otherwise you will waste away. It's an elixir of sorts."

"What's it made of?" Loxa's curiosity was not yet stilled.

"That is something for when you are back in a workroom, with an Apothecary. The effects after directly taking it makes the patient weary. You're going to have to watch over me for the next day, we'll not be leaving this spot until the day after tomorrow. Make sure the fire is banked well during the night and do not try to rouse me. I'll not need food or anything else. If someone comes, tell them that I have a pestilence, the excuse should keep most uneducated people away. If it's soldiers of the Foot or Riders, then we're in trouble. I must not be moved, but if they insist—and they probably will—tell them that if they want me to survive to be brought before their king, it is imperative that I be carried gently."

All the while Scetis had been talking he had been arranging his bedding, close to the fire. He lay down with his last words and folded his arms around him. He looked up into the face of his young apprentice.

"You must do this. Give me your word before I go to sleep," Scetis urged Loxa.

"I promised my life to you, Master, as your apprentice. I will make that promise again. I will watch over you and protect you," he stood tall with the responsibility being placed on him and it settled on his shoulders lightly.

"Good night then, guard me well. Oh, and Loxa, note down any changes in my body as I sleep, this specific elixir has not been fully studied," Scetis mumbled, once more regretting taking on Loxa as his apprentice. Thoughts of his own apprenticeship came to him as his mind began the slow descent down into darkness and the restorative sleep that only the distilled venom of a urodela could procure.

Sometime during the night Loxa woke to moaning. He looked across the dying fire at his master who was still very much asleep, but now his body was shivering, and his teeth chattered. Getting up he threw some more wood on the flickering flames, hoping to increase the heat it was putting out. Rummaging around in the large bag he pulled out the spare blanket and threw it over the top of Scetis. There was sweat beading off his stubbly head and dripping down in great streams.

Scetis moved suddenly, curling himself up into a ball, his arms pulled into his body and his knees almost touching his chin. He moaned again. Loxa raced around the fire and grabbed his own blanket to cover his master. He started to rub his back and limbs trying to get as much heat as he could into the tightened and knotted muscles he could feel under his touch. He was getting scared of these effects, the thought of his master dying slowly crept in, and then remembered what Scetis had asked him.

After putting another couple of logs on the fire, he pulled out a notebook, bound in black leather, and a charcoal pencil. Quickly he noted the time of the night and all the noticeable effects the elixir was having on his master's body. When he was sure he had them down he sat at the head of his master to watch over him for the rest of the night. He had to make sure Scetis did not die.

A deep and mournful bell clanged lazily near Loxa and he opened his eyes, unaware he had fallen asleep. His head came up quickly and he regretted it immediately. The pain in his cramped neck muscles radiated out and he rubbed it to ease the ache. Looking around he saw the large head of a cow nearby; its mouth was working as it chewed the grass it had found and looked back at Loxa with large brown eyes.

"Go, shoo!" Loxa got up and waved his hands at the cow. "Go on, get out of here!" His words became louder when the bovine refused to move.

"Who are you?" a boy of about ten asked as he came from behind a tree. "What are you doing here?"

"What does it look like? We stopped here the night; we're only passing through. My brother is sick," Loxa told him and hoped that the boy would believe his lie.

"Sick? What's wrong with him? I can go fetch my mam if you like, she's a healer of sorts," he offered.

"No, he has some sort of pestilence, I can't move him, and I don't think it would be a good idea if you were to come too close. That's why I was trying to shoo your cow away." Loxa gave a quick backwards glance at Scetis and then back to the boy.

"It's catchy then?" The boy's eyes widened at the word pestilence and he hurriedly stretched out his arm from where he stood for the lead rope around the cow's neck to pull it away from the two strange men.

"I don't know. I don't want to risk it."

"Best I tell mam then. Come on cow, move," he encouraged the animal.

Slowly the large head turned, and the bell began to chime once more as the cow followed the boy. Loxa could see that he was in a hurry to get away and was pleased when they had left. But the thought of the boy bringing his family there was not a happy one.

Turning back to the slowly dying fire Loxa banked it up again and soon the blaze danced merrily in its stone confines.

The boy was soon back along with a woman. The moment Loxa saw her he knew she was not a person to be lied to easily. Dressed in soft cloth leggings and boots almost up to her knees, a loose shirt that was kept close to her body by a tight-fitting vest and a belt that was tied around her waist. The belt held a knife in a sheath and her hand rested on it. She had the bearing of someone who had been trained well to use it. On the other side was strung a leather pouch.

"You there, what are you doing on our land?" she called out. Her voice was demanding and strong, a little deeper than he had expected.

"Please mistress, my brother is sick, we had to stop for the night so I could tend to him," Loxa said, standing now from where he had sat at the fire. He took a few steps to put himself in between Scetis and the two strangers.

"What are his symptoms?" she demanded.

"Fever, sweats, shivering, tight muscles and there is an odor to him."

"What sort of odor?" The woman instinctively placed a handout to bring her son back behind her.

"A sweet one, almost like honey," Loxa replied telling her the truth. It was a new development that he had noticed only a short while before they had arrived.

"It sounds more like a poison than a sickness. Have you been foraging for food as you've travelled?"

"A little, to supplement our own dry rations."

"Did you pick mushrooms?"

"We did, we found some yesterday morning and ate them last night. My brother said that they were fine."

"It seems your brother doesn't know anything about plants. Can you describe the mushrooms?"

Loxa had to wrack his brain trying to remember the different mushrooms Scetis had tried to teach him. Only one poisonous one came to mind and he described it.

"They were small and growing in clumps on a rotten log. Their caps were brown, although some were nearly yellow. When they were cooking, they had a sweet smell."

"Galerina Grief. They're poisonous." The woman untied the bag at her waist and tugged at the leather cord that held it shut. "You need to steep this in water and give it to your brother in small sips. If he survives the night then he'll live, but if his fever worsens then even a Physician from the Convocation could not help him."

In her hand was a small woody looking substance. She held it out to Loxa to take.

"Thank you, mistress." He took the piece of bark from her hands and looked at her.

"Boil the water and let the bark steep for a little, until the steam goes off the water. You need to give it to him when the water is completely cold. Do not try to add more water to cool it down faster, it will only dilute the effect of the treatment."

"Can I ask how you know to do this?" Loxa asked.

"No, you cannot. Why are you travelling off the King's road?"

"We were escaping from some bandits," he said evasively.

"Bandits? Alright, do you need food?" the woman asked him, and he got the impression that she did not believe his story.

"We don't, thank you. We bought supplies in Hunndaidh before we left."

"When was that?"

"It was three days ago."

"Three days? You've not come very far then."

"My brother began to feel unwell yesterday and we slowed up a bit. Then the men started to follow us, he thought it would be best to hide and wait for them to either pass us or—"

"Alright, give him the tea and he should come right, if the poison has not affected him too badly. If it has, our home is that way," the woman pointed to where they had pillaged the stores. "We'll help you bury him," she told him quietly.

"I don't think it's that serious," Loxa told her, trying to keep his voice even.

"If you are still here tomorrow afternoon, then it will be a settled matter," she told him. "Brete come, you still have work to do before your studies."

"Yes Mam," the boy smiled at Loxa and then turned to follow his mother.

"Thank you again for your help," Loxa called after them.

"None needed, young man. Look after yourself." The pair walked away.

Loxa turned back to the fire and immediately began to prepare the tea as the woman had suggested, until he remembered that it would not do any good to give it to Scetis. He tucked the piece of bark into his pack and then stirred the fire a little more before checking on his master. He was happy to see that his earlier symptoms were beginning to ease.

"Water," the breathless whisper escaped his lips as he lay under the blankets. Scetis' throat was dry, and it hurt to swallow. The ability to produce saliva to moisten his cracked lips and mouth was not there and he coughed a little. "Water," he called again a little louder.

"Master!" Loxa was there at his side as soon as his eyes opened and was holding a water skin to his lips.

Scetis tried to grasp the bag with shaking hands as the water spilled over his tongue and down his throat. Between gulps he breathed deeply while Loxa held his head. With the immediate thirst slackened somewhat, Scetis struggled to rise, Loxa helped him to sit up, pulling the blankets up around his still shivering shoulders.

"Were we disturbed?" he asked, reaching for the water skin once more.

"The woman and a boy from the farm were here. I said you had eaten some Galerina Grief," Loxa reported while banking the fire up against the still night air, somewhere nearby an owl called out.

"Good cover. Were you also keeping notes, like I asked?" Scetis looked up at the boy and pulled the blankets around him, clenching his teeth against the chattering.

"I did, Master. Including what you uttered while you were asleep. I also noted down the times of any changes in your condition, I didn't know if that was important or not," he reported.

"Well thought out. You've done well." Scetis drank deeply again from the skin. "You are not suited as a Trader; I don't know why Wradech insisted to Tavae that I take you on. You have an Apothecary's mind; I'll find you a proper master when we get back."

"The man who took me from my family said that I should become one. I don't know why I was put with a Trader." Loxa poked at the fire with a stick.

"You didn't want to leave your home, did you?"

"No, I didn't. I wanted to take over from dad. My eldest brother had gone to the army, my sister was set to marry the boy from the next farm, and it was my duty to take the farm on. Now that falls to one of my younger brothers or sisters."

"I was taken from my family," Scetis said quietly while staring into the fire. "I was six and my mother could no longer feed us. She sold me to be a slave in that place."

Loxa sat on the other side of the fire and stared through the leaping flames at his master. The flickering light casting shadows over his pale face and deepening the dark shadows under his eyes. He held his breath a moment and wondered if Scetis would continue. Just after he had entered the Convocation and into the service of this man, he had heard whispers of his beginnings. So many rumors and conjectures of where he came from and how he had risen from the slave's quarters.

"It is not a place for a child," Scetis went on. "It should not have been so easy for her to sell me."

Scetis looked up suddenly, realizing what he was saying. He took a deep breath in through his nose and straightened his back. The pale blue eyes which were sunken into his skull and red from the drug that was running through his veins, stared at Loxa. His jaw clenched and the muscles quivered at his memories, trying to keep them under control.

"I wish you better than I, Loxa. I will make sure that you are put into the tutorship of a practitioner who will treat you kindly. You shall be no mere Trader. No, the truth of it runs through you and is so evident to one of our trade. I see great things for you now, so much greater than you could imagine. If I do this for you, you must promise me that you will work your hardest, learn all you can and more. You must do this and become who you are supposed to be. In my dreams Loxa you become the highest, and I call you master."

"That cannot be, Master," Loxa said, shaking his head as a small smile curled at the corners of his mouth.

"An effect of one component of the elixir is a clearing of the mind and insight into what should be obvious. I see it in you, and I will make sure you get there, but you have to promise me that you will do as I ask." The stare intensified and the almost gleaming eyes burned into Loxa's own.

"I do promise you, Scetis, my Master," Loxa replied.

"That is all I ask. Now sleep. I'll watch the rest of the night." Scetis pulled one of the blankets off his shoulders and held it out to his apprentice.

Promise

The smell of reptiles filled the air, along with the chirping of two small creatures and the sound of their soft scales rubbing against each other, as they tumbled in the nest. The pile of hay they played on was surrounded by their mother's tail, just in case they were to tumble out onto the hard, stone floor. Screamer nudged them with her nose gently and yipped at the pair. Each of the whelps stretched their tiny wings and flapped them awkwardly.

Wick stood at Muniath's side watching the baby dragons and laughed. They were like a couple of puppies in their play. Muniath glanced sideways at his newly appointed apprentice and gave his own small laugh.

"Go introduce yourself," he said quietly.

"But won't Screamer be defensive of her babies?" The smile slipped from his mouth as he looked at Muniath.

"She won't hurt you; she knows you already."

Wick turned back to the large mother dragon before him and took a tentative step towards her. Screamer brought up her head and looked at him, blinking a couple of times. As he raised his hand, she brought her head to meet it and cooed softly to him. The scales under his palm were slick and smooth, and they gleamed in the torch light of the dim cavern.

"Screamer," her name escaped his lips and a stream of images passed from the large beast to his mind. They were fast and flickering and he was unable to make any sense of them.

"It will come with training and time, Wick. Just let her get to know you first and be comfortable with you."

"You said she knows me already, how?" the boy asked in wonder.

"Your dreams. That is how we first start to communicate with them. They are very good at finding those with the skill to speak with them. It is almost as if the dragons are seeking us out deliberately, to make us understand them." Muniath was now beside him, his own hand reached up to stroke the large head of Screamer.

The image of the two baby dragons were firmly implanted in his mind and he looked down at the pair. They were sitting on their haunches staring up at him with dark, almost black looking eyes, their wings were tucked into their sides.

"Go ahead, she wants one of her babies to be bonded with you. This is important, Wick, she trusts you with her children," Muniath told him quietly.

"But surely one of the Riders without a mount should have first pick," he protested, uncertain in his role.

"In normal times, yes, but this is a special moment. You are going to be a Dragon Warden and she wants the honor of seeing one of her offspring bonded with you."

"But which one, Muniath?" Wick stared at the two whelps.

"You need to touch each one, it will come to you. It's an instinctive process Wick; trust what's there inside you."

Very gently he placed a hand on each head and waited for some sort of sign. It did not take long for him to see which it would be. His hand pulled away from the gold and red hatchling and he picked up the gold and green. The little male dragon shivered excitedly in his hands and wriggled a little to nestle himself in Wick's palms, the bond slipped between them almost immediately and a contentment lay itself over him like a blanket.

"Well done. Now you can learn from the start how to care and nurture a dragon. He is your responsibility from now on, and as soon as his mother will allow him to leave the nest you will have the training of him. With my help of course." Mun placed a hand on the boy's shoulder and looked down at the small creature.

Screamer nudged the remaining dragon in the nest forward and then brought her head around to Muniath. He locked his eyes with her for a moment and drew in a great breath, letting it out shuddering with emotions.

Almost without knowing what he was doing he reached out and the small whelp leapt into his palm, gripping tightly with small, clawed feet. It raced up his arm and onto his shoulder. The small head rubbed up against his cheek and Muniath pulled it away to get a better look at it.

"I am honored, Screamer," he told the dragon.

If Wick thought that his duties were to be training and observing Muniath, he was sadly mistaken. He was to learn from the bottom up, just as any new Warden had. Mucking out and bringing in fresh bedding for the mounts. By learning what each species of dragon ate and preparing their meals, but this did not concern him.

Working for his mother and with his grandfather had given him a good grounding and a solid work ethic. He knew that to keep his apprenticeship he had to work hard, and he was loving every minute of it. Just being around the dragons was amazing for him. His dreams were only fleeting things but being beside the dragons and learning each beast's personality and the traits of each species was beneficial.

Every spare moment he had was spent in the company of Screamer and her whelps. The dragon which had been bonded to him would race to the edge of the nest as he entered the cavern and sit chirping to him. The baby still did not have a name, but Muniath had promised that it would come to him as he grew to know the small dragon.

Wick had already started mind-sharing with the creature, but the images were still getting muddled along with Screamer's. When he entered this time, he found Muniath sitting against the wall with the gold and red on his knee, his hand resting on the small head. The Warden looked up and smiled at his apprentice.

"You've finished your duties for the day then?" he asked, his attention going back to the small dragon.

"I have, sir," he replied, coming to attention and waiting for any more orders Muniath might have for him.

"Good, you can have the rest of the afternoon off to do with as you wish. You could stay here and get to know your charge, or you could go visit your mother. How long has it been since you saw her?" Muniath once more turned his gaze to his foster-nephew.

"It's been a couple of weeks, Uncle Mun." Wick turned his attention to the other dragon, nestled in the crook of its mother's tail. He went carefully and nodded his head in acknowledgement of Screamer and then picked up the whelp. It had grown considerably since they had first been introduced and was now heavier in his arms.

"That's about a week too long. Mae will not be happy that you're ignoring her and then I'll hear about it. Spend some time with your charge but go surprise her for dinner. You'll not be needed again until tomorrow morning."

"I will, Uncle Mun." Wick came to sit beside him as the young dragon immediately began to seek his mind. There was one image that kept invading the others, the image of a dark emerald-green egg.

"Are you seeing it too?" Muniath asked him quietly and his eyes went up to Screamer.

"I don't understand what it means." Wick shook his head a little.

"Screamer still misses her other child. Dragons are fiercely protective of their young, and when something happens to one of them, they mourn just as we do."

"Is it just the females who do that, I mean, because they give birth to them?" Wick pulled his finger out of the small dragon's mouth as it began to bite down on it. Its teeth were starting to come through and they were needle sharp.

"No, the males do also, though to a lesser extent. Raker knows he has more offspring, he also knows that one of them is missing and we do not know what happened to it," Muniath sighed.

"But we do, it went through the portal in the Hall of Secrets. It can't have survived, that's what the other Riders are saying."

"That is the reasoning the King has laid down, so I don't go hurtling after it, but I have a feeling. You know we can sense where a dragon or its egg may be in the world?"

"I do. The dragons have been calling me in my dreams since I was little."

"I feel that the egg survived. I feel it out there deep inside me. It is out there, and Screamer can sense it too."

"But we can't go after it; there's no way back," Wick protested.

"No, there is no way back," Muniath mumbled a little and then fell into silence. The dragon in his lap climbed up his chest and placed its head on his shoulder, almost as if she were comforting him. His hand came up and stroked the neck that was starting to lengthen.

Across the cavern, Screamer looked up at Muniath and gave a little cooing cry, her green eyes had a great sadness and longing in them.

"Stay and get to know your little one, but remember to visit you mother, Wick," Muniath said, as he got up, holding his dragon to him carefully. He returned the little one to her mother and then stroked the large head of Screamer. "I'll find out what happened to it, Screamer. I promise on my life. I know that he is still alive and if I can, I'll bring him back so you can see him for yourself."

The reflective mood Muniath had slipped into followed him from the caves that afternoon. He had spent the next hour after leaving Wick and Screamer going through the caverns and checking on all the beasts. Inspecting the new security measures that he had insisted on took another half hour, he found some things that needed adjustment and saw to them himself, not wanting to leave the safety of the dragons to anyone else. The guilt that he was not there himself when the eggs were stolen still weighed heavily on his conscience.

Going down the stairs that lead to the citadel, the urge to get drunk was overpowering him. When he reached the bottom, he stood at the junction; onwards lead to the citadel and palace, right lead to the town and left lead to his family home. With a deliberate action he turned to his left and followed the path down the side of the mountain to the large house that sat on the banks of the lake.

The white and grey stood out against the lush green of the trees that surrounded it. Walking around the large stone building he remembered growing up in the house, running through the many halls, chasing his older brother, or being chased by his younger sister for something he had done or taken from her. He remembered their laughter and their arguments, it all seemed so long ago for him. Time had changed things.

Both of his siblings were being groomed to eventually take over each branch of the military. Venicones was to succeed their father as General of Riders, and Ide was to follow their mother as General of Foot, once Domnall Gerarailt had stepped down. It was their destiny to stand behind the King as his advisors and Generals, having the ultimate responsibility for the safety and protection of the realm. Muniath was happy about that. He could not think of himself in a position with any more responsibility than Master of Dragons. The dragons were his life since he was that small boy.

Muniath stopped at the wall of the outer courtyard and looked out over the lake. The water rippled with the wind that funneled through the large valley and he watched the birds as they swooped, looking for insects to catch. He tried to still his mind and push the nagging thoughts of the lost egg from him. It would do him no good to dwell and think of it too much. He had been ordered to leave it and forget, but he could not ignore the pain Screamer was still in.

"A copper for them?" the voice of his sister Ide spoke behind him.

"You wouldn't understand," he replied, not even looking around at her.

"I might understand more than you think. Try me," she challenged him.

"It's my own troubles, Ide, and I don't want to worry you with them. I have already caused you pain and distress for my actions against Orcades."

Ide placed her hand over the top of his that rested on the wall. "I know what he said, and I do understand how much it hurt you. I am my father's daughter too, you know. Just because I am in the Foot doesn't mean I don't understand how hard you took your losses."

Muniath turned his head and gave her a brief smile. "Thank you."

"It doesn't mean that I fully forgive your actions either, but I do understand."

"When does Orcades come back?" Muniath asked, trying to turn the subject a little and sniffed, blinking back tears that were starting to sting at his eyes.

"The King has sent him on a six-month stint to the farthest outpost on the border." Ide gave her own great sigh.

"Has he written? Sent any word to you?"

"No, nothing yet. But he will, I'm sure he will." It was her turn to look somber.

"What on earth do you see in him? You must know what sort of man he is?" Muniath asked her.

"I have heard the rumors, but I love him, Mun. When he is with me, he is kind and attentive."

"But he doesn't like it when you talk back to him; when you challenge him on things."

"I know he has his faults, but I am sure I can smooth out the rough edges he has. I have already seen some changes," she said trying to make it sound brighter.

"Mother and Father aren't happy."

"Yes, I know. But they have accepted him. Why can't you?" Ide's eyebrows were knitted together as she tried to understand why he had so many objections to Orcades.

"Because I am your older brother and overprotective of you, my dear sister. And I can also see he will hurt you."

"But what of you, Mun? When will a girl turn your heart into water? Or is your mind too full of dragons to be caught?" she gave a little laugh as she teased him.

"I don't have time for all that."

"No, you don't. You're either up there in the caverns with the dragons, or in the whorehouses. You won't find someone our parents will approve of in there you know." The smile that lit up her face made Muniath give one in return.

"No, but they are so much more fun than the good girls Mother and Father approve of," he chuckled and winked at her.

"You and Ven are the same. Though I think he has his eye on someone."

"Who?" Although this news did not surprise Muniath, he didn't want to give away his own suspicions on where their older brother's affections lay.

"I'm not telling, just that I have had reports of our brother being seen somewhere a lot in the last few weeks." Ide moved away back towards the house.

"Are you going to tell me?" he asked as he followed her inside the house.

"I will give you three guesses," Ide granted him, as she started to take off her cloak and gloves. She waited for him to ask with a small smile on her lips, laying the cloak and gloves on the back of a chair.

"I'm no good at this sort of thing, you are just going to have to tell me," Muniath told her, giving up quicker than she thought he would.

"If it doesn't involve a dragon, you're useless," she laughed at him. "Who has been a constant in our lives, and we treat as a sister?" Her laughter still carried through her words.

"Mae?"

"Of course. Ven has always liked her." Ide went to the sideboard and started to pour herself a glass of wine. She looked up and saw her brother staring at the carafe. "Mun, it will do you no good to go back to drinking."

"But one small one, wouldn't hurt." He took a step closer to the glass decanter.

"Do I need to tell mother to hide it all."

"I am not that bad, Ide." Muniath turned away and stared out of the window.

"Is it worth the risk though, you've been doing so well, Mun. You've kept away from the drink, away from the whorehouses as well. But you still seem so distant from us all. You used to laugh so much."

"That's all changed. Life can't be all about laughter and joy."

Ide came to stand beside her older brother. "No, it can't, but you are allowed to smile once in a while."

"I smile."

"Not lately. It's the egg isn't it?" she asked him quietly.

"He's out there; I can feel he has hatched, and it is growing without guidance or care. I fear that it will be found and killed in ignorance. It's strange, the dragon feels more than just a combination of Screamer and Raker, I can even feel the temperament of the animal. He is gentle, but strong. He will be an amazing mount for someone, even better than Tempest, I think. And that was a one in a million dragon," he smiled at the memory.

Ide placed a caring hand on his arm. "We all miss, Cara."

Muniath closed his eyes for a moment. "I know you do."

"Are you able to tell me what happened? We don't know and you were completely insensible to give a good account before," Ide whispered.

"This is a report I should give father." He shook his head a little.

"Think of this as practice. A way of getting it sorted in your own mind," she prompted.

Muniath continued to stare out the window, his gaze unfocused over the scene in front of him. He was unable to see the very familiar paved terrace and wall of his home, the low bushes, and the lake beyond, that stretched to the other side of the valley. He did not register the large mountain that rose up high on the other side, capped white with ice and snow that remained there all year round. Instead, his mind saw another mountain. "Cara was not supposed to be there; she had insisted—demanded even—of Arcois that he take her. She was keen to prove herself. Ide, I knew she was in love with me, I knew the real reason she pushed her way into our mission." Muniath swallowed hard as the emotions were threatening to overwhelm him.

Ide stayed where she was, the grasp on his arm moved to his hand and she held it, gently while she waited for him to continue.

"We had reports of a wild Great Black taking up residence in a crag in the western mountains. It was the first one we had heard of for some time. Arcois wanted the eggs that he knew she had given birth to. He wanted the offspring to bolster our species pool, a fresh bloodline to mate into ours and create stronger and better dragons. We had both felt it when she had given birth, and where we could find them. What we could not predict was how much that wild Black would defend her roost."

Muniath's hand slipped out of his sister's comforting one and he moved to the sideboard and the glass she had left lying there. He picked it up and with one swallow, drank it down, enjoying the smoothness of the rich red wine as it slipped so easily down his throat. He placed the glass gently back on the wooden surface and then turned back to her.

"The Black rose up before us. I was supposed to slip in behind her while Arcois and Cara kept her busy. It felt like I was no more than a thieving Trader as I neared the roost and saw the four eggs there. I heard a scream, saw Tempest and Fury along with Swift rise up with their wings beating furiously above the Black. Arcois and Cara were creeping up on her from each side. I thought they had the situation in hand. One against three dragons and two humans, it should have been an easy operation."

Muniath's hand went to the decanter and pulled the stopper out. Ide crossed the room and gently took them out of his hands, firmly placing the stopper back into place and then steered him away from the sideboard. He sank into one of the deep chairs there and his hands went through his long hair, pushing it off his face and turning saddened dark eyes up to his sister.

"We did not feel the male's presence. As far as I can tell, Arcois did not know he was around. Our focus had always been on the female and her clutch. He came swooping out of the sky, taking out Fury first. His jaw clamped around the old Red's neck, I heard it crack. He then turned on Tempest. They grappled together. Swift kept in place, trying to keep the female from fully attacking Cara and Arcois. She did a good job in protecting them, I was so proud of my Blue. But seeing the death of Fury made me freeze. I heard a call from above and Tempest's wings were tattered, he fell from the sky, unable to keep himself in the air. The Black swooped down on him; his claws dug deep into his back. I saw scales go flying with the force of the attack. Tempest tried to fight back, tried to bring his head around to tear at the Black, but the large male was dominating the fight. He bit through Tempest's slender neck, his head came flying off and blood was spurting everywhere.

"The Black bellowed as it still clenched the body of Tempest in its talons. The spray of fire it sent out almost reached Arcois and Cara. I called out a warning and raced to help them against the two dragons. Swift was trying to keep the male away but being a blue, she was slender and while agile, she was no match for a Black, let alone two. The two Blacks converged on her. Arcois tried to attack the flank of the female and was knocked aside by her large head. Cara tried to climb on her back, I have no idea what she was thinking she could do.

"Swift went down between the two dragons, and I watched in horror as the Black male picked Cara off the back of the female. I can't—" he broke off, shaking his head, his shoulders heaving.

Ide reached his side and placed her arms around him, pulling her still grieving brother to her and holding him tightly.

"She died trying to prove herself to me," he whispered.

"She died being who she was, a Rider. What happened next, Mun?" Ide asked gently, her eyes spotting two people in the doorway who were listening in.

"I ran to Arcois, while Swift was being killed. I dragged him to safety, they didn't seem to realize that I was there. I managed to get his armor off, little it did to protect him. His chest was caved in and there was blood coming from his mouth. He was struggling for breath, and tried reaching his knife. I could see in his eyes what he wanted me to do, but I couldn't. How could I, Ide? Take his life—my mentor and friend? I couldn't do it. I held him as he died."

"You did what you could for him. Arcois would have understood," Ide tried to ease his terror and fears.

"I waited until dark and made the long journey back. It was the most humiliating and shameful day when I walked back into the citadel and had to tell the King that they were dead, three dragons and two Riders. With me, a Dragon Warden just out of my apprenticeship, the only one to live without a scratch on me. I hated myself—I still do. I miss them, Ide." Muniath pulled himself away from her embrace and turned stricken eyes to her. "I am sorry for what I did later, when Orcades made that remark. I should have been more understanding and the better person, but how could I when I blamed myself for their deaths. After being dragged before the King, especially being so drunk, I couldn't face anyone. My shame was absolute, and it still is."

The movement of the two people at the door caught his attention and he stood as his parents came to him. His mother wrapped her strong arms around her youngest son and held him. His father placed a caring and large hand on his head, tears in his own brown eyes for his son.

82

Growing

The long trip home was fraught for Teagan. She was almost certain that the baby dragon would be discovered in her bag; that he would make a noise or suddenly appear at the feet or lap of one of the men in the four-wheel drive they were all confined in. But it did not. He stayed in the bag and she could sense he was asleep and content for now. This was a strange sensation for Teagan, to be so melded in thoughts with a creature. There had always been a tugging and an awareness when she had held reptiles in the past, especially when she had the honor of holding the Tuataras in the breeding programs. This though, was something else. It was like she was reading the dragon's thoughts.

The four-wheel drive pulled up the long drive to her home, set in amongst the trees and tucked away in the cradling arms of one of the hills in the Upper Hutt Valley. It stopped outside the door to a rundown looking house, with its peeling, pale green paint on the walls, and jungle-like overgrown garden. There was no sign of anyone home.

Pushing on the door of the car, Teagan gathered the backpack with its precious cargo hidden away inside and started to climb out.

"You take it easy, Teagan, rest that ankle and we'll see you in the office in a couple of days," Eric said, giving her a smile from the driver's seat.

"I will. See you." She hopped out, favoring her right ankle and the sprain she had incurred. Phil jumped out of the back seat and went to the rear door to pull out her large hiking pack, handing it to her.

"Do you want me to take it in for you?" he asked her, still holding onto one of the straps.

"No, I can manage. But thank you for the offer, Phil." The reasons for not letting any of these men inside had little to do with what was in her backpack.

Phil nodded and climbed into the front seat she had just vacated. The car backed up, Eric expertly putting it into a three-point turn in the small, confined space, before heading back down the dusty, gravel driveway. Teagan stood, giving them a wave goodbye, until they were out of sight. Heaving the hiking pack onto her shoulder she hobbled to the front door and carefully climbed the short front steps.

The brown, dust-laden door squealed in protest of being opened and the interior was dark and dim in stark contrast to the brightness of the sunny day outside. Placing down the large pack in the hallway she walked further into the small two-bedroom house. The scuffed floorboards creaked under the pressure of her weight until she reached the first door in the hall. Teagan put a hand on it and pushed it open. Inside was empty of any human life. A rumpled bed lay in the middle of the room, a set of drawers with some of them open and clothing scattered around in dirty heaps were all that greeted her.

Moving further in she passed the second and third doors—her own bedroom and the small bathroom—to get to the back of the house. It was one large room, sitting, dining and kitchen all in one. In one of the large chairs, with the footrest extended and in an almost prone position, lay her father. His face grizzled with stubble of a couple of days growth, showing predominantly whiter now than the dark brown it had once been. He wore creased and stained clothing, and he was snoring loudly.

Teagan went to the kitchen and opened the fridge door. The food she had prepared for him was still sitting in the containers on the shelves, untouched. Pulling out one, she opened it and then pulled around her backpack. Reaching in she disturbed the little creature and held it in her hands. Gremlin looked up at her with blinking and sleepy dark eyes that were changing. They were no longer the fully black eyes she had first seen, but now had a hint green and silver running through them.

Pulling at the sausage that sat in the container, along with vegetables she had prepared for her father, she started to feed Gremlin. The food was soon gobbled up greedily. He started to purr and stretched out his wings, flapping them as his back arched and his tail straightened, so much like a cat that Teagan smiled at the small creature.

Carefully she carried him to the couch and placed Gremlin down on the cushions. Limping her way over to her father she placed a hand on his arm and gave him a small shake. He snorted in reply, still very much asleep and she shook him again. His head moved from side to side and the snoring stopped for a moment. Taking in a deep breath, he then let it out in a loud whoosh. The stench of his bad breath and the effects of the alcohol were stomach churning for Teagan, and she turned her head.

"Papa," Teagan called out while waving away the fumes. "Papa!"

An eye opened to show her the bloodshot white that had been concealed under the lid. A lazy smile creased one corner of his mouth as he woke and realized his daughter was back.

"My darling girl, you're home," he whispered, his throat raspy from the last couple of days of being in a stupor, caused by the amount of whiskey he had consumed. The remains were littered at the side of his chair in mute evidence of the bender he had been having, no sign of a glass at all and Teagan surmised he had drunk straight from the bottle.

Straightening himself up in the chair, he pushed the footrest into the chair once more and stood unsteadily to greet her.

"Papa, why?" Tegan shook her head at him, disappointment etched in her eyes.

"I couldn't stand that job anyway. Bunch of no hopers grinding away day to day, out in the sunshine all day, fixing roads."

"Papa, you quit your job again?" she demanded.

"Sort of." Tharain told her scratching at his stubbly chin.

"You got fired." Teagan turned and hobbled over to the couch and Tharain followed her with his eyes. He was about to protest about being fired when he spotted the baby dragon.

"Oh god, I think I have overdone it this time," he said in a whisper as he fell back onto his chair, his eyes wide as he tried to focus on what was next to Teagan. "I'm hallucinating."

"No, you're not. You're seeing what's really there." Teagan picked the dragon up in her hands and held him out to her father. "I found him in the remains of the forest fire we went out to inspect."

"But it can't be here. How is it here?" he demanded his hand reaching out and then pulling back in fright that it might actually be real.

"I don't know."

"There are no dragons left in this world." Tharain shook his head.

"Well, there is now. All my dreams were real, weren't they Papa? I do remember the life we had before, in the castle, the dragons with riders on their backs?" Teagan looked at her father hard.

"They are my girl. They are very real, just as real as that little one you are holding now," he said in wonder.

Gremlin looked at him and blinked a couple of times. His wings extended and he started to flap them, gaining speed and wind underneath them, before lifting off and over to Teagan's father. He landed on the arm of the chair and Tharain pulled back a little. Gremlin cooed at him.

"You're far too young to be flying yet," he said in surprise. "Turn the light on, Teagan, let me have a look at it properly." Without even really thinking he reached out and stroked the little head.

Teagan hobbled to the switch and flicked it on. The light above burst into life and sent out its golden glow into the dim room. It was only when she was coming back that he noticed her injury.

"It's nothing, Papa," she told him before he could voice his concern. "Just a slight sprain. I fell down a hole and twisted it."

Tharain turned his attention back to the baby dragon once more, his eyes eager and more alive than Teagan had seen them for some time. "Let's have a look at you then."

He placed a finger under the chin of Gremlin and tilted his head up. Tharain examined his eyes and opened his mouth a little, spying the small teeth that were coming through already. He ran a hand down the spine, careful not to catch his fingers on the protrusions of sharp spiky horns that were there. Picking up each in turn, he examined the feet and sharp claws, testing each one. Very carefully he spread each wing, looking at the very thin membrane and making mental note of the veins that ran through it.

"At first, I would have classed it as being a Green, but he seems too dark. His eyes tell me that he's come from some cross breeding, possibly a Red or even a Gold and Red. The traits are all there, but it seems to be mainly a Green and I would estimate he is no more than a couple of weeks old. His teeth are starting to protrude."

"Papa, will you help me raise him?" Teagan asked him.

Tharain turned his eyes to his daughter. "You cannot be serious? Dragons are no longer on this earth for a reason. You have read their fairy stories, heard their myths and legends. If it were to become known it even existed here in this world, then it will be hunted."

"But Papa, Gremlin is only a baby."

"You've named it?" he demanded.

"I have, why?"

"It is too early for naming. That comes only after being with them for some time, not a matter of days. And…and he should be at least four times the size of this before he should be even attempting to fly. Teagan we cannot keep him, where could we hide such a creature here?"

"I know of a few places in the forest where he would be safe," she told him eagerly. There was a hesitation to her father, she could see that he was almost persuaded to her idea, and it was the first time in years that she had seen him so interested in something. "Please Papa."

"No. You have not had time to bond with it yet. It must be done soon, while it is still young."

"Papa release your grip, you're hurting him," Teagan told him quickly.

"How did you know that?" Carefully he stood with the whelp in his hands, Tharain went and sat beside his daughter and looked deeply into her bright green eyes. "You have it! I've been so blind all these years. You have the skill and I made it impossible for you to follow your destiny." Tharain carefully placed Gremlin in his daughter's lap and took her face in his workworn hands. "I am so sorry, my girl. I am, so very, very sorry. It is there, you have the silver, your eyes glow with it. But I don't know why you still have it; it should have left you by now. You should have been a Dragon Warden."

"I don't understand, why are you sorry?"

"My stupidity, my avarice, it denied you your birthright. Our coming to this world was my fault, if I had not begged King Urmond to spare my life so I could raise you, you would now be in amongst the creatures you have an affinity with. A Dragon Warden."

"Papa, please, I still don't understand," she pleaded with him.

"After your mother died, I sunk to levels I am so ashamed of. She was the light of my heart and I lost her too soon. I drank to ease the pain, which led to gambling, and I lost heavily. I became indebted to men who I should never have been associating with. They threatened me, threatened you, my precious girl. Each time I saw you I could see your mother—" A tear escaped his eye and got caught in amongst the bristly whiskers on his cheek.

"They said, if I could not pay them in coin what I owed them, then they would take a dragon egg. I struggled with that for such a long time. I tried to pay them back with what I could borrow and scrounge up, but they decided that they would not take it. They wanted an egg. By the time I agreed, I was deeper into debt with them. I know I was an idiot." Tharain put up a hand to stop her from speaking. "By then they were demanding two eggs. It was easy for me to get them. When Fury had laid her new offspring, I made my way up and inspected the clutch, as was part of my duties. I talked to Arcois, the Master of Dragons and he was happy. The brood was a cross between a Red and a White, it had never been done before and he was sure they would make an excellent breed. He had been trying to breed a Red and Blue for years, but they had never taken. He believed it was the next step. I crept up there one night. I had checked on you to make sure you were asleep. Then, like a thief I went, forever taking the steps that I cannot undo. I stole the whole clutch, delivered them to the men, who were delighted and promptly let me out of my debts. But I could see they would not let go of me. I turned and fled, covered in my shame."

Tharain stood and went to the kitchen. Leaning on the bench he dropped his chin to his chest and Teagan waited until he got himself under control. Scooping up a glass from beside the sink, he turned the faucet on and then drank deeply of something other than whiskey for the first time in days.

"When you came to watch the Riders leave, they were going to search for those eggs. I had no idea that the Trader had already been caught with the eggs in his possession. I thought he had got away and my deed would go unpunished. I should've known better. My cousin Urmond deserves the title King. He is of the old-born. In some ways I was relieved that I had been caught, but then I thought of you being parentless, growing up an orphan at court. I could not bear that, leaving you behind, my only connection to Gael. I begged him to spare my life, I got down on my knees and I begged him. I should have gone to the executioner along with the Trader that day. I'm sorry, Teagan. I have brought nothing but hardship, shame and degradation to you. I have not been a proper father; I have not provided for you like I should have. I have wallowed in my own self-pity. I see that now. I am sorry, my daughter," he whispered to her.

Teagan placed Gremlin back on the couch and went to her father, as he slipped down on the floor. Great sobs wracked his thin frame, for the first time she noticed he was not the man he once was. He had been strong, fit and had a presence that demanded respect from those around him. Now he was broken, sad, and worn out. She knelt beside him and held him tightly as he crumbled before her eyes.

For years it had been Teagan who had held them together, she could see that he had not adjusted well to their life in this world. As she spoke of the dragons in her naïve way, he had told her to stop making up stories, to stop dreaming. That there was no such thing as dragons. She had thought his words were meant to help her adjust to the new life, but they were really to hide his shame and to forget what they had been sent from. As she had grown, she took on more of the responsibilities while he drank more and more. It was Teagan that made sure the bills were paid on time, that there was food and not just booze in the cupboards.

Teagan held her father, their roles now reversed so totally. Child-like he clung to her for acceptance and forgiveness. She gave it without even thinking about it. He was her father and she loved him. This was the life that had been dealt to them and they would continue, hopefully now better.

Tharain emerged from the bathroom, cleaner, sober, and more upright than he had been in a long time. His face was newly shaven, and he wore clean clothes. He was smoothing back his hair when he entered the living area, and he watched his daughter in the kitchen as she cooked.

"What about the food you prepared for me?" he asked her, stepping towards the fridge to open it.

"I saved the meat for Gremlin, but the rest was ruined," she said in reply, turning to face him.

"I'm sorry, for being such a burden to you."

"Will you stop saying that? You've apologized enough today, Papa."

Teagan turned back to the meal she was preparing and Tharain went to sit on the couch and marvel at the baby dragon that lay curled up there. Gremlin twitched in his sleep and made a snorting sound. A puff a white smoke curled out of his nostrils.

Over dinner they ate in silence. It was as he was pushing his plate back away from him that he looked up Teagan.

"He's a fire breather," Tharain raised his eyebrows at her.

"I figured that. What did you mean when you said I had the skill?" she pushed her own plate away as she spoke.

"One way to tell is in the eyes. Of the Old-born there are tell-tales in the eyes. They glow brightly, almost luminescent and they have some silver flecks about the pupil. The Old-born could all talk to dragons, just as we are now, and they were the original Riders. They tamed and bred them to wage war on their neighbors and the Realm was founded by them. Legend has it that they all rode great Blacks, the fiercest of all the breeds. As the Old-born were starting to dwindle they mixed with other races. Soon only those that have dragon blood running through their veins could communicate with the beasts. It starts with dreams I'm told, and as they grow, a connection is usually made with the dragons, which becomes permanent. Now, if a child who has the skill, and has the Old-born blood, is not bonded with a dragon by the time they are eighteen, then it leaves them and so too the traces of silver in their eyes."

"So how come I can visualize what Gremlin wants? I am 22."

"Of that I am not sure myself. There must be a reason for it lingering in you. Maybe it's to do with the fact that we were sent here, so far from the dragons. But it does not change the fact that the baby dragon on the couch cannot be allowed to live in this world, Teagan. Keeping it secret, being able to feed him as he grows, these are all going to be very difficult."

"I know I can do this."

"Where would you keep him?" Tharain asked his daughter.

"There's a gully in the hills that would be perfect. It's away from people and any hiking tracks. It has water, and I am sure I can make up some sort of shelter for Gremlin."

At the sound of his name the whelp looked up at Teagan. He chirped and then rested his head back down, his eyes still on her.

"You don't know the first thing about his breed, or any breed of dragon for that matter."

"You can teach me. Please, Papa," she begged him.

Tharain leaned back in his chair and looked at his daughter speculatively. The years of trying to deny their previous life had all been for nothing, he thought to himself. She was destined for something else, this daughter of his, and he could see that immediately. The skill was there, and he wondered at never seeing it before. Then he remembered that he had not really been paying attention.

Now he sat there looking at his grown-up daughter and wished he could have those years back. Tharain regretted the times he sought solace from the neck of a bottle and gambling away money that was meant for food and bills. He really looked at his daughter who had supported him and never complained once about what he had put her through, making her grow up faster and have more responsibilities than a girl of that age should ever have. How could he deny her this?

Closing his eyes as he came to his decision, he shook his head. "I just hope that you and I don't come to regret this, but I'll help you raise Gremlin. You know he'll become harder to handle as he grows and being a fire breather, he will cause even more problems that you won't have answers for."

"Thank you, Papa!" Teagan exclaimed and she ran around the table to throw her arms around his neck. "Thank you, thank you, thank you!" she repeated, punctuating each with a kiss on his head.

Gremlin looked up from his seat on the couch and cocked his head at her excitement, then joined in by flapping his wings and making squeaking sounds that were meant to be a roar.

Teagan carefully followed the small markers she now no longer needed through the dense forest, as she hiked her way into the outer blocks of the hills that surrounded the valley she lived in. The calls of the birds were all around her, the trilling sounds of tuis and thrush along with the smaller native birds of her adoptive home. The forest was wet and dripping from a recent rainfall and she eagerly pushed through the undergrowth to reach her destination.

Teagan became aware of the dragon before she saw or heard him. Gremlin's eagerness at her visit grew as she neared and was translated into excitement. Their bond had strengthened in the early days of his growing. At first Teagan had kept him at their home, she fed him and looked after him, making sure he was warm and happy. While she was at work, Tharain took over and began the training the little dragon would need.

Now it was six months on. The summer had given way to winter and the nights were cold and chilly, the storms that blew in from the south brought with them snow falls that blanketed the mountains and hills.

Gremlin had grown quickly and was soon too big to keep at home. He filled the little house with his fast-grown girth and while he could still fit through the door, the father and daughter had soon agreed it was time for him to go to the gully.

Tharain had also changed in that six months. He had helped his daughter build a crude shelter for the dragon deep in the forest; had advised her how to train him properly and what he needed to survive. There were no more empty bottles of whisky in their rubbish, and he was healthier and happier. Teagan loved this new side to her father.

A deep, low roar sounded in front of her and Teagan smiled, sending out a thought of calm and patience. Parting the last of the bushes that hid the clearing, she stepped through and the dragon raced up to her. He nudged her shoulder with his head, and she placed loving arms around his sinewy neck. Not only was he getting bigger, but his form was changing also. Gone were the baby black eyes, now they were emerald and silver and were cut through with the long black pupil. The color of his scales had now deepened to a rich emerald, with a faint silver edging to them. The horns which ran down his spine were elongating and hardening, one on the very top of his head was turning a silver color. His neck was not the only part of his body to lengthen, his toes were long and tipped with black claws, his tail was the same length if not a little longer than his body and ended with a flat section, like a spear tip. The wings had grown like great sails on a ship and they had thickened. The muscles that controlled them extended around his chest which had broadened. But the biggest difference was the head.

The short, almost lizard-like face which held such expression as a baby, was now long. The jaw had grown and was filled with razor sharp teeth, the eyes had been moved back to the side of the skull, and Gremlin's nostrils had widened. But his enthusiasm and his love of Teagan had not changed. He still acted like he was little and Tharain had told her that was because she had babied him too much when she had first found him.

He cooed at her now, a deep rumbling from within as he delighted in her touch and comfort. It had taken a lot to convince him that he needed to be there in this cold, wet place, but he came to accept it from Teagan.

"I have some food for you, are you hungry, Gremlin?" she asked him, and he pulled away from her to go stand in the middle of the clearing.

Teagan pulled off her backpack and placed it down in front of her. Opening it up, she pulled out raw beef ribs that came in long strips with the meat still on them, a tail with the skin still on and other off cuts. Carefully she tossed each one to the dragon. She had learned the hard way that you should never leave your fingers too close to a dragon's meal.

The meat had come from a butcher her father had started to work for. Each night Tharain would scavenge what he could from the bins to bring home, telling his new boss that he had dogs and was not wanting to waste anything.

With the meal done Gremlin moved to his shelter to wait for Teagan, while she cleaned the clearing. She got to work clearing away his waste, which he was kind enough to do in one spot, along with this she buried any evidence of things he had brought back to the clearing.

Once her chores were complete, she entered the crude lean-to and began to sort his bedding. She straightened the old sheets and blankets they had gathered from second-hand stores and pulled out the last of the bale of hay her father had hauled for her the last time he had come with her.

Gremlin waited until she was finished politely, and as soon as she was done nudged her with his large head.

"Fly!"

Teagan could hear his longing for the open sky above them, and it matched her own. The pair returned to the center of the clearing, Gremlin holding out a foot to help her hoist herself onto his back. There was a spot between his neck and the shoulders which was devoid of spines and she settled herself there.

With a hissing sound like material being rubbed against itself, his wings spread wide and were raised up, ready for the first beat down to gain air underneath them. The muscles that were protected under the hard, glossy, green scales moved under her touch, they bunched and released like springs as Gremlin lifted then lowered them to gain the air he needed under the membrane.

The sound of the movement of air as they billowed out was a loud whooshing, and she gripped tightly to two of his curved spikes as Gremlin lifted them off the ground. The first time they had flown together it had been exhilarating and freeing. She loved the experience of being at one with him, their minds joined as they swooped over the trees, racing from one end of the gully to the other and back again. He had clawed his way high into the sky and dove down fast, the clearing hurtling towards them, before he flared his wings and brought them safely back to the ground.

This time she wanted to go further afield. She urged him forward and up, over the hill, and he raced down the other side into the next valley. The wind buffeted her face and her bright orange hair escaped the ponytail. Gremlin gave out a roar as he beat his wings to gain speed,

Teagan could sense him wanting to lay down a stream of liquid fire and pulled his thought away from it.

They climbed into the sky and circled lazily, his wing tips moving only slightly to change the direction. Teagan leaned down and hugged his neck, resting her cheek against his cool scales, reveling in the dragon's delight in the freedom he had, but also seeing the desire to see more; go further.

All too soon she was asking him to land. With great regret they headed back to the clearing and Gremlin's home. The landing was soft, and it took her a moment to realize that they were back, before slipping off his back.

"Papa is coming tomorrow. I have to go away for work for a few days. You be good and behave yourself for him, please. I know it frustrates you that you cannot communicate with him, but he tries."

Gremlin passed on the image of flying and her father. Teagan nodded to him. "I'll tell him of your wishes, Gremlin, and I'll be back as soon as I can."

With a final hug and caress of his head she turned, picked up the empty pack and started the trek out of the forest and back home. She could sense the loneliness emanating from him and it saddened her that she had to keep him so isolated.

Crossing

Shivering still with the lingering effects of the elixir, Scetis looked down at the border crossing over the wildly rushing river. Earlier that morning the pair had been woken by the sound of thundering hooves of a new patrol of Foot that had come in to relieve those stationed there. The large black dragon which they had seen the last time they had tried to cross was nowhere in sight, and for that he was thankful. It would be easier to get through without it.

Scetis and Loxa had moved on from their campsite where he had been affected by the restorative drug. After Loxa had told him the woman would be coming back to check on him, Scetis had decided that it would be safer for them to move on, even though he was still weakened by the effects of not only the poison, but the lifesaving elixir itself. That first day they had ambled along, his feet dragging, and they had not made much ground, but were far enough away from the farm for him to feel safer.

They had spent the next few nights huddled against the cold beside small fires, deep in thickets and groves of trees. They tried to follow the road but keep off it as much as possible. Until they reached the crossing.

He watched as the two Lieutenants brought each other up to date with what was happening. Beside them stood two other men and Scetis recognized them as the guards who had discovered himself and Loxa in the Hall of Secrets. The hunt was still on and these two men were going to be making the crossing far more difficult.

"What are we going to do, Master?" Loxa asked him quietly.

"Together is not going to do it. We'll never cross with those two men who can recognize us. We're going to have to split up." Scetis rubbed a hand over his stubbled jaw and the sleep from his eyes as he thought about their problem. "I want you to go first. You're more innocent looking and have that perpetual scared look about you that most young boys have when dealing with someone in authority. Show them your bags, but keep that medallion hidden. You're also going to need a good cover story."

"I'll tell them that I am heading to relatives who live across the border. It's not unusual for a nephew to go help out on another farm in the family," Loxa suggested.

"It's a good story," Scetis agreed. He looked down at the crossing once more and saw the relieved patrol mount up and start up the road which lay below the pair.

"Get across that river, and out of sight of the control box. Hide yourself away in a thicket and wait for me to reach you. It's the only way to get across." He once more scanned the sheer cliffs that separated one side to the other, surrounding the only pass through the mountains. It would be impossible to clamber over the rocks and mountains without being seen at the crossing.

"How long will you leave it to cross after me?"

"It will be a good hour or so. I don't want them to think we're in anyway travelling together."

"What story will you use?" Loxa asked curiously.

"That of a Physician, returning back to the Convocation."

"But won't they have your name on a list."

"Ah, but the patient had a long, drawn-out illness and I entered the realm before the nasty business of someone trying to steal the precious dragon eggs, such a dreadful affair. If I offer them the information first, it will let them know that the person I was treating was someone in authority and privy to secrets. It will put them on the back foot." The smile he gave Loxa was lopsided and once more his eyes gleamed slightly in a way that made the boy turn away from his gaze.

"Gather your things and give me your medallion." Scetis held out his hand to the boy and slowly Loxa reached into his shirt and pulled out the metal disc attached to a thin leather cord.

"What if something happens? I'm going to need that to get back into the Convocation."

"And you'll have it back before you cross. Just give me a minute to change the appearance." Scetis looked up and saw that Loxa had not moved. "Well, get on with clearing up. I don't want to be all day crossing that damned river."

The boy stepped out of the thicket they had hidden in throughout the night. Loxa shouldered the bag onto his back and started out down the dusty road. Scetis watched him from the safe confines of the thick bushes, he had no doubts that the boy could make it across. He was an innocent and still acted like it. He could see his apprentice was nervous and watched as he kept touching the spot where his medallion lay under his shirt. The Trader, again, told him under his breath to be calm.

It did not take Loxa long to make it to the inspection point. A guard stepped out, his hand lazily resting on the pommel of his sword that was strapped to his side and raised a bored hand to bring the boy to a halt. Loxa stood facing him, shifting his weight softly from one foot to another in his nervousness. The guard demanded to see in the bag and Loxa took it off, opened it and held it while it was inspected.

Scetis could see them talking, Loxa was gesturing to the other side of the river and the neighboring realm, the guard nodded at his story and then waved the bag away. Loxa shouldered the bag once more and kept his hands away from the medallion.

"Good boy," Scetis whispered from his hiding spot.

Soon the guard stood aside and waived Loxa on. He nodded to the man and started out, keeping his steps easy and unhurried. He stepped onto the bridge when a shout came from the guard house and a figure stepped out. It was one of the men from the hall. Scetis held his breath.

Loxa turned back to the man, his face started to frown with the demands that were being made of him. Slowly he retraced his steps and came to stand before this new guard. Scetis could see him inspecting his face, he reached up and turned the boy's head from side to side, peering into it, before releasing it again.

The man gestured to the shirt Loxa was wearing, and he opened it. Sitting against his chest was the medallion. The new guard picked it up and held it while he inspected the ruins on it. As he was doing this a woman came out of the hut. Her long hair was caught up in a high ponytail that trailed down her back and gleamed a glossy black in the sunshine. The marks of her office evident on the leather breastplate she wore and the trimming of her cloak. She also looked at the disc, taking in the markings before curtly telling the guard to let it go, and waiving Loxa on.

The subtle changes Scetis had made on the metal disc had worked and he let out a long low breath. The markings were still for an apprentice, but changed slightly to make them appear older, like it was a family heirloom handed down to the younger generation. It had not taken much to make it so, and only a true member of the Convocation could discern that it was in fact a current disc.

Loxa was turning and heading away from the small group of three. He reached the middle and turned back to see if they were still watching. The pace of his steps quickened only slightly as he headed to the other side. There was a small conversation with the guard from the other realm and he was soon on his way. Scetis continued to watch him until he was out of sight.

Turning back to the small campsite he continued with his own preparations. They had divided the bundles up and he was now carrying his own clothing and bedding. He picked up the burgundy vest and gave it a flick to try and get the creases out of it. The leather pants he had on were starting to show their age and wear of the last week, as they had gone from one hiding spot to the other, but they would have to do.

Scetis sat down on a rock and pulled his leather boots off. They were starting to crack from the constant wear and were dull and scratched. He picked up a rag and spat on them, carefully cleaning the ingrained dirt from the leather, and bringing them back to a semi-shine, before pulling them back on.

The white linen shirt was the last clean one he had. He had hoped to change into it before they reached the gates of the Convocation, so he would be in some order of respectability, but there was a need for its use now. Shrugging on the vest he did up the buttons and noticed the once tight garment now hung loosely on his frame. He finished cleaning up the campsite, hiding their fire pit by burying it and making sure no trace had been left behind.

Looking up at the position of the sun he sat back on the stone to wait. Practicing patience was not something he was used to. As a child he had often been scolded and punished for it. His hands, which were balled into fists, with knuckles turning white, were held tightly on his knees, and he closed his eyes. Evening his breathing, Scetis went through all the possible scenarios of how the meeting down at the border would go.

After seeing the guard examine Loxa's face he knew he could possibly be recognized. The different actions played out and he dismissed some as being too impossible, too impractical and beyond his capabilities. His mind wandered as he plotted and then a shout rang out, echoing off the shear sides of the surrounding mountains. Opening his eyes, he waited a little while. He could hear a commotion below him and got up to see what was going on.

On the road below a team of horses and a cart, laden and covered by a protective canvas sheet was being driven by a large man. A whip was in his hand and he was using it liberally to urge the horses on the rutted road. Following behind were two other men on horseback, their armor was light and they each held a sword at their hips. They looked bored and uninterested in how the teamster was treating his animals. They were hired guards, sell-swords, and men probably without any morals, especially regarding the lives of others.

Scetis watched as the small group was stopped at the border. More Foot came out of the house to inspect each individual and the contents of the cart. The Rider also joined them, looking into each face careful. Scetis took his chance, while they were distracted with such a commotion.

Picking up his bags, he slung them over his shoulders. Carefully he made his way out of the thicket and onto the road. At first, he kept to the short shadows of the midday sun through the trees that overhung the road. He was finally spotted by a Foot soldier, who beckoned him over.

"Good day, sir," Scetis greeted him with a slightly crooked smile.

"Good day, where are you travelling from?" the soldier demanded, not really interested, only echoing the words he was supposed to ask.

"I've been in Hunndaidh and now returning to the Convocation of Mystical Medicine," Scetis replied.

This got the guards attention. "Are you a Physician or Trader?" he asked, his hand going to his sword.

"I am a Physician and am returning from tending a very important client."

"When did you enter our realm?" the guard looked around as he spoke, searching for someone to call as back up.

"I entered over a month ago. It was a very drawn out and complicated illness. My client is now recovered enough for me to leave him."

"A month, you say?" the guard spotted someone and called them over.

"Yes, a month. Can I inquire as to why you are asking me these questions, never before have I had them asked when leaving?"

"You make this trip quite frequently then?"

"I have had the need to occasionally, when an important client requests the help of the Convocation."

Scetis saw who the guard had called for. The woman he had spotted earlier, he could now see the badge of her office, giving her the rank of Lieutenant. Her armor was tidy and immaculately kept, he could see she was proud of her rise and achievements, and then she turned her eyes to him. They were a deep brown, almost black, matching the color of her hair.

"What is it, Ero?" she demanded, the cloak she wore billowed out behind her as she walked briskly towards them.

"This is a healer," the man told his superior officer.

"A Physician, Ma'am," Scetis corrected him.

"Your name Physician?" she demanded.

"Scetis Mordha," he bowed to her, seeing no reason to hide his real name. "I am a Practitioner Fourth Class of the Convocation of Mystical Medicine."

Scetis reached into his shirt and pulled out the medallion that proclaimed his status. Tugging it over his head he handed the disc to the lieutenant. "And who do I have the honor of addressing, ma'am?" he asked politely.

"Lieutenant Ide Magaoidh," she inspected the carved disc. "When did you arrive?"

"As I told your colleague here, it was about a month ago. A very important client of the Convocation needed my attention."

"Who?" Ide demanded.

"I'm sure he would prefer that his name be kept out of public knowledge. The illness was one that was protracted and of an embarrassing nature."

"I will ask again, Physician Mordha, who?" her hand went immediately to the pommel of her sword.

Beyond Ide and Ero there was a commotion at the cart as the guards were inspecting the contents. Their attention was taken for a moment and Scetis thought to try and slip passed them, but Ide was soon turning her eyes back to him.

"It was Councilor Laighin."

"And the nature of this illness?" she demanded.

"It was a matter of sexual nature, a disease one may pick up in the seedier parts of town. I would not wish to embarrass you, Lieutenant, by going into all the details."

"I am no milk maid, Mordha, I do not embarrass easily. But you don't need to go into more detail. Do you know of any Traders that have been visiting our realm recently?" She eyed him speculatively.

"I don't really associate with the Traders, ma'am. They are a lower branch of the Convocation," he paused a moment and then made his eyes go wide, dropped his voice in a whisper and carried on. "Ahhh, this tightening of security will have to do with the recent theft."

"Theft?" The Lieutenant's eyes narrowed slightly.

"The—" he looked around a moment to see if anyone was in earshot. "The stolen precious items that occurred a few weeks back, only I heard that they were recovered."

"How would you hear?" Scetis could see the suspicion rise in the Lieutenant.

"The Councilor had many guests and I was present for some of those meetings, ma'am. So, is it?" A small doubt began to creep in that his offering of knowledge of the event would not ease his way across the border, as he had hoped and planned for.

"It is, only one was recovered, however. Wait there." Ide demanded and then turned.

Scetis watched her go, admiring her form and the way she walked, although the armor was very masculine in form, on her it only enhanced her natural attributes, he thought. These thoughts disturbed him a little as they almost distracted from what was happening around him.

Ide soon returned with the Rider guard, who was already looking at Scetis. His eyes were squinting and Scetis could tell that he suffered from a form of short sightedness, he hoped this would work in his favor as they had not gotten that close to the guards while he and Loxa had made their escape from the hall.

"Take a good look, Vist. Is this the man you saw?" Ide demanded.

The man stepped closer to Scetis and peered into his face. Unlike his treatment of Loxa, Vist did not grab Scetis' face to examine it closer. The man stank of reptiles to Scetis' acute nose, his breath also reeked of something else, a compound that was used to hide an injury.

"How did you get injured?" Scetis asked, hoping to fluster him.

"I'm not injured," Vist immediately protested.

"But you have the smell of Actaea Racemosa. Have you been preparing it correctly? Because it can have severe side effects if you consume some parts still in their raw state." Scetis raised his hand and pulled down the lower lids of Vist, who immediately pulled away.

"I don't use the stuff," he protested, looking to Ide for help.

"What's this?" she demanded of Scetis.

"His breath smells of the use of the plant. If I can smell it, it means he has been ingesting large amounts of the raw material, which affects the eyes to start with and other symptoms are likely to develop within a day or two. You need to stop using it straight away, I suggest you seek other ways of masking your pain. Is it your back, or a leg?" Scetis ran a critical eye over the man and how he was standing.

"Vist?" Ide turned to him.

"I don't know what he's talking about," Vist protested loudly.

"I think you can go Physician," Ide waved him away and Scetis left them standing there.

Making use of his chance to escape, he skirted around the cart and passed the hired guards, who were still seated on their horses and quickly made his way to the bridge. Scetis kept an ear out behind him, just to make sure he would not be called back and interrogated more. His foot landed its first step on the wooden bridge and he hurried up the small incline as it rose over the swift, deep, cold water below. The sound of the river was loud, and it masked the noise behind him. He was almost at the center when he heard his name.

"Physician Mordha!" It was a commanding female voice that called.

Scetis turned slowly to watch her stride towards him, holding something in her hand. She reached the bridge when Vist caught up to her and whispered something to the Lieutenant. Her eyes were hard when they turned back to Scetis and she continued, with Vist coming up behind.

"You forgot this," she told him, pushing the medallion out in front of her, the cord swinging with each step she took closer.

"My thanks, ma'am," he said bowing his head to her and reaching out to take it.

Ide's free hand came out and clasped his wrist as he took hold of the medallion. Her grasp was tight, and her eyes narrowed.

"Vist claims you are the man in the Hall. Was it you?" she asked quietly, just audible above the sound of the water below them.

Scetis gave her an equal stare, his eyes began to gleam again slightly, and he heard her intake of breath at the effect. His mouth turned up at one corner, stretching his lips over his uneven teeth. With a quick motion the medallion was tucked into his shirt, and his now free arm pulled her sword from its sheath at her hip, he flicked it out and ran it straight through Vist, who stood shocked at the blade sticking through his chest.

The sound of pulling it out, as he twisted the blade and it grated on the bone it had sliced through was lost, but the blood as it came pouring out of him was not. It ran freely from his wound, running down his torso and his leg. He tried in vain to stem the flow of the severed artery, his face turned a deadly shade of grey and he collapsed to his knees.

Ide made a lunge at the arm Scetis held the sword in, she was stronger than she looked, and he struggled with her. The skirmish and the collapse of Vist drew cries from the other guards and Scetis knew that it was a fight he could not win; one lone man against so many Foot guards.

Scetis looked down at Ide and grinned now.

"Feel like a swim?" he asked her. With all his might he threw himself at the railing to the bridge. It was old wood, long gone to rot and not replaced by either realm. He dragged her with him, while they still contended for control of the sword. The sound of the barrier snapping made Ide's eyes widen as he continued to stare into them. The shock of the fall and the impact into the raging waters that came straight from the melting snow higher up in the mountains, was great. It sucked what little breath either had remaining in their lungs, as it hurtled them down the great stream cutting between the mountains.

Ide's hands were still clamped on his wrists, not to restrain anymore, but in self-preservation. The sword he had taken from her was wrenched out of his grasp and was lost to the bottom of the river and the stones there. Scetis struggled with the panic coming from the woman and he managed to get them both to the surface of the water.

The weight of her armor and cloak were pulling Ide down, she choked back the water that constantly covered her face. Scetis reached for her side and pulled at the straps that held it onto her body, his fingers were becoming numb, and they could not work properly to undo them.

Quickly he reached to her belt once more and pulled on the knife that was there, the fight was ebbing from her body as she struggled to keep her head above water and breathe in the precious air that would keep her alive. Pulling it free he carefully sliced through the straps, he dropped the knife so he could help her out of her breast plate and cloak.

The weight dropped away, and Ide surfaced. She took in a very large gulp of air and started to cough. He grasped her around the waist and held her up as the water pushed them through the great chasm with vertical sides. There was nowhere they could try to get out of the cold water. Her arms went around his neck and held on almost pushing him under in her still raging panic.

The roar started shallowly at first, it was dull and just audible. But soon it began to get louder, until it reverberated off the sides of the water cut stone. Billows of small droplets soon were visible, rising into the air and floating away from the straight drop that they were heading towards. Ide looked at him as she became aware of the danger that was looming up before them.

"Just hold on to me," he told her and then turned to face what was to come.

The edge came hurtling up on them, the water turned white as it mixed with the air while it plunged down into the depths. It was not as steep as he had first thought. The sound had been increased in the confined space and they were soon bobbing to the surface once more. The pool under them was deep and despite the amount of water pouring down from above it was almost calm.

"Why did you save me?" Ide asked him, still holding on tightly to his neck and starting to shiver.

"I am not a murderer," he said, not meeting her eyes.

"But you killed Vist."

"Yes, but I don't kill women."

"That may be your downfall," she said harshly through chattering teeth.

"You were not going to kill me, he was, I saw it in his eyes. The other symptoms of overuse of Actaea Racemosa is a tendency for rashness and inability to judge a situation. He was about to pull his sword and disregard your safety to get to me. So, in a way, I protected you."

"I don't need protection," her teeth were chattering badly now, and she tried to pull her arms away from him.

"Keep holding on. Our body warmth together will keep us alive long enough—I hope—to find somewhere to get out of the water." His grip around her waist tightened and Ide relaxed against him. The sensation was not one he had ever experienced before, as he had never been with a woman, or anyone for that matter.

The water continued to carry them swiftly through the v-shaped gap, the years of erosion evident on the walls. The stone around them was dark and left little to hold onto. A bend was fast approaching and as they turned, a little beach appeared where the water flung around one side. Scetis set to swim with one arm while still holding onto Ide to gain the ground they needed to pull themselves up on the gravel strewn piece of land.

He pulled her out of the water and up as high as they could before collapsing under her weight and the exhaustion of their efforts. Scetis breathed deeply, he looked up at the sky so far above them and saw a slice of blue. It was still afternoon, but soon night would be falling, and it would get cold in this place.

Looking around he found a meagre supply of wood pushed against the rocks on the downstream side of the beach. He hauled himself to his feet and started to collect what he could. Piling it up against the sheer face of the rock wall he pulled off his bags, then started to rummage for his flint. Everything inside was swimming with the water that had seeped in.

Soon a fire was going, only small and flickering, but it drew Ide to it, and she crouched down, holding her hands out for its growing warmth. She watched this strange man as he searched through the bags and pulled things out. Wringing out the wet clothing, and unwrapping parcels in waxed cloth.

"At least we can eat tonight," he said glancing up at her, taking in her wet linen shirt and the long hair that hung down over her chest. He averted his gaze, the sight of Ide in this state was evoking thoughts that he did not need. He placed more wood on the fire and sat back against the wall on the opposite side of her.

Alarm

Muniath reached up and patted the red scales of Scorcher. Venicones had said that his mount had seemed a little off the last couple of days and was worried about him. Down at his feet the little dragon had followed him and was keeping very close, while they were with the larger male dragon. Scorcher gave a low rumble at the small whelp, though it was not so small now. Both of Screamer's children had grown rapidly in the last week.

"So, what is the matter with you, my boy?" Muniath muttered as he began to search the dragon's mind. Images of a Blue flitted through them and he laughed.

"I see. You're lovesick, not ailing in any other way," he patted the Reds head. "I'll see what we can do about your ailment, Scorcher. Rain may want you; we will just have to see. But I am not sure you will get any whelps from the mating. A Fire and a Water type might just be unattainable, but it would make for an interesting union."

The large dragon before him made another noise and then lowered its head down to the young one. The small dragon slowly edged her way to the big Red and stretched out its lengthening neck to touch the nose of its senior. The small dragon chirped happily at the Red and rustled her wings. A shimmer of color went along the small body and Muniath knelt beside his new young charge.

"He does not want to play with you, little one. You need to find your nest mate if you want to do that. Go on, off back to your mother." He stroked her head and watched as she alternatively tried to fly and ran out of the cavern and headed back to Screamer.

"Muniath!" the call was loud, and it sounded like the person was out of breath.

"In here with Scorcher," Muniath replied.

Venicones entered at an almost run and stopped so he did not alarm his mount. He gulped a few times before he managed to get enough breath in his lungs to talk.

"It's Ide, there's been an incident at the border, the Trader, he was there, she tried to stop him, and he took her with him into the river." It came out all in one breath.

"When?" Muniath demanded.

"Late afternoon yesterday. Father has ordered a search, all mounts in the air as soon as possible. He and the King are on their way now, even Urmond is going to search."

"I've not heard the alarm."

"I wanted to tell you first. Go ring it and I'll get Scorcher ready." Venicones moved past his brother heading to where the tack for his mount was stored.

Scorcher reared up alert to the sudden panic and concern that was emanating from Muniath now. He looked at his older brother for a moment and then went running.

Out in the main cave he raced to the entrance and the large bell that was hung there. He grasped the rope tightly in his hand, before pulling on it with all his might. It moved slowly as the bell heaved to the side, the large clapper inside hit the outer edge with an ear-splitting sound. Muniath released the rope so that it would swing back the other way. Again, and again he pulled on that bell rope. The sound sent out to the farther reaches of the valley. Many people began to pass him as they entered the Eyrie to go mount their own beasts.

From within a loud cry called out. He saw Scorcher with his brother on his back, lumber out of the cavern. Coming to a stop under one of the openings in the roof, the great beast spread his glorious wings and began to beat them. They rose from the earth and up through the opening, before angling off down the valley.

Muniath stopped ringing the bell and raced back down the cave system. He stopped at each cavern to make sure the other Riders were doing what they should and then hurried them out before going to saddle his father's mount, Raker. He was just leading the dragon out when two men strode towards him.

"My Lord King, General," Muniath greeted them.

"Muniath, are they all away?" Galanan asked his son.

"They are, just yourself and the King's mount remain," he reported.

"Good. My King, would you mind if I did not wait for you?" Galanan asked.

"Of course, go find your daughter, I will be right behind. Muniath can help me saddle Screamer," Urmond told his friend.

Without waiting for another word Galanan was gone and Muniath was heaving out the heavily ornate saddle that belonged to the king. Screamer waited patiently as he placed it on her back, while Urmond secured the guiding reins to her head.

"Is it too soon for her to leave her young?" Urmond asked as he finished the last strap.

"No, they are old enough now to be left for a while. I'll have Wick watch them."

"And you, what will you be doing?" Urmond came to stand in front of the Master of Dragons.

"I'll be going down to the General's office and taking charge."

"Good. Until you are mounted yourself there is nothing you can do. Nothing, do you hear me."

"I don't know what you mean, Sire," Muniath was genuinely confused.

"I know you have been brooding on the lost egg. You will not get it back; it probably has perished by now."

"It hasn't, I can feel it."

"Even from this distance?"

"Yes, Sire."

This news gave Urmond a moment of pause. "I still forbid you to go looking for it. I cannot afford to lose another Master of Dragons and leave me with only an apprentice."

"I will do as my King commands." Muniath bowed to Urmond and followed both Screamer and the King out of the cavern.

As he watched them leave, Wick came running from the entrance. His hair was plastered to his face and he was out of breath.

"I got here as soon as I could, is it true?" he panted.

"It is. Look after the two young ones, I need to go somewhere."

Muniath briefly laid a hand on his apprentice's shoulder before passing him and heading out of the Eyrie and down to the town. With hurried steps he found his way to Meara's tavern and entered. The talk inside was raised with excitement about the news from the border. Some looked at the opened door and recognized Muniath and called to him for news.

He waved them away, telling them he could not help as he did not know anything himself. Muniath instead headed out to the back rooms and found the person he was looking for.

Taran was hauling in a basket full of freshly dug vegetables for the pot that night. Muniath took it out of his hands and placed it on the table for the older man.

"My thanks. But you shouldn't be here, you should be out there looking for Ide. Is there any news?" Taran asked.

"I only just found out; I've heard nothing more and I am on my way to my father's office to take charge there, if I can. Before I do though, I wanted to talk to you."

"Me? I can't help you; I am a Rider no longer remember." The old man sat down heavily at the table and began to pull the basket towards him.

"No, I need your experience. With the portals." Muniath leaned on the back of another chair and waited for Taran to reply.

"This is about that other dragon?"

"It is. It's still alive and from what I can feel, flying already. Its littermates are only now testing their wings. Taran it's special. It's different from the other dragons. It's more advanced and highly intelligent," he said excitedly.

"All dragons are intelligent." Taran raised an eyebrow at him.

"But this one is different. I can't tell you how without actually seeing it for myself."

"But that would mean going through the portal, and you have been forbidden to do so." Taran stopped washing the dirt of the carrot in his hands and looked up the younger man. "No, I will not help you get into the hall and go through that portal."

"But I can get home again." Muniath released the chair and sat down on it. "When the King banished Tharain and his daughter, he gave her a necklace. It has a charm on it that will open a temporary portal to bring the wearer and whoever, or whatever is with her, home. If I could find Tharain and Teagan, then I can get us all home again with the dragon."

"And how would you find them?" Taran asked him.

"The dragon is the key. It can't have survived by itself without help, no matter how special it is. I believe that Tharain or his daughter has found it and is looking after it."

"How can you be so certain of that?" Taran threw the carrot back amongst the pile in the basket.

"I can't, I just have this feeling. I have to try."

"You have responsibilities here. Or did you forget the promise you made to my daughter?"

"No, I've not forgotten. But will you help me when the time comes, and Wick is far enough along to take over for a while?"

"Come see me then and we'll talk more. I am not going to promise you anything right now, Mun. It would be foolish for me to do so. But you can promise me something," Taran pointed a finger at the younger man.

"Anything."

"When you do decide to do this foolish and rash act, you leave Wick behind. You do not allow him to follow you in any way. I will not have Mae lose someone else because of a dragon. It would kill her."

"I know it would, and gladly make that promise, sir. Wick will know nothing of my plans. The fewer people who do know the better. The King will try to stop me, and I think I have a way around that. I'll have myself banished."

"You can't do that, that would kill your mother. Your last depressive bout worried her sick. She would come in here and ask after you every day, you didn't know that did you?"

"No," he shook his head slightly. "I had no idea."

"She wasn't the only one."

"Father?"

Taran only nodded his answer to Muniath. "Your father came to me the other day, we sat here at this very table, drinking like old Riders do, reminiscing and telling tall tales. He told me what you went through. He also told me how proud he is of you." Taran paused a moment before continuing, "If you do this, shame yourself so badly that you are banished then his pride will be for naught. There has to be another way."

"I have thought through so many different ways, and the one I am known by and the one the King has already warned me against is attacking Orcades."

"Why would you do that? The man is a pompous ass and I wish I could shake some sense into Ide about him, but he is the King's nephew. No, if you are going to do this then that option is out. You must leave him alone." Taran punctuated his words by tapping on the table.

"Alright, I will. For now." Muniath bowed his head and covered his face with his hands. "I hate this, stymied at every turn. Unable to ride to rescue my sister, unable to go save the young dragon," he looked up at Taran. "Unable to have the satisfaction of punching in that overly chiseled face," he grinned.

"When everything is settled, you and I will go have a little chat with Orcades. But only when things are back to normal, and before he has a chance to marry Ide," Taran chuckled back. "Now, you have duties. As third in command you should be at your father's office to receive updates and organize things. Galanan and Aideen would expect it of you."

"Thank you, Taran. I'll think on your advice." Muniath stood and held his hand out to the older man, who took it and held it firmly.

Once released Muniath turned and left the room. Taran looked after him as his hand absently picked up the knife on the table and began to play with it.

"Mun is going to get himself and you in trouble, old man," Mae said quietly from the shadows before entering the room fully.

"I'll curb his enthusiasm until he is thinking straight. I knew you were there, that's why I extracted that promise from him."

"But Wick will follow him, you know he will. He idolizes Mun and my boy is as thick headed as his father was, and his grandfather is." Mae placed her hands on his shoulders and gave them a squeeze.

"He is at that, but Mun will keep him safe, I know he will. He keeps his vows and oaths, he really is not that bad a man for a womanizer," Taran chuckled and looked up at his daughter.

"Yes, and any decent woman would stay away from him because of his ways," Meara told him as she moved to the stove and the pot that sat over the flames.

"But he isn't the one for you."

"I'm pleased you think that Father," she chuckled as she began to stir the stew that bubbled away.

"No, there is another who you have caught the eye of." Taran swiveled in his seat to look at her.

"I am in no rush for matrimony again. I have Wick to think of, and you." She continued to stir the large pot.

"But you cannot be on your own, I am not going to live forever, and Wick is growing fast. Already he's lodging in the barracks with the other Riders."

"Please stop, Father," she asked quietly resting the spoon on the side of the blackened pot.

"You know who I'm referring to. He did nothing to stand in the way of you and Nabarus, he even encouraged it. All the while his heart was breaking in two."

"Father, stop."

"No, I won't, not when your happiness is at stake. Do you feel anything for him?"

"I don't know, and it's a matter which will never come to pass. His mother will see to that."

"Why would Aideen object?"

"Because I am his foster-sister. Father, I thank you for your concern, but it is not warranted. I'm happy here in this place I built up with my own hands, without the help of a man at my side. Just because I live alone, does not mean I am lonely."

"We shall see," Taran told her.

As Muniath strode through the halls of the citadel, guards of both Foot and Rider snapped to attention as he passed them. Approaching his father's office door, the two Riders that were stationed there brought their sabers up to attention, from where they had been resting on the floor. He stopped before them.

"Is there going to be a problem with my entering the General's office?" he asked them formally.

"No, sir, you have been expected," the man on the right said. He moved quickly and opened the doors for Muniath.

As the guard was about to shut the door Muniath spoke up, "Keep them open, there will be runners coming and going. Also go set them to man the flyway, I am expecting the first report to come in soon."

"Yes, sir, and if I may, I am sure Lieutenant Magaoidh will be found soon."

"I thank you for your thoughts."

With the guard gone to follow his orders, Muniath turned to his father's desk. It was unusual for papers to litter the top of the polished surface, and Mun could sense the haste and urgency of the General's departure to find his only daughter. Going around to the seat, Muniath stared at some of the sheets to find the daily reports from the many Rostra that lined the border of the realm. Bundling them up he moved them to the side of the desk in a tidy pile.

"Good, you're here. Have you had any word yet?" Aideen said coming into the room, nodding to the guard that still remained.

"No, Captain Magaoidh," Muniath reported, coming to attention. "We have not had any news come in yet, but I have set up the runners for when they do."

"She will be found; Ide is strong and smart. If anyone can survive going down that river, it will be her," she said stoically, Muniath, though, could see the worry etched in her eyes.

Muniath came from behind the large desk and put his arms around his mother. He heard a small sniff from the confines of the embrace and Aideen was soon pulling away from him, nodding her thanks.

"You're right, Mother, she will be found, and she will be safe," he told her, trying to put as much positivity into his tone as he could.

"General Gerarailt wants all communications with the border sent through to him as soon as they have come in," she told him, once more gaining her composure.

"It will be as he wishes then, Captain." Muniath stood to attention as he spoke.

"We are of equal rank Mun, you don't need to do that." Aideen gave her youngest child a small smile.

"Yes, I do, you outrank me in many ways, Mother," he told her with a lopsided grin and a wink.

"Get to work," his quip raised a smile to her own lips. "I am about to ride to the border crossing. That Trader can't have been on his own; there were two when they broke into the Hall. Someone has failed in their duties."

"I wish you a very speedy journey, and I wish there was more that I could do."

"You are where you should be right now; where you're most useful to the search. Your father and brother will find her, I am sure of it." Aideen gave him a quick nod of the head before turning and heading out of the door.

Muniath was not alone for very long. A boy of about eighteen came running in, clutching a leather cylinder. He held it out to his superior.

"Thank you, go back to Flyway. There may be more coming," he instructed.

"Yes, sir." The boy gave a hasty salute as he was already turning to run back to his post.

Prying the lid of the tube off he reached inside and pulled up a coiled piece of paper. Laying it on the surface of the desk he unrolled it and studied what was written there. The news was not hopeful, and the witness statements were damning for one of the Riders.

Rolling it back up Muniath stalked out of the office, pausing briefly to talk to the guards.

"Any runners come, send them straight to General Gerarailt's office," he ordered.

"Yes, sir," they both saluted, and he left them to their posts.

The Riders and their command were situated in the west wing of the Citadel, closest to the gate leading up to the Eyrie. The Foot, on the other hand, were in the east wing, along with the stables and extensive armory. Muniath crossed the courtyard between the north wing and east and could already hear the clang of the blacksmiths at work. The smells were different in this part of the Citadel, with the animals that were kept here, not just horses, but falcons and dogs. Just as he could communicate with the dragons high above them, there were those that also had the same ability with other animals.

Entering in through a side door, the sudden darkness from the bright sunshine outside made him blind for a moment, but he knew the way. He garnered stares from soldiers of the Foot in his Rider garb, but he ignored them. Most greeted him by name with a nod and those who were young and inexperienced recognized his rank and saluted.

The door to the office he sought was open and he nodded to the guards posted outside. They let him through without interference and he placed the parchment in front of the man behind the desk.

Domnall was grey now, and his hair was thinning, but still he commanded respect. He looked up at Muniath and pulled the parchment to him, unrolled it, and read.

"So, your witness was no good then?" he asked as he dropped it to the desk once more.

"It seems not, sir," Muniath replied.

"No doubt your father will deal with him, I can't say I pity the man. To be on duty while so doped up, what was he thinking?"

"His duty, sir."

Domnall waived Muniath into a seat opposite him. "One of my best Lieutenants is now lost—and I mean not to make you lose hope—but possibly dead in the river."

"I know my sister, General. She's a fighter and will work to her last breath to stay alive. I can only hope that the Trader who dragged her with him will not be so lucky," Muniath's anger was building with his words.

"I want you to stay in the Citadel tonight, Mun. While the King is away, I'm in charge. I don't want to have to try and pull you out of a beer barrel to get you to work. Ide needs you."

"Thank you for concern, General Gerarailt, but I'll not be taking that chance. I know my duties, and I'll not be going back down into that particular hell again."

Travel

The cool wind whipped at her face, making her cheeks redden under its sting. Teagan sat on the back of Gremlin and smiled broadly; her teeth bright in the moonlight that shone from high above. His wings were extended to their fullest and they silently glided along the gullies and over the hills, covering vast distances with only a few strokes of his powerful wings.

The scales shone and almost sparkled in the magical light of the moon and they were toughening up. As Gremlin grew, his body changed. His scales that used to be soft now had gaps between them that overlapped, almost like armor. Long, gripping claws sprouted on the tips of his wings, and what she could only call the elbows. The tail had sprouted spikes where the flat flesh had been, and the horns on his head were large, curved, and very sharp.

Their minds were one, and they celebrated together this freedom they had found in the sky. Although, only a couple of weeks prior, they had almost been discovered as they flew the valleys near Gremlin's roost. The decision had been agreed between them that they would only fly at night. Just as they did in this moment.

Gremlin's wings clawed at the air, pushing them on further and further afield than they had been the previous nights. In the distance the scenery was changing, the valley below was widening, and there was a gleaming river running down it. They followed it like a path and soon it brought them to the sea. White rolling waves pounded and churned beneath them and Gremlin banked wide to come back around.

Teagan looked out in the distance and could see lights from towns and houses in the distance, car lights lit the ground in great yellow arcs, and she recognized the coastline. Especially the island that sat offshore.

Her father had brought her as a child to the beaches a few times when he was sober enough and had saved a little for a holiday. She had fallen in love with that island and its shape. Teagan remembered telling her father that it looked like a dragon. He had told her to stop thinking of such nonsense.

The dragon-like shape loomed dark against the stars and moonlit sky. The water around it sparkled and danced with the waves as they pushed to shore. It was still magical to her.

Gremlin banked again, gliding in slower and slower circles until he landed on the soft black sand of the Kapiti Coast. The small particles of dry sand flew up in a cloud from his large claws, as he came to a skidding stop. Teagan leapt down from the makeshift saddle her father had found and adjusted so it would fit the wider back of the dragon. She walked around to his large head, placed a hand on his cheek, and lay her head on his.

"That was a wonderful ride, Gremlin, thank you," she spoke to him directly with her mind.

"It was so freeing. The smell of the water is pleasing, and the ground is much different underfoot," he thought back. Teagan had to quickly step out of his way as he danced around on the beach.

Their means of communication had started hesitantly, at first. The occasional word and meaning derived from it graduated to more simple sentences. Now their thoughts were linked, and they could speak more freely of what they needed from each other.

Teagan pulled her head away and walked to the edge of the water. The waves that crashed to shore were larger than normal. They were the heavy remains of some unseen storm out to sea, beyond the large island before them. The wind tugged at her hair and she breathed deeply of the salt enriched air. The sound of the surf pounding in front of her and slowly sliding back out over the dark sand set her at ease.

"What is that place?" Gremlin asked, coming up behind her.

"That is Kapiti Island," Tegan replied.

"It has some meaning for you, I think."

"It does. It was the first time I was introduced to the conservation work of the forests and birds of this country. My father brought me here to this coast when I was about twelve and we managed to get to go across to the island. I always think it looks like the back of a dragon, but father told me I was being silly."

Gremlin made a snorting sound and turned to look down his own back, the spikes that grew there and the drop down to his tail.

"It does not look like my back; I think you have a very good imagination."

"Maybe I do, or I was remembering my childhood," she said quietly, her hand automatically went to the pendant at her throat. The silver and green jewel caught the moonlight and for a moment it seemed to the dragon that the emerald glowed.

"I have seen you wear that before, what is it?"

"It was given to me before we were sent here. The King himself placed it around my neck to remember the world we were to leave."

"There is something to it, something else I can sense," Gremlin brought his great jaw closer to her and sniffed a little.

"It's a trinket only." Tegan let out a great sigh. "We'll have to come back another night. It's time we were heading back to the forest."

"I wish I could see more of this land," Gremlin gave his own sigh and then bent his foreleg to help Teagan once more gain her seat on his back.

"I'm due to some holiday time soon. We could travel the country. There are many places that are very remote, and people are scarce." She settled herself on the saddle once more and held onto two of the large spikes on his neck. Her father had wanted her to use reins, but with their connection she had decided that they were unnecessary.

"That sounds like a very good idea, Teagan, I look forward to it."

Gremlin moved away from the edge of the water and started to beat his wings. Clouds of loose sand were soon stirred up and Teagan squinted her eyes against the stinging particles. They gained air again, rising higher and higher above the beach. Instead of heading inland as she initially indicated, Gremlin turned and headed out over the sea. He glided out to the island and slowly circled it.

As Teagan looked down, she saw the hut that the rangers used, the light spilling brightly out of the windows. They sped passed it fast and came to the other end of the island. The dim light that shone from the moon above cast dark shadows deep into the forest-laden island, revealing its rugged beauty. With a couple of strong beats of his wings, Gremlin was once more heading inland and over the hills and valleys.

This time the excitement was dulled to her, seeing the island again had reminded her of how much had changed in her life. She thought about that fateful day again, the day they were banished. Each time she did, a new part of the memory came to her. The racing up the steps to her father's arms, seeing the dragons, mounted, and flying passed and the salute from the Riders. The sound of the marching feet of the soldiers that had come for her father, the long walk to the throne room and seeing the King sitting looking so grim on his chair.

Gremlin's wings beat again, keeping both dragon and rider aloft on the swirling winds. The dragon shared the loss and pain coming from the rider on his back and he carried on, keeping her safe from harm and prying eyes. He beat against the sudden up drafts and saw the distant lights from the city that they lived near. He circled around it, keeping away from the farms and the roads, until slowly he began their descent down into his clearing.

Teagan slipped from his back and began to unbuckle the saddle. Gremlin stood calmly waiting for her to release him from the straps. It had been awkward at first when Tharain had first placed them on his back, but he had gotten used to the sensation of the saddle and the weight of the girl was not too much for him. As the straps fell away from his back, he gave a shake for a moment and then he began to lumber his way to his bed.

"I am looking forward to our flight, Teagan," he told her, yawning softly.

"Yes, it will be an adventure," she replied as she stowed the riding equipment. She walked back to the crude shelter and Gremlin settled himself in for the night.

The shelter had been rebuilt many times as the dragon had grown, her father often commentating that he had never seen a one of his kind grow as fast as Gremlin did.

"Teagan, I know you are sad and wish to go home." The words were accompanied with a low purring sound from deep within his chest.

"I am going home now, but it does not mean I don't want to be here with you." Teagan was confused with his words.

"You long for the other world, where we come from."

"You have opened my eyes as to what could have been. Papa tells me that if we were there, I would have been apprenticed to the Master of Dragons and I would have talked to many dragons."

"Am I not enough?" he gently teased her.

"Of course you are, Gremlin." Teagan crossed the gap between them and hugged his neck. He placed his head gently on her shoulder.

"Go home then Teagan and sleep well. I will see you tomorrow and we won't talk of our homeland. We will plan instead our great adventure and the sights we shall see," he tried to cheer her up.

"That we will, Gremlin. Good night." She kissed his cheek and then released him, turning away and walking into the forest along the well-worn track that had developed since she had brought him to this valley.

When Teagan arrived at work the next day, she had immediately gone to try and book some time off while the weather was still warm. She was met with a little resistance at first from Eric, only because he could not stand to be left with Mark and Phil for company, he told her jokingly. Her leave was soon granted.

She took the books she borrowed from work into the forest that night, along with a large map of the country. Together Gremlin and Teagan mapped out a route to take around the country, picking places to stop that were remote and planning when they could travel by day and when it would be necessary to only be about at night. There was much to see, and her spirits were lifting with each suggestion.

Gremlin was pleased to see her enthusiastic and not thinking about her past again. Although he could not read the runes, she called words, he could see the pictures. Her enthusiasm was infectious, and he was eager to be off.

Tharain came with her the night they were to leave. He had with him a bag strapped to his back, which was of equal size to the one Teagan had with her also. Gremlin stood in the center of the clearing and waited for them after he heard their footsteps out in the forest. A thrill passed through him at the thought of moving further afield, it was an eagerness he could also sense in Teagan. But the worry from Tharain overshadowed it all.

"Go get the gear and we'll start to saddle him up," Tharain said to his daughter as he dropped the pack from his back. He walked up to Gremlin and was very formal in his greeting to the Dragon. "Good eve to you Gremlin, I hope you are well."

The dragon dropped his head, bowing to Teagan's father. The man approached Gremlin and lay a hand on his neck.

"Look after her, boy. She's all I have," he told Gremlin gently and quietly so Teagan would not hear.

Gremlin in turn gave a little snort of assurance and hoped that the man would understand the meaning. Tharain patted his neck and then went to help Teagan saddle the dragon.

Soon both packs were attached to the saddle on either side of Gremlin. He tested his wings to make sure that he had full use of them, and the bags would not impede his movement in any way.

"Now, you be careful. He's not small anymore and if someone were to spot the two of you, it…well it could have consequences you are not willing to face." Tharain pulled Teagan into a hug.

"I'm not a child anymore, Papa. We'll be careful. Remember his eyesight is great and can see for miles in all directions. He'll give me enough warning if there are people nearby." Teagan pulled away from her father. "I want you to promise me that you will take care of yourself."

"I promise. I have not touched a drop since this all started, and I don't mean to start again. I'm fitter than I have been in some time, and clearer of head."

"It was a blessing the day I found Gremlin in the burnt forest. He's helped us both."

"He has indeed. Now go, before the moon rises. You can be away over the Cook Straight without being seen. Enjoy the trip, I expect a lot of stories when you get back."

"See you in a week, Papa." Teagan reached up and kissed her father's stubbly cheek and then turned to mount the dragon.

Gremlin nudged Tharain's shoulder and there was a look in his reptilian eye that comforted the old rider. His daughter would be well looked after.

Tharain stepped back as Gremlin began to move his wings. They stretched wide and billowed up as the wind caught beneath the leathery membrane. The breeze it created ruffled the hair on his head and the forest around him. Slowly the pair began to rise into the night sky, and they were soon a dark shadow against the starlit night. He saw Teagan wave and they headed off into the darkness. Tharain watched them go and then turned to the track and headed home.

Gremlin dropped low over the expanse of water of the Cook Strait which separated the North and South Islands of New Zealand. The waves were lines of ripples, ever moving across the deep water. Before them the South Island's shadow grew. The mountain ranges reaching for the sky became brighter and brighter as the crescent moon rose in the east like a great shining arc, so big and so yellow as it appeared on the horizon. They could see the craters and forms that covered the surface of the lunar object. Teagan only spent a little time watching it as it hauled itself away from the earth's horizon. She turned her attention back to Gremlin in order to guide them to their first destination: The West Coast.

The Marlborough Sounds flittered away underneath them, a collection of small and large islands; the shores of which were scattered with little shacks and holiday homes. Some were large and grand, with long jetties spreading out into the bays that protected the properties. Others were just shacks of four walls and a roof, some looking like they would fall down from the next good gust.

The flight was so freeing, and Teagan watched it all pass far below, as Gremlin climbed once more to avoid a hill that loomed up before them. Out in the distance they could see lights on the shores, and on the water as people enjoyed their pleasure craft and yachts. Teagan sent a suggestion to Gremlin that they move further out and away from the shoreline, in case they were spotted.

They passed over D'Urville Island and could see the lights of Nelson on the left in the distance. Gremlin pushed on, his wings never tiring as they passed over the waters of Tasman Bay, heading for their first stop and rest for the night, before pushing on down the West Coast to Farewell Spit. A long narrow piece of land, pointing out and curving around, protecting Golden Bay from the Tasman Sea.

Finding a place to land on the very top of the last rise, Teagan slipped from his back and stretched. Gremlin sank to the ground, his breath only slightly faster than normal.

"Oh, that was so amazing, Teagan. It is so beautiful," he told her wondrously.

"It is, and even better to see it from the air."

Teagan went to one of the packs and pulled out a package, unwrapped it and handed the meaty contents inside to Gremlin. Delicately he took it from her hands and gulped it down, only chewing it slightly. She saw to his needs first before satisfying her own thirst and hunger and sat down beside him as they stared at the moon. They watched the rolling waves crashing on the shore far below, the white as they curled, catching brightly in the light.

"How much further tonight?" he asked her.

"Just a little more. The coastline is not very heavily populated, not on this side of the island anyway. I thought we would stop on the edge of Kahurangi National Park. It's dense and there are not many beaches. There are a few huts we must be careful of; at this time of the year, they'll be used by hikers and possibly some rangers as well. I thought we could find a decent sized beach to land and stay the rest of the night and day, before heading off again tomorrow night."

"That's a good idea." Gremlin stretched his neck out and shuffled his wings.

"Are you in pain?" she asked him.

"No, I would tell you if I were. I'm just stretching out my muscles as you did when we landed. If you are ready, we should go, I'm eager to see more."

"I'm ready," she smiled at his impatience and stood with him.

They were soon in the air again and heading down the coast. Gremlin was crying out into the night his delight, letting go roar after roar, while he darted from the hills and shoreline, out over the rolling Tasman Sea.

He climbed high and then dropped low, making Teagan cry out with his delight as she clung to the horns on his back. The sharp cliffs loomed up and Gremlin used the updraft to climb high. She clung to his back as she began to slowly slip with the near vertical angle, her knees and feet pushing harder into his sides and slipping on the slick scales.

Teagan's scream was one of pure exhilaration and was completely lost in Gremlin's roar. She marveled at his strength and speed, at his sheer delight in freedom. As he crested the top of the cliff she was laughing and enjoying it with him. Gremlin banked away to the right and headed south down the coast, gliding along. Teagan let go of the spikes she used to hold onto and raised her arms in the air. The wind buffeted her face and arms, threatening to unseat her, but she was enjoying the moment too much to worry or be afraid.

Lazily and slowly, they played their way down the coast, the white wave caps crashing against the narrow shoreline and cliffs that they passed. Using their connection Teagan guided Gremlin to a spot where they could stay for the rest of the night and the fast-approaching day. She could hear his acceptance as they neared the spot and used the updrafts to gently bring them down to the shore. It was a mix of sand and pebbles and the high tide mark was well and truly visible with a line of driftwood that was thick and bound together.

Teagan soon set to work building a fire pit, while Gremlin began to choose pieces of wood. Using his mighty jaws, he broke up the larger pieces and placed them down beside his companion. Soon there was a small tent set up for Teagan and an area cleared for Gremlin.

She was searching through the packs for the lighter Teagan knew she put there, when she heard a whoosh and a bright golden light. Looking up from her task she saw a fire merrily dancing in the pit and Gremlin looking out to sea. She laughed and pulled out the meal provisions for herself and the dragon.

They ate in companionable silence as they watched the sky lighten with the rising sun. The birds in the forest behind them woke early and began their day, filling the air with sweet soaring music. The sound of the waves crashing to shore only added to the sound, and it was soothing.

Teagan leaned against Gremlin, who curled his tail gently around and protected her from the day with a wing. His head came to rest on his front paws and they both fell asleep, stomachs full and minds overflowing with their long flight.

Teagan had timed this trip well. When they set off the moon was still building to its fullest and gave them the greatest of light as they travelled. They saw many things under the cover of darkness and beneath the watchful eye of the Earth's nearest neighbor. One of those sights was the giant crags of rock sticking up out of the water, the remnants of an old and long forgotten shoreline. Large and powerful waves were rolling in from the Tasman Sea, crashing onto the shear sides, shooting up white walls of water. The pair circled for a long time, gliding on silent wings, before Gremlin came to rest on the largest. The power of the force of the waves shuddered up through the rock at their feet, and the salty mists drifted over them. Both Teagan and Gremlin were drenched from the sea spray by the time they flew up and off into the night.

Further south they went, occasionally seeing the lights of little and large settlements. But always they kept away from human occupation. On their third night they reached Fiordland National Park. They moved past the ever-popular Milford Sound and entered the park through Doubtful Sound. Gremlin dropped low over the relatively calmer water, his occasional wing beats leaving the only tell-tale sign of their passing. In a small, secluded bay, they came to rest on the beach and made for the tree line just as the sun was rising. They quickly set up their camp, but Teagan had stopped putting up the tent for herself, now preferring to sleep under the protective wing of the dragon.

It was a good while after they had fallen asleep that she woke. Gremlin had moved and was alert. Teagan opened her eyes and listened carefully to what had brought him out of a deep sleep.

"Fresh meat," Gremlin let her know. "I smell a large beast."

"It's probably a deer. Do you want to go hunt it?" she asked him now sitting up.

"I've never hunted; you and your father have always provided for me. Am I allowed to hunt?"

"You are, Gremlin. Especially deer, or wild pig, they're destructive creatures in the forests, they're not native to New Zealand."

Teagan stood and moved out of his way. Gremlin had become intrigued with the idea of catching something for himself and she could sense it. He looked to her then the forest.

"You can go and hunt, I'll wait for you here. But be careful though, the forest can be enclosing and there may be other hunters out there. Humans with guns."

"Thanks for the warnings. Get some sleep Teagan, I'll be back soon."

Gremlin rose to his feet and headed further into the forest, his green scales soon disappearing into the deep shadows of the dense foliage, but she could hear him.

"Go quietly, otherwise you'll frighten it," Teagan sent the thought to him as she settled herself down beside their small fire and fed it a few sticks.

As she looked into the dancing flames their connection was still strong and Teagan closed her eyes to concentrate on it a little more. The startling revelation that she could see through his eyes almost made her break it. The vision was so different to her own human one, but she could still make out the tree trunks and bushes. Then a great shot of bright light flared. It was like a heat signature. Gremlin had paused as he looked at the creature. Tegan could clearly see that it was a deer, a large buck with a great rack of antlers. One that had lived a long and prosperous life in the New Zealand forest.

"Quietly," she coached him. Teagan had never been against hunting, especially those creatures that ruined the native plants and other creatures that lived in the forests.

Gremlin moved a little closer, careful where to place his feet, making sure he kept his wings in tight to his body and control of his tail. They watched together as he neared the buck, who seemed oblivious to the large dragon and continued to feed on the undergrowth.

"How will you attack it?" Teagan asked quietly.

"I could use fire," he mused.

"No, you'll set fire to the forest. Your jaw and tail I think would work better."

"Stun it with my tail spikes and then a killing bite to the neck would bring it down quickly and quietly. But I still need to get close to be able to do that. It will sense me."

"You are already within striking distance of the tail. The only way you will know how, is by doing it. Even if you fail this time, you will have learned what not to do next time. Try it, Gremlin," she urged.

The determination she experienced through their shared connection increased. His confidence was not as high for the success of the kill, but it was not so low as to hinder his performance. Teagan sensed him getting ready, the muscles in his tail began to tighten in anticipation of the strike and she held her breath.

It moved so quickly. One moment it was spread out the back end of him, then it flicked around the side, under his right wing. The spikes penetrated the tough hide of the buck and it immediately went into flight mode but found itself stuck. Gremlin lashed out with his neck, bringing his jaws and sharp rows of teeth down on the exposed neck of the deer. It went limp under the pressure as the neck snapped in two.

For the first time Gremlin tasted fresh blood and meat. He waited while the life force left the creature due to his actions and it filled him up with a sense of purpose. The natural instincts were awoken, and he immediately began to devour the buck, bones, organs and all. The only thing that was left when he had finished his first feast, was the antlered head.

Teagan was with him through it all. She could sense his accomplishment and his pride in the kill. The rush of adrenaline coursed through his veins and made his muscles twitch to do it again. The act of him eating his prize did not revolt her as it would have in others, it was only natural. He was a predator; the buck was his prey. To have left it to rot into the earth would have been wasteful. But now she was also aware and warier of his natural instincts.

The dragon landed in the middle of the clearing that was his home, the forest to the sides moving slightly under the pressure of the wind caused by his massive wingspan. While Teagan and Gremlin had been away, the dragon had grown even more. His muscles were now honed with the work that had taken them on their tour of the country. When they had left, she could still see traces of the baby dragon he had been when she had first found him, but now there was only the adult. He was enormous, his head now fully formed, with armored plates and spikes that curved backwards, his eyes large and double lidded. The armor plating going down the vulnerable neck to his massive chest. The spikes which were a single line down the back of his neck were many now, culminating in the two Teagan used as hand holds.

The wings which sprouted from his shoulders were wide and the membrane had thickened. They glistened in the moonlight and the hooks which protruded from the ends and the elbows were sharp and he had found uses for them when he hunted. The tail which spread out behind Gremlin's large hind quarters was quick and whipped behind him, the sharp spikes at the very tip were effective and his hunting was now perfected.

"Home," Gremlin breathed and waited patiently while Teagan dismounted and began to unclasp the saddle and packs from his back.

"Yes, home," Teagan replied, sounding almost sorry that they were.

"It'll be nice to sleep in one place. I want to thank you, Teagan, for our journey. I've learned a great deal since we've been gone."

"You're welcome, Gremlin," Teagan said as she yawned widely.

"You're welcome to share my nest tonight, it's a long walk for you to your home," he offered.

"That's very kind of you, Gremlin, but I should get home to Papa. He's expecting me tonight." Teagan once more stroked his long head gently, and Gremlin leaned into her touch. "Sleep well, my friend."

Watching as he turned and tried to enter the shelter, she thought they would need to make a new one and mentally was making a list in her mind regarding what material they would need. Gremlin sighed and coiled himself up in the entrance, placing his head on his front feet, his long tail circling around and Teagan could hear his breathing deepen as he headed to sleep.

After settling both packs on her shoulders, Teagan turned and left the clearing and made her way down the track. The dim light from the nearly spent moon filtered down through the thick canopy of the native trees and forest. An owl called out mournfully into the night and the sound suited her mood. She was home and had to go back to work. The freedom they had both reveled in flying around the country had been amazing and she had loved it. Teagan also wished they could fly during the day, she wished that they were somewhere that Gremlin could be free to come and go as he pleased, that he was not something to be feared and strange.

The track led her to the back gate of the house she shared with her father. The lights blazed in the back of the house and she noticed that the yard seemed to be neater than when she had left. Reaching the back door, she pushed it open and the smell of hot food assaulted her senses. She shrugged off the packs and left them in the laundry room as she made her way into the kitchen.

"Papa, I'm home," Teagan called out.

"Welcome back, you are just in time for dinner. How was your trip?" Tharain asked, coming to meet her from the front of the house. He wore an old shirt and shorts, which were covered in paint, the same color was smeared on one of his cheeks.

"What are you doing, Papa?" she asked him, laughing a little.

"I'm sorting the house. I thought it was about time that your room and the rest of the house got an upgrade," he told her proudly.

Teagan moved past him as he winked at her and walked down the hallway. The smell of paint became stronger the closer she got to the bedrooms and she pushed her door open. Her eyes widened when she saw what he had done for her. The room was no longer shabby and tired looking, but elegant and very girly. Where once piles of books had been stacked along one wall now a large set of shelves stood and all her precious books were lined up, their titles on the spines proudly on display. The color of the walls were a slight green tinge and the bed was covered with an embroidered quilt and a dark green throw blanket.

Looking around she was amazed at the work and thought he had taken to make it beautiful. Turning she found him behind her and threw her arms around her father's neck.

"Thank you, Papa, I love it,"

"You're welcome. I had hoped to have my room finished as well, but unfortunately it was not to be." He kissed her forehead and pulled her off. "Now you must be hungry, the stew should be done, it's been in the slow cooker all day. And you can then tell me all about your travels."

The meal was wonderful and Tharain marveled at her stories. He was most interested in the changes she had described in Gremlin. How his hunting had gone and the development of their talking to each other. When Teagan mentioned about being able to see through the dragon's eyes he sat forward.

"Are you sure you weren't just imagining it?" he asked intently.

"No, I saw the heat signatures of the animals he was hunting. I even saw my own when he returned to camp. Humans give off a different signal to other animals," she told him as if she were reporting a finding to her boss.

"Explain it to me," Tharain asked.

"Well, a deer shows up a deep red, a pig is a shimmering blue, and a goat or sheep is green."

"And a human?"

"I showed up as a silver color."

"Silver?" he asked.

"Yes, well varying degrees of silver, just like the animals. It depends on where the hottest parts of the body are showing. Now that I come to think of it, where the heart should be was the hottest point, the brightest," she said curiously.

"Amazing," he said with a long low breath.

"What is?" Teagan began to clear the plates and glasses from the table.

Tharain looked up at his daughter. "I don't think there has been anyone that can do what you say you can do with Gremlin. A normal Warden can make their intentions known, they have a rudimentary communication link with a dragon, but to hold a conversation and see through the eyes of the beasts is unheard of. There is something very strange going on here, Teagan."

"What's so strange? Gremlin won't hurt me, Papa," she said as she moved into the kitchen and put the dirty plates into the sink.

"I know he won't, I trust him. And it's not that that I am worried about. It is how you communicate; you say you can converse just like we are now. That is unusual. I spent many long hours drinking with the Master of Dragons. He and I discussed what it's like to have the skill in communing with dragons. What you are describing is far more ability than he had."

"Maybe it's because I found him so young, the link developed with no other dragon around. Could it be that he has learned from me, and not the other way around?" she asked him.

Teagan's head was slightly cocked to one side and to Tharain at that moment his daughter was the image of her mother. Quickly he pushed down the pain of his loss once more and tried to focus on what his daughter had asked him.

"It could be. He has learned so fast, he was flying far earlier than he should have, and he has grown very quickly. He would still be with his mother if he were in our realm, learning how to be a dragon from her. If it is because he didn't have that influence, then this could be a whole new way to train a dragon." Tharain pushed his hand through his greying hair. "I wish we had a Warden here we could discuss this possibility with."

"Don't go blaming yourself, Papa. What happened was in the past and nothing we can do now can change the circumstances." Teagan could see the self-admonishment in him for their current situation.

"I know that, but—"

"No buts. We are here and we will just have to figure it out for ourselves." Teagan turned back to the sink and turned on the tap to begin washing up.

Tharain watched her for a moment, admiring the strength she had in her. A strength that he knew he did not possess. After a moment he helped her to tidy up, they worked in silence as they had on so many nights previous as she had grown.

At first coming to this world had been strange for them both. He had tried to keep it together for her, and he had for a good while. They had found their feet with Tharain finding work and Teagan attending school, once their lives had become 'normal' in the eyes of those that they found around them, it was then that he had slipped. The drinking started as having one with the men he worked with at the end of a long day, then it became two. Soon the drinking made its way into their home, but he tried hard to hide his drinking from his daughter. He would wait until she was asleep to drink himself into the same state. But he soon lost control.

The first job he had was not a great one, it was menial hard labor. The men he worked with were nice to the stranger with a strange accent and they took him at face value, never inquiring into where he and his daughter had come from. At work he became known as Terry as his true name was hard for the New Zealanders to pronounce. Those men soon became concerned when they detected the smell of alcohol on his breath during the day, and he became clumsy with it. They did all they could to protect him from their supervisor, but soon it outstripped even their kindness. Tharain was fired and it only added to his shame.

The pair moved around a lot in those first few years. Every time Teagan would mention something from their past, his shame would ooze to the surface and spill over as he told her to stop making up stories. Tharain knew his outbursts hurt his daughter, but it pained him even more when she brought them up. The reminder of his high status, of the loss of his beautiful and kind wife.

Gael had been so beautiful, with flaming red hair and a quick and ready laugh. As soon as he had seen her, he had fallen under her spell. They were apprentices together, and soon there was a rivalry that built between them, born out of their mutual admiration and growing love. Tharain had thought then that she would not look at him, being the youngest son of a fisherman, after all she was cousin to the future king.

It had been Urmond who had seen the budding relationship, who had encouraged Tharain to pursue Gael. They were all the same age, all apprentices at the same time. Urmond had pressed the issue and soon the couple were starting to see each other on their time off. When Urmond had risen to the throne after his father had passed, it was he who wrote up the decree of marriage for his cousin, long before the couple had come to seek permission for Gael to marry. As a member of the royal family her hand was not her own to give away, it was a commodity to be used in negotiations with other realms or even with high-ranking families within their own. There had been talk about Gael marrying a nobleman's son, but Urmond put that matter to rest with his decree. He happily stood by the couple and was even happier when they asked him to be their daughter's Parraine.

Tharain remembered the discussion he had had with his old friend on that fateful day he was brought before him. The discussion on what would happen with Teagan and he thanked whoever had been looking down on him that Urmond had allowed him to take his daughter with him. He did not like to think what would have happened to him if Teagan had not been there to guide and help him. To pull him up out of the stupors and depression that plagued him.

Now she was there beside him, a fully-grown woman who could never become who her skills now proclaimed her to be. A Dragon Warden. Her talents in that area had blossomed and come out in full, thanks to the arrival of Gremlin in their lives. But those skills should have been lost when she turned eighteen. He looked at her sideways for a moment and she yawned loudly.

Taking the dish that was in her hand he told her; "Go for a shower and get to bed. I'll finish up here tonight."

"Are you sure?" Teagan asked as she yawned once more, covering her mouth with a suds laden hand.

"I am sure. Good night, Teagan, I'll see you in the morning." Tharain leaned in and kissed her forehead.

"Good night, Papa." She wiped her hands on the towel and then headed to the bathroom.

As he watched her go, Tharain wished again for a way to get back to the world they had left. He knew he would not be welcome back, but his daughter might be, especially if Urmond was still King.

River

Scetis' eyes were closed, but he was far from sleep. Their meagre supply of wood was fast diminishing and the fire burned low between him and the Lieutenant. He could hear her move uncomfortably on the pebbly shore. The smoothed rock at his back chilled him further and he shivered involuntarily.

"They will come looking for me. For my body if nothing else," her voice was low and slow.

When Scetis did not reply, Ide looked over at the man who was the cause of their predicament.

"Did you hear me?" she said louder.

"I did," he replied, shifting his weight.

"You will be going before the King."

"You should conserve your energy."

"There is no way you can get away with this."

"I think I will. Once I'm back at the Convocation, I will be safe. We are already out of the realm you so diligently serve and getting permission from my hierarchy to allow those beasts fly into their lands will be difficult."

"You have no idea who I am, do you?"

"When people say that kind of statement, it usually means that they have a very high opinion of themselves, which does not equate to their real status." Scetis turned his head to her and opened his eyes. Her brown ones reflected the dying fire, but also burned with their own supposed authority.

"I am First Lieutenant Ide Magaoidh, daughter of First Foot Captain Aideen Magaoidh. Daughter of Rider General Galanan Magaoidh.

Sister to First Rider Captain Venicones and Master of Dragons Captain Muniath Magaoidh."

"That sounds like a strong lineage, or a family of overachievers," he told her with as much disinterest as possible.

"And betrothed of Second Foot Captain Orcades Braonáin, nephew of King Urmond."

"Then I am sorry for you. Captain Orcades Braonáin's reputation is known far and wide. Your marriage will be a very unhappy one for you."

"What do you, a thieving Trader, know of it?" she demanded.

"Let's just say that it is widely agreed that many a border brat bears his resemblance," he gave her a crooked smile as he spoke.

Ide suddenly stood and loomed over Scetis with her fists balled up, ready to strike.

"Sit down and conserve your energy. It's going to be a long night and we'll be going back into the water as soon as the sky lightens enough for us to see," he told her mildly.

Ide turned and stalked away, her boots crunching in the loose stones. Scetis could see her in the faint light that filtered down from above. Her arms were wrapped around herself protectively and she deliberately kept her back to him. The long dark hair that was still caught up in a ponytail hung down her back, contrasting against the white linen shirt, which almost glowed against the dark rock on the opposite side of the river. It was messier, with locks of hair now loose, a stark contrast to how it was that morning when he had first seen her.

There was something about Ide. Even though Scetis was well into his thirties, there had never been a woman who had caught his eye. Fellow apprentices at the Convocation had all lusted after each other during their training but being with another human in that way had never appealed to him. But now there was something in the way this woman held herself, something in her bearing that intrigued him.

Quickly he squashed that line of thinking. He would only be in her company until he had the chance to get away, and that would be the next day, hopefully. The river that now passed them at a great rate, fed a large lake when it finally emptied from the canyon they found themselves in. As soon as they made that lake, he would leave her and head straight for the relative safety of the Convocation, and Scetis prayed that they would protect him from King Urmond and his Riders.

The revelation of who her parents and brothers were had unsettled him somewhat, although he was unwilling to let her see it. She was no ordinary Foot Lieutenant. She was near enough to kin to the King. He had heard enough about General Galanan and King Urmond to know they would not give up looking for her. But that was a worry for the next day. They would have to ride the cold water out to the lake. Only by combining their body heat could he ever hope of both of them overcoming the extreme cold of the water.

Ide was coming back to the small fire, it glowed softly, sending flickering shadows up the stone wall behind it. He watched her as she moved towards him. Her arms were still wrapped around her body, trying to comfort and keep the cold out. They only managed to enhance her figure, and he closed his eyes to it. But the image was already burned in his mind.

Sleep had not overcome him, instead Scetis remained awake the whole of the night, and at the first lightening of the sky, he stood and began to cover the remains of the fire. It had died sometime just before the false dawn and the embers had flickered for a little while longer. He pushed the stones over the top of it until he was satisfied that there would be no evidence left behind.

Crouching down he placed a hand on Ide's shoulder and gently shook her awake. Her eyes flew open with a start and she tried to move away from his touch.

"Time to go," he told her softly as he stood then moved to the edge of the river, placing his bags back on his shoulders.

"I am not going anywhere with you," Ide shook her head determinedly.

"You will be going with me. You are going to be my safety net to get away from your family and their search." Scetis did not even turn as he waited for her, his voice loud and echoed off the sides of the canyon.

"I would like to see you try and make me," her voice was defiant as she stood to face him.

"Please do not make me hurt you. At heart I am still a Physician and it goes against all of my training." Slowly he turned back to her.

"No, you are a filthy Trader."

"You know nothing of my life. I am a Trader now, but once I was a Physician, also an Apothecary. The life of a Trader suits me for now, it gets me away from the simpering, pampered and over indulged people I had to treat. My talents were too valuable to waste on the truly needy, on those that had real ailments."

Ide stopped in her tracks as he stared at her, the venom of his words stabbed at her as she realized, she had made so many assumptions of this man.

"That still does not change the fact that I will not be going with you." Ide folded her arms across her chest.

"Yes, you will. I will not have you tell your father and the King who I am."

"So, what are you going to do with me once we get out of this place, kill me?"

Scetis tore his eyes from her, the idea of taking her life did not sit well with him. He had killed in the past without even thinking about it, the Rider who had recognized him being a case in point. The thought of killing her made his stomach knot and clench uncomfortably.

"I will not kill you," he told her softly.

"Then why take me?"

"They will not find me once we make the great lake. But between then and now, I need you as assurance they will not hurt me." Scetis looked back at the woman. He could see she would not be easily persuaded to follow him willingly into the water.

Quickly he crossed the space that divided them, put his arm around her waist and scooped her up with his other. Her arms became unfolded immediately and she began to hit him with all her might. Purposefully he walked into the water, the cold of it soon spilling over the tops of his boots and making him gasp as it sent its icy spears into his bare flesh. The further in he waded the more she protested, yelling and hitting at him, until he was deep enough to drop her.

The splash that came up from her body washed over him and he grasped her by the arm and brought her back to the surface and to stand on the unstable shelf of pebbles under their feet. Ide spluttered and wiped away the water from her face and then spat at him.

"We are going, and we are going now," he told her flatly and then guided her further out, to where the current was swift.

It soon took them off their feet, he held her closely to him, their bodies pressed against each other, her breathing quickened, expanding her chest as she came to grips with how cold the water was. He did not look at her, only the way the river was carrying them.

Around mid-morning Scetis looked down at the woman in his arms. Ide was pale, her lips had a blue tinge to them, and she was shivering violently. He looked back up at the sides of the canyon and judged that they still have quite a way to go to be thrown out into the lake. Many a pebble bar had passed them by in the hours they had been in the water, but now the water was sluggish and filled the canyon from one steep side to the other. Further on he saw another sharp bend was coming. He prayed there was somewhere they could get out of the water, somewhere that had wood for a fire so they could at least warm themselves a little.

His wish was granted. As they rounded the bend, Scetis saw it and immediately started to kick to get to the small mound. Just when he thought that it would pass them by, Ide roused a little from her stupor to help, using up what energy she still had to get them to safety. Together they managed to reach the rocky outcrop at the bottom end, and they pulled themselves out of the water.

Leaving her panting on the stones Scetis went in search of wood, finding some jammed into the craggy rocks that had fallen from above at some point, probably when the river was in flood. The fire was small to start with, quickly he fed it, using up more wood than he normally would have, knowing that they had to go back into the water.

Once the fire was large, he went and picked Ide up, moving her closer to the flames and the heat it was now putting out. He started to rub her hands and arms, trying to get the blood circulating faster into her chilled and stiffened limbs, and to warm her up. He pulled her boots off her feet, which allowed a great flood of water to spew from the stiffened leather. Underneath her socks were plastered to her skin and he gently removed them, wrung them out a little and placed them by the fire.

Starting at her toes he began to massage her feet, working up to her ankles and then legs. When he reached her thighs, she opened her eyes, warm enough now to become aware of what was happening to her and who was touching her.

"Stop," she protested weakly.

"You need to get warm," he pushed her hands away as they tried to stop his ministrations. "If I don't, you will die. Your body will become so cold that the blood will stop flowing and once that happens your heart and your mind shut down. Now lie still."

His teeth were chattering away in his own head as he worked on her. His limbs were heavy and tight from the time in the water, but still he tried to warm her first. As the fire burned away beside them, it helped to revive Ide a little and soon she was sitting up. Carefully she took his hands in hers, taking them away from her body. She started to rub each one, trying to give back to Scetis what he had given her.

Water dripped down her face from her hair, and she brushed the drops away with the back of her hand. Scetis reached up and wiped one away from her cheek with his thumb. Her skin was soft and smooth under his touch and he was soon cupping her face with his hand. His eyes took in her whole face, the way her long eyelashes framed her dark brown eyes, her sculpted eyebrows and the fullness of her lips. They were slightly parted, and her breathing was coming in shallow quick pants.

Gently, Ide reached up and took his hand from her face and released it. Scetis' eyes were still on her, taking in every detail until he realized he was making her uncomfortable. Quickly he leaned back and away from her, he pulled off his bags and rummaged around in one of them for something to eat. The stillness and quiet between them was thick with only the sound of the river and the crackling of the fire to fill the void.

"Tell me about you," Ide requested of him. She was curious about this man. There seemed to be so much more to Scetis than she had first thought. His revelations of changing professions had been the first clue that he had more hidden away inside.

"There's nothing to tell," he told her unwrapping packages of spoiled food. Only a small wheel of cheese had survived.

"There is always something to tell."

"Then you go first." Scetis set about cutting the cheese and handed her a portion.

"Alright, I am the youngest child, my two brothers have far outstripped me as far as rank goes, but I made their lives growing up a hell. Now I am the comfort for one who has lost so much and the other who cannot have the woman he loves."

"You said one of your brother's is Master of Dragons. Is that Muniath?" He bit into his piece of cheese and refused to look at her.

"It is."

"I heard about his troubles."

"I figured you did, that's why you took the opportunity to take the eggs." Ide paused to eat for a moment. "Why did you, when the risk is so high?"

"I was ordered to. Our Regulator sent word down that it was for an important client."

"So, the order came from the highest."

"It did; it always does when it is to do with something so precious. I have never tried to take an egg from a dragon before and it had not been done for some years. I knew the risks and consequences of my actions."

"But you did not do it alone?"

"No, I did it on my own."

"So, who was in the hall with you?"

"No one of importance. He should not worry you at all, he is not suited for a life as a Trader and I mean to fix that as soon as I get back."

"He was your apprentice?" Ide asked surprised as she finished her meal.

"'Was' being the operative word. Forget the boy, for he is only a boy and should never have been with me. I feel that he was placed in my care for some reason and that reason was to hinder me, to make me sloppy and careless."

"It almost worked. It seems you have an enemy in the Convocation."

"I do, and I already know who it is." Scetis sat cross legged by the fire, his hands stretched out to gather the warmth from the flames.

"Who?"

"It is a matter for me and me alone. It does not concern you."

"But it does. You are desperate to get back there, and you are taking me along for the ride. Tell me your story," Ide demanded again.

"It is not short enough for this small stop we make before we go back into the water."

"Start it then, I am not going to give up, I never do."

Scetis looked up at her through the flames and could tell that she meant what she had said.

"I was young, only six when my mother sold me into slavery, and I was bought by the Convocation. She could not afford to keep me; she could not afford to feed herself. So, I was the solution." Scetis kept his eyes on her while he started his tale. "I was taken to that place, it looked so large to my young eyes, set in the lake with the long bridge out to it. So tall I thought that the topmost towers must touch the sky. I would never see the view from those towers in my childhood. I was instead taken to the lower levels, where the slaves are kept."

"They keep slaves?"

"You did not know?"

"No, this is news to me. Sorry, please go on."

"At first it wasn't too bad. I was placed in the care of a woman, who was kind and she looked out for me. When she became sick and they refused to heal her, she died, and I was then put to work. I scrubbed floors, took out their refuse and was kicked, hit and sometimes worse, but mostly I was just ignored. I was a thing, lower than even a rat in that place."

The intensity of his stare was strong, but Ide did not break it. She waited patiently for him to carry on.

"I was cleaning a room, it had medicinal herbs and compounds and I understood that there were experiments going on. I was examining the table and what was on there, when the Apothecary came into the room. He was one of the kinder men, Tavae is his name. He recognized my curiosity, slowly he gained my trust. It was hard won too. Up until the age of ten I had been abused by so many people of rank."

Scetis cleared his throat, the heat from the fire started to penetrate the shirt he wore, warming him more, but not enough to calm his uneasiness of talking about his past. He watched as Ide took her long hair in her hands and began to ring it out, watching the water tumble in drops from those dark strands, illuminated and sparkling in the light from the flames.

"What did he teach you?" she prompted.

"He taught me to read, to recognize herbs and plants and their medicinal value," Scetis heard himself say staring into the flames. "Next he taught me the uses of some animals and their parts. Tavae asked permission to train me formally. He told the hierarchy that he could see the gift within me. I was elevated from the slave pit to the apprentice quarters. If I thought my days of being abused were over, it was nothing to what happened when the others found out that I was once their slave, the treatment I received I hid from Tavae, I didn't want to worry or disappoint him. But he had his way of finding out. I was taken out of the dorm and placed in his rooms.

"Tavae had another apprentice. He was older, almost out of his time and already looking for a new master to further his training to become a Physician. For some reason he took an instant dislike to me. Wradech came from a wealthy family and his place had been paid for well. He knew my master and I had a relationship he could not understand and as soon as he finished his time with Tavae, he arranged for me to be placed in the apprenticeship of another.

"This master was not so kind, but I learned all I could from him. He was a Physician and I excelled. In time even he could see the talent I had for it, but when it came time to choose the path I should go down, the hierarchy ignored my wishes and pleas. Instead of helping the poor and those that needed it most, I was sent to the Elite School. It was decided that my talent would have been wasted on those that could not pay for it and so I was fed to the wealthy."

"Not all of those who are wealthy take advantage of their station," Ide told him honestly.

"I am aware of that, but they are in the minority and usually have humble roots. The people who I was to treat ate to excess, indulged in things that they had no idea of what affected their bodies. They abused themselves and those around them. They are the ones I despise. They take up the resources that should be shared amongst those that cannot pay for the privilege."

Time was hushed between them while Ide took in his words. He appeared to have no feelings, no emotions and was driven in his purpose. But after hearing the start of his tale she could see an underlying passion that was denied to him. Scetis' life had been a hard one, but he was driven by a basic instinct to help.

"What happened then? How did you become a Trader?" Ide asked him quietly, wanting him to go on and continue his tale.

Scetis looked up at the sliver of sky above them. It was deepening in blue, and he judged that it was now just after midday. The fire danced merrily in the ever-moving air around them and they were now both warm.

"There is no need for you to know that information," he told her quietly.

"But there is, how can I understand why you act the way you do, if I do not know your past."

"And from what you have told me of yourself, I can judge that you throw your affections away on a man who is useless," he spat at her, hoping to deflect her from one of the most painful moments in his life.

"You know nothing of why I love him."

"But do you love him, or the status that he will give you. Is he your way to the top? Because he will never allow that to happen. His eyes are on the throne, did you know that? He is always looking for a way to get closer to it."

"How do you know this?" Ide demanded.

"Because he was one of the spoiled rich children I used to treat. The thing about a Physician or even an Apothecary is that most rich people believe they are just servants, so they do not check what they say in front of them. His mother is the ambitious one. I'm surprised she allowed the betrothal between you. She wanted him to marry his cousin, the Princess Orlagh."

"I know about the proposal, King Urmond denied it. He said the connection was too close for them to marry."

"It is. So why choose you, why allow her precious son, who she hopes will be king one day to marry you?" Scetis asked, he began to wonder how she had not asked these questions herself.

"Our family is well known; we are military people."

"And there is the answer. She hopes that you will lead the military in backing her son's claim to the throne. She knows that your family will be faithful to you and your wishes. I would check her connections very carefully if I were you, especially with certain people in the Convocation."

"What are you trying to tell me?"

"That you and your family, along with good, King Urmond and his daughter, are all in danger from people who you do not see and do not know. They will use you as their pawns to gain power and that power will ultimately lead to the downfall of not only this realm, but many more. Their goal is not to rule your realm, their goal is to subjugate it, to use its resources and rid this world of the beasts that they have no way of controlling."

"They will never win; they will never be able to even try to get their hands on it." Ide shook her head at the thought.

"I hope you are right," Scetis replied wearily.

Looking out over the water that had changed slightly in color, he thought about those that had wanted him out of the way. It was a complicated plot and he thought he knew who the architect of it was. It was about time he did something about his old teacher's first apprentice.

With the decision made he stood and went looking for more wood. The search was more to be doing something, rather than just sitting on the uncomfortable and damp pebbly ground. When he brought back a small bundle Ide looked up at him.

"If what you say is true, then come back with me and lay the charges at the King's feet. He will listen to you," she pleaded.

"And then carefully cut off my head. No, thank you." He dumped the pile beside the fire and began to feed it.

"He is a merciful man. I remember what he did with the previous General when he was caught stealing eggs."

"Yes, General Tharain Loinsigh. A pawn in the same game that started so long ago. Apparently, it did not take much to bring him to his knees and make him do what they wanted him to do."

"My brothers and father were there when they were exiled."

"They?" Scetis asked.

"Yes, they. General Loinsigh and his daughter."

"They exiled his daughter?"

"Of course. General Loinsigh insisted. Look," Ide paused for a moment, "I don't even know your name."

"You do, I gave it to you at the border. Scetis Mordha," he said bowing his head a little.

"Scetis, our King was merciful. He could have kept the girl and raised her in the court, but King Urmond saw that she needed her father. That's what Muniath always said anyway."

"I don't think they knew about the girl, but then she wouldn't have mattered to them." Scetis said but not to Ide.

"Who?" she asked, clearly puzzled by his remark.

When he looked up, he shook his head. "It's not something for you, only a little more information for me."

"I don't understand."

"No, you wouldn't. But that is of no mind." He looked up again at the gap between the sheer faces of the rock and took a measurement of the sun's position. "It's time to go."

"No, I don't want to go back in the water, please." Ide stood, her hands rubbing on her thighs.

"I am afraid we must. It is not much further and once we are in the lake, you'll be free to go. I'll even give you the flint so you can make a fire."

"Please, no." She shook her head, her eyes wide.

"This is not what I would expect from a First Lieutenant of the Foot," he chided her.

"It was worth a shot," Ide shrugged her shoulders, and she dropped the desperate façade she had been playing out. She pulled her socks and boots back onto her feet and moved away from the fire to the edge of the river, watching the flow as it sped by. "Are you ready?" she asked, glancing back at him.

Scetis did not bother to put the fire out, instead he picked up the bags and slung them over his shoulders, crossing the straps over his chest and back. He kept his eyes on her as he walked the short distance between them.

"I am now," he said his voice low as his arm went around her waist and they walked together into the water.

The pair clung to each other to keep warm, Ide looked up into his blue eyes and noticed the silver that rimmed the dark pupil. She averted her gaze when he turned his to her.

"Tell me more about your life, it will help pass the time," she asked him, already starting to feel the warmth leach away from her body.

"From when?"

"How did you go from being an Apothecary to a Trader?" Her body started to shiver, and she felt him hold her closer.

"Wradech had his family wealth at his disposal and with his interference, I did not stay with Tavae long."

"You've already told me that. He was a Physician and was hard on you," Ide reminded him.

"So, I did. When I came out of the apprenticeship with him, my skills had grown and I had caught the eye of the hierarchy, they set me up to treat the wealthy. My master's first apprentice did not like how far I had come, how successful I was. Especially how his own wealthy patients were leaving him to come and see me. He poisoned me. Tavae found me, almost dead, he moved me to the rooms of a friend of his, a Trader. Together they ministered my poison and brought me closer to life. But there is no cure for what he gave me. Every month, I must take an elixir to keep me alive; to stop the poison from attacking my veins. A compound so deadly that one drop will kill if not taken correctly. It is the culmination of all our knowledge, the Physician, an Apothecary and a Trader."

"What is it made of?"

"The ingredients would mean nothing to you, I doubt you could even identify most of the plants that go into it."

"You doubt my intelligence?"

"No, I do not doubt that at all." His eyes once more connected with hers. For a split second she saw them flare with light, she wiped her eyes and thought it was just the light from the sun.

"So, you became a Trader?"

"Etain took me in and trained me secretly. When she thought I was ready she went to the hierarchy and asked that I apprentice to her. They were confused at this point and my sickness was quickly given as the reason. They agreed and now here I am."

"What about the boy? You said he should not have been apprenticed to you?"

"No, he should not have. Again, another of Wradech's plans. He had gone to Etain, who is now the head of my order. The request was formally given that I and an apprentice should be given the task. Wradech had now risen by means of bribery and corruption through the ranks and now sits as Chief Physician in the hierarchy of the Convocation. He is one step below our leader, the Regulator, and I do not know that he knows of the request Wradech sent out. Our Regulator is Tavae, he did not like the idea of dealing with such things, he understood the importance of the animals. But Wradech has his eyes firmly on Tavae's seat, and he will stop at nothing to reach the top. I am afraid of what will happen if he does."

"So, this Wradech is part of the plot to overthrow, not only my own country's throne, but the Convocation as well?" Ide moved position, changing her grip on her arms that were about Scetis neck, and their bodies moved against each other as she did so.

"Yes, I believe he is, he is power hungry." He moved his own grip on her and became embarrassingly aware of other stirrings as their bodies pressed against each other.

Ide lapsed into silence as she thought about this new information. It was important that she make it back to see the King and give it to him. "How much further?" she asked him, looking down the canyon at yet another bend.

"It won't be long now; I can feel the current picking up again. When we get to the drop, you must keep hold of me. We will be dropping down a great way into the lake. If you let me go, I can't guarantee that you will survive. Again, together we will have more of a chance."

Ide nodded her head, the trust for this man was building slowly. So far, he had not seemed to have lied to her. The actions at the border bridge were of self-preservation on his part and he had not intended to take her hostage. She had fallen into the river with him, because she had refused to let him go. Now as she looked at him, she once more did not want to let him go.

The cold was affecting her more than before, having not really become dry earlier. She shivered in his arms and he pulled her closer to him. She could hear him talking but it sounded mumbled to her ears and so distant. Lifting her head, her vision swam as she tried to concentrate on his face and what he was saying, but all she could see were those eyes, so penetrating and blue.

"Ide, wake up, I need you to be aware of what's going on, we're coming to the waterfall," his words finally broke through the fog of her brain.

Scetis shifted her in his arms, holding on tightly with one arm while the other came up to her face and held it. "Wake up, Ide," he called again.

"Waterfall," she repeated to him.

"Good, keep awake. I can hear it; it will be just around this bend." Scetis looked down the river and at the fast-approaching bend. He could hear the roar of the water and soon they were around it.

The canyon widened but the flow of the water quickened and pushed them on to the edge. Through the clouds of water vapor, he could make out the lake and the land beyond. He was almost home.

"Hold on tightly," he told her and gripped his hands together behind her back.

"How much of a drop is it?" she asked him, now fully awake and aware.

"A long one. Whatever you do, do not let go of me once we are over and back in the water. You will need my strength to bring you back to the surface." His eyes were still on the horizon and the drop off. The roar of the water going over the edge was so loud now and encompassed all their senses. The power of it thrummed through them as they neared it.

"Don't let me go," Ide pleaded with him, pulling her own gaze from the edge back to him. "Don't let me go."

"I won't," he told her. Quickly he pressed his lips to hers, they went with the water and tumbled over the edge. He held her; their lips locked as they fell through the streaming white water.

Scetis broke the kiss and managed to turn them so he would land first. Their eyes were locked onto each other's, and then the water came up to meet them. It was a hard landing, and it knocked the breath out of Scetis. But he clung to Ide, to protect her. His mind was only on making sure she survived the fall. Her hands slipped their grasp from around his neck at the impact and their bodies were pushed deep into the water of the lake. He refused to let go of her, his hands firmly grasped around each of his own wrists. Scetis fought the urge to take in a breath that would take his life. He tried to keep his head and push them back to the surface, his kicks diminishing as it felt like they were not getting nearer. The force of Ide's own desperate kicking beside him, helped them to rise faster and take that first much needed breath of precious air.

Gasping he broke the surface, and still Ide clung to him. Water streamed from their faces and they both coughed up what water had managed to make it into their lungs. He wiped his face and looked about. To their right, a sandy shore was close to them and he began to swim with her towards it. Gaining their feet, he used it to haul them out. Ide's strength was almost all used up and he noticed again the blue tinge around her lips.

Scetis made sure she was safe on the shore and went to find wood. He started the fire with the first load and went looking for more. Bundle after bundle he brought to it until the fire raged and was large. He pulled her up the shore, placing her gently down beside it. Carefully he tried to squeeze the water from her hair, and once more began to rub at her hands and arms, trying to get the circulation back into her limbs.

Ide opened her eyes to him. "Go," she told him quietly.

"I want to make sure you're alright first," he replied, still trying to get her warm.

"They will be here soon. Go, now before they can find you."

"You don't want to take me back?" he asked, still holding her hand.

"No, I don't. You have to stop them from your side, I will not allow my King to fall."

"Thank you," he said softly. Scetis dropped her hand and stood. He started to walk away from the fire but stopped. He returned to her and knelt beside her. Carefully he took her face in his hands and brought his lips to kiss her once more.

"I will never forget you, Lieutenant Ide Magaoidh."

"And I will not forget you, Scetis Mordha," she said breathlessly.

Releasing her he stood and left her side. Ide watched him go.

Found

Muniath was leaning back on a chair, his feet up on the desk in front of him, his eyes closed, and his breathing even. At a casual glance anyone would think he was asleep, but he was far from it. His mind was solely on the safety of his sister. When he concentrated on her he could sense she was still alive, it was like he was searching for a dragon, and knew within his heart that she was alive. He toyed with it a little while, as he tried to see if he could find others in his family.

His father and brother were together, their mounts were getting anxious and wanting to fly. Muniath calmed their minds and went in search of his mother. She was there, riding hard on a horse, speeding towards her husband and son, her desperation was growing at the lack of knowledge of where her only daughter was. The pride Aideen had for his sister exuded from her. He also gained the knowledge that Aideen had held back from her daughter, that she had made Second Captain.

Another face suddenly appeared before him. This one he had never seen before, a woman, with long bright ginger hair and striking green eyes. She was not dressed like someone from the realm, and she smiled at him, it was a smile he could not refuse and found the corners of his mouth twitching in response. Her skin was smooth and tanned, like she was used to being outdoors and there was something very familiar about her. Muniath found his eyes roaming her body, taking it all in and recognized the stirrings of attraction for her.

"Sir?" a voice queried, breaking his thoughts and the vision of the woman.

Muniath opened an eye and looked at the young Rider apprentice before him. He was only around eighteen, fresh faced and trying to grow facial hair, which was coming in patchy.

"What?" he asked as he lifted his feet off Domnall's desk and sat up straight.

The apprentice held out his hand, which held a leather cylinder, the red wax seal was still intact.

"Where is General Gerarailt?" he asked thickly, his mouth dry.

"I believe the General is talking to the King, Sir."

"King Urmond has come back?"

"Yes Sir," the boy said, still holding out the communication.

"Why wasn't I told?"

"The General asked us not to, he said you needed sleep." The boy thrust the cylinder forward once more.

Muniath took it and dismissed him to go back to his post on the flyway. Cracking the seal, he pried open the lid and pulled the paper report out from it. His eyes scanned down the page and then grew wider. Immediately he was up on his feet and running from the General of the Foot's office. His foot falls were lost behind the pumping of his heart as he made his way through the corridors of the Citadel, heading to the throne room.

He did not see the two guards as they came to attention and saluted when he passed through the doorway to enter the large white room with its many columns and banners. Two men stood at the other end, one in formal uniform and the other almost like a peasant. They turned his way as he entered and waited for him to approach.

"My Lord King, I bring news," Muniath said formally.

"Just tell us Mun, there is no need for formality right now," King Urmond bade him.

"Word from the General. He says that they have found the remains of a fire down river, it appears that two people were camped there overnight, and some pains were made to cover the fire from us. Scorcher discovered it. They carried on down and found the embers of another fire, this one had not been covered at all. He believes from the reports of Venicones that they are both still alive and heading for the great lake."

"Thank any god you wish that Ide is still alive. But the lake is not our territory, getting her back is going to be difficult," Domnall said to them both.

"The Regulator will see sense; I've found him to be a sensible man and very accommodating in allowing us to search in the lands controlled by the Convocation. I can't see a problem there. Also, Ide is a resourceful woman. I believe she has the capabilities to look out for herself. What worries me is the man she is with. We don't know anything about him except that he is a Trader and cannot be trusted."

"If he hurts her, I swear I'll hunt him down," Muniath swore.

"It will not only be you Mun, but you'll also have us all at your back," Urmond said, placing a caring hand on Muniath's shoulder. "I'm sure that we will find her soon. In the meantime, I'll draft up a letter to Regulator Stiobhard requesting his assistance."

"Thank you, my Lord King," Muniath said and bowed low in appreciation.

"Enough of that, now back to work, the pair of you. There is still much to organize. Domnall, on your way back to your office can you stop in at the Councilor for Works and tell her that I wish to see her and her underlings this afternoon, in my office."

"Yes, Sire." Domnall bowed and turned heading out of the throne room.

As Muniath went to do the same Urmond called him back.

"Mun, a word before you go."

"Yes, Sire," he responded.

"Shall we walk in the garden for a moment, I won't keep you long and that letter has already been drafted, I did it in case we found something."

"As you wish." Muniath followed his king out of the side door and into the formal garden beyond. He remembered the last time he was there and smiled when he saw the dog Bili laying on the green grass, his belly exposed to the warm sunshine.

"Muniath, there is something I wish to ask you and I want it to go no further than the two of us," Urmond started.

"What is it, my Lord King?"

"I think we can dispense with all that Lord King palaver, don't you? We've known each other long enough and our families are close."

"Of course, Urmond," Muniath smiled back.

"Good. Now what I want to ask you, you can never, ever let on to anyone else. It is very important that I have your word on this, Mun." Urmond moved to the marble bench beside the wall, which gave a good view of the planted gardens with all their color. Bili got up from his sun soaking spot and made his way over to Urmond with his tail wagging and tongue lolling from his mouth.

"If I can be of any assistance, I will make that promise." He sat beside Urmond and scratched the dog's ears absentmindedly.

"You are Master of Dragons because you possess skills others in our nation do not. You can communicate with the dragons and feel their needs. Can you do more than that?" Urmond clasped his hands together and looked down at the dog, rather than at Muniath.

"I'm not sure what you mean." Muniath hoped that his apparent confusion hid the knowledge of what his king was talking about.

"In our Realm there used to be those in your position who could do more than just haltingly communicate with Dragons. They could converse with them and track them no matter where they were in the world. There were also those that could track people," Urmond added hesitantly.

"I can track dragons; you know of this already. I have also been able to communicate with them long distance. I did just now with Raker and Scorcher, they were wanting to be in the sky, and I calmed them." Muniath stood and walked over to a rose bush, it had large, bright orange blooms all over it, weighing down the stems. He plucked one and held it in his hands, the color reminding him of the image of the strange woman he had just seen.

"And the other I spoke of?" Urmond watched him carefully.

"I'm not sure."

"Mun, I can feel it in you. You can track people, can't you?"

"I can tell you what part of the road my mother is on and that my father and brother are right now standing by the broken bridge arguing. Venicones is wanting to go after Ide and bring her back, while she may still be with that man. I can tell you that he wants to be the one to kill him."

"And what of your sister? Can you feel how she is feeling?" Urmond asked urgently.

"I know she is alive; she is further away."

"Try, reach out to her, Mun. Like you do with the dragons." Urmond urged him.

Muniath sank to the soft, sweet smelling grass under him and closed his eyes. It was the first time he actively sought out someone, every other time had been while he was half asleep. The first time he had done it was like he was dreaming. Now he pushed through that barrier that seemed to want to hold him back, he reached out to find his sister.

The cold seeped into his flesh first, it flowed around him like a fast-moving river and Muniath shivered with it. It invaded his bones, and he could feel his teeth chatter loudly in his mouth. He clenched his jaw tightly against it and tried to push the sensation aside so he could concentrate more. There was not only cold, but warmth, he felt it sustaining Ide, keeping her alive as the waters pushed her down river. Muniath tried to see her, tried to find exactly where she was but it was no good. It was all dim and her awareness was slipping away.

Muniath opened his eyes suddenly before speaking. "She's in the water and it's so cold. They're sustaining each other with their combined warmth."

"That does not sound like the actions of a man who was wanting to kill her," Urmond said leaning forward. "Did you get anything else?"

"No, her energy is ebbing away in the cold water. If they don't get out soon, she'll die of it," Muniath said getting to his feet and starting to move away.

"Mun, stop right there," King Urmond commanded.

"But, My Lord King, I know I can find her."

"I only stopped you to say, take Screamer, she trusts you and you will get there quickly on her back. Now go and save your sister, and when you get back, we shall talk more about this." Urmond waved him away and watched the younger man go.

Muniath ran quickly through the palace and out into the citadel. He made all the short-cuts he could until he found the path to his parents' home and ran down the many steps. Once inside he climbed the stairs to his bedroom, flung the door open and yanked on the closet door. Pulling out the items he needed, he hastily and with fumbling fingers donned his Rider Uniform. The leather breastplate had a stylized dragon cut into the thick layers of leather, the greaves that protected his shins and knees were the same deep green decorations as on the plate. He next placed the belt around his waist, pulling it tightly and set the sword that it held in place against his thigh, tying the cord to keep it there.

With not even a glance at himself in the mirror to check that he had placed everything correctly, he was out again. The trek up past the citadel, palace, and town along with the turning up to the mountain behind them seemed to take ages. He reached the entrance to the Eyrie and through the security barriers. Racing along the stream that cut through the caves, he made it to Screamer's cavern. Wick was dozing beside the wall and at his side were the two young dragons and they raised their heads at his entrance. The boy came awake at their movement and immediately stood.

"Uncle Mun!" he cried out. "What's happening?"

"I'm taking Screamer, under the King's orders to go get Ide. I know where she is," he told Wick as he started to saddle the gold and red dragon.

Wick did not say another word but rushed to get the reins and started to attach them to the dragon, who waited patiently and understood their urgency.

"I'll look after your young until you get back," Wick reassured her with a gentle stroke of her face. The dragon in turn gave a chirp of acknowledgement and trust.

With the dragon now ready to fly, Muniath led her out into the main cave. He placed her under the first of the great openings in the roof and carefully mounted the large beast.

"First to the border and my father," he told her, "and then to find Ide. I'll guide you."

"Be safe, Uncle Mun," Wick called after him while the two young dragons pushed their scaled heads into his hands and gave their own calls.

The great gold wings unfurled and stretched out; slowly they lifted, and the muscles contracted under Muniath's legs as Screamer started the downward stroke. A few more strokes and they were rising out of the opening, the rock and scrubby bushes giving way to clear sky. With an almighty push of her wings, Screamer pushed them forward, the image of where they needed to go already in her mind. Muniath held tightly to the edge of the ornate saddle, trusting her to lead them on. He clung with his legs as she dove downward, the mountain streaking past in a great rush as she picked up speed. Levelling out, she followed the great long lake that lay between the steep mountains until it started to become a narrow river.

Great stretches of green fields now rose up and covered the valley floor. Crops in differing stages of growth, showing green, gold and brown fallowed fields. They flew over farm steads and the faces of herders lifted their heads to watch their passing, many waving at the Rider and dragon, their herds scattering a little at the passing of what was once their predator.

The journey did not take long and when he reached the border crossing, he arrived to see his mother dismounting her own horse. Her head looked up at the gold and red dragon landing. Coming from around the building were Venicones and Galanan.

"What are you doing here? I need you back at the Citadel. Who did you leave in charge?" Galanan demanded.

"The King sent me, Sir," Muniath told him as he dismounted.

"What is it?"

"I know where Ide is," he said standing to attention in front of his family.

"We know by the lake."

"I can pin-point her; I know exactly the position."

"How can you know?" Aideen asked him.

""I'll explain later, we're wasting time. The more we argue, the further away they are getting, and the closer Ide is to dying," Muniath argued.

"We are unable to, it would be a breach of the treaty for us to fly so far into their lands."

"King Urmond is sorting it out. I'm leaving with or without your permission father, Ide is fading fast in the cold water. If she is to survive then I need to get to her now." Without waiting for this father's permission Muniath leapt onto the back of Screamer and she was already preparing for flight.

Galanan looked at his youngest son and then at his wife. Indecision played on his features, thoughts of a General and that of a Father fought with each other.

"Ven, go with him. One can save Ide and the other capture that man. I want him back here in one piece. You are not to harm him; he is to stand before the King for judgement." Galanan urged his eldest son.

"We'll find her." Venicones told him emphatically as he rushed to his own mount to catch up to his brother who was already in the air and heading down the canyon.

Scorcher soon caught up to Muniath and Screamer, and the two creatures sped along the canyon, banking and twisting with its many turns. Scorcher took the lead and Muniath could see his brother pointing and presumed he meant to show him the first stop their sister and her captor had stopped.

Further on they flew into the afternoon, Screamer let out a roar that echoed loudly off the steep cliffs. Muniath risked looking down at the water and could see the depths and the jagged rocks that were hidden there, he could also see how fast it ran. Closing his eyes for a moment he searched for her and found Ide quickly. She was now on a bank with a fire raging beside her. He saw her shivering and desperately trying to get warm once more. The man was kneeling beside her. Muniath paid attention to his facial features, burning them into his memory.

Screamer responded to Muniath's urgent need to get to them quickly and pushed harder through the canyon. They rounded a tight bend, so tight that the two dragons' wings were almost vertical with the tips almost dipping into the water. The bend ended and before them the canyon widened, and a billowing cloud of water blocked the view beyond. Droplets sprayed the dragons and Riders alike as they raced through it. They burst out the other side to the view of a lake far below. The waterfall roared its way out of the cleft in the mountain as they left it behind, circling around in a desperate search for the beach where Ide now sat beside the roaring fire. As Muniath looked at the waterfall he shuddered and wondered how the pair had survived such a fall.

Raising his arm, Muniath pointed to the nearest shore, curling from the beach was a pillar of blue smoke. It caught in the wind and was pushed away and dispersed, but it was the sign they were looking for. The dragons banked at the command of Muniath, and they were soon landing on the soft sandy shore of the lake. The brothers dismounted before the beasts had even come to a halt and ran to the large fire.

With her arms wrapped tightly around her legs and hugging herself, they found Ide. Her eyes were closed as her head rested on her knees, her hair was still dripping wet, and she was pale with blue tinged lips.

"Ide!" Venicones came to a skidding halt beside his sister and hugged her tightly to him. Muniath was already tugging off his cloak and began to wrap it around her shoulders. Venicones let her go and did the same, then rubbed her arms and back trying to get the warmth that the material held into her.

"Where is he?" Venicones asked her gently.

Ide did not respond, and he looked to Muniath, who was already scanning the scrubby bush covered land that surrounded the lake.

"He's gone," she said in a small, shaking voice.

"I'll find him," Muniath said, already heading back to Screamer.

"No. Let him go," she said to him in a voice that was a little stronger.

"But he—"

"Let him go," she told him again, this time looking up at him, her eyes wide. "He is not the enemy."

"But he stole the eggs, he took you captive," said Venicones, pushing the wet hair from her face.

"There is more to the story than you know. I need to get back to the King. There is news I have to tell him."

"What is it?" Venicones asked.

"For the King alone." Ide closed her eyes again and shivered violently.

"That man still needs to answer for his actions, he broke our laws," Muniath told her.

"Scetis was used, just as General Tharain Loinsigh was. Just shut up and get me warm. Have you got any food?"

"No, we don't." Venicones put his arm around his sister, while Muniath sat on her other side, mirroring his brother's actions.

The afternoon had marched on while they warmed Ide enough to mount one of the Dragons. Venicones pulled her up to sit before him with the help of Muniath and they waited while their younger brother climbed up on Screamer. Scorcher filled the air with a great cry that carried out over the water as he beat his wings. Sand shifted and the ashes of the near dead fire spread out as they lifted off the shore, making their way back to the border crossing.

The trip did not take as long as it had seemed when they went to find her. Venicones held on tight to her still trying to keep her warm and safe as they flew, and soon they were dipping down to land beside the border control hut. Ready hands helped Ide down from the back of the dragon and she was rushed inside to the warm fire that was burning there. Venicones tossed his reins to Muniath to deal with his mount as he followed their sister inside.

Carefully Muniath thanked both dragons for their efforts of the day. He stroked their necks and checked them over, making sure neither had taken injury.

"Mun," his mother called to him gently so as not to frighten the beasts.

With one last pat he left the dragons to greet his mother with a hug. "You did well today. Thank you for bringing her back to us."

"Has she said anything about the man?" he asked her as she linked her arm and started to walk back to the hut.

"No, she only says that she will talk to the King alone."

"She said the same to us. Also, something about him being used in some plot," he provided.

"This is a mess." The pair entered the hut and the smell of food cooking assaulted made his mouth water. His stomach growled loudly with it.

The family spent the night in the border control hut and returned home at first light, their mother following along behind on horse. Ide had been home for a couple of days and under strict instructions for bed rest, of which she complained and refused. Her interview with King Urmond took place the day she arrived back. It had been a long interview, and both looked troubled when they came out of the King's private office.

Muniath had tried to get their sister to talk about her ordeal and what had happened to her, his imagination going immediately to dark places when she refused. She tried to placate him by letting him know that nothing bad had happened, that the man had been kind towards her and had not tried anything else. When he mentioned to her that he could see him and track him she looked a little troubled, but underneath he also detected her own curiosity about him.

Return

Scetis pushed his way through the thick underbrush of branches laced with small sharp thorns, which cut and scratched at this exposed skin and caught the fabric of his once white shirt. But none of it caught his attention. The touch of her lips on his still lingered in his memory; the softness of her skin under his touch haunted his thoughts. Ide had not pushed him away, had accepted that kiss and touch, and he thought had reciprocated as well.

These stirrings were strange to him. Never in his life had he had any attraction for another human being. Many in the Convocation who knew him—or those whose advances had been spurned—surmised he was either attracted to the other sex, or that there was something wrong with him. Scetis was not one to show his emotions easily. He had learned at a very young age, while still a slave, that to show emotion was to invite ridicule, hatred, pain, and abuse. That side of him he had tried hard to keep at bay, to keep himself safe. He had even held a lot back from his mentors, but then, they did not demand that he show them affection, only loyalty. That was one thing he could do. He was fiercely loyal to those that had helped him; cared for him in any way. He would die trying to save them.

Now he was fighting his way back to them. Scetis pushed aside yet another thorny bush, which whipped back at him after he had let it go. It landed on his back and he grunted with the pain as the thorns dug into his flesh, tearing it and causing the fabric to soak up the blood that sprung from the wounds. Scetis ignored them again. He would have Tavae deal with them when he got back.

That was his focus; getting to the Convocation and seeking out his old master. They had to stop Wradech's plans. When he had first heard of them, he had not worried. The kingship of a small realm was nothing to him. Whomsoever sat on the throne did nothing to change his life and what he did. But now that he knew that the plans included Ide, it was different. There was a push to do something about his old tormentor, he had to stop Ide marrying Orcades, and in turn becoming yet another pawn in the game.

Ide.

Scetis' mind again wandered to her. The shape of her face, the darkness of her eyes, the way her mouth was set as she pondered something. Her hair, which was thick and long, the way it moved in the water. He also thought of the way her body fitted against his, how she had clung to him, so close, her heart seemed like it was beating inside his own chest. The thoughts made him stop and he took in a deep breath. He could not afford for these emotions to overtake him and he forged on through the dense brush in front of him.

Ahead he could hear the rattle and creak of a cart going down a bumpy road. Scetis doubled his efforts and finally stumbled out beside a well-used small track. He landed heavily in a ditch beside the road and pulled himself up the other side. Mud from recent rains clung to his clothing, surprising the farmer who was coming back from delivering his goods to market.

Pulling on the reins he called the plodding horse to a halt and stared at the sight of the battered and dirty man who had stumbled into his path.

"What you want?" he called out to Scetis.

"Help, please," Scetis replied as he took a step towards the horse and cart.

"Just you wait right there a moment. What sort of help you be want'n?" he called again.

"I need to get to The Convocation."

"I can see that! You're a right mess, you are."

"Can I ask for a ride?" Scetis called to him.

"It also looks like you're on the run. I can't tell if it be to or from. Which one is it?"

"To, I promise you. I had a little trouble on the road, I am a Trader of Mystical Medicine."

"Is that right?" The man sat there looking at the bedraggled Scetis before him. "You got proof of that?"

"I do, Sir." Scetis immediately dug under his shirt and pulled out the medallion proclaiming who he was. The changes he had made with the wax were now gone and it was back to its original state.

"Bring it here, I can't see that far, young man." The farmer beckoned him on.

Scetis jogged the distance between them and pulled the medallion over his head then passed it up to the farmer.

"Mmm, it seems to be in order, though I've only seen a couple in my whole life. Does this say you're a Physician as well?" the farmer said as he handed it back.

"It does," Scetis replied as he placed the medallion around his neck.

"Get up on the back then, I'm not head'n in the direction of that place of quacks, but you're welcome to come home with me, and we'll see to your wounds, give you food and a place to sleep this night. Then you can be on your way in the morn'n."

"That is very kind of you, sir." Scetis said heading to the back of the cart and climbing aboard.

"You got a name?"

"Scetis, sir."

"I ain't no sir that's for sure, call me Uen."

"Thank you, Uen, for your kindness."

"That's what we're put on this world for, to help those that need it." Uen flicked the reins and the horse once more began to pull the cart.

"Not many in the world think the same as you do," Scetis called to him.

"Aye and that is the shame of it. If more people cared about their fellow man more than the gold that was in their pockets, the world would be a better place," Uen grumbled.

"It would indeed, my friend. It would indeed." Scetis leaned back against the side of the nearly empty cart and closed his eyes for a moment. The sound of the metal shod, wooden wheels on the dirt track, and the movement as it lurched from one rut to another, soon lulled him to sleep.

The hand that shook him awake was gentle and Scetis' eyes flew open. It was the first decent sleep he had had since the night before falling into the water with Ide. He sat up and looked around at the small farmyard that surrounded him. There was the usual well-built, but run-down farmhouse, with a barn across the yard that looked in much the same dis-repair. But it was neat and tidy.

"You're back, Dah," a young man called out as he came limping out of the barn.

"That I am. And Son, this here is Scetis, he's stay'n the night. I want you to put the horse away and unload the cart, then come inside and start supper will you. Our visitor is in a bad way and needs tend'n to."

"Right away." The boy nodded and then went to the horse.

Uen helped Scetis down from the back of the cart. The muscles in his body all seemed to be protesting after being allowed to rest for a moment and he had stiffened up. His pride though, would not allow him to accept Uen's help into the house and he brushed him away gently.

"Suit yourself," Uen said with a bit of a grin, and headed inside, waiting at the door for Scetis.

The inside of the farmhouse was comfy and had that well lived-in feeling to it, like generations of Uen's had made it their home. Uen ushered him to sit by the fire that was barely going in the grate under a large stone mantle. A stack of wood sat to one side and Uen pulled a few logs out to place on the ash and charred wood, encouraging it to flare with some kindling. Scetis lowered himself onto a stool that seemed to be used as a footrest for the larger wooden chair that sat on one side of the hearth. As gently as he could, Scetis pulled off his bags and lay them down at his feet.

"Get that shirt off and let's be hav'n a look at what's what," Uen told him as he poured water into a cup and brought it over to him. Scetis took a gulp of the sweet tasting liquid and then placed the cup down beside him.

As gently as he could, he began to peel the shirt from the dried blood on his back. He winced as it pulled on the wounds and refused to come off.

"Hold still." Uen returned to the jug and brought it back with him. Very slowly he dribbled the water over Scetis' back It soaked into the material of the shirt causing the red to run again.

Uen placed the jug on the floor and gently began to ease the shirt away from the wounds. With the scabs now softened it came away easily. With a bit more encouragement, it was off his back and Uen stared at the slashes which were laced in and over much older scars. He did not say a word about them to Scetis, but picked up a clean cloth, dipped it into the jug and went about cleaning the new ones.

While he worked, Scetis opened one of his bags and rummaged through it, pulling out his leather case. He did not expect anything inside to be of use any more and his fears were well met. Water sloshed around inside most of the little vials and the powders that were held inside, some of them ruined. One container was untouched by the immersion in both the river and lake, and he twisted the top off. Inside a pungent ointment sat, it was a deep yellow in color, and he handed it to Uen.

"Put these on the cuts once they are clean. It will help to fight any infection that may have got in," he instructed.

Uen sniffed the ointment and pulled his face away quickly from the smell.

"What's in it?" he inquired, dipping a finger into the jar.

"A bit of this and that," Scetis answered then winced as Uen began to apply it to his back.

"Trade secrets is it?" Uen said, giving a little laugh.

"Something like that," and he winced again.

The door flew open, and the boy entered, carefully carrying another load of wood as he did. With his foot he kicked it shut behind him and then proceeded to dump the wood by the fireplace. He turned and stared openly at Scetis back.

"How'd you get all them scars?" the boy asked.

"That's rude, Pont, go wash up and get the dinner started," Uen told his son without looking up from what he was doing.

"Was just asking, Dah," he said sulkily and went to do as he was told.

Scetis studied the boy as a way of blocking out the pain that he was going through. Pont looked to be no more than twelve years of age, and Scetis noticed again the limp in his left leg. It was something the boy seemed to be used to living with, not a new injury, but one that did not seem to hamper him in his every-day life. Pont moved around the small kitchen area, laying his hands on things without looking for where they were with the practice of someone who was used to the work. Soon the room was filled with the smell of frying ham, eggs and the smell of a loaf of bread set by the fire to warm.

Uen finished applying the ointment and then went to a cabinet in the corner, where he pulled out strips of material. Slowly and as gently, he began to wrap the lacerations to keep the air from them. When he was finished, he washed his hands and then poured two mugs of ale, handing one to Scetis.

"My thanks," he said as he raised it to his lips.

In short order, the meal was served and Scetis had to pace himself, so he did not eat it too quickly. His short rations from the past two days had not been enough to keep his toned body satisfied. When he was finished Uen looked at him and recognized someone who had gone without food for a little while.

"Help yourself to more if you wish, Scetis, we have plenty to share." The older man pushed the plate of ham towards Scetis.

After his second helping Scetis finished his mug of ale off and sighed. As he stretched the wounds began to pull under the bandages and he tried not to wince with the pain.

"What's wrong with the boy's leg?" he asked as Pont went to clean up after the meal.

"His leg got broke when he was little. We couldn't afford a Physician so we set it as best we could. But it don't seem to mind him much," Uen told him.

"Would you allow me to examine him?"

"I can't pay you; we only earn enough to feed ourselves and get a few little luxuries to make life bearable."

"I don't want your payment. You have taken me in and tended to my wounds, I would like to repay the favor." Scetis offered.

"Well, that would be right kind of you. But I don't think there is much you'll be able to do now, the injury as I said, is an old one."

"If I can help, I would like to."

After the dishes were cleared away, Pont stood in front of Scetis. He examined the way the boy stood and noted that one leg appeared to be shorter than the other. Running his hand down the left leg he found through the thin fabric of Pont's leggings the knotted muscles that had been pulled out of place, and underneath the tight flesh a distinctive lump where the bone had knitted back together wrong.

"There is something I can do, but it would mean that the bone will have to be broken once more," Scetis told Pont.

"No, I'm alright really, it don't bother me much, sir," he told him, shaking his head and going a little white at the thought.

"But son, if he can fix it, then I think we should do it, don't you?" Uen asked him.

"No Dah, I'm fine. I don't need fixing." Pont backed away from Scetis. "I got to go make sure the animals is fine."

The boy turned and fled the house, the door banging shut behind him. Uen sighed deeply and poured another mug of ale for the each of them.

"He still thinks it's his fault," he sighed deeply sitting back down in his seat by the fire.

"How did he get injured?" Scetis asked.

"He was playing by the river; it has a high bank and fast flowing water. His Mam was there with him picking wild celery and strawberries. Pont got too close to the edge and it fell away, his leg was twisted under him and he was screaming something fierce. I could hear it in the field I was work'n and I ran, but my Aeilnor jumped down to help him before I could get there. We'd some rains and the earth was soft, and I didn't know that a nanaue had come down from the hot springs further up. I kill them as soon as I know they are there.

"Aeilnor had got between Pont and the creature, she was trying to hold it off with a stick, but they are like their deep-water cousins the shark with their vicious teeth and sharp claws. She did everything she could to defend the boy, to save him until I could get there. It had her by the throat by the time I fell down the bank and she was dead. I slashed out with the reaper I had in my hands and imbedded it in the thing's head. But they don't know when they are dead, them creatures. There was nothing I could do for my wife. I raced passed and picked the boy up and got him back up the bank and then went back to do what I could for my poor Aeilnor."

Uen drank deeply from his cup and held it in his hands as he stared into the dancing flames in the grate. The wood moved slightly, sending glittering sparks up the chimney and making the fire crackle in the quiet of the room.

"That is a sad tale. I am sorry for your loss," Scetis said quietly drinking from his own cup.

"So," Uen said, rousing himself from his own pain. "You can fix my boy?"

"I can, but he is moving freely and does not seem to be in any pain from the injury. If I do this then he will be laid up for at least six weeks and there could be the chance of infection."

"Ahh, we have harvest com'n up. I can't be doing without him; it costs too much to hire one of the layabouts from the town."

"When the harvest is done and winter is in, send me a message at the Convocation. I will gladly come back and tend to him for you," Scetis offered. He then pulled out the jar of ointment from his bag and tossed it across the room to his host.

"I can't be go'n accepting this, it's too expensive." Uen tossed it back to his guest.

"You can and you will, basic treatments should not cost the everyday man anything. It was a hard thing for you to treat your son after losing your wife. Any Physician of any worth would have offered their services for free in such a case. I would have, at any rate. Keeping medicine for only those that can pay is wrong."

Scetis once more threw the jar to Uen. He held it in his hands and then turned his creased and worn eyes to the younger man, a tear forming in the corner and spilling over his weather-beaten face.

"I thank you, Scetis. You are a true and honest man. I will gratefully send word when harvest is over. My boy does not need the reminder of the day his mam died."

"It is I who thanks you, for taking in a bedraggled stranger."

Morning dawned to a sky that was ribboned with high white clouds, stretching from horizon to horizon. Scetis looked out at the farmyard and heard the rooster crowing in the hen house. The world was waking. He stretched a little and already the cuts on his back were easing with the help of the ointment. Turning south he looked to where he knew the large building of The Convocation stood jutting out into the great lake. It would take him all day to get there by foot.

Ducking back inside of the house he found Pont up and already stoking the fire. The boy did not look at him and seemed to be trying to avoid Scetis altogether. Uen entered behind Scetis having visited the privy and was yawning loudly. The father and son did not say anything to each other and Scetis watched them as they worked together and could see that words were not needed between the pair. They were bonded not only as parent and child, but by their combined grief.

Over breakfast Uen turned to Scetis. "I can take you as far as the next town, which is 'bout half-way to The Convocation. I have some business there and have been mean'n to get it out of the way for some time. This gives me a good excuse to go there."

"I appreciate the offer, thank you." He then pulled out a piece of parchment he had filched from Uen's crude desk and passed it to him. "I also have this. It's a complete list of ingredients and how to prepare it into the ointment that I gave you last night. That jar will not last you long."

"You would share your secrets with the likes of us?" Uen asked as he unfolded the instructions.

"I would, and anyone else who is in need of my care."

"My appreciation then, Scetis." He laid the paper aside and then stood. "When you are ready, I think we should be on our way. I'll just go hitch the horse to the cart. Pont you know what needs do'n today, so get on with the work. I'll bring you back something, boy."

"Thanks, Dah." Pont got up and immediately began cleaning away the mess.

Down the road with the farm fast receding behind them, Scetis settled himself into the seat beside Uen on the cart. Again, it rocked and rolled as it went over the ruts in the road. It creaked and moaned as it moved, though there was silence between the two men.

It continued this way for some time before a thought crossed Scetis' mind.

"The nanaue, do they come down this far from the hot springs often?" Scetis asked the farmer.

"Not often, except for when we get lots of rain. We've not had another since and before that the last one was when I was a lad," Uen answered him and flicked the reins in his hands to get the horse to pick up speed it was slowly losing.

"Has no one gone to wipe out the population there?"

"Why would we? Up there in their valley they ain't hurt'n no one. They have plenty to feed them and they keeps pretty much to themselves. They have all the heated water from the springs they could wish for. A nanaue will only attack if it feels threatened, or it's desperate for food. Which is what's most likely the case with the one that killed my Aeilnor."

"There are some parts of them which are useful in medicine."

"I take no store in that mystical medicine. If a plant can't be reduced to fix what ails you then we have no business cutting into animals for their so-called magical parts."

"Take it from me, my friend, there are some that would pay a great deal for parts from animals."

"A great deal is it?"

"If you are interested, I can put you in touch with my Trader Master, she'll be very interested in whatever you can pass her way."

"Mmm, it would have to be done so as not to hurt the group that's there now, just one or two a year could give us a bit extra," Uen said speculatively.

"It could indeed. Shall I pass your name on to her?"

"You could do that, and we would welcome a visit from her." He grinned at Scetis, appreciating the help this stranger had given him.

The parting in the next town was not long. Scetis and Uen shook hands, and he made the farmer promise to send for him once the harvest was over and winter was setting in. Uen clicked the reins of the horse and moved down the road towards the center of the small town and the markets that were held there, while Scetis watched him go. Hefting the bags into place and being careful not to annoy the wounds on his back, he headed down the road that would take him to The Convocation. Looking up at the position of the sun, he gauged that he would arrive at his home in the middle of the afternoon.

The pace he set himself was an easy one and many times he had to move off the side of the road to let fast moving men on horseback with the colors of messengers on their backs. A few carts carrying supplies also lumbered past him, one or two offering him a ride to the bastion that held all the schools. Scetis declined cheerfully their offers, the sun was warm on him and the day seemed bright and easy, he wanted to enjoy it just a little more, before being plunged once more back into the intrigues that went with The Convocation of Mystical Medicine.

The land about him that was like soft undulating waves of green and golden crops, small hills and vast ancient trees soon flattened out, and as he crested the last hill the view became clear. The great lake, whose opposite shore was just able to be seen in the hazy distance, sat glistening and shimmering in the afternoon sunshine. Rising from what had once been a large island, was the stronghold. Its towers reached high above the water in tiers, each roof a different color against the beautiful blue of the sky. The walls were made of a sand-colored stone and appeared to gleam gold in the light from above. The main part of the stronghold was centered in the middle of the island, this was the seat for the hierarchy and the living quarters of the Regulator. It was surrounded by a large turreted wall, with four rounded towers at each corner. Below this, the various schools sat with large stone buildings, each trying to outdo the others in grandness. Under these monuments to their own self-importance, sat small buildings, interspersed with green spaces for the gardens of medicine. This was the area that Scetis liked the best. The people who resided there were good folk who tended the earth and cared about the medicines they produced. These were the Apothecaries.

Scattered around these last structures sat a town of sorts. It lined both sides of the street that ran around the outer edge of the island. Tied up to some of these buildings were boats, used for fishing and transport across the lake. No Physician would ever dream of living down in this area. This was where the common folk lived, the people who did the laundry, prepared the food, made the clothes, and other trades useful to The Convocation. And leading to it all was the causeway.

The great structure had been built on a naturally occurring shallow area that led to the island. At some point after The Convocation had begun on the island, a bridge had been built. It had been wooden, and only just above the water line. Over the centuries, the water had rotted the wood away, and it was then replaced by a more permanent structure. Someone had been put in charge of the design and they had released their great imagination. Arches gracefully curved between each supporting pillar. Columns lined the sides and intricate filigree metal work had been commissioned to fill the spaces between. It gave a beautiful impression as a person crossed the causeway, like they were entering some long-lost civilization, that they were enlightened and rich.

The richness was right. Some of the hierarchy of The Convocation, especially the Physicians, coveted their gifts and their skills jealously, pandering more and more only to those that could afford their services. The Physicians held themselves aloft of their fellows in Apothecary and Trade. They were becoming a danger to the whole idea of The Convocation of Mystical Medicine. They had become more and more secretive and unwilling to share their information, issuing edicts forbidding the giving away of medicinal secrets. They were intent on taking over the hierarchy and were unhappy the Regulator had risen from the Lower Tier Hierarchy above higher personages.

Tavae had been most embarrassed when the role was offered to him. He had thought himself too lowly and not suited for the job. At that point, the Physicians were just starting their take over, and those that were in charge could see what they were trying to do, and he was their answer. The elevation of Tavae from Lower Councilor to Regulator had angered quite a few, including his old student, Wradech Foghladh. Tavae was known to believe that The Convocation should be one and not separate, and that their practices should be spread wide and offered to all, not just those that could pay for it.

Scetis now stood before the beginning of the causeway. He looked down the long bridge as The Convocation loomed large before him. His feet moved and soon he was walking towards it. The foot and cart traffic had increased in the afternoon and was interspersed with ornate carriages, carrying the ill rich to see their Physicians. Some loudly proclaimed which family they came from with garishly painted family emblems, while others were darkly painted. He could pick out some that held those in authority and would duck his head so he would not be recognized.

At the end of the causeway a gateway was the only portal onto the island. Out the front stood two guards who were bored with their post and were more intent in staring at the lengthening shadows than those that were passing through. Scetis joined the end of one group who was chatting away and managed to slip passed the ill attending guards.

Having grown up on the island and starting life as a slave gave Scetis a certain advantage. He did not think it wise to just make his way to the main stronghold and try to walk through the gates the way he looked right then. Instead, he sought out the tunnels that had been dug into the hard rock the stronghold sat upon. He was soon slipping into the ranks of slaves and servants that used them as their main thoroughfare to get from one part of the island to the other with little hassle and speed. Scetis knew these corridors and tunnels like the back of his hand.

The first stop he had to make was his own meagre quarters in the Traders Enclave. This was located just below the Apothecaries, in a small sector. It was walled off to protect those that were based inside. He still had to be careful as there were people inside the enclave that were in the pockets of those who were wanting to take over. Ducking and slipping into niches which would hide him from people coming towards him, he finally made it to his rooms and retrieved the key from where he had hidden it.

Before Scetis even slipped the key into the lock, he examined the door closely including the mechanism of the lock. Nothing had been tampered with and the hair he had put in place was still where it should be. Carefully he turned the key and the door sprung open, he walked inside and shut it behind him quietly. Standing with his back to the solid wooden door he looked around to see if anything had been disturbed since he had been gone and was thankful everything was still in order.

The room was bare. It had a pallet bed which was pushed up against one wall and held a thin mattress and a few blankets, underneath a chest containing his clothes was kept. The bed was tidily made and undisturbed. At the end a small table sat with a battered metal jug and basin on top. The small desk up against another wall, with the plain wooden stool pushed underneath was still clear of papers. The shelves on the third and fourth walls held various jars of dried plants and animal parts, and a few were pickled in a greenish liquid. Other objects sat sparkling in the sunlight that filtered into the room from the only window above the bed. Crushed minerals and ores sat in rows of vials, all standing at attention like soldiers, ready for use.

Scetis took off the bags which were slung over his shoulders and placed them carefully down at the end of the bed. Crouching down he opened one and pulled out the leather case and placed it on the desk. It would need to be gone through and everything replaced, but that could wait. The first thing he had to do was to try and get an audience with Tavae. His old Master needed to be warned of what was happening in the other realm. He was not sure how the plot to overthrow King Urmond and the take-over of The Convocation were linked and why, but he knew they were.

Quickly he pulled the chest from under the bed. A clean set of clothes were soon laid out on the bed before him. Stripping, he unwound the bandages that Uen had carefully placed on him and threw them in the corner to be dealt with later. The jug still had some water in it from the last time he was there, carefully he poured it into the basin and retrieved a cloth from the chest.

After a hurried wash and change of clothes he was heading out of the door, placing his tells before locking the door and pocketing the key. Footsteps could be heard from around the corner of the corridor, and he headed away on silent feet. The entrance to the tunnel that would take him up to the higher stronghold was easy for him to find and he slipped under the tapestry that depicted a farm scene and entered.

Inside it was dim and musty smelling. It was little used as there was no need for the servants or slaves to make the trek up to the stronghold from this part. The use of it was mainly for Traders and their clandestine meetings with those in higher authority when they wanted something harder to attain or illegal. Reaching out with his hand his fingers brushed the roughly worked stone as he travelled through the dark and he knew the way without fail. It wound its way up and many offshoots and junctures intersected it, making sure he passed those that were lighter and often used so he would not be seen.

Unerringly, he made the turn that would take him to the private quarters of the Regulator, and he waited at the entrance to the set of rooms. This specific tunnel came out in the bedchamber. Scetis listened at the door, trying desperately to hear if Tavae was there and if he was alone. He could hear nothing. Still not trusting what he could not hear, he reached up and carefully removed a spy hole he had placed in the door. Inside was flooded with the setting sun, and the room glowed a golden orange color from it. The sunlight catching on the shiny surfaces gave it a very opulent visage.

There was no one inside the chamber and he pushed on the hidden door. It opened without a squeak, or any rasping on the thick carpet which covered the floor. The click that the secret door made when he shut it was barely audible and he looked to the door to the outer audience room, where Tavae conducted most of his business. Pressing himself up against the wall the door was fitted into, he waited and held his breath. Beyond the door there were voices, they were companionable sounding, not directive, and shortly he heard a call of farewell and a door shutting.

Carefully he opened the door just a crack and looked at the room beyond. Opposite and with his back to the large ornate windows sat

Scetis' old Master. Tavae looked up at the door with the movement and shook his head.

"Come in, boy. No point hiding in there, there's no one here who will harm you," the old man called to him.

Scetis smiled as he recognized the words that Tavae had first spoken to him before taking him on as an apprentice.

Planning

Muniath strode into the citadel with his sleeveless work cloak billowing out behind him as he moved. The white linen shirt underneath was tight fitting as were the black leather pants. His long hair was tied back neatly at the nape of his neck. The summons from King Urmond had come just as he was about to leave home to climb up to the Eyrie to start his days' work.

It had been well over seven days since Ide had been rescued and her promotion to Second Captain. He and their brother had both tried to find out what had happened and what she had told the King and their parents. The level of security in the palace and the citadel had slowly been increased. Leave had been cancelled and the brothels and inns in the town had been ordered to close their doors early each night. Even Meara had been no help with any gossip she may have heard at her establishment.

It appeared to Muniath that nearly every door throughout the citadel now had either a Foot or Rider guard, and in some instances, both. As he passed them, he received their salutes and nodded his acknowledgement. Some of the guards appeared to be very young and he recognized the Rider Apprentices.

Turning the corner to head towards the throne room he was met by a page boy.

"Master of Dragons," he bowed.

"Yes?"

"My Lord King requests that you meet him in his private office," the young man informed him in an official tone.

"My thanks," Muniath told him, then turned aside from the corridor that led to the throne room.

For Urmond to summon him to such a private room did not bode well. In the palace there were three rooms which Urmond used to conduct the affairs of the realm. The first was the throne room, which was for public and international matters. The second was his official office, where he met with his councilors, advisors and heads of the military. Then there was his private office. When Urmond entered that room no one was to disturb him. It was where he conducted the secret business of the land and where his own personal correspondence was conducted. For him to summon Muniath there meant that it had to be very important, and now he wondered if it had to do with the matter they had talked about in the garden.

The guards outside the door snapped to attention as he approached, and one carefully knocked on the door. The door opened almost immediately and Urmond himself stood there holding the handle.

"Master of Dragons, thank you for coming so quickly," he greeted and gestured for Muniath to enter.

"As my Lord King commands," Muniath replied formally and entered the room.

The room was in ordered chaos and very unlike Urmond's neat and tidy official office. Stacks of leather clad books towered on tables, and the desk was a mess of clutter and papers hastily pushed into piles. A pair of large comfy chairs bookended the fireplace which lay empty and unlit. The windows looked at the mountain and had a clear vision of the steps that led to the Eyrie, they stood wide open to allow the entry of the cool clear mountain air. The walls were lined with shelves, only some of which held more books, others held personal gifts from family and those close to the King.

"Please sit, Mun. Can I offer you something to drink or eat?" Urmond asked him.

"No thank you, Sire, I had only just eaten when your summons came."

"Good, we can get down to it then." Urmond sat on one of the chairs and Muniath lowered himself into the other. "You know Mun, in this room, we are just two men meeting to discuss what we may," Urmond said.

"I understand, Urmond," Muniath reassured him.

"I am happy you do. The reason I have summoned you here is to talk about a matter of great urgency and security. I presume that Ide has not told either yourself or Ven what occurred to her?"

"She has not, which is not like our sister."

"Ahh, that would be my doing. I asked that she keep the information from both of you because I didn't want you or Ven to go off and try to deal with the situation, until I had a chance to think things through."

"And that situation is?" Muniath prompted.

"There is a threat to my crown."

"Who?" Muniath demanded sitting on the edge of his seat.

"It is that reaction I was hoping to avoid," Urmond chuckled.

"It was a little reactionary," Muniath agreed and sat back again, trying to relax.

"It does not matter who, only that the threat is there. The who will be dealt with in due course."

"So, what is the nature of the threat?"

"A direct overthrowing of my line. It has influences from outside of our realm and it is the reason I have asked you here. It seems that there are those who wish to rule both countries and the stealing of Screamer's eggs was part of the plot."

"I can't see how?"

"The only reason I can think of was to test our defenses, security, and response to a threat. That or they were trying to sow discord between our two nations."

"The Convocation is involved," Muniath surmised.

"I believe the Regulator is not behind it and possibly has no knowledge of the plot. But I do have reason to believe that it stems from some in the Hierarchy."

"This information came from the Trader who endangered my sister's life?"

"It did. And I am inclined to believe the intelligence. I received a letter from the Regulator this morning, giving me a warning and telling me what this man had told him. The Trader was an apprentice of Tavae's at one point. It seems he was ordered by some in the Hierarchy to steal the eggs. He was being thrown to the nanaue it seems. They thought he posed a threat because of his relationship with the Regulator."

"So, what do you wish me to do?"

"I understand that you know what this Trader looks like?"

"I do. I saw him through Ide's eyes."

"Then, we have work to do." Urmond looked around him at the books that lined the shelves. "In these works are hidden treasures. Writings of my ancestors from when the realm was first formed. In amongst these writings are notes about taming the first dragons and the skills of those that have become known as Dragon Wardens."

Urmond turned his blue eyes to Muniath. He was not sure, but he could have sworn that they glowed slightly.

"You want me to read all these?"

"Not all, I can direct you where you need to go. What I want you to do is put into practice what you learn from them." Urmond left his seat by the unlit fire and went to stand by the windows before carrying on.

"What I am going to tell you cannot leave this room. No one in our realm must ever hear this from you, unless you can recognize the same skill in them. Not even my own heir, my daughter, can know this information. I had hoped that she would possess it, but the blood line has been watered down too much now. There have been too many diplomatic marriages for it to have continued." He turned back to Muniath who was still waiting. "When this realm was founded, the original rulers were a race apart from the normal people. They were human in semblance, they talked the common tongue, and their bodies were akin to true humans, but they were not. The race that originally ruled were more closely related to dragons."

This last statement hung between the two men. Muniath was disbelieving at first, but soon saw that Urmond was serious.

"But your line—"

"Yes. I am a direct descendant, and my child does not share that blood. The Dragon Wardens and those that possess the skill are all descended from that line. Your sister told me something very interesting when she reported to me. She told me that this Trader's eyes seemed to glow at one point during their journey. I believe he is of that line and I wish to talk to him, face to face. I need to know if he is." Urmond took in a deep breath, he seemed to be holding more information back, and Muniath was not inclined to press him further. "There is another task I wish you to take on. One that I have previously forbidden you to do. I need you to go and bring back Teagan and the young dragon."

"What of her father?"

"If he still lives, Tharain can come home, but he will never again have the status he once had. Teagan is my family and I sense she is born of the true dragon line. I need to get my house in order. There are things that need to be done and steps taken to ensure the throne is protected. I am not the throne; I am only the one whose ass is currently sat on it. This realm must not fall. If it does, the dragons will be free from our influence and will rebel. It would be devastating not just for this realm, but this world."

Muniath let out a long sigh as he took in all that Urmond had told him. This news that he himself may not be truly human dawned on him. Urmond was watching his reaction and nodded.

"Yes, you are a descendant and in some small part, so is your whole family. The silver around the pupil gives it away. These are two perilous and fraught tasks I have set you, especially going through the mirror to that world. You will have to rely on the skill to find them. You have the right to say no to my request. I am not going to command or give you a royal decree. This is something you must decide on whether it is worth the danger you will face."

"I will gladly do both. I will know the Trader by sight, that will be a reasonably easy task, and to be honest with you, Urmond, I had always intended to defy your order on the other."

"I know. You have even discussed it with Taran. Except, on his loyalty and obedience I can count on." Urmond gave Muniath a little chuckle." I thought you might have ideas on that matter and asked Taran to keep an ear out for me."

"He never let on," Muniath said with a smile.

"Again, at my request. I wanted to see how far into the planning you would get. But unfortunately, events have overtaken matters and I need you to do this first."

"I'll have the Trader here by the end of tomorrow," Muniath declared urgently.

"He can wait. The Regulator has assured me of that. I have also given my own promise that he will not face charges when he gets here."

"But My Lord, he did steal the eggs in the first place."

Urmond put up a hand to stay off further protest from Muniath. "I am aware of the crime he has committed. But he is worth more to both this realm and The Convocation alive."

"I don't know what I am going to tell Screamer then, I promised that she could have him for supper when we found him."

"You should never make rash promises without knowing if you can fulfil them first. Especially to a dragon," Urmond told him.

A polite knock came at the door and Urmond opened it. Standing on the other side was a page holding a tray with three cups and a steaming pot precariously balanced. He nodded his head and entered when Urmond stepped aside. Behind him, walking with a stick to aid his steps came Taran.

"Come in, I'm pleased you were able to join us, old friend," Urmond greeted him.

"It is my honor, My Lord King, for you to remember an old and damaged Rider," Taran replied.

"I already know you were acting as a spy for our King, Taran," Muniath said, stepping forward to shake his hand.

"Ahh, I am sorry about that, Mun. But when the King commands we must obey."

"Yes, we must," he replied as he watched the page carefully lay out the cups and pot, then bow before heading out the still open door, Urmond closed it firmly behind him.

"So Urmond, why have you dragged my broken ass all the way up here?" Taran asked, all formality gone from his address.

"Yes, well if I could trust a place closer to your establishment we would meet there."

Taran eased himself down onto one of the chairs at the table and pulled the pot towards him. Carefully he poured the dark liquid that was contained inside into the three waiting cups. Urmond and Muniath joined him, each taking a cup for himself. Muniath drank deeply of the beverage that was steeped from the new shoots of the Dragon Tree. The rich taste, both bitter and sweet, raced over his tongue and warmed him from the inside.

"So, this has to do with the insane scheme of Mun's then?" Taran asked.

"It does. You have made a study of all the worlds which are connected to our own. What I need you to do for me is to teach Mun about one."

"The one called 'Earth'?"

"Yes."

"We've not had contact with the people in that world for many, many centuries. That portal was destroyed when the last dragon died there. If you remember the history, they were not happy that we would not send eggs through to repopulate, and you also should remember why," Taran said darkly.

"I do, but it is not me who needs the lesson, Taran. Once again, my room and books are available to you. Mun needs to know everything he can before he goes to find Teagan and the dragon."

"I hope you are a quick study then Mun, because I hate repeating myself," Taran told him.

"I remember, Taran. It was you who trained me to fly." Muniath paused for a moment. "And I think you may have another use, while I am away."

"For what?"

"Wick. He is still yet to get on the back of a dragon. Depending on how long I am away, he will need instruction."

"Will he have learned enough of the skill before you leave?" Taran asked him.

"He has learned a lot already, but I'll make sure he has enough to be going on with." Muniath then turned to Urmond. "When do you want me to leave?"

"As soon as you are able. Come back and see me here tonight and I will start with what we discussed earlier. Right now, I'll leave you to your instruction." Urmond got to his feet and placed a hand on Muniath's shoulder. "I have faith in you Muniath."

The instruction that morning with Taran surprised Muniath. The knowledge Taran had gained and was giving, was backed up by the books that lined the room. He would send Muniath off to get a book so he could emphasize his point and never erred as to where the book was located. When they were finished with it, he would insist it go back immediately to the spot it had come from.

At the end of their intensive session, Taran rose to his feet with the aid of his stick. He looked directly at Muniath when the younger man finished putting the books away. "All this information on Earth is out of date though. We have no knowledge of what has happened to their people since the portal was smashed on their side. I have a feeling that our King wants Teagan and Tharain home partly so he can fill in what is missing. He never liked the idea of sending them away into the unknown. Your confirming to him that they are still alive has only excited his thirst for knowledge."

"I hope I don't disappoint him then."

"You had better not. The realm—indeed if not this world—depends on it," Taran told him bleakly then walked to the door. His hand was on the handle but he stopped before opening it. "When is Ven going to ask Mae to marry him?"

"I don't know. What goes on with my brother is as much a mystery to me as it is to you. Do you want me to have a word with him? And is Mae open to the idea?"

"We've talked briefly of it. She doesn't think that Ven is serious."

"We all know that's not true. Leave it with me Taran."

"I would like to see them both happy," Taran opened the door and left Muniath standing, pondering the problem of his brother's apparent shyness when it came to their foster-sister.

By the end of the afternoon up at the Eyrie, Wick was exhausted with the exercises Muniath had set for him. They were designed to open his mind more, so that he was receptive to the brief flashes the dragons sent to let them know what they needed and their current mood. Muniath was pleased with how the boy was progressing.

Their constant companions while they were in the cave system were the two small dragons. Each one now stood near shoulder height on Wick, who was fast growing to be as tall as Muniath. The pair of dragons were playful, and their personalities were now developing. Sting was almost a direct copy of Raker, the sire of the pair. While Fleet was developing into a cunning and quick dragon. She could devise ways of slipping away from their mother to be with either Wick or Muniath, or whoever was in the caves. She could sense their presence as soon as they entered through the barrier by the stairs. Neither dragon strayed far from their mother, but soon they would need to be in their own caverns. Muniath could sense the impatience of Screamer in wanting her own space once more.

Out in the wild, dragons were usually solitary creatures, only coming together to mate. The mating ritual would last for months before the female would acquiesce to the male. He would only stay a few more days to make sure the female had produced the offspring, then leave her to bring them up. The offspring would then stay with their mother until they had learned all they could from her.

In captivity however, these lessons were different. The dragons did not need to hunt, as they were provided with ample food. Their flying lessons were delayed until they were large enough to carry the weight of a Rider. The first person to ride a dragon was usually a Dragon Warden. This was important to forge the trust and bond between them. Only when the Dragon Warden was satisfied would the Rider who was paired with the dragon be allowed to mount it for the first time. This short flight always occurred in the gallery near the entrance, instead of the training platform the Warden used.

Muniath looked at Wick and the young green dragon who was looking over his shoulder and could see the instinctive connection they already had. The gold and red nudged his hand, she enjoyed the sensation of being stroked and she purred as Muniath indulged her.

"That's enough for today, Wick. Make sure that the dragons are fed and watered for the night, and make sure these two understand to stay away from the older ones. They're not as tolerant as some. Then you can have the night off. Go see your mother, she worries you aren't being fed enough in the barracks."

"Thank you, sir," Wick answered coming to attention, but grinning at his uncle.

Muniath left him to his duties and made for the entrance. Behind him he could hear the clicking of talons on the smooth rock floor. He turned and faced Fleet.

"Back to your mother, young one."

"Fly." The word was as clear as a bell to Muniath and he stared for a moment. *"Fly,"* it came again.

"Fly?" Muniath asked quietly back.

The young dragon became very excited and bounded towards him. *"Fly, fly, fly,"* she said over and over, her head now on his shoulder.

Muniath placed careful and gentle hands on her extending neck and pulled her away from him.

"I don't know how I can understand you," he said with some wonder.

"Brother," Fleet said softly, and it sounded full of longing.

"Sting?"

The dragon looked at him in the eye, her bright blue blinked a few times at him.

"Brother," she said again.

A flash of an image assaulted Muniath for a second. It was a densely wooded area, and he did not recognize any of the plants. But it was not the flora that interested him. It was the deep green iris and a pupil of silver that stared at him. Muniath stepped back from the image and the gold and red dragon before him.

"Brother," Fleet repeated, satisfied she had got the message across to him.

"Who was that?" he asked her.

Frustration swamped him in waves emanating from the little dragon and he heard her sigh with it. *"Brother,"* she said more emphatically.

"That was not your brother, he is back with Wick."

"Brother." The thought was once more reinforced with the image.

"Could it be?" he mused as the thought of the third and lost egg came to him.

"Brother!" She became excited again as she heard his thought.

"So, the feeling I have is true. He is alive."

"Brother." This time the word came as pleading.

Muniath placed a hand against the smooth scales of her cheek and she leaned into the touch.

"I will find him. The King has asked me to," he told her. He was unsure how much she understood but was surprised by her reaction to the news.

"Brother, brother," she said excitedly. Fleet butted her head against his gently for a moment and then scampered away back down the gallery. She stopped and looked back at Muniath and bowed her head to him respectively. *"Brother thanks."*

Entering the private study of the King later, after a quick clean up and meal, Muniath was still amazed by the interaction. Urmond sat behind his desk, a sheet of parchment in his hand and he looked up at the younger man.

"You look a bit perplexed, Mun. Is there something I can help you with?" he asked.

Muniath looked at his King. "I think you are the only one who can help me," he said then remained quiet for some time, his eyes straying to the entrance of the Eyrie so high above even this tower in the palace.

"I can't if I don't know what the problem is to start with," Urmond said breaking the silence between them.

"Fleet spoke to me."

"Screamer's girl?"

"Yes."

"What did she say?" Urmond asked very quietly and expectantly.

"At first she said 'fly'." Muniath paused as he debated with himself about saying more, now wondering if he had dreamt the whole encounter.

"Then?" Urmond prompted.

"Then she said 'brother'." Muniath turned to Urmond. "But it couldn't have happened."

"What makes you say that?"

"It must have been my imagination."

"Did anything else happen?" He waited expectantly.

"An image."

"Describe it to me," Urmond urged him.

"A forest. A dragon eye. The pupil was silver. But how could that be? The pupil on any dragon is black, the silver is the line around it."

"She definitely said brother?" Urmond was now standing in front of him.

"She did," he confirmed.

"This is important, Muniath. Did she say anything else?"

"Yes, before she went back to Screamer she said, 'brother thanks'."

"She can communicate with him," Urmond said in awe.

"Who?" Muniath looked at the King. "Surely you don't mean the missing dragon?"

"Yes, I do." Urmond suddenly crossed the room to the shelves nearest his desk. Reaching out he pulled on a book and laid it on the work surface. Opening it carefully he beckoned Muniath over to read it.

"Aloud," Urmond instructed and then moved to the window, staring up at the Eyrie.

Muniath looked at the page and the neat writing that was scrawled across it, then cleared his throat.

"'The Dragon King is a magnificent beast. He stands at least two feet taller than the largest of the breeds. The color of his scales is a gleaming deep emerald green and a face festooned with small spikes. But the most striking feature of this special dragon is his eyes. They gleam green and the pupil is silver. He is skilled and very dominant. Our Master suggests that he not be tamed but be released into the wild. According to the old lore, it is prophesied that the Dragon King will only be born in answer to a direct threat to the throne, and the line of those who sit on it. But we will need to study it further.'"

Muniath turned the page and looked further on in the book, but the page after was blank as was the rest of the book.

"There is no more," he informed Urmond.

"No. I know that. It was written by King Uerd, my ten times great grandfather. I have never found any other mention of a Dragon King in these writings," he indicated the shelves.

"So, what does this mean?"

"It means that the threat is real, more real than I even realized. How is Wick coming along? Do you think you could leave him now?"

"Now? No, he is nowhere near ready to be left in charge of the dragons," Muniath protested.

"I am afraid that it will be necessary. I do have the skill, not as great as yours, but enough so I can take on his teaching."

"Sire, that is not necessary."

"But it is. I will not have the Eyrie unattended. I am the King, it is my role to serve this realm, and in this I can help. I need you to leave almost straight away Muniath, it is imperative that we get that dragon back on our home soil. He was born to protect our world; he cannot do it when he is on another."

"It will be as you wish then, my Lord King," Muniath bowed deeply to Urmond.

Compulsion

A cold southerly wind blew around the parking lot, strong enough to set the streetlights dancing with it. The shadows were deep beyond their golden, orange glow and the drenched ground beneath sparkled in their light. Teagan left the warm interior of the DOC offices, hearing the click of the lock as it set itself back into place when the door shut. She looked around her at the deepening night, the sky full of scudding clouds, dark and threatening, leaving gaps between them showing the first stars of the evening. She pulled her backpack higher onto her hunched shoulders against the onslaught of cold air, as it buffeted her and tugged at her hair.

Pressing the remote, the lights flashed on her small car for a moment as it unlocked and just as she pulled on the door the heavens opened. Quickly she leapt into the front seat and slammed the door against the nasty weather and sighed. The cold always made her sluggish, just wanting to curl up in a blanket and hide herself away. Dumping the bag on the empty front seat she inserted the key and turned it. The car whirred a little and she turned it off. Once more she tried to start it, but it refused to catch. Taking a deep breath, she went about turning everything off she could think of, the radio, the lights, even the heater. Praying under her breath, she turned the key again. The car tried to start, but it was getting slower and slower as it turned over.

The knock at her window made her jump and she saw Mark peering in at her, getting drenched in the downpour. Teagan rolled the window down a little so they could talk, but not let in the cold rain.

"Open the hood, I'll have a look for you," Mark said grinning at her.

"Ok," she told him and reached down for the hood release. She heard the clunk as it opened and Mark raced round to the front, pulling it up and securing it so it did not fall on his head. Through the narrow gap at the bottom Teagan could see him checking leads on the battery and other things on the motor.

"Try it again," he yelled out trying to be heard over the increasing storm.

Teagan turned the key in the ignition again. Once more it whined and whirred, but it still did not take. Mark dropped the hood down and made sure it was secure, before coming back to the driver's door.

"I think the battery's flat; I'll give you a ride home," he offered.

"You don't have to, I can get my dad to come get me," she protested.

"Don't be stupid, it's a shit night, and you aren't that far out of my way. Come on," he said as he opened the door for her.

Teagan grabbed her bag and stepped out into the cold again. Mark shut the door and took off before her to one of the office four-wheel drives he had the use of. The lights flashed as he unlocked it. As he was about to get in the driver's side, he looked back at her, she was still hesitating.

"Come on, you're getting drenched," he called, as he disappeared inside the cab.

Pressing the lock button on her set of keys she raced over to the passenger door and it opened just as she got to it. Mark was still leaning over and moved as she got in, dumping her bag at her feet while she reached for the seatbelt.

"Hopefully all the traffic should be gone by now," he said as he started the vehicle up. The sound of the diesel engine was loud, and he reached over to turn off the radio which blared out. "Sorry, nothing like a bit of AC/DC to get you going in the morning."

"Can't say I really like them myself," she told him quietly.

"So what music are you into?" Mark maneuvered the car out of the staff parking lot and onto the slick and rain-drenched road. The lights from the truck lit up the falling rain, making them sparkle like fireworks as they moved through it.

"I'm more a book person than a music fan."

"You gotta listen to something, have you got any favorite bands?" he persisted.

"Not really. I like music in the background, like Enya or Celtic music."

"Enya? Really? I would have picked you as liking more boy bands than that stuff," he gave a chuckle.

"Boybands? Give me some credit," she laughed with him.

"So, what do you like to do on your time off? I mean, we really haven't gotten to know one another."

"We spent all that time in the forest only a few months ago."

"I know, but well, Eric and Phil were there as well," he shrugged, glancing over at her as he drove.

"There's not much to tell. Actually, I go hiking a lot in the forest behind the house."

"You really enjoy your work don't you."

"Of course, don't you?" Teagan asked him. In the brief flashes of the overhead streetlights, she could see him trying to come up with an answer.

"Well, yeah, I do. It's a good job, I'm the outdoors type, I couldn't stand it if I were in an office all day. Eric is a good guy to work for, he's not as demanding as some of them."

"So why did you join DOC?"

"It seemed like a good fit. Don't get me wrong, I do care about the environment and the wildlife, we have a shocking history in losing species here. I do enjoy it, most of the time. But I wouldn't call it my life. I like getting home and spending time with my friends."

"It's all I ever wanted to do. I've always looked after injured creatures. My dad always complained about finding lizards and birds in the house."

"You and your dad are close then?"

"I suppose you could say that."

"What does he do, or is he retired?"

"He's still working. At the moment he's working in a butcher's shop." Teagan hoped that Mark would stop with the almost interrogating questions. Looking out the windows she could see that they were almost past the harbor and heading into the valley. The lights from Petone were bright.

"Teagan, I was wondering if I could take you out sometime?" Mark asked quietly, she saw from the corner of her eye he was biting on his lower lip while he waited for her reply.

"I don't know," she stammered. The question had come as a shock.

"We could go out on Friday after work, or Saturday. I thought we could go to the movies and maybe get something to eat," he said hopefully.

Teagan's face reddened with embarrassment, she did not know how to handle the situation and shifted a little uncomfortably in her seat. She thanked the darkness for hiding it. But surprised herself.

"Sure, Saturday sounds great," she replied slowly.

"Really? You want to go out with me?"

"Mark, why ask me if you thought I would say no?"

"Because I wasn't sure. I mean, I hoped you'd say yes, but I thought you'd say no. You never stay for work parties and you don't really socialize much. No one knows much about you," he said quickly.

"I guess no one except Eric has ever tried to get to know me." Now she had given her answer she found herself looking forward to going out on Saturday. It had been a long time since she had been asked out, not since she was at school.

"I've wanted to for a while, but I thought you preferred Phil."

"No, actually I didn't think of either of you in that way."

"Sweet. So, I'll pick you up at about six or do you want to meet me in town?"

Teagan could hear the excitement in his voice, making him stammer a little and trip over the words.

"If you could pick me up that would be lovely," she told him.

For the rest of the drive through the valley and up the narrow hill road to reach her house they discussed the movies that were playing. By the time Mark stopped the car they had decided not only which film they would see, but where they would go afterwards to eat. Teagan reached down and pulled her backpack onto her lap as she unclipped the seatbelt.

"Thanks for the lift, Mark, I'll see you tomorrow at work," she said as she opened the door.

"See you tomorrow and I'll take a look at your car in the morning."

"I'd appreciate that."

As she was stepping out he stopped her. "Hey, do you need a lift in the morning?"

"No, I'll catch a ride with my father. Thanks again, Mark." Teagan smiled at him and shut the door. She did not look back as she ran through the rain to the front door and stepped through it. The sound of the noisy diesel engine revving and moving off did come to her as she shut it and the nasty night out.

"I'm home, Dad," she called out.

"Just in time, dinner's ready," Tharain called back to his daughter.

Teagan dumped her bag just inside the door to her room and carried on down the hall towards the kitchen.

"When is my dinner, Teagan?" Gremlin spoke to her in their joined mind.

"As soon as I've eaten, I'll be there," she sent the thought along with the smile.

The large double doors, engraved long ago by some unknown artists, opened wide. The heavy key sat in Muniath's clenched hand, the chain from which it hung swung freely. He had just retrieved it from his brother, after Venicones had hidden it and kept it safe since the Trader and his apprentice had broken into the secret and dangerous hall. The darkness inside was a deep black and he could not see the end of it. Two Rider guards stood on either side of him, each holding a torch. With a nod from Muniath they entered the hall and touched the dancing flames from their torches to the sconces that were placed between each set of mirrors. As they flared into life their light bounced around the room, shining off the highly polished surfaces and illuminating the carvings of dragons around the frames.

Muniath turned to Urmond and held out the key to his King. Urmond took it and placed the chain around his neck.

"I'll keep it safe until you return. You know how to get hold of me," the King said, placing a hand on his shoulder.

"I do, my Lord King."

"Go with speed and go safely." Urmond stepped away so Muniath's parents could say their goodbyes.

The reason for his mission was still a secret, so too was the portal he was to enter. He could see the worry in his mother's eyes, but she tried not to show it, instead giving him a smile and a hug.

"Get back home soon Mun, and don't do anything stupid," she instructed as she released him to shake his father's hand.

"What your mother said, Son," Galanan said gruffly. "And when you get back you can report to me why it was necessary for me to be kept out of this mission." He raised an eyebrow at his son.

"I will, Father," Muniath agreed.

Once his farewells were said he turned back to the hall. The two guards had returned to their posts at the entrance and his parents had followed them. Only a few of the sconces had been lit, but it was enough to make out the mirror he needed. He remembered the first time he had seen it, when Tharain and his little girl had gone through. The memory of his thoughts at that time now haunted his mind, how he was glad it wasn't him going through. Now it was. Taking a deep breath, he stepped through the doorway and marched down the hall. He could hear Urmond walking a little distance behind him, but did not turn to look at his King, only on the spot before the portal.

Standing before it he saw the slight shimmer in the reflective surface. His own image stared back at him, and he took in the clothes he wore, the bag on his back and his dark hair. They were his everyday clothes. A white linen shirt, with a hooded vest cloak over the top, his dark soft leggings which were tucked into his highly polished boots. In his bag were things he thought would be useful, his double-bladed knife, a spare set of clothes, and some food. Also tucked in with these belongings was something special. Venicones and Ide had both said their goodbyes in the house, and Ide had given him a token in case he could not make it back. On a cord of leather were two of Fleet's baby scales. She had found them in his room and worked hard to make something of them for him to take.

Now it was time to focus on leaving his home, his family and everything he knew, to head to a world no one had come back from for centuries. Muniath took in a deep breath.

"I'm ready," he said, instilling his words with confidence that was just teetering on the edge of cowardice.

"Good luck," Urmond replied.

With a curt nod Muniath stepped forward towards the mirror. He watched as his image grew before him and hesitated for a moment before taking the step up onto the frame to enter. He watched, fascinated as the toes in his boot disappeared into the silvery liquid. The surface stirred and waved with the action, like a pond on a still day. Another deep breath and this time he held it and clamped his eyes shut.

It was cool on his skin, like a gentle head wind was gusting, there was a slight resistance to the liquid as he pushed his way through it. Muniath opened an eye as he kept walking and then the other as he saw a myriad of lights, all colors of the rainbow dancing around him. They flashed and swirled, making him squint when they got too close and became too bright. Still, he walked on. The breath now burning his lungs he wondered how long it would take to break through to the other side. Then he was tumbling forward.

The ground beneath his face was dark and damp, it had a rich scent to it. The leaf litter that nearly covered it was unlike any leaves he had seen before, they were flat and wide, while some were like his homeland, long thin needles. Pushing himself up he gulped in the air to replace that which had rushed out of his lungs when he landed. Kneeling in this strange land he looked up at the treetops, so high above him. It was day here, the sun streamed through the gaps in the canopy and the sky was a deep blue. He became aware of the sounds next. The calls of unfamiliar birds he could not see in the heights above him. The wind rustled their branches and whistled around their trunks. It was cold.

Muniath got to his feet and spun around, taking in the area, trying to remember where he was. Everything seemed to look as if it had been burnt not long ago, a matter of months maybe. Taking off his bag he rummaged around inside and pulled out the double-bladed knife.

Tugging at one of the blades he pulled it out and stepped to the nearest tree. He carved a character into the charred bark and wood, an 'M'.

Moving back to the center where he had landed, Muniath quickly scraped away at the dirt with his boot, making an 'X' on the ground. He hoped that it would still be there when he needed to go back, along with Teagan, Tharain, and the dragon. When he finished his work, he stood still in the center. With his mind he pushed out like Urmond had instructed him the night before. He willed his thoughts to find the dragon. There were no doubts in his mind that if he found the dragon then he would find the girl and her father.

While he searched, the image of the little girl, Teagan swam into his mind. Her bright orange hair and the solemness of her eyes. She had only been in his company for such a short amount of time before being banished with her father, but her whole being had made an impression on him.

Shaking the image of the child from his mind he tried to make it work properly and focus on the dragon. The flash of vision that Fleet had impressed upon him seemed less like an invitation from the lost dragon, but more like a challenge. Standing in the forest he shivered and did not know if it was from the cold of his surroundings that was creeping under his clothing or the sense of the near human like qualities he had coming from the dragon. Clearing his throat and closing his eyes he concentrated again.

The thought and image tugged at his mind and he turned on the spot to find where it was coming from. Using it like a compass, to guide him where he needed to go. His foot moved, taking the first step in finding the dragon, Teagan, and Tharain. Opening his eyes, he followed the trail. His mind now skipped to his memories of the disgraced general. He remembered a man full of vigor and commanding presence. Everyone knew he had vices, but the shock which had run through the Company of Riders was enormous. That one of their own, the leader that they all looked up to, could be brought so low. It was humbling. The gambling and whoring dens business had declined a little after the incident and an investigation led by his father could turn up no sign of the men Tharain had been gambling with, but rumors were flying.

The underbrush through the trees became dense as he pushed his way through. There were delicate looking ferns, some which seemed to reach up to the sky, standing tall and shielding the ground with their widespread fronds. They were all jammed in together, their woolly looking trunks rough under his touch. Above him he could hear the flap of many birds, their calls all strange to his ears and he listened to them. Some resembled the birds of his world, a small cheeping sound, but others were musical and bell like.

Muniath walked what seemed like hours. Clambering up the sides of hills, steep and dark in the shadow of the dying sun, then slipping down the other side, leaving great swathes of cleared leaf litter in his wake. In the bottom of another valley he stood, a stream ran down the center of it, tripping over stones and leaving its own note to the music of this strange land. The sun was now well and truly dipping below the horizon, the temperature of the air was dropping rapidly around him, and the shadows were deepening. Finding a small clearing he stopped and bent to drink from the stream.

It tasted earthy and cool, and it slackened the thirst he had built up from the trip through the portal and walking. Shaking the remaining water from his hand he stood and looked around him.

"Seems like a good place to stop for the night," he said out loud, then chuckled as he realized there was nothing to hear him.

Using his foot, he scraped away the dead leaf litter on the ground at a flat spot and brought up rocks from beside the stream. He set them down in a circle then went in search of sticks and bits of old wood for the fire. With the job done he pulled out the flint from his backpack and started to strike, small sparks jumped as he used the back of his knife. One caught and very carefully he tended to it, blowing on it gently and waiting to see a flickering flame before feeding it more fuel. Gently he placed the now leaping flame into the pile on the ground, waiting for it to take hold. Soon a merry fire was dancing before him, radiating warmth.

Along with the small rocks for the fire, Muniath had also hauled over another, this was larger and flat on one side. He had placed it carefully by the fire and now sat on it. His stomach chose the moment he sat to send out its message that his body needed feeding as well. Muniath had no idea how long it would take him to find the dragon, and carefully unwrapped a food parcel from its wax cloth covering. Inside was cheese and in another was a small loaf of bread. Pulling out his knife again he made a slit in the bread and placed the cheese inside, then put it down on one of the stones to warm by the fire.

The sounds of the forest settling as the night descended was hushed and calm. In his home there would be the sounds of night creatures coming out to fill the void left by those that inhabited the day. Here was a different matter. There seemed to be no animals in this forest, only birds, and small flying insects. Above him the wind gently brushed the tops of the trees, sending them sighing and bending slightly, but it did not penetrate down onto the floor of the forest, for which he was grateful.

The meal was small, but it did satisfy, and warm food always had that effect on him. While he had fresh water, he drank from the stream instead of the flask. He pulled out his blanket and wrapped it around his shoulders, then banked the fire up. The light from the flames sent shadows to dance and flicker around the small clearing. The sound of the stream, along with the slight popping sounds coming from the fire began to lull him to sleep. His eyes became heavy as he sat by the fire, his hands clutched the blanket closer and his head nodded onto his chest.

As he slept, he thought he could see the forest from above. It was like he was on the back of a dragon; except he could not see the neck and head. Rising from the treetops was a column of blue smoke, which dissipated quickly with the wind and under the foliage he could make out something bright orange. Muniath circled again around the area, he could clearly hear the wing beats of a large dragon, but again could see nothing of the mount under him. He banked again and then the dragon called out. The cry was deep and rumbling. Then he woke.

Muniath's head came up with a start at the sound and looked around him. The fire had died somewhat and the light it emitted was dim in the deep darkness that surrounded him. He shivered and pulled the blanket tighter around himself.

"See you tomorrow," a deep voice spoke in his mind, just like Fleet had done.

Immediately he stood to his feet, the blanket forgotten and falling to the ground.

"Where are you?" he demanded out loud into the quiet of the forest.

"Tomorrow will be soon enough." Then it was gone.

The bird calls in the morning when Muniath woke were deafening. The fluttering of the wings was loud and sounded close to where he lay. Prying his gritty and still tired eyes open he looked up at the canopy above him. The sky had the steely look of just the beginning of dawn and there was a blanket of light grey clouds. The branches of the strange trees were moving, but not from any wind, instead, they were set to dancing by the number of birds that were hopping and making short flights from branch to branch. The air was cool under the branches and Muniath pulled the blanket up higher to his chin to guard against it, only to find that it was damp.

"It must've rained," he mused out loud.

Pushing down the rain sodden blanket, Muniath sat himself up and looked around him. Somewhere to his right he heard movement. It sounded like a large animal crashing through the underbrush. Immediately he jumped to his feet, tossing the blanket from him to give the freedom to move. Muniath tried to see through the trees and bushes, but they obscured his view too much. The noise was getting closer, he pushed out with the skill hoping that the commotion was being made by the dragon he was seeking. He touched the presence of him, but he was further away than the creature that was now heading his way.

Bursting out from a large bush, crashed a large creature that looked similar to the deer at home, only it had large branch-like horns sprouting from its head. The creature looked back at Muniath, seemingly just as surprised at seeing him in the clearing. It sniffed the air slightly and then moved slowly on delicate and spindly legs to the edge of the running water. Lowering its head, it drank quickly and then gracefully leapt the small stream, disappearing into the forest on the other side. It had made no challenge to him; made no noise and he had no name for the creature. For the first time since arriving in this foreign world, the vast strangeness of it made him aware of how utterly alone he was. A wave of sympathy washed over him for Tharain and his young daughter Teagan, and also for the dragon.

"Come!" a deep voice commanded, and Muniath recognized it as the dragon. With it came a strong compulsion to obey.

Turning back to where he had camped the previous night, he set about shaking out the damp blanket before stowing it into his pack. Checking the remains of his fire, he kicked at the long dead ashes to make sure it was truly out. Satisfied he left nothing behind, he shouldered the pack and set off in the direction of the urgent call. Once he was on his way, a happiness washed over him, and he tried to reason out why that was but could make no sense of it.

All day he pushed on, only stopping briefly when he judged it to be midday and the hunger pains were getting too sore. Muniath ate hastily and drank his fill from the stream he had found and then pressed on. He walked into the afternoon, hoping that he would find the dragon soon.

Teagan was still cursing the cost of the new battery for her car when she pulled up the drive to her home. The car was starting to cost her far more than it was worth she decided. Opening the door and pulling her bag with her, she stumped up the front path, trying to get the dried mud from her boots she had acquired from her trip into the Rimutaka Ranges to release an owl which had recovered from its injuries. That was the part of her job she enjoyed the most.

Reaching the door, she pulled the boots off and entered calling out as she did, "I'm home, Papa."

"How's your day?" her father called back.

"It was amazing, you remember that owl that we were treating?" Teagan asked as she walked down the hall.

"I do, how is it?" Tharain was in the kitchen cutting up vegetables, the knife in his hand a blur as he sliced some carrots.

"Really good, we released it today."

"That's brilliant," he grinned up at her.

"Did you manage to get the meat for Gremlin?" she asked, pouring herself a glass of water.

"I did, it's ready to go. There's still time for you to go feed him before dinner, but I don't know how long that lot will last him. He seems to have grown so much on your travels."

"He has. I think it was the hunting," she said before gulping down the water.

"I think we're going to have to find some other alternative to feed him, what I bring home is not going to be enough soon. I have never seen a dragon grow so quickly and the way you two communicate I'm sure is not normal. Do you ever get scared around him?" Tharain paused in his preparation of their meal to look at his daughter.

"No, I trust him. Gremlin would never hurt me."

"I wish I knew more about them; I must admit my own training was more about getting on the back of one and staying on. I loved and cared for Justice, and he seemed to understand what I wanted him to do, but there was not really a connection there."

"What type of dragon was he?" Teagan asked, happy that her father was now willing to talk about the creatures.

"He was a black. They're indigenous to the realm and are a mountainous dragon. Justice was large, with a big, barreled chest and a massive wingspan. He knew how to glide on the updrafts and didn't need to beat his wings very much to keep him aloft. Blacks don't have four legs like Gremlin does, they have two massive hind legs, with sharp claws. Their forelegs are part of their wings. They have claws attached to them and they use them to their advantage when clinging to the side of a mountain. They can also be deadly in a fight." Tharain had a far-away look in his eye as he spoke of his mount.

"Could he still be alive now?" Teagan waited for her father to come back to her.

"No, possibly not. The Black live only thirty years in the wild. In captivity it's a little longer and Justice was already in his twenties when we left. It was his offspring which brought us here." Tharain sniffed a little at the bad memory and carried on chopping.

From experience Teagan knew it was no good trying to get more information from her father after his last words. He would brood on that memory for a little while, and she hoped it would not lead to a bottle. When Gremlin and she had arrived home after their journey around the country she had gone looking in all his usual hiding places and was pleased to see they were all empty. Her only worry was that he had found another place to hide a stash of alcohol from her.

"I'll go feed Gremlin. Be back soon," she told him and wasn't sure he had heard her.

Out in the laundry room the pack was already loaded up and she could smell the meat inside. It had that not quite fresh, but not spoiled smell to it that she had learned to live with. Walking out the back she put on her boots for home and headed into the forest to the track. It led up the hill, along the ridge a little, and then down into the next small valley. The sun was already just about set over the hills opposite, and the air was getting chillier as autumn marched determinedly into winter.

Muniath could sense the creature was near, the immense power that had enveloped him from the call was getting heavier and heavier to bear. It urged him and pulled at his mind. At one point he found himself running to get to his destination quicker. He had to stop himself and take a few deep breaths. He pressed on again, pushing his way through the scrubby bushes, ignoring the branches as they swung back and hit him.

Reaching the top of a hill he managed to get a view of what lay ahead. Off in the distances, beyond the next hill was what looked like a town, a large town. The sun was setting, and it was directly in his eyes, making it hard for him to see properly. He looked up at the sky and saw the blue deepen. At some point during the day the cloud had either been burned off or moved away, leaving behind only the bright blue. His feet did not pause for long and soon he was heading down the steep slope of the hill, slipping and sliding as he went on wet, dead leaves. The speed of his descent soon quickened, and he tried to arrest it by reaching out for the spindly trees that grew there. They bent under the pressure and weight of him, and the bark cut at his hands.

Muniath suddenly burst out into a clearing at the bottom. It was wide and looked well trampled. He stopped dead in his tracks, his eyes taking it all in quickly. At one end sat a shelter of sorts, cobbled together with what looked like old bits of a building and deadfall from the forest. Inside was a collection of mud stained and rumpled blankets.

At the other end, coming through a large opening, was an enormous head, the sound of the body which followed was loud as it pushed through the bushes. It was a dragon. The most magnificent dragon Muniath had ever seen. The scales gleamed a deep glossy emerald green, the spikes that festooned his face were delicately curved around his head, only adding to the majestic way he held himself and moved. The green and silver eyes when they turned to Muniath were piercing and he had the urge to kneel before this creature.

"So, you have finally come," he spoke inside Muniath's mind. The voice was deep and rich and went perfectly with the dragon before him. The dragon moved closer to Muniath on large and deadly clawed feet. But unlike other dragons he had known, this one did not make a sound as it walked. *"Did I make a mistake in sending for you?"* he asked Muniath. *"My sister was under the impression that you could help me."*

Muniath shook his head a little. "No—I mean yes, I can help you. But I'm confused."

"I believe you are. All will be explained to you when Teagan arrives. You will stay here until she does, Muniath," the dragon commanded.

Muniath was surprised that he knew his name, but then everything was surprising to him about the situation he found himself in. "Have you been named?" Muniath asked.

"My true name is written in the heavens. But here in this world, which has no other like me, I have been called Gremlin."

"Gremlin?" The word seemed strange on his lips, and Muniath spoke it again to try it out.

"Are you a little slow?" Gremlin asked, trying to figure out if Muniath was a little touched in the head and not who he thought he was.

"No, it's a strange name, that is all."

"It is the name of an unseen creature that causes havoc and mischief," Gremlin made what sounded like a little chuckle deep in his throat, then paused a moment and lifted his head, looking to another path that Muniath had missed when he first entered the clearing. *"Behind me, and do not speak a word,"* Gremlin commanded as he moved his great bulk

around. Muniath had to jump out of the way of the massive tail and the sharp spikes that grew on the tip.

"Afternoon, Gremlin," a feminine voice called out from the other side of the hulking beast.

"Afternoon to you, Teagan," Gremlin said formally and bowed his head to the newcomer.

"How was your day?" Muniath heard her ask and the sound of something heavy being dropped to the ground.

"Surprising," Gremlin responded, then stepped to one side to reveal Muniath.

Muniath stood just as he had only moments before when he had first met Gremlin. Before him this time was a vision from his dreams. Her hair was pulled back tightly but was the same color as it was when he had first met her just after her ninth birthday, when Muniath was sixteen and just started his apprenticeship. She stood tall and lithe, and her large green eyes were wide at this newcomer's appearance. Her stance, which at first was relaxed, suddenly shifted to one of defense. He could see she had never been trained how to fight but had a natural instinct for it.

"Who are you?" she immediately demanded from him.

"Teagan," the command in Gremlin's voice caught her attention. *"There is no need to be concerned."*

"You know him? How?" she asked, still wary of the stranger.

"I have been aware of you both since even before the moment my egg was formed inside my mother. Not only you, but also one other who helped me get to this world," Gremlin told her. "Nothing I do is without reason. I called Muniath here."

Teagan turned her eyes to the stranger, and they narrowed slightly. "Muniath?" she repeated the name. In turn he nodded that it was his name. He could see her mind furiously working and the memory came back to her. "I know that name," she said very quietly.

"We met, before you and your father went through the portal. I sat with you outside in the palace garden. You had a puppy with you."

"Bili," she said, the memory still playing out in her mind.

"He's still alive. The King took him in to be his personal dog."

Teagan shook her head a little to dispel the memories that were flooding back from her nine-year-old self.

"But that still does not explain your presence here. Were you banished as well?"

"You are not listening, Teagan," Gremlin broke into their thoughts. "I called him."

"No, my Lord King sent me," corrected Muniath.

"Where do you think he got the idea. You are both needed. You two and one other are the only ones who I can communicate properly with. Though the other does not know it yet." Gremlin turned his large head to Teagan. "It's time to go home and set the Dragon Realm in order once more, Child of Dragons." Gremlin bowed his head to her, till it was almost touching the ground.

"I still don't understand, Gremlin—" Teagan stammered at his action.

"*After I have eaten I will explain it all,*" Gremlin said as he sniffed towards the bag she had brought with her.

Teagan bent to pick the bag back up and found another pair of hands there, lifting it out of hers. Their eyes met and she saw for the first time the silver glint that she had only seen in her own set. His were a deep brown, so soft and friendly looking and she remembered the wink he had given her in the Hall of Secrets. He had been so kind and gentle with her back then. Muniath gave her a little smile as he saw the last of the memory play in her eyes.

"Thank you," she said, quietly going a little red.

The blush spread over her cheeks and Muniath thought it made her look even more beautiful. Teagan tore her eyes away from him and began to open the pack as he held it. Reaching inside she pulled out the racks of bone and discarded flesh from the butchers her father worked for. Each piece she handed to Gremlin, who chomped and swallowed the whole bag full quickly. Teagan wiped her hands on her pants and then closed the bag once more, taking it from Muniath and placing it beside the track that headed for home.

Teagan had been aware of his eyes on her the whole time, and she experienced a little fluttering sensation, like small butterflies were beating their wings inside the pit of her stomach. Mark had looked at her in a similar way, but she had never experienced a similar reaction to it that she was now getting. It puzzled her a little.

"Now, you wish to know what is occurring, Teagan and Muniath. Come, sit, and I shall explain myself to you." Gremlin moved over to his bedding in the crude shelter and sat down. His front paws crossed over and his head erect, just missing the ceiling. Muniath and Teagan did as they were bid and sat down on the ground before the dragon. They waited patiently for Gremlin to begin speaking again. *"I believe, Muniath, that Urmond has told you what I am?"*

"He has, but we did not have time for him to explain it in detail," Muniath replied to the dragon's question.

"Then I shall start at the beginning for Teagan's sake." Gremlin settled himself in more, rustling his large green iridescent wings until he was comfortable.

"Dragons have been on many worlds for as long as there have been any. We were birthed from the great fires within those worlds, leaping forward from the very bowels of the planets through the volcanoes and the flowing lava. We have changed and adapted to our environments, becoming the many breeds that exist—or in some cases no longer exist. We ruled over the worlds and there was peace among us. But we did not count on the coming of humans. A council was called, a great meeting of Dragons. It was decided that we would send out some of our own in the shape of man to take charge of the war-like beings. Young dragons were molded by our magic and both of you, Urmond, and the other I spoke of, are the last of that kind, although there are some lesser mortals who possess a little of the skill as you call it. It is the diminishing of that blood that now makes the Dragon Realm in danger. Man was too greedy and wanted to dominate everything. It is their nature, and they cannot help it. There are some who wish to share and look after those that need it, but mainly it is only the fear of loss and the instinct of survival that burns inside the others.

"It is this instinct which now pushes some to take over that which they do not understand. Our old lore has been lost; the dragon ways have gone by the wayside to be replaced with those of man. The dragons do not breed as much as they once did, and they will die out if this threat succeeds. The Realm must be led by one of dragon blood that is almost pure. The magic that was used then has long since died out on all worlds." Gremlin looked between the pair of them.

"I am the last of the Great Dragons, my spirit is reborn when the Dragon Realm is threatened. The last of the Council's magic was used on me so that it might be so. I have come because of this new threat. It is the task laid before me to right this wrong, to make sure that we are not lost and not destroyed. A world without dragons will become like this one. Tearing itself apart with greed and malice."

"What must we do?" Muniath asked, the knowledge Gremlin had imparted was still sinking in.

"For the moment, we must go back to the Dragon Realm. It is imperative that the threat be banished."

"But there is no way back. The portal on this side was dismantled when the last dragon died on this world," Teagan said.

"And you hold the key Teagan, or rather you wear it," Gremlin told her gently.

"Wear it?"

"The pendant that King Urmond gave you just before you went through," Muniath spoke up. His eyes went to her throat, but the green shirt was buttoned high, and he could not see anything laying there.

Teagan's hand went immediately to her neck to reassure herself that the jewel was still there, hidden away. She looked between the dragon and the stranger she just remembered and then dipped her hand into her shirt and pulled it out. It gleamed in the last light that filtered down into the clearing, the emerald gem still bright and the silver dragons on either side seemed almost alive.

"You can't mean this?" Teagan looked down at the pendant swinging on the fine silver chain.

"I do indeed, Teagan," Gremlin informed her.

Dream

The small room felt like it was closing in and becoming too confining for Scetis. As he lay on the basic pallet bed with his hands behind his head, legs crossed at the ankles and staring up at the discolored stone ceiling, the walls seemed to be bowing in. A cell was an apt name for the room and that is what it had become since his return to The Convocation. He had been under strict orders by Tavae to not leave the little room he had not been in since his apprenticeship with the Regulator ended. The room was attached to Tavae's old set of rooms. Scetis could still smell the compounds of minerals, animal parts, and plants that had seemed so magical to him as a child. These same things were still considered magical out in the wider world, but they had long lost their mystery to him. The rooms which now lay empty were still the domain of Tavae. Even though he was now the Regulator, he was still expected to keep up his studies every now and then, or to check the findings of others. That was the purpose of these rooms now.

Tavae was concerned over the news that Scetis had brought to him. He had leaned back in the large chair behind his equally impressive desk and took on the familiar pose of pondering a problem. This reflective pose, for some reason, made the younger man calmer. The information was now shared and with a man he trusted. His once Master had ordered him into seclusion at once and had sent a message to Urmond the King in The Realm.

It was now several days later, and impatience was starting to grow inside him. He was not used to just sitting around with nothing to do and had even found himself cleaning the old rooms. On a couple of evenings Tavae had joined him, bringing him news. He had received a reply from Urmond asking that Scetis return to The Realm, promising not to hold him responsible for the theft and assuring his safety. Scetis had been dubious at this news but agreed to the terms. Tavae told him to stay put until he could organize a cleansing of the Hierarchy, but he did not go into detail about how he was going to go about it.

With eyelids drooping, Scetis began to doze as he contemplated all that had happened in the last few months. Then his mind turned to the one image he had been trying hard to ignore. Ide. She had invaded his dreams; in some they were so clear he could almost believe he was with her. Her eyes: the deep brown with the small silver flecks that seemed to sparkle when she had looked at him, the way his body responded to that look. When he woke from those dreams it always made him frustrated with a mix of being disturbed and disappointed that he could not be with her.

Now those thoughts were released. The sensations he did not want were pressing on him, making him acknowledge the desire he had for Ide. These were emotions he had never experienced before. His childhood had made him close off all display of eagerness, wanting, or desire. His experience at the cruel hands of others had made him who he was. He did not enjoy personal relationships; he had learned all he could from the masters he had, and only Tavae was in any way dear to him.

Ide. Scetis now remembered her long hair trailing down her back, as dark as her eyes and thick. He remembered how even though it was tied up high, the length nearly reached her buttocks. The hair contrasting against the white of her shirt, which when wet clung to her athletic frame and highlighted her tanned skin. The image of her sitting on the shore of the lake huddled in on herself, wet and shivering beside the fire he had built came to him. The soft brush of her lips on his as he kissed her.

The image changed. Ide was now dry. The surroundings had shifted. He now saw her sitting on a wall, looking out over another lake, the wind lifted her hair that was down and spilling over her shoulders in a dark curtain. There was a far-away look in her eye and a small smile played on her full lips. She stirred something in him, and his eyes flew open to stop it.

"Come!"

Scetis shook his head, certain that he was still half asleep. The word had boomed inside his mind and was commanding. The urge to get up right away and start heading towards that voice was very instinctive and he found himself sitting on the side of the bed. Again, he shook his head.

"Come!" it demanded again, louder, and more firmly.

Looking across the room his eyes came to rest on his knapsacks, hanging from a hook on the wall, along with a new leather cloak. This time he was on his feet and standing in the middle of the small room. The compulsion was real and for him slightly frightening. Never before had he reacted this way, always he had been in full control of his thoughts and actions. Each one carefully deliberated.

The door handle was in his hand and twisting wanting to be doing something else, before he could succumb to that demanding voice once more. He stalked out into the main room, with its tables and fireplaces. The shelves were all neat and dust free once more thanks to his work, and the labels on the jars were replaced with newly written ones and in some instances the contents replaced for fresher specimens. The light from the large window flooded the floor with sunlight, small dust motes danced in the beams and the room swam in his vision for a moment. The picture of a deep emerald, green dragon stood before him briefly, then it was gone. The beast had been large, much larger than a normal dragon and its green and silver eyes stared intently at Scetis.

Out in the corridor beyond those familiar rooms was the usual sedate quiet of the late afternoon. Most in the School of Apothecary were making use of the last of the warm autumn weather to be out in their gardens, preparing the ground for the winter crops. Scetis almost ran to the entrance of the hidden tunnel that would lead him to the Regulators office and made his way through the darkened passageway. He burst out into Tavae's bedchamber and stood looking around him for a moment. The door that led to his office was slightly ajar and he could hear voices coming from beyond.

"He must be dealt with soon then?" a woman's voice asked.

"Yes. Urmond will not wait long before he sends a beast and Rider to fetch him," Tavae replied.

"What did you promise the king to gain the assurances Urmond would not kill him?"

"That is none of your concern and will remain a secret for now. All will be revealed in due course, Etain," he said hastily.

At the revealing of who was with Tavae, Scetis relaxed a little. Etain had been his Trader Master and who had helped Tavae heal him of the poison Wradech had almost killed him with. Pulling the door open he quickly made sure no one else was around and stepped through the opening.

"What are you doing here?" Tavae demanded getting to his feet. "I told you to stay out of sight."

"I have to talk to you," panted Scetis, out of breath from his haste to get to his friend.

"What's happened?" Etain said seeing how pale he was. "Is it the poison?"

Scetis shook his head and swallowed deeply, trying to gain his breath. "No. Something else."

"When are you due your next elixir?" she asked, now coming to examine him.

"Not for another week or so," he fended her off gently. "I'm fine physically. Can I talk to you alone, Master?" Scetis asked Tavae.

"Yes, of course. Do you mind Etain if we take this up another time? How about this evening?"

"That would probably be wise, Tavae. Call me if there is anything I can do in the meantime." Etain then turned to Scetis. "You look after yourself, young man."

"I will, Master," he said, giving her a little bow and grateful that she was leaving.

Etain had been kind to him, but by the time he had entered the apprenticeship with her, he had learned to wall himself away from everyone. He had learned as fast and as quickly as he could about being a Trader and then went out on his own as soon as she had made him a Journeyman.

Once the door was shut on his old Trader Master, Scetis sank into the seat she had just vacated and the warmth that she had imparted to it. He rubbed a hand over his eyes and his heart started to calm.

"So, what is so wrong that made you race to my office, and burst into the room while I was with someone? Which could have been dangerous. You don't know who it could have been."

"I waited to be sure, when you said her name, I knew I would be safe."

"I am still waiting to hear what was so urgent," Tavae prompted him.

"A voice, not just a voice, but a command."

"That is not much to go on, Scetis, you're going to have to go into more detail. You have become sloppy since you took up being a Trader." Tavae returned to his seat behind the desk and sank into it. He leaned his elbows on the desk and placed his fingertips together.

"I was in my room, lying on the bed. Then a voice called out to me. At first, I thought I was dreaming, that I was half asleep and imagined it. I found myself sitting on the edge of the bed. Then it came again. A deep commanding voice. This time I was standing in the middle of the room looking at my bags."

"What did the voice say?" Tavae's eyebrows were knitted together with this news.

"It said '*Come!*' I found it difficult to resist the urge to pack my bags and go off."

"Describe the voice for me."

"Deep and resonating. Like it came from the depths. It was honeyed but firm and demanding."

"Was it spoken aloud in the room or in your head?" His eyes narrowed with the question and he pressed his fingers to his lips.

"I cannot be certain. I would like to believe—no I hope—it was out loud. But I fear that it was within my head." This thought did worry him, he had never heard of anyone communicating in such a way, and the ulterior explanation of himself going mad, he did not want to think about.

"The elixir you take each month, so little is known of side effects. This could be another symptom of that coming out. When did you take it last?"

"As I told Etain, I am not due a dose for another week."

"I'm not sure I like this new development. Is the voice talking to you now?"

"No, only those two times, before I ran here."

"Mmm, leave it with me. I'll study it for a while. It's a pity the notes that your apprentice made were lost to the water, I would've liked to have read them."

"You could always send for him, Tavae. I'm sure he would give you a first-hand account of what he witnessed. I found Loxa to have a quick mind and his recall of facts and information was even a match for me."

"Loxa has been sent home for a little while, and I've found him a new apprenticeship already. He'll start it when he gets back in two weeks. Are you sleeping?"

"It seems to be the only thing I can do at the moment. Are you sure I can't move around a bit more?"

"Yes. I'm not sure still of the extent of the plot. I need to prepare and find those that are in the thick of it. Go back to the rooms and use them to keep you busy. You said that your leather case had been damaged, and all the compounds lost. Set about replacing them and making up a new batch of elixir. I know you've already reorganized everything, are you missing any ingredients?"

"Everything I need is there, thank you." Scetis knew by the tone in his old master's voice that he was being dismissed and not to prolong the process.

"It will not be long now and then you can move around more. Then it will be time for you to go to Urmond and answer his questions, though I do not know what you could tell him of it that has not already been conveyed to him in my letters." Tavae shook his head and came around the desk to stand in front of Scetis. "Don't worry about it, Scetis. I'm hoping this time next month our houses will be cleaned, and the plot destroyed."

Scetis response was automatic and due to his training. "Yes, Master." He nodded his head.

Tavae released his shoulder and went back behind his desk. "Go back to your room and stay there. Do as I suggested, the time when you will need a new supply of elixir will be soon. Concentrate on that."

"But what about the voice?"

"A figment of your imagination, or dream, nothing more. You know the compound for a peaceful sleep, make some of that as well."

Scetis hesitated to leave after the dismissal from Tavae. He wanted to say something more, how the voice had seemed so real, but something was holding him back.

"Was there something else?" Tavae adjusted his red robes of office as he sat back down.

"No, Master, there was nothing else. Thank you for your assessment and wise words." Scetis bowed shallowly to Tavae and then headed back into the bedchamber.

"Make sure you close both doors behind you firmly, Scetis," Tavae called out and the younger man did as he was told.

Once he was back in the familiar rooms, he looked around the shelves. Soon a collection of jars with an assortment of contents sat on the long and stained bench, grouped together to make the different compounds he lost. Scetis started with the easiest to make, the sleeping potion. The work was automatic and kept his mind busy as he made sure that the correct measurements were made. Most of the potions and powders he made from memory, but the more dangerous he made sure to find the correct directions in the books that lined one wall. The most difficult of all was the elixir that kept him alive.

The distilled salamander venom was kept in a glass jar, but the lid was sealed with lead. Pulling on a pair of thick leather gloves and using a pair of pliers, Scetis set about prying off the seal. It came away in a long strip, which he placed in a waiting metal bowl to be melted and used once more. Before he opened the lid, he tied a cloth over his mouth and nose, then pulled the gloves back on again. Taking up the jar, he held it out before him, as far away from his body as possible. With a quick twist the lid came off the top, placing it down on the workbench.

He then took up a measuring spoon, the smallest in the collection. He dipped it in, capturing the slimy green liquid within and then carefully poured it into a large vile, big enough to hold enough elixir for four months. It clung to the sides of the small bottle and the spoon, which he then dropped into another waiting bowl, already filled with the counteracting liquid for the poisonous venom.

Carefully he placed the lid back on the jar and carried it over to where the lead would be melted, and the jar dipped into it. Back at the workbench, he added the other prepared items one at a time in the correct order. Placing the stopper into the vile he shook it in his gloved hand until the green tinged liquid turned red. Taking up the prewritten label, he coated the back of it with a brush dipped in glue and then placed it neatly and squarely on the vile along with the other medicines, but slightly apart.

Scetis' clean-up was thorough and stringent. Each surface he had used was scrubbed and then rescrubbed again, the smell of the harsh cleaner filled the air, and he opened the windows to air the room out. The leather case he had used since coming out of his apprenticeship had been ruined with the immersion in the water. The vials would have to remain where they sat until he could make a new one. Then his eyes fell on a curiosity.

It was a book, leather bound with gold lettering on the outside of the spine, just like any other book on the shelves. But he remembered the day Tavae had shown him his latest curiosity. The thick book was not what it seemed. He pulled it from the shelf and laid it on the bench. Gently, he undid the metal clasps holding the leather straps closed, and they sprung free, as if they had just been attached. Scetis opened the cover to find paper leaf pages sitting there, bound and attached to the outer leather casing. Moving these pages, he came to what he knew lay hidden inside. Leather clad little compartment drawers with tiny bead handles. There were eleven of these compartments surrounding a larger one in the middle, made especially for a bottle, with a leather cord to keep it in place. The whole interior was wooden and highly varnished, gold leaf delicately decorated each individual drawer and the surroundings. He had admired the workmanship it had taken to make this object when he was younger, and now he admired it once more. It was just what he needed.

Picking it up he took it over to the collection of compounds, potions, and powders. Standing it on its end up right, he started to pack the small drawers with his evenings work. The final potion to go in was the elixir. He placed this into the empty slot and made sure the cord was securely tied to keep it in place and safe from breakage. Closing the cover, he snapped the clasps back into place and then looked at the book. With care he carried the book over to the small room he was once more using as a bedroom, and to the two bags he liked to use on his travels. Scetis slipped it into one bag and flicked the flap back to cover it.

The hour was very late, but Scetis had not realized he had worked so long. The mixing and making of these medicines calmed him. But now the hunger pains began to bite deeply. His stomach grumbled and it groaned loudly with the lack of food. Since his return, he would slip out and use the tunnels to go to the kitchens to filch a meal. The way was as well-known to him as any other tunnel in the bored-out mountain the Convocation sat on. Yet, most of the Physicians, Apothecaries, and Traders had no idea that these were here, that only a few steps away the slaves were busy going from one place to another, doing their bidding. Scetis was happy about that.

The door to the kitchen was just ahead, he could see the light coming from a gap at the bottom, spilling out over the well-used floor. From beyond there was noise, the bakers now hard at work once the cooks had finished. The smell of the rising dough came to him along with the memories he associated with it. He placed his hands on the wooden surface and pushed. It swung open on well-oiled hinges without a sound, and he looked inside the warm room. No matter what the weather outside, the inside of the kitchens were always sweltering hot from the many ovens and open fire spits. Scattered on the other side of the large, cavernous room, busy making the bread and other delicate cakes for the next day, were an assortment of men and women, also some children in various stages of their own apprenticeships.

This group had grown used to his wandering during the night. Some smiled and waved, but most ignored him and let him get on with what he needed to do. Scetis sliced off slabs of meat from a haunch that had been taken off the roasting spit and placed it on a plate. The pattering of running feet from behind him made Scetis turn, coming towards him was a child with bread that was left over from the day.

"My mistress warmed it through for you, sir," the girl said with a smile.

"Give her my thanks then, little one," he gave her a half smile and produced a coin from his pocket. He held it out to her.

The girl took the coin in a floured covered hand and grinned up at him. "Thank you, sir." She bobbed her head and then turned, running back to her Mistress.

With a full stomach and an evening's work behind him, Scetis was tired. He lay on his bed, the blankets pulled up only partially covering his bare chest, his eyes closed and his breathing even. Sleep was slowly taking him, and he fell into it gratefully. The dreams he had that night were mixed, never before had he had dreams which were so vivid. In one he was flying high above a forest. Curiously only one moon was high in the sky, full and bloated against a backdrop of stars. The wind blew on his face as he sped along, the sensation of being totally free and alive, was one that he had never experienced before, and he cried out with the pure joy that spilled out from inside.

The cry that escaped his lips was not his own voice. It was a resonant rumbling roar that filled the sky, it burned down deep inside his own chest. It was like a fire was welling up, so intense and he had the urge to set it free.

"*No, not for you,*" the voice spoke to him in his mind.

"Why not?" he asked.

The voice chuckled deeply at his question. "You're not built the right way, Scetis."

Somehow, he was pushed out of the dream and the disappointment at finding himself back on solid ground overwhelmed him. Looking around he found himself by a lake, it shimmered in the night, both moons were now present, showing just small slivers of themselves and glowing green and blue in the inky blackness above him. The sound of something hitting the water and splashing caught his attention and he turned to where the sound had come from.

Standing right on the edge where the bank met the mountain lake was a figure, he recognized in the dim light. Her hair was down and blowing in the gentle breeze, she wore a tight-fitting coat, synched at the waist and flaring out in an asymmetrical skirt over a tight pair of breeches tucked into highly polished boots. Her arms were wrapped around herself and he remembered the same stance from their trip down the river.

Another sound made her turn from him. The sound of hard soled boots clipped along towards them. Scetis watched as a cloaked figure approached. In his hand he held a torch, flickering flames sending eerie light over his features and Scetis gasped. For a moment the man who was so determinedly marching towards Ide looked like Wradech Foghladh, Tavae's old apprentice and Scetis' tormentor. But the face was not quite right, the nose was longer and broader, the chin slightly wider.

"Orcades, what are you doing here?" Ide greeted him.

"Ide is that anyway to greet your beloved?" he grinned at and wrapped an arm around her waist and pulled her to him.

Scetis watched, his anger growing as the man placed his lips on hers. The lips he had kissed and now wanted only for his own. He moved to approach and grab the man, to pull him away from Ide and keep her safe from him.

"*No. Wait,*" the voice commanded again.

"But…" he started.

"*Wait!*" The command was reinforced this time and Scetis found he could not move.

Repeatedly he tried to scream at her, but no sound escaped his throat. He had to watch as Orcades held Ide.

"Enough, Orcades," Ide said, trying to keep her tone light.

"It is a romantic sort of night, how about a dip?" he asked suggestively.

"It's too cold and late in the season for that." Ide managed to extract his arm from around her.

"Then we shall walk back to the house and have a drink. Are your parents at home?"

They started to walk away from Scetis, and he found he could follow, but get no closer to them.

"They are, and they will be pleased to see you. When did you get back? I thought you were meant to be away for a few months more?"

"I was, but my uncle agreed to let me come home early. Are your brothers at home or are they on duty? Only, I had heard that Muniath has not been seen for a week. Has he gone on another bender?" He placed his arm around her shoulders and moved the torch as far from her as possible.

"No, I believe that he was sent on a mission by the King."

"Where?"

"I don't know, Orcades. Have you heard my news?"

"What news?"

"I have gained a promotion. I made Second Captain; we're equals now."

"Not for long," he smiled down at her. "Once we are wed, I plan to get you with child as soon as I can, lots of them."

"There's no hurry is there?" The concern in her voice was great.

"Why not, my cousin is in no hurry to marry and produce an heir for the throne, she is too enamored of the beasts to give any real thought to her obligations to the crown. That then leaves me and any children we have. I've been thinking, there is nothing really we have to wait for, so why don't we move the wedding up; make it as soon as possible."

Ide hesitated a moment before she answered. "I would rather wait until all my family are back from their missions. Please, Orcades, you can't expect me to leave them out of our day, all three of us are close."

"No, of course not. We'll wait until both Venicones and Muniath can be here."

Their steps brought them to the stairs that led up to a large house, which loomed over gardens and walls. Lights flickered in the windows and somewhere music was playing.

"You can go no further and can hear no more. You must come to me. You must find me, Scetis. It is important that Orcades and his cousin's plot fails. It is important that Ide and he never have children. Come to me, Scetis," the voice echoed through his mind as he found himself in blackness.

Scetis sat on the edge of the bed and ran his hands over his face and head, trying to dispel the voice that had called to him. It was still there; the command was so sure and steadfast now in his mind. Quickly he pulled on a few items of clothing and his boots, then slipped out of his room and made his way to the corridor. On sure feet he found his way to the main shared garden for the Apothecaries, it was supposed to be used for contemplation and discussion, but hardly anyone went there. It was now more a monument to the army of gardeners who kept up the hedges and flower beds.

Stepping off the path he walked into the center of the carefully clipped lawn. The lush green grass was washed out and almost grey under the small curve of the blue moon high above, the green had already dipped below the horizon. Scetis took in a deep breath, the breeze was coming straight off the lake and the view was perfectly framed by two large trees which sat in opposite corners of the walled garden. Their branches reached high into the air, the leaves now turning as the autumn season took hold. Out beyond the wall, the water of the large lake reflected the moon and the many stars that were shining in the cloudless sky.

With a heart that was still hammering in his chest at the sight of Ide in the arms of Orcades, Scetis breathed deeply trying to get the emotions once more under control and button them up, to bury them deep inside. He could not afford to lose his head and let them get the better of him. That way only led to pain.

Walking around the grounds he did not notice the cool air that was chilling his skin, nor the dew that was starting to settle on the greenery and grass underfoot. By the time he had made the third circuit his heart was back to normal and he could think calmly. This voice that had invaded his dreams—he decided—was just that, a dream. He put it down to the combined effects of some of the ingredients he had been working with earlier.

"There you are," a whispered feminine voice called out urgently behind Scetis.

Turning quickly to face the intruder into his silence he saw Etain moving towards him. She looked worried and was moving quickly, her haste immediately had him concerned.

"Etain?" He took a step towards her.

"Scetis, you have to leave, tonight," she said breathlessly to him covering the distance between them. "You are in grave danger."

"What are you talking about?"

Etain grasped his arms and held on tightly. "You have to leave, Wradech has discovered you are back in The Convocation. He is organizing his men to find you even now. You must leave."

"How did he find out?" Scetis grabbed at her wrist as his old master turned to leave.

"There is no time to explain," she said trying to pull her wrist free.

"There is always time, Etain. You taught me that, now how did he find out?" he demanded again holding onto her firmly.

"Someone from the kitchens told him. He came bursting into Tavae's office while I was there and demanded that Tavae tell him where you are. But he would never give you away, now can we stop this and get your things so you can escape." Etain finally managed to free herself and then made for the building. She stopped when she realized he was not following. "Now! Scetis, you don't have much time."

Scetis raced after her and they entered Tavae's old rooms together. While Scetis bundled clothes and blankets into his travel bags, Etain gathered some things in the work room. In a drawer she found an old and battered leather case. Inside it she placed various herbs and powders, things she thought he could use. She knew his talents and that he could find most things he needed along the way but thought to give him enough to treat the minor injuries or ailments he might come across.

As he exited his small cell, she pressed the leather case into his hands. "It might come in handy," she said breathlessly.

"I don't need it; I've already resupplied my own case. Etain, you saved me once, now only to save me again. I don't know how I can ever thank you," he said as he pushed the case back to her.

"Just stay alive, until this whole mess is worked out." Etain followed him out of the rooms and down the corridor.

Scetis stopped at the tapestry that covered the secret tunnel entrance, he pulled her into an embrace, it was something he had never done before. The feeling seemed natural, and normal. Tavae had become the father he had needed and, in some ways, Etain the mother figure. She hugged him back.

"Do you know where you will go?" she asked, pulling away from him.

"No, I don't. I'll find somewhere and hide out."

"There is a place in the mountains which borders The Realm. It's my mother's house, go there. Travel to Ima Drakoni, the house is on the other side of the village and you can't miss it, it's large. When you get there ask for Nora Óhaodha and tell her who sent you, she will take you in until everything is sorted."

"Thank you, Etain," he said once more, before lifting the tapestry and heading into the dark tunnel.

Moving on silent feet, Scetis held his bags close to him so they did not make any sounds. He tried to keep his breathing even and shallow, while listening for footsteps in the darkness. Lights shone dimly from some of the more well used tunnels, and he avoided these as much as possible, all the while making his way down into the bowels of the hill.

As he descended the air became stale and had that fetid smell of bodies living in close and not too hygienic quarters. It was mixed with the less desirable smells of jobs that were kept well away from those that lived higher up in the social ladder. Scetis would always remember those smells, they would stay with him forever. He skirted around the outside of the main slave quarters, keeping to the darker spaces. As a child he had explored every inch of this level and knew it by heart.

The last opening was the one he was looking for. He could see it in the dim light, could see the deeper darkness that would swallow him up and help him escape the island that was his home. But he could not reach it. Two guards came from another tunnel behind him, their torches throwing bobbing light into the gloom and illuminating the shadows. Scetis pushed his way back up the tunnel he had come from and hoped they would not be too picky in their search of the slave caverns. He watched as the light came closer to the opening, he could hear their feet and their mumbled voices.

"This is bloody useless," one said to the other.

"We're being paid to find him and that is what we will do," the second man said in a more authoritative voice.

"We should just take the money and leave," the first whined.

So Wradech and Orcades had hired mercenaries. This news surprised Scetis and adjusted his thinking about the road ahead of him. He was going to have to be cautious as he made his way to the mountains.

"And have the Captain on our tail, I don't think so. You're just too bloody lazy, that's your trouble. All good when things are quiet and you can play your dice games, but as soon as we get hired, it's nothing but moan and bloody groan."

"Your nose is too far up the Captain's ass. *'Yes sir, no sir, anything you say sir,'*" the first sang in a high voice.

"And look where it's got me, third in line. Now shut up and get looking," the second said as they reached the entrance to the tunnel Scetis was hiding in. "You go down this one, I'll take the next and meet you back here."

Scetis saw the light from the torches split, as one moved on while the other hesitated at the entrance to the tunnel. He backed up, trying to keep to the darkness, but it was not needed. The guard entered the tunnel and leaned against the wall. He dipped a hand into a pocket and pulled out a small cloth drawstring bag. Fumbling and trying not to drop his torch he managed to get it open and began to pull out small leaves from the pouch. Scetis recognized them immediately, it was Actaea Racemosa in its raw form. The guard slipped two of the leaves into his mouth and began to chew them. The man was an addict.

"Cind!" the second guard called out some time later. "You finished?"

"Yeah, like all the bloody rest, nothing here," Cind grumbled as he pushed himself off the wall and back to the entrance.

"Did you check it properly?"

"Of course, I did," Cind grumbled, and the pair moved further back.

Scetis let out the breath he was holding. He moved to the entrance and stole a look as to where the two guards were. They were heading back up the corridor, the torches flickering as they went sending shadows to dance around them. He crept out and ran on quiet feet to the tunnel he wanted and raced down the slipway.

The steeper the tunnel grew, the damper it became. Underfoot was slippery and wet with a thickening layer of moss and slime. Scetis' feet slipped on the surface and he slowed down, grabbing onto the rough-hewn wall beside him for balance. Somewhere up ahead he could hear water gently lapping and the gentle bump of a wooden boat tied to a pier. Carefully he made his way forward until he came to the edge of the water. Soft light crept in from somewhere further along and he spied the little narrow boat, that would seat one comfortably and two at a pinch. It was nodding away on the small waves and bumped slight against the wooden pier it was tied up to.

Scetis trod on the first few boards of the little jetty, the wood creaked loudly under his weight, but it held. It was ancient, already old when he was just a boy. Others had told him it was originally used by those not wanting to be seen coming and going to The Convocation. He had used it occasionally himself after he became a Trader.

Grabbing the rope that held the boat fast to the mooring he felt the knot he had tied himself months ago. It was damp and had swollen, making it difficult to untie, but it soon fell way into his hands. Gripping the side of the boat he tossed the rope in and carefully climbed into it, then waited for the rocking to stop. He hated boats.

Scetis pushed the boat away from the pier and took up the paddle and he dipped the edge into the water and pulled on it. He waited a few seconds feeling the boat move slowly forward as he headed to the entrance which was hidden by a turn in the tunnel. The stench of the littered water which washed in through the entrance clawed at his nose, his answer to it was to pull the shirt up to cover most of the stench and breathe shallowly. He pushed the paddle into the water again and pulled on it with greater force, wanting to gain the fresh open air. The boat lurched forward towards a mass of foliage, thick ropy vines which were covered in large, flat green leaves. The tip of the boat pushed into the vines, parting them like a curtain, and he had to use one arm to help maneuver through them.

Scetis could see the other side and gripped one of the vines to halt the boat. He used it to swing sideways and thrust his head through the last layer. Fresher air washed over him, and he breathed deeply as he took in his surroundings. The world outside was dark, the light from the fortress and surrounding tiers illuminated the greenish water for some way out. The building above him was lit up and music spilled out of its many windows, along with the laughter and talk of the people inside. Another rich person doing whatever they wanted and ignoring the advice of the Physicians they had come to see and knowing the type of party that was going on, the Physician was probably in attendance.

No one would even take any notice of a small one-man boat floating on the water far beneath them. It would just be another worker or slave on an errand for someone else. He placed a hand on the handle of the paddle, the other on the shaft. Pushing it deep into the water he pulled against it, his muscles bunching under the pressure and he left the protection of the vines. He pulled the paddle out and moved it to the other side, repeating the action over and over, never looking back at the hill that had been overtaken by man and buildings.

Scetis soon was out of the reach of the light and the noise of the party had long since fallen away. The darkness of the night overtook him, and he blindly paddled through the even murkier water to the shore that he was sure was there. He paused a moment, resting the paddle on the side of the boat, and looked up at the sky. The stars were still out as was the sliver of the blue moon, now hovering just kissing the mountainous horizon that was his destination. The opposite way the sky was slightly brighter as the sun was making its way into the new day.

Instruction

The darkness had never really ever bothered Teagan, even in the blackest of rooms she had always been able to see details, outlines of objects; just enough to be able to navigate around obstacles. On the way home from the clearing, it was like that, she was sure footed, having taken the path many times helped her. Behind her, Muniath was not doing so well. He tripped and stumbled on the roots that protruded across the path, and she could hear the mumbled curses under his breath.

It had been a shock when she had seen him. It was like a ghost rising up from the past, she recognized him, but didn't at the same time. Teagan now remembered him fully from that final day in The Realm. He had been kind, gentle even, and she also remembered the wink and smile he had given her just before going through the portal with her father.

"The path turns here," Teagan called out to Muniath.

"It would be fine if I knew where 'here' was," he complained.

Teagan walked towards him, the glow from his body heat was a bright yellow, making it very easy to find him. Taking his hand in hers, she raised it up and placed it on her shoulder.

"Follow me and don't let go. We are not far from home now," she told him.

"How can you see in the darkness?" he asked as they moved on down the track.

"I have always been able to see in the dark." Teagan made sure she did not walk too fast, so that he had time to collect himself if his foot caught on a raised stone.

"Gremlin called you the Child of Dragons. It could have something to do with that," he said.

The touch on her shoulder tightened a moment as Muniath found a lower spot on the path. His words seemed more to have something to say than really trying to find answers she thought.

"I don't know, and until Gremlin tells us more, I can't tell you," she replied.

Again, the pressure increased on her shoulder, only this time he did stumble. With reflexes that were quick, Teagan turned and caught him before he could fall. Her arms wrapped around his chest, his hands clasped her shoulders, the weight of him almost bringing her to her knees. Pushing up she got Muniath back standing up, but he did not let her go. Under her touch she felt his muscles through his shirt, could smell him, her breath quickened for a moment until she shook her head and pulled away from him. One hand still resting on her shoulder.

"Only a little further," she said swallowing hard and her heart racing, almost trying to escape the confines of her ribs.

The pair did not talk for the rest of the hike back to the house. They moved through the last of the forest and Muniath's hand slipped from her shoulder as the light from the house illuminated the surroundings.

"My thanks for helping me," he spoke quietly, now moving to stand beside her.

"You're welcome. It's not much but it's home," she said as she moved to the back gate and pushed it open. The protest from the rusty hinges called out into the night and she made sure she shut it behind them.

Opening the back door, she could smell the food her father had been cooking. Her stomach growled loudly at it and she moved into the kitchen. "I'm back," she called out.

"It's in the oven. What took you so long tonight, did you go flying?" Tharain asked as he came from his bedroom. He saw the stranger standing behind his daughter and stopped.

"General Loinsigh, it is good to see you again," Muniath greeted him.

"General?" Tharain shook his head at this. "Who are you?"

"Papa, this is Muniath."

"I am Aideen and Galanan Magaoidh's son. I was just an apprentice when you were exiled." Muniath moved from behind Teagan and held his hand out to the older man.

Tharain's eyes narrowed slightly, and he stared at the offered hand. "What are you doing here?" he demanded.

"King Urmond sent me."

"Sent or exiled? Don't lie to me boy, if you are here it's more likely that you were exiled. What crime did you commit?"

"No crime, sir. I'm telling only the truth, our King sent me to find yourself, your daughter, and the dragon."

"He knows about the dragon? How?"

"The eggs were stolen; one was recovered, and the other was seen being thrown through the portal into this world. I wanted to come immediately to retrieve it, but he would not let me. Now there is a threat to The Realm, and he wants you all back."

"He threw me out of his Realm. What makes you think I would want to go back?"

"Papa, please. How many nights have you spoken of one day going home?" Teagan interjected between the two men.

"When I was drunk and weak, and I would remember all we had lost." He turned his eyes to her.

"Now we have the chance."

"You want to go? Your life is here, your work which is so important to you, friends…"

"What friends? You know I have not had anyone I could call a close friend. Acquaintances, maybe, but not friends. My work, so I found out today, was just an extension of the skill. A way of me channeling that part of me into something constructive. Papa, please listen to Muniath."

"Has he seen Gremlin?"

"I have. It was Gremlin who guided me."

"What was your apprenticeship?" Tharain demanded.

"I am now Dragon Master."

Tharain stepped back from the two people before him and went and sat heavily in his chair. He looked up at Muniath and could see his father, his old friend, in his stance and features.

"How is Arcois? He must have retired then, if you're Dragon Master."

"I am sorry to tell you that Arcois has passed," Muniath informed him. Teagan watched as a deep sadness crossed over his face for a moment.

"I am sorry to hear that; he was a good friend." Tharain passed a hand over his face. "Sit. Are you hungry?"

"I am," Muniath answered, realizing it had been several hours since he had eaten last.

"Teagan get our guest something would you," Tharain asked, his daughter still staring at Muniath.

"Yes Papa." She turned and went to the kitchen, keeping an ear out on the conversation in the lounge.

"So, Gremlin talks to you as well?" Tharain asked Muniath.

"At first it was more commands," he responded.

"Then tell me what is going on?" Tharain demanded, a little of his old authority seeped into his voice.

"King Urmond sent me. There is a threat to the throne. He has asked me to bring back both Teagan and you, as well as Gremlin."

"How? There is no portal."

"I have the key, apparently," Teagan said, pulling a plate of food out of the oven. She picked up a knife and fork and brought them out to Muniath.

Taking them from her, Muniath smiled his thanks and began to eat with enthusiasm.

"What key?" Tharain asked, as he noticed how his daughter was looking at this newcomer, and he was returning that look.

Teagan dipped her hand into the front of her shirt and pulled out the pendant. "Do you remember when I was given this?"

"Yes, I do, and who gave it to you. It's the reason why I have never let you sell it when we were down." He flicked his eyes at Muniath, who did not seem to notice.

"According to Muniath and Gremlin," Teagan resumed quickly to hide any embarrassment her father had felt. "It's a key of sorts. It will open a temporary portal to take us home."

"What is the threat Muniath?" asked Tharain, shaking his head.

"There is a part of the Hierarchy of The Convocation of Mystical Medicine which wants the throne of our Realm and the lands. From what I understand, they wish to dispose of Urmond and replace him with his nephew Orcades. But there is a problem. Not only will it bring total devastation to the Realm, but it threatens all worlds. The Realm, or as it should be called, The Dragon Realm, is the seat of power. This skill that I, and Teagan, have is diminishing because the original rulers were not human. Dragons formed some of their young to be in our image, they thought that it would help in dealing with them. If a person who does not have Dragon Blood in them takes the throne, then the dragons will die out and the world will become like this one."

Tharain sat back in his chair. His eyes flicked from Teagan who was now sitting beside Muniath and the son of his former friend. This world he had found himself in was ripping itself apart, disease was rampant, as was the greed in people's hearts. The weather patterns were changing and becoming dangerous, and wars were ravaging cultures and races.

Teagan watched her father. She could see his mind working and waited for him to come to the same conclusion as herself. They had to go back to the land of their birth. They had to help those that had once cared and loved them.

"Gremlin is no ordinary dragon, is he?" Tharain finally said after some moments of silence.

"I don't believe he is. When the Dragon Realm is threatened a special dragon is born, a King of Dragons. He is that dragon."

"I knew he was different. I've never seen a dragon with a silver pupil. It's unnerving sometimes the way he looks at me, as if he can see into my soul." He looked intently at Muniath. "Did our King tell you how to use this key?"

"He has." Muniath placed the last forkful of food into his mouth and began to chew.

"And what of me? Will I be beheaded as soon as I step foot back in that world?" Tharain asked quietly.

"No Papa," Teagan broke in.

"The King has given his word that you will not. But you will not have the status you once had," Muniath informed the old General.

"Urmond is a man of his word. But to hope that things will be fine when we get there is just too much. I won't be going." Tharain shook his head.

"Papa, you have to, I won't leave you here."

"Teagan, there is too much pain and shame there, I will never be acknowledged by those that I once called friends, I would be shunned and alone."

"You won't be alone, Papa, I'll be there," Teagan cried and launched herself across the room to kneel by her father's chair.

"I'm sure my mother and father will not do that, nor Taran. Sir, there are people who still remember you fondly and still count you as a friend. I believe Urmond is one of those men." Muniath sat forward, placing the empty plate on the seat beside him. "You will be in no way friendless."

"Let me think on it." His eyes were distant and pinched with thought.

"It'll be alright, Papa," Teagan said as she stood, giving her father's hand a slight squeeze of comfort and support. After gaining no further response from her father on the matter, she turned to Muniath, "The only bed we can offer you is the couch you are sitting on; I am afraid it is not very comfortable."

"It's better than the bed I had last night." Muniath picked up the plate and took it to the kitchen.

"Blankets are in the hall cupboard, Teagan. Make sure our guest has everything he needs for the night. I will bid you goodnight sir, I need a night's rest to think on things." Tharain bade him. He kissed his daughter on the cheek and then left the pair looking after him as he headed to his bedroom.

"Would you like a drink? A tea or coffee?" Teagan asked automatically.

As Muniath came back around the bench he was looking to where Tharain had disappeared. "I take it he did not handle the transition to this world well?"

"That's an understatement," Teagan whispered her reply with a wry smile, and she passed him to enter the kitchen to put the kettle on. She moved around making a cup of tea for them each and brought it back out.

"Thank you," he said as he took the cup from her. "So how did you adjust?"

"With great difficulty on my father's part. This world is so different from The Realm. There may be no dragons, but there are other things that will kill you just as effectively."

"Other beasts?"

"No, man-made things. They don't go about on dragons or horses here; they have developed a vehicle that you can maneuver to take you from place to place. It is called a car. I'll show you tomorrow." Teagan was about to take a sip and stopped. "Tomorrow. I can't go to work tomorrow." Quickly she placed down the cup and pulled out her phone, dialed and left a message for Eric before tucking it back away.

"What's that?" Muniath asked curiously.

"You have much to learn young padawan," Teagan smiled as she quoted one of her favorite movies.

"I don't understand." He shook his head.

"Tomorrow morning we'll go through all the marvels of this world, I promise." Teagan sighed and sipped her tea.

"You have obviously adjusted." Muniath sat back and rested an ankle on the opposite knee.

"I did. I think children are more resilient than adults to change. Papa made it quite clear when we first arrived that I should forget our old life, and reprimanded me when I would bring things up, like dragons."

"He hit you?"

"Papa has never hit me, and he never would."

"But he found it difficult to adjust."

"He soon learned about the many forms of alcohol here. He drank quite a bit to forget, but how could he with me here?"

"You looked after him?"

"As best as I could, while trying to figure everything out. We started in a small farming community, they all thought we were odd and kept asking where we had come from. Then someone asked if we had been in some sort of cult and broken free. Papa clung to that idea to explain away our unfamiliarity with the technology we were faced with and how things worked. I did get one kind woman ask if my father had taken me from my mother, but I explained to her that mother had died when I was five, and she accepted that. Though I could never be sure if she believed me."

"So how did you end up here, with a dragon in the hills behind you?"

"We moved a lot; Papa couldn't hold a job for long. Sometimes he would quit drinking and things would be fine, but then I would come home from school and find him passed out, with an empty bottle beside him. I got after school jobs to help out, and we managed. I worked myself through university and started working for the Department of Conservation. It was on one of our inspections of a forest that I found Gremlin, and I brought him home. Papa has not had a drink since. He found himself another job and has been steady with it. I believe Gremlin has helped him. It was a blessing the day I found him."

"He is much larger than the normal dragon."

"Gremlin is a lot more of everything than a normal dragon is, I believe, from what Papa has told me."

"His brother and sister are still juveniles, while he is fully grown."

"And they are in your care. That is what a Dragon Master does, isn't it?"

"Yes, it is my job to care and train the young dragons, and then make sure they are cared for by their Riders. Also, the mating and cross breeding."

"But they are in the decline?"

"Not as many eggs have been laid in the last few years, which has me worried."

"Tell me about training dragons."

Their talk lasted long into the night and Teagan soaked up as much information as she could on the subject of dragons. Muniath on his part found her a willing and apt pupil. It helped, of course, that she had already raised Gremlin—or rather, Gremlin had brought out the skill in her. It was somewhere around three in the morning when Muniath had started to yawn as he talked, and Teagan fetched him some blankets and a pillow before retiring to her own room for the night.

Coming out of her bedroom the next morning, Teagan could hear her father and Muniath talking quietly. She stopped for a moment to understand what they were saying, hoping that Muniath was convincing her father to leave with them. But knowing how stubborn Tharain could be, she still doubted that he would be coming with them.

"It is a strange device and I still marvel at how it actually works. But it can be entertaining and educational. We've learned a lot about this world through that contraption. Here, you press this button, and it will change it to something else." She heard her father say.

"Amazing!" Muniath marveled.

Teagan stepped into the lounge and watched as Muniath was furiously pressing a button on the television remote, his eyes as wide as saucers as he watched the flickering images change before him.

"I see you're corrupting him already. Just because you're addicted to watching it, doesn't mean you have to turn him into a couch potato as well, Papa," Teagan laughed at the pair.

"I remember you being glued to it as well, Teagan. Good morning, did you sleep well?" Tharain asked her with a grin.

"I did, when I eventually got to bed. I'm sorry I kept you up so late, Muniath," she said as she went to make a coffee.

"What?" Muniath asked, his eyes still firmly watching the screen. "Last night? Yes, it was late, but I didn't mind. You were curious and curiosity should be rewarded with answers."

"You're late if you are going into work," Tharain said looking at his watch.

"I'm not, I rang and left a message for Eric letting him know already." Teagan came back into the room and leaned against the bench. "So Muniath, do you want to watch that screen all day or do you want to see where we live. I thought I would take you for a drive."

The remote was soon passed to Tharain and Muniath stood to face Teagan. "I would like that. Is the world out there like it is on that contraption?" he asked, pointing to the television.

"In some ways it is, in others it is just as different as our two worlds are. Don't believe everything you see on that screen," she laughed a little at his enthusiasm.

"Well, if that dragon wants feeding tonight, I had better go into work." Tharain stood, turned the television off and threw the remote onto the couch. "I'll leave you two to your tour and, Teagan, can you please pick up a few items, I've put a list on the bench already."

"Yes, Papa."

After Tharain had left for the day and Teagan had made herself a hasty breakfast, they were ready to go out into the strange world Muniath had come to. He followed Teagan out of the door and to the car. She unlocked it remotely and then opened the door for him. He stood staring at the contraption, not ready to sit in the seat that was plainly there.

"How does it work?" he asked her, bending down trying to see underneath.

Teagan gave a little sigh and then opened the hood of the car before stepping back to show Muniath the mechanics of the engine bay.

"The motor ignites the fuel which then turns something or another, and the motion is then sent to the drive box thingy, and that propels the car forward, or backward."

"You don't know how it works?" he said peering into the dim filled cavity.

"Sort of, someone tried to explain it to me once. But I prefer animals and plants to mechanics, and you don't really need to know how it works to drive it." She shut the hood making him step away. "Get in and we'll go."

Teagan watched as he looked at the side of the car, trying to figure out how to open the door. A smile almost escaped her as she opened it for him, and he entered. Going around to the driver's side she climbed in and automatically reached for the seatbelt.

"Put your seatbelt on," she instructed.

"Seat belt?" he echoed.

"This," she said, pulling on her own and pushing the end into the clasp, giving an audible click.

Muniath twisted in his seat and found the belt. He tugged on in and then pulled it across him, shadowing her movements.

Teagan placed the key in the ignition and turned it. The car came to life with a little rumble and sputter, before igniting and idling. She quickly glanced to see his reaction.

"You ready?" she asked.

"As I'll ever be," he grinned.

Putting it into gear she pulled away from the house and the car bounced down the driveway to the street. Muniath's eyes were wide as he took it all in and his hands were clasped on the dashboard to steady himself. Teagan pulled out onto the street and drove slowly around the backroads of the suburb where she and her father lived. The houses were spaced out nicely as it was an older suburb, all with neat fences showing the borders of their gardens. She could see his head moving as he tried to see different things.

As she sat waiting at an intersection, another car was coming towards them, crossing over at the same time and she could hear the intake of breath from Muniath as they did.

"It came so close," he gasped.

"Yes, they do. And occasionally they collide, if you're not watching what is going on around you," she said so matter-of-factly that he gaped at her.

"They collide?"

"On occasion and depending on how fast they are going, the result can just be a little dent in the body of the car, or it could mean death for the driver and passenger."

"And these things are legal?" he cried out.

"People die on dragons, don't they?"

"They do, but only rarely."

"Are they legal in that world?"

Muniath gave a little laugh. "I suppose you are going to say that these contraptions are the dragons of this world."

"You could say that. They come in many different varieties and some vehicles can fly, those are called planes, or helicopters. But they can wait for another time. If there is another time." She tried to smile encouragingly at him. "Just sit back and relax."

Teagan turned and entered a main road, where the traffic was heavier, and she could see from the corner of her eye that he was trying to relax. She drove him around not only the suburb but took him into Wellington City as well. The tall buildings loomed high and large, but he was used to tall things, coming from the mountains, and having the citadel and palace towering above him all his life. As they drove through the city he compared it to The Realm, describing the architecture and the town that serviced it. The people who were important in his life.

Listening raptly, Teagan drove on and they headed out back to the Hutt Valley. Following the line of traffic. As they entered her suburb again, he turned to her eagerly.

"Can I have a go at driving?"

"I'm not sure."

"I've been watching what you've been doing, the movement of your feet and hands, I think I can do it."

"You probably could, this being an automatic makes it easier than a manual." She bit her lip as she weighed up the request. "Alright. When we get back to our street."

Teagan pulled up to the curb by the driveway to the house and turned the car off. They swapped seats and she told him how to adjust the seat a little, so he was comfortable. Then she set about explaining how to drive a car, what the mirrors were for and what to look for on the dashboard. Quickly she did up her seatbelt and instructed him to start it.

The lesson went far better than she had expected. Muniath was a quick learner and soon was gaining enough confidence to reach the speed limit for the road. They drove around and around the block and he was very disappointed when Teagan would not let him go further, explaining the laws of the road and how he didn't have a learner's permit.

Carefully he maneuvered the car up the drive and parked in front of the house. After the car had been turned off he sat there in wonder, his hands still resting on the steering wheel.

"Amazing," he said under his breath.

Teagan just laughed at his reaction, then said, "I think dragons are better."

"So do I," a rumbling voice proclaimed to them in their minds. "Now if you two have finished playing, I think a little more instruction is required."

Muniath and Teagan looked at each other and got out of the car.

Safe

The jingle of the pouch of coins was decidedly lesser than it had been only moments before, and even more so than when Scetis had first left The Convocation. Having left so suddenly he had not had time to actually prepare supplies to take with him. So for the moment he was willing to pay for food as he went, and for anything else he needed.

The boat he had left far behind him, hidden in amongst a conveniently and carefully planted patch of reeds for when he needed it next, and had walked for a day and a half inland towards the mountains that were the natural border between The Realm and The Convocation. They loomed over the land, large already, their tops sprinkled with the never melting snow which glowed brightly in the sunshine, and as the day waned they glowed bright pinks and oranges fading into deep purple.

Scetis looked around him at the busy market of the village he had found. Sheep were crying out in pens nearby; a group of musicians strategically placed outside the only inn in town were playing a merry tune that danced its way through the throng of people who had come to town to sell their wares. Smells of baking bread, roasting meat, and other delectables wafted on the slight breeze and made his mouth water. Stall holders cried out their wares and the prices over the top of the noise. Brightly colored awnings flapped lazily on whatever air managed to penetrate the crowd. Children ran laughing through it all, enjoying a moment of freedom from working with their parents. The festive air was further continued by the small stage and a troupe of players acting out a story for the enjoyment of the crowd, who jeered, clapped, and laughed at the appropriate times.

These were scenes Scetis had seen before on his travels. It was a once-a-month grand fair where people bought silly trinkets for loved ones, or hard to come by commodities. He had no memories of them from his childhood, so he stood back, chewing on the heel of the warm loaf he had just bought while he watched the children of the farms and the town playing together. He envied their natural ability to make friends, to look past their differences and just enjoy each other's company. From the moment Tavae had taken him on as an apprentice, he had told Scetis that he was talented and different to other children his age. All through his time with his old mentor, and even beyond, he had reiterated it to him. Scetis now could see how it had helped mold him into the man he was today. He felt a slight pang of loss for what could have been.

Walking on, he passed the hawkers trying to get him to stop and buy something for his sweetheart, for his mother, or sister. Scetis shook his head at them and carried on, still looking at their wares for the unusual and rare item that might be useful to him. His eye caught on a pendant, which hung from a hook. It was silver, the gem that was set within was a deep green, caught between the claws of two fighting dragons. Each dragon eye was set with a smaller emerald. The wings of the dragons were extended, and their tails were entwined at the bottom.

"A beauty ain't it sir?" a man cooed as he took it down off the hook. "And cheap too only twenty bronze and it could be yours." The man was old with wispy white hair. One eye was glazed over with a cataract and he had several teeth missing. The robes he wore were clean and well maintained, only a little evidence of mending here and there. His wrinkled face smiled up at Scetis as he held it out for the younger man to see the details more clearly in the sunlight.

"It is very beautiful," Scetis agreed, his hand moving to touch the amulet, before pulling it away. "But I have no one special to give it to."

Scetis went to move away but the old man stepped in front of him. "I can see that you really admire it young man. How's about I drop the price? Fifteen bronze. And you don't worry about getting a sweetheart to wear it, I'm sure a man as good looking as you will have someone soon."

"The offer is tempting good sir, but still—" Scetis mind went to Ide for a brief moment and the temptation to buy it for her grew.

"Ten bronze then," the old man spoke over the top of him.

"Ten? May I ask how you came about it?" Scetis asked looking at the old man closely.

"I came by it honestly. T'was was sold to me by a man quite some years back, he had a run of bad luck at the cards and needed the coin in a hurry like." The old man pulled away protecting the pendant in his hands.

"So why keep it for so long?"

"Because I took a fancy to it. Now I find myself in need of the coin to pay the Physician."

"What's the matter with you?" Scetis eyed the man up and down more closely.

"What's right more'n like it." The old man laughed abruptly, causing Scetis to give a rare smile. "I has a painful 'ruption of the gut, young master, not the first I've had looked at neither. So, you see it'll take a pretty fair amount of coin to pay the Physician to fix it." He turned and placed the pendant back on the hook.

"If you make that pendant five bronze, I'll examine you and see what I can do," Scetis offered.

"You don't look like no Physician to me, young sir. You looks more like some out of work farm hand," and the old man dismissed him with a wave and a derisive laugh. Scetis pulled his amulet out from under his shirt and held it out for the old man to see through his one good eye. "Well, I never. Then that puts a different spin on things. How much did you say, young master?"

"Five bronze."

"A bargain indeed, but the coin I will be saving will indeed be a match for that. I will take your kind offer, young master. I can meet you after the market has closed in the inn if you like, once I pack up shop."

"I'm not staying at the inn; I am only passing through today. Do you have a house in the village?"

"No, sir, I lives a little ways out of the village, on a small farm holding."

"I can help you pack up at the end of the day and travel with you," Scetis offered.

"That would be right nice of you. What you say your name was?"

"I didn't. I am Scetis."

"Scetis what?"

"I don't truly have a family name, well at least not one that I can remember. I just go by Scetis Mordha."

The old man gave a short bark of a laugh. "Someone was having a joke on you, Master Scetis Mordha, with an ancient name that means more. I'm Farmer Elpin Depaor. And if you could meet me back here when the sun is an hour off setting, then we can get going."

"I named myself." Scetis replied with a crooked smile. He could not help but take a liking to this man. "I would be honored to do that for you Farmer Depaor." Scetis gave the old man a small bow and then wandered off into the market, making a note as to where Elpin's stall was located.

As the day diminished, the noise and activity had gotten to Scetis. He had always enjoyed his own company more than that of crowds and put up with the farmers who had done their business and were now well on the way to being drunk in the tavern. The owner of the inn had seen the necessity of spilling out his bar onto the square of the town as his patrons swelled, quickly filling the inside and then out. The barmaids were young and quite a few times had to swat away wandering hands of those that became bolder with drink. Scetis scowled at this behavior, and when one patron would not get the hint his advances were not wanted, he had stepped in. He hauled the drunken man up by the collar of his worn and stained tunic and tossed him out onto the street. When the farmer came to, he shook his head to clear it and stumbled, looking through bleary eyes to see who it was that had assaulted him. By this time everyone else was laughing at him and Scetis was no longer around. The young barmaid was looking at where he had disappeared and smiled in appreciation.

The sun was judged to be at the right moment and almost as one the stall holders was packing up. Scetis found Elpin as he finished putting the last of his stock into a box. He helped the old man to dismantle his hoarding and awning and place them in the back of a rickety hand pulled cart, followed by the boxes of goods. When Elpin went to pick up the yoke, Scetis stopped him and took his place.

"Lead the way, Farmer Depaor," and they moved off with the others who were heading north.

As they went they talked companionably about life in general, never once getting into anything personal, and it wasn't long until Elpin was leading him off the main cobbled road onto a dirt one that was straight as an arrow to a stone house, with a newly thatched roof.

"It was that damn roof that caused this 'ruption I now got," Elpin told him, subconsciously rubbing his stomach.

"Do you live by yourself?" Scetis asked as the cart got caught in a rut and he had to pull a little harder.

"My dear wife is there, bless her soul. Can't believe she hung on with an old bugger like me," he laughed a little. "There she be now."

Elpin waved out as the door opened and a woman with long grey hair stepped into the doorway. She had the stance of one used to being on fishing boats and she waved back.

"Roz, this here is Scetis, and he says that he can cure me," he called out to her.

"Cure you of what old man, your wandering ways?" Roz laughed. Her voice sounded raspy like one who had yelled a lot over their lifetime.

"Scetis this here is my common-law wife, the delightful and beautiful Rozenn Ómurchadha. The love of my life and the only woman to catch my eye."

"Your good eye that is, that's why the other is all blanked off," she laughed again as Elpin took her in his arms and planted a dutiful kiss on her lips.

"She kept telling me no, whenever I asked her to marry me. Since we was kids she's been telling me no. And then one day there she was in front the lake, her boat sold and asking if I was still interested. I think she was only after my holding and my money." He gave a great theatrical and conspiratorial wink to Scetis.

"It's true, he finally wore me down. Brought me in from the water and the job I had dedicated myself to and made a semi honest woman of me." Rozenn hugged him back.

"Well don't just stand there lad, put the cart in the shed round the back and I'll help you bring in the boxes." Elpin extracted himself from Rozenn's arms and walked with Scetis around the back.

The inside of the small house was neat to an inch of its life. He could see the tell-tale signs of someone who has been used to living in confined quarters and everything had a place. The two men walked through the back door and Elpin indicated the scrubbed wooden table to place the boxes down on.

"So, do you want to examine him before supper or after?" Rozenn asked, wiping her hands on a cloth. She was in the middle of preparing food and the smell of the meat cooking in the oven was tantalizing.

"I think before and depending on how bad the hernia is then I will treat him before as well, if it won't interrupt supper of course?" Scetis asked.

"Be our guest, the sooner the better, then he can stop his belly aching about it. You can use the table; I'll go get a clean cloth to cover it." She headed to a set of drawers by the door and opened the bottom one.

Elpin and Scetis moved the boxes they had just placed there, and he got the old man to lay down on the table. Lifting his tunic, it was more than obvious to Scetis that the *'ruption'* as Elpin called it was a nasty one and needed fixing urgently.

"It's in the same place as the last one, son. I don't think that Physician did a very good job of fixing me last time." Elpin complained.

"No, he didn't. If it were treated properly in the first place, it wouldn't have opened again. I am sorry, Elpin, but I am going to need to open you up and put you back together."

"You go right ahead, and never mind what he has to say." Rozenn told him before Elpin could utter a word. "But before you do, I want to see your credentials and know how much this is going to cost us."

"It's not going to cost you and Elpin anything, Mistress Ómurchadha. It's included in the price of a pendant Elpin has promised to sell me."

"That dragon one with the emerald love, you know the one I mean," Elpin said from the table, still clutching the hem of his tunic in his two hands.

"I do know it. And your services are worth more than that trinket Master Scetis," she told him.

"My services are worth what I say they are worth. I will share them with whomever I wish. The skills of the Physician should be available to all people, not just those who can pay."

"Then you have our most grateful and humble thanks. Also, I insist you stay the night, then you can check on Elpin in the morning and I can see you off with your pack full of what we can spare."

"I would be most grateful to accept your offer." Scetis bowed his head to her. There was no point arguing with a woman like Rozenn, she was too used to being her own boss and getting her own way. "Right then, I'll give you something to knock you out for a little while, and when you wake, you'll have a new scar."

"Another to add to the collection, just get on with it Scetis, I'm not getting any younger," Elpin told him, his grin was more a grimace at the coming pain, and he looked up at the rafters stoically.

The procedure went well and did not take long. With the help of a surprisingly strong Rozenn, they moved Elpin to the bed in the corner of the one room house and she dished up a dinner for them both. The food was wholesome and plain but tasty and welcome after the small, rationed meals he had since leaving. He found Rozenn to be a humorous woman and she even managed to make him smile a time or two with some of her bawdier jokes. After, Scetis cleaned the dishes as his way of thanks for the meal, while Rozenn leaned back in her chair at the table.

"So, are you married, have a sweetheart? Is that who the pendant is for?" she asked him, reaching into her pocket for a pouch and a pipe.

"No, neither. I saw the pendant and it spoke to me; I suppose you could say."

"I suppose it would, you're having the silver in your eyes." Rozenn dipped her pipe into the pouch and pulled it out, tampering the shredded leaf in, before leaning over to the fire and pulling out a taper and lighting it.

"I am not sure what you mean, Mistress Ómurchadha."

"Call me Roz, everyone does." She puffed on the pipe a time or two and sent out a cloud of blue smoke. "The silver around your pupil. You have dragon blood. Where're you from?"

"I don't know." He came to sit at the table with her and refused the pouch she offered. "My mother sold me into slavery when I was small. I grew up in The Convocation."

"A sad tale, but you've risen to master three tiers. How'd that happen?" Roz asked. As Scetis outlined his life as briefly as he could she did not take her eyes off him once. When he had finished, she puffed a little more on her pipe and regarded him with critical eyes.

"Tavae Stiobhard, the Regulator?"

"Yes, he was my first master. Then I studied to be a Practitioner under Picti Ómuireadhaigh, he was a fair man who I have a high regard for, and he is now a member of the Hierarchy and was one of the men responsible for appointing Tavae as Regulator."

"I've heard of him, I sold a lot of my catch to the Convocation regularly, I got to know a lot of the cooks." Rozenn puffed away on her pipe.

"After I had finished with Picti, I ran into a little trouble and found myself under the tutelage of Etain Óhaodha."

"How did you find her?"

"More than fair, patient and caring."

"That is not how I would describe her." Rozenn stood and tapped her pipe out into a bucket by the door. "The Etain I used to know was a spoiled child."

"You knew her."

"Very much so. I am a cousin of sorts, through marriage. The times that we met I found her to be willful and nasty. Several times I caught her being nasty to the younger members of her house."

"That does not sound like the Etain I know. She cared and cured me after I had been poisoned."

"Who poisoned you?"

"It doesn't matter who, she and Tavae saved my life."

"She may have changed," Rozenn said speculatively.

A groan from the bed had both of them turning. Elpin moved, his hand going to the source of his pain. Scetis jumped up and crossed the room to his patient and pulled the hand away.

"Calm now, Elpin. I will give you something for the pain, if you move you will ruin all my hard work," he told him gently.

"Well, give it to me man! Don't just stand there like a great dolt," Elpin mumbled through a groan and gasped at the effort it took to speak.

Going to his bag, Scetis took out the leather case and looked at the little jars. Plucking one out of the band that held it in place he asked Rozenn for a cup of water. Carefully he measured out a small amount of the powdered crystals that were contained within and then stirred the water vigorously.

"Take this in one go, make sure the cup is empty," he explained to Elpin, as he helped him to sit and get comfortable.

The old man raised the cup to his lips and loudly gulped it down greedily, in a hurry for the pain to subside. Handing the cup back to Scetis, Elpin sighed and relaxed a little. Scetis had noticed this behavior before, where a patient after taking something they were told would help ease pain, would relax as soon as they took it, even though the actual medicine would not work for several minutes. The power of the mind was usually half the battle in some cases, he thought to himself.

"Now relax and no overdoing things. You can start moving around in a day or so, but no heavy lifting," Scetis warned him.

"Stop your fussing, that's what Roz is for," he grumbled, still drowsy from the compound Scetis had given him to sleep and he closed his eyes. Soon he was snoring once more.

Scetis and Rozenn sat back down at the table and she pushed the jug of home brewed mead across to him. He poured himself a good measure and drank it down, the honey liquid slipped down his throat easily. While he placed his cup back down he remembered a comment that Rozenn had made at the beginning of their conversation.

"You said I had dragon blood, what do you mean by that?" He played with the lip of the cup as he looked up at her with his blue and silver eyes.

"You would be one of the old people. They say that there is dragon blood running through the veins of those with silver in their eyes. It's an old tale and you saying that the pendant spoke to you made me think of it."

"A likely tale," he scoffed at her theory, but the notion played on his mind. The only other person he had seen with silver flecks in their eyes had been Ide and she was sister to the current Dragon Master of The Realm.

"It is, indeed, a tale to tell children in their beds." Rozenn drank the last of her drink and then stood. "I'll get you some bedding, there's room in the shed if you don't mind sleeping out there."

"The shed will be fine, Roz, I thank you for your hospitality." He also stood.

"I didn't have much choice, the old man there does these things from time to time. But you, young man, are a blessing. My thanks for performing the procedure on Elpin, the worry of coming up with the coin was weighing heavily on him."

Scetis bade Roz goodnight, his arms laden with blankets for the night. As he settled down on the hand cart in the shed, he thought about his journey. So far he was thankful that he had not met with any of the soldiers he knew were searching for him. Scetis also thanked fate for throwing Elpin and his problem in his path and giving him somewhere safe for the night.

Sun beams shone through the gaps in the shed. Long shafts of light cut across the small space brightening the inside. One bright stream crept along the sleeping form of Scetis as he lay on the cleared off hand cart, his blankets only half on as he slept. Finally, the dazzling stream made it to his eyes, and they squinted a little as he stirred and moved, the blanket finally slipping from his body. He carefully opened them and looked about, remembering where he was and the conversation of the previous night. As it had become normal for him his mind then wandered to Ide, wondering what she was doing.

"I can show you," the rumbling voice said in his mind and it chuckled a little.

"Who are you?" Scetis replied out loud.

"You need to hurry; we will be in The Realm soon. I will guide you along the way."

"What do you want of me?"

"You will find out when you get to where you need to go." Then the presence was gone.

Scetis stared up at the gleaming dust making the sunlight visible, seeing the motes dancing with the drafts that infiltrated their way into the small building. His hands went to the back of his head as he returned to his reflections of Ide. Outside he heard a door open and footsteps, a metal clang announced the lowering of the bucket into the well. He heard the splash at the bottom and then could hear the creak of the handle as Rozenn began to lift it out—at least he hoped it was Rozenn and not Elpin.

Sitting up, Scetis stretched out the bunched-up muscles in his back and shoulders. The surface of the cart had been hard, but it was better than sleeping on the ground. Sliding his way to the end of the cart, he stood and pulled his blanket with him. After making sure he had packed all his belongings he headed out of the door, which squeaked in protest as he pushed on it. Letting it go it banged back in place behind him, bouncing a couple of times before he slipped the latch to keep it closed.

The yard was clean, and the flower beds were well maintained. There was order everywhere and he believed that was down to Rozenn and her habits of a lifetime. He stepped across the hard-packed dirt to the house and knocked gently on the door.

"It's open and we're decent, just," Elpin cried out loudly with a chortle.

Scetis entered and smelled the frying meat on the stove. "Good morning. How did you sleep?" he asked his patient who was still reclining in bed.

"Like a log. You wouldn't want to leave a bit of that stuff you gave me would you now, son, it might help a little."

"I'm sorry, I cannot. It is only to be used to make sure the patient is knocked out. But I can recommend some herbs steeped in hot water before you go to bed. Some are in your garden outside, that should help you get to sleep. May I see the wound?"

"Help yourself, son, it's your handy work," Elpin said as he pushed the blankets down and lifted the shirt he had on.

"Could I bother you for some hot water, Roz?" Scetis asked Elpin's wife.

"Of course, you can, I have it on the boil now." She took a bowl to the stove and lifted off a kettle, poured a little in and brought it over to Scetis, along with a clean cloth and a bar of homemade soap. Setting it down she stood back to watch how he worked.

Washing his hands carefully and then drying them on the cloth Scetis then gently, and with as much care as he could, lifted the bandages off the wound. He looked and prodded it softly, testing his stitches with his fingertips.

"Can you see this redness here," he indicated with a finger to Rozenn, "That should reduce in a day or two, as will any swelling. I'll give you some ointment to place on it to guard against infection, I want you to clean it twice a day and put the ointment on it."

"I can do that, I've treated enough of my own battle wounds to know what I am doing," she told him, holding out her hands, showing the scars of multiple wounds she had attained during her career as a fisherwoman.

"Good. Then I know he will be in capable hands." Scetis took up a corner of the cloth and dipped it into the water, softly he dabbed at the wound taking in how much Elpin winced with it.

"You're not going to leave me in her hands, are you?" Elpin said, cheekily throwing a quick look at Rozenn. "She's got a touch like a dragon she does."

"You keep your comments to yourself, Elpin Depaor, or all you'll be getting for breakfast, midday, and supper will be gruel," she flung back at him good naturedly.

Scetis finished dressing the wound again and placed the bandages back in place. He reiterated his instructions about light work and plenty of rest, which he hoped the old man would take to heart but knew he probably wouldn't.

"I'll make sure of it, Scetis," Rozenn said as she started to dish up the breakfast, bringing over a plate for Elpin to eat in bed.

Scetis cleaned up the bowl and closed his leather case. The ointment he promised was in a little jar, wide enough just to dip a finger in, this he placed on the table for Rozenn.

"If you need more, I can give you the formula for it, it doesn't take many items to make, and you should be able to find most of them in your garden already."

"That would be most kind of you Scetis, now eat," she told him as he sat, and he did as he was instructed.

The breakfast things were cleared away and Scetis made himself useful once more with helping in the clean-up. When he was finished, he picked up his bags and turned to the couple.

"The pendant," Elpin cried as he tried to get out of bed.

"Which box is it in?" Rozenn asked him, making sure to push him back down.

"In the black one, right on the top. It's in a green silk bag, you can take that too, all part of the price," he hinted.

"Ah yes the price." Scetis pulled out his pouch and measured out five bronze coins, which he handed to Rozenn. "I thank you again for your hospitality."

"Oh stop your thanking there, son. It's us who're grateful. I just can't wait to see that old Physician's face when he asks how I is." Elpin chuckled a little at the delightful thought.

At this Scetis became a little nervous. The thought that this couple might inadvertently give his position and where he was heading away was creeping up on him.

"I would be most grateful if you did not mention my name," he said very carefully.

"I wondered why a master of the three trades was wandering around and without a horse or carriage," Rozenn said. "What did you do?"

"I have done nothing, it is what others who wish to point the finger at me, want to do. I would rather that I remained anonymous so they cannot find me."

"Don't worry your head, son, we won't be telling anyone who you be. I'll tell that squirmy Physician that I cured myself," Elpin laughed, clutching the wound site. "He thinks he's in for a nice little pay packet, but he's gonna be sore disappointed."

"I'm pleased you will be able to have one over him, Elpin. Take care and look after yourself, both of you." Scetis held out his hand to the old man.

"If you get out of this trouble of yours, you come back and sees us. Then we can have a proper drink together." Elpin returned the handshake.

"Thank you, Scetis, and I agree with Elpin. Come back and see us when you can, then you can tell us all about your adventure." Rozenn smiled and embraced him. This took Scetis by surprise and he quickly hugged her back before letting go.

Rozenn walked him to the door and watched as Scetis made his way down the long track back to the road. He turned once and found her still standing there watching. She waved and he lifted his own hand in farewell, then turned back to the road and headed north.

The road north was not as busy as he thought it was going to be. Only a couple of times had he needed to step off the road and conceal himself in the shrubbery at the side to hide from the sound of horses heading his way. The road was cobbled and wound its way like a meandering stream through the flat pastureland. In some instances, it was faster to go across the field to meet back up with it, as it took a bend which wound its way back on itself.

The mountains that were his destination loomed larger and larger on the horizon. The landscape changed slowly around him. At first there were only a few little hillocks, and small bumps mainly in the landscape. These soon started to grow as the land bent and buckled, as if the base of the mountain were spreading out and was pushing all before it. The air was beginning to chill as autumn truly took hold. The trees around him were all changing color, turning from lush green to varying shades of browns, oranges, yellows, and reds. The last of the berry bushes were starting to ripen and he made use of them, trying not to dip into his purse to feed himself.

Higher and higher the foothills became. He puffed his way up the side, sticking to the road and the shock in his legs, making it hard on his knees as he walked down the other side. Occasionally he stopped and brought out his sling when he saw a small fluffy creature bounding through the long grass. He cleaned and cooked these straight away, no matter what time of the day. A hot meal was better than none and the animals were enough for one.

A village could be seen as he made the top of a hill early one afternoon, getting closer and closer each time he made a rise high enough to see. It was perched on the very side of the steep slope that started the mountain. The wooden structures all had sharply pitched roofs, with shutters and sturdy glass in the windows. A few people could be seen in the streets. Women were talking together and going about their business, the men did the same. The elderly gentlemen sat outside the tavern already, enjoying the autumn sunshine before the winter set in. Boys and girls ran around, one was hurrying a herd of goats to their pasture. As they neared, he hailed her.

"What's the name of this place?" he asked.

"It be Ima Drakoni," the girl responded, tapping the hind quarter of one of the goats to get it to move along.

"Is Planirana nearby?"

"Keep on the road that goes through the village, you can't miss it on the other side," she said as she passed him, the goats bleating out their protest at being moved.

"My thanks to you," he called out to her, she only waved her response and kept the herd moving.

The road steepened as it climbed through the village. Many a face turned his way to look at him as he passed, he nodded and said 'good afternoon' politely as he made his way through the village. Not many smiled at him and from the old men he only received scowls as they looked at him from under bushy eyebrows, holding their tankards close as if he would snatch them away from their hands. Again, another nod and a greeting called, only the briefest of nods in return did he get, but he was not concerned about these village folks. It was the large house which was starting to make itself known to him. The odd glimpse of a cone shaped roof, topping a tower peeked out from behind an outcrop of rock. Each turn he thought he would see more, but the house was tucked away in a protective embrace of the mountain itself.

Rounding one more corner it suddenly loomed up at him. As the girl had said, you couldn't miss it. It was tall, elegant, and there was a romanticism about it, like the stories that children were told. A ragged flag waved in the afternoon wind that moved around the side of the mountain, a black dragon on a background of bright yellow fluttered around the pole it was attached to.

The actual house was more like a castle and he noticed that it was built with a gap between the side he was on, and the other. A bridge of wood was stretched across the great divide and he walked across it, his footsteps echoing into the chasm underneath. The door stood before him, thick and large, bound with great metal bracings and large rounded heads of the nails, made for a formidable barrier.

The sound of his knock on the door was muted and lost in the wood. Scetis stepped back a little and noticed a large chain with a circle attached to the end. Grasping it tightly he pulled on it and heard from within a loud and sustained clang, that seemed to reverberate in the very stones at his feet. The sound of many locks being slammed back from their places with great difficulty echoed through the thick partition. The creak of the door indicated how much it needed maintenance. It continued to protest at the movement for some time before a face appeared from the darkness of the room beyond. It was an elderly face, but not so old as it showed the man who wore it should be retired. His hair was sparse and wispy and almost completely white. His dark beady eyes took in the travel worn image of Scetis as he stood waiting to be admitted. The man was dressed impeccably in an old-fashioned doublet, breeches, and silk hose. At his throat a cravat was fastidiously tied and held in place with a pin made of gold, yellow topaz, and black onyx, denoting the colors of House Planirana. The man cleared his throat and brought himself up to his full height.

"Yes?" he inquired in a tone that was superior and looked down his long, hooked nose at Scetis.

"Good afternoon, sir. I am wishing an audience with Lady Nora Óhaodha," Scetis asked just as formally.

"My Lady does not see vagabonds. Be away with you, young man." The old man went to shut the ponderous door and Scetis reached out to stop him, his strength outdoing that of the servant.

"I bring word from The Convocation of Mystical Medicine, in particular from Lady Nora's daughter, Etain," Scetis informed him quickly.

"If you would give me the message, I will pass it on," he said imperiously, holding out his hand for the expected written message.

"It is a verbal message and one of great importance. Also, it is for Lady Nora's ears alone," Scetis said still holding onto the door to keep it open.

The man hesitated, his hand still putting pressure on the large door and Scetis could see he was torn between sending him away and going against his mistress' wishes to let him in. Finally, he relented and stepped aside, unbarring the entrance for Scetis.

Stepping through the portal into the dim interior it took Scetis only a moment for his eyes to adjust. The air inside had that long shut up smell and the distinct damp air feeling of not many people residing within the large building.

"Who can I say is calling?" the old man asked while the door banged shut and he slid the bolts once more into their places.

"I am Physician Scetis," he told the man, deciding that the title would serve him better than just his name. "And you are?"

"Gant, Sir. If you would follow me." Gant started to enter the house proper, his steps not as sure as a younger man's. Age was catching up to him and there was nothing in Scetis' bags that could halt the passage of time.

The staircase that wound up the side of the once grand entrance hall was highly decorated. The handrail was elaborately carved with interweaving dragons. In each gap and on each surface that was not regularly touched by human hand, was thick with a layer of dust. Scetis took in the frayed and fading tapestries that lined the walls and the travel worn carpet under his feet. On the next floor, a corridor with four doors leading off faced them. Gant unerringly led Scetis to one and motioned for him to wait as he knocked loudly and then entered.

"What do you want now, Gant?" an aged woman's voice warbled weakly from within.

"A messenger, My Lady, he says he comes from Etain." Scetis saw Gant bowing deeply and formally to the woman who was not in eyesight.

"Etain? Well send him in, what are you waiting for?" she demanded becoming suddenly excited.

Gant turned to Scetis and waived him in. Stepping through the doorway he looked about him at probably the only room in the house to be kept in any sort of order or livability. It was warm with a large fire set under an enormous marble mantle, with two dragons winding up each side. The dragon motif was evident everywhere. This was a family who was proud of their history with dragons. Facing the woman, he took her in. An elderly lady whose hair, a stunning silver in color, was elaborately styled each morning, faint traces of makeup tried to defy her age, and a mode of dress which suggested she had not kept up with modern fashions for some time. A book lay on her lap and her keen eyes were staring back at Scetis.

"This is Physician Scetis, My Lady," Gant introduced him.

"Please sit Physician, can I offer you a drink, maybe something to eat?" Lady Nora asked.

"That would be most welcome Lady Nora, if it is not too much trouble," he said and bowed his head to her, acknowledging her higher status.

"Gant, can you see to it please?" Lady Nora instructed and waived her servant away.

"At once, My Lady," Gant bowed dutifully and then he stepped out of the room, shutting the door on the pair.

"Please sit, Physician, it looks like you have had a hard journey," the elderly lady said and indicated a seat near her.

"Thank you, My Lady, but I think I will stay over here. It was a very difficult and long journey, and I would not want to offend you with my travel scents," he said diplomatically as he sat down on the nearest seat to him.

"You will have to rectify that shortly. Now I believe you have a message from my daughter?" she prompted.

"I do indeed. Etain and I are very old friends and when she discovered I was to come this way; she bade me pass on her regards to her mother. Also, she wished me to tell you there is trouble afoot and humbly ask that you take me in for a little while until the said trouble is taken care of."

"Intrigue in The Convocation," she said eagerly sitting forward a little, the book that was on her lap, slipped off and fell with a thud on the floor, unnoticed. "So, young man, what sort of trouble are you in and can it have dire consequences for this family?"

"There is a selection of Hierarchy that wish to take over not only The Convocation, but also The Realm. I became aware of it, and I have been asked to go see King Urmond to relate to him in person all that I know. I believe some do not wish me to do so."

"That is more than just a little bit of trouble then. That is high treason, both here and in The Realm. It has been so long since I travelled to The Realm. It would be good to go back and see where the family has its roots," Lady Nora pondered.

"My Lady, I do not wish to involve you in this conspiracy," Scetis said quickly.

"It will be no trouble at all young man. If you travel with me they would not dare stop you at either border. My house name—in fact my very name—is enough to ensure your safety. I don't know if you are aware, this family is closely related to King Urmond Cionaoith, we share a great grandfather."

"I was not aware, My Lady."

"Yes, very closely related."

The door opened once more, and their conversation halted. Gant entered closely followed by a young girl, neat as a pin in a plain black dress and starched white apron. Her hair was firmly pulled back from her face and tucked up under a white cap. In her hands she carried a tray, with a steaming pot and two cups, on a plate lay various cakes and slices and, on another sweetmeats, and pastries. Carefully she placed the tray on a little table close to her mistress and then dropped a small curtsy to Lady Nora, before being ushered out quickly by Gant.

"My butler's grand-daughter. I don't mind a little nepotism; it's good continuity for an old lady such as myself. She reminds me of her grandmother at the same age, who was my hand-maiden." Lady Nora sighed wistfully at the memories and then turned to Scetis once more. "Will you pour please, Physician?"

"Of course, My Lady, and please call me Scetis." He stood and moved closer, kneeling beside the small table and picked the pot up. The smell of the steeped taraxacum root was heady and rich, the person who had prepared the root knew what they were doing. The liquid was dark, and it was obvious that it had been steeped for a little while, timed perfectly to be at its best in color and taste.

"Help yourself to something to eat. Going by your appearance I think your fare along the way was rudimentary at best." She arched an eyebrow as she accepted the steaming cup from Scetis.

"It was, My Lady, but also being a Trader, I am used to finding my own meals as I travel." He picked up a pastry and his own cup and began to eat where he still knelt.

"A Trader also? Were you one of Etain's apprentices then?"

"I was. She was very kind to me; in fact I owe her my life. She saved me, along with Tavae."

Scetis sipped his cup and the bitterness had indeed been steeped out, leaving a rich and full-bodied flavor rolling over his tongue. It warmed him as it seeped down into his stomach and he bit into a pastry from the tray. Lady Nora reached out a hand ravaged by rheumatism and slightly shaking to pick up a small cake.

"I have some things in my bag which would ease your pain, My Lady," he offered.

"I thank you, young man, but I am well cared for. Etain sends along an ointment and infusions for me to take and apply to help."

They ate and drank in silence, the fire crackling and settling in the grate was the only noise, apart from the odd slurp. Carefully she handed her empty cup to Scetis who placed it back on the tray.

"So, I am to take you in for a while. In that case I will have Gant set up a room for you to use. You may have the run of the house. There is an extensive library my husband built up, he was very fond of books. The older the better, he used to say. He had his agents out hunting for the rarest and most obscure tomes he could find." She looked him in the eye and her own blue ones widened a little. The silver was faint around her pupil, but it was still visible.

"Dragon-blood!" she exclaimed sitting forward. "Who are your people?" she demanded, reaching out and taking his chin in her bent fingers.

"I don't know Ma'am. I was sold to The Convocation as a child," he replied, startled at her action.

"Your eyes proclaim your heritage, Scetis. You are of Dragon-Blood. The silver is there, and it is in large quantities. How I longed to see it in my own children's eyes when they were born, but it was not to be. I am the last in my house to have it. Do you remember nothing of before you were sold?" Lady Nora's eyebrows were knitted together, causing more lines to appear on her already creased and time worn face.

"I only remember my mother a little. I don't know where we lived. I remember the day she sold me, telling me to be good and to go with the man whose hand clenched my own." Scetis looked down at his hand and rubbed it unconsciously with the other.

Lady Nora sat back and stared at him. "Something is afoot, and you made your way to my door for a reason I believe." Reaching out a hand she pulled on a length of cloth and somewhere in the house a bell rang. "When Gant gets here follow him. He will show you to a room where you can get cleaned up and use for your stay here." Her eyes did not leave his own for one moment and when he looked back up at her, he could see the intrigue and hope that lay within them.

The door opened shortly after the bell had stopped ringing and Gant stepped in. Scetis stood. Lady Nora gave her instructions to Gant and Scetis bowed graciously to her, picked up his bags and left the room with Gant closing the door behind him.

"This way, sir." Gant led the way back to the staircase and it carried on up to the next floor. He stopped at the first door and opened it. Inside was palatial and dated in décor. A large bed occupied most of the room, with a thick down cover and canopy rising over the top. Heavy dark green curtains hung from the almost black stained posts in the same material as the canopy. A large chair was placed by the fireplace, which had only just been lit and was still struggling to catch with small flames dancing on the wood. On the other side of the fireplace a door stood open and Scetis could hear movement from within and the sound of water being poured in a continuous stream.

"Your bath is being prepared for you, sir. If you have anything you wish to have laundered, leave them by the bath and Keira will tend to them once you are finished," the old man advised him.

"Thank you, Gant, and I'm sorry I have given the household staff trouble," he extended his hand to Gant, who looked at it warily, before taking it. "I mean no harm to your mistress or to anyone in this house."

"I thank you for your honesty. But I will reserve judgement until we get to know you a little better."

"The bath is ready now, Grandah," Keira said, coming into the room and dropping a small curtsy to Scetis and her grandfather.

"Run along then, child, there are other tasks to be performed before the evening meal. Come back later and take the dirty clothes to the laundry when Physician Scetis has returned to Lady Nora's company," Gant instructed.

On closer inspection the young girl looked to be around seventeen. Her dark brown eyes flicked up to Scetis and back to her grandfather as she passed him and gave him a little curtsy before heading out the door. He noticed that she blushed furiously at his gaze and decided to make sure he was never alone with her.

Gant left the room shortly after Keira and as the door latch clicked into place, he stepped up to it and turned the key that was in the lock. For the first time since gaining entry Scetis let out a long sigh and leaned against the door. He had found safety for now. The bags which were still clutched in his hands he dropped into the chair by the fire, as he neared the only other door leading out of the bedchamber. He stood in the frame and looked inside. It was a small dressing room. In the center sat a large copper bath, one that was permanently fixed in place, with a plug in the bottom to keep the water in. Rising up at the head were two taps. The house was not as old as he had thought, either that or they had been retrofitted for the comfort of the occupants.

Quickly he disrobed and entered the bath. The water was hot, but not quite scalding. Wisps of steam rose up from the surface of the water, eddying as he moved and sank down into its depths. Scetis leaned back and enjoyed the sensation of the hot water seeping into his weary body, easing the aches and pains that he had accumulated on the journey there.

As it did when there was nothing going on around him, his mind sought out Ide. The dreams he had been having of her on his trek had been vivid and so real it seemed as if he could reach out and touch her. In some of them it seemed she was aware of his presence near her as her eyes searched around. He had looked at the wealth of long dark hair as it moved with her, her dark eyes were warm and inviting. He missed her in his arms and ached to have her with him.

Scetis' eyes flew open as he felt his body stirring at the thought of her and shook his head. He had to get these feelings under control. She was not for him, was far too good for the likes of him and would not even welcome any notion of such a match.

A deep rumbling laugh ran through his mind and he recognized it. It had become familiar to him and right then a welcome distraction from the thoughts of Ide.

"It is the other way around, Scetis. Ide will be a good match. And do not be so hasty to judge her feelings for you." The owner of the voice gave a throaty soft laugh.

"Does she dream of me?" he asked the voice quietly.

"Of course."

"But why? Why would a woman of such birth, training, and grace dream of me?" he asked confused, but the voice did not answer, only laughed some more as it faded from his mind.

Stirring now with the luxury of laying in the bath no longer holding any pleasure, Scetis quickly washed the dirt and stench off his body, with vigorous and quick motions and then stood. He stepped out onto the soft towel laid out on the floor and picked up another that had been draped across the arm of a chair that sat beside the tub. He dried the water from his skin and hair and then wrapped it around his waist before moving back to the main room.

The fire had grown while he had been in the bath and he placed another log on it to keep it going. The heat radiated out and touched his already warmed skin, Scetis took a step back and went to his bags, pulling out a clean set of clothing. Hastily he donned the attire and ran a hand over his scalp. Where he should have felt clean skin he now felt stubble, his hair was in desperate need of shaving once more, but it was a job for another day.

Sitting on the edge of the big four poster bed, Scetis watched the flames merrily dancing in the blackened grate. The two lesser dragons that sat on either side seemed to move in the flickering light coming from the fire. Their eyes were set with stones of a silvery tone, highly polished and picking up the light. Scetis stood and went to the one on the right, his fingers already brushing the head and the eyes that stood out in relief. The stone was smooth and cool to the touch.

"Steel," he said out loud with some wonder. He would have expected them to be inset with a gem, not a metal. Scetis pulled his hand away, the stone the dragons were made of was warm under his touch, a lot warmer than they should be with only a small fire in the grate.

He did not want to think of why that was. Some old stories from the woman who had cared for him when he first arrived at The Convocation, returned to him. Stories of dragon forged metal.

Scetis stepped back, went to his bag and the leather case that appeared as a book. Inside he found the ointment he wanted and pushed it into the pocket of his soft leather vest. He looked around the room and made sure that his things would be safe, then turned to the door. The lock slipped easily as he turned the key and he opened the door. As it shut behind him he slipped the key back into the lock and made sure it was safe. Then tucked the key into his inside vest pocket. He may have the assurances of the lady of the house that he was safe, but that did not mean he needed to let his guard down.

Convincing

The daily excursions were interrupted by Teagan's work. While she was home, Muniath would ask endless questions about the world, learning as much as he could. His thoughts were only to report to Urmond how much this world had changed without dragons and how much of their information was now out of date. He was only sorry that the portal had been destroyed, and the magic for making a new one was lost.

His time while Teagan and Tharain were at work was spent mostly in the clearing with Gremlin. The large green dragon was a font of knowledge on dragon lore, and spent a lot of time with Muniath, making sure that he remembered it correctly. There was so much more than Muniath could have ever imagined. The history of the worlds was not what he had been brought up to believe. The fact that the portals were now hidden from common knowledge only indicated to Muniath that humans were fast taking over, not only from dragons, but from Dragon-Blood.

That was a term he was still getting used to. In such a short span of time he had gone from thinking he knew everything about himself and his ancestry, to finding out he was only part human. He remembered as a child being taught fastidiously by his tutors about his lineage. It was long, and much had been made of the tenuous links from both his mother and father's sides to the crown. His mind flicked through his memories. Scenes and words long forgotten were soon brought up and he had a suspicion that these memories were being sorted and rifled through by Gremlin in order to learn more about him.

Gremlin lay on the ground basking in the warm rays of the sun in the autumn air. The light from above glinted off his scales with each breath. His tail curled around him, covering his clawed feet and his sinuous neck bent a little, as his large horned head lay on the ground. His enormous wings were open slightly to gather what heat they could and pump it through his reptilian body. His breathing was deep and even. He looked like he was asleep, but Muniath knew better. He could sense a mind at work, always turning and searching. Muniath pushed forward with his mind to find what Gremlin could be thinking, what he was looking for. Only to find himself laid out on the ground.

The force of the mental push had the desired effect immediately. Muniath pulled his thoughts away from Gremlin's and he lay on the damp earth breathing heavily from the impact. This was something new, never before had a dragon ever expelled him like that. Occasionally he would feel Screamer push back when she was feeling testy and wanting to be left alone, but this was something else.

"You still have a lot to learn," Gremlin told him as he opened an eye and showed the glinting silver in the pupil. "You are still a fledgling, being taught what is what. Do not attempt to fly too soon, Muniath, your wings are not strong enough yet."

"Then teach me," Muniath said as he sat up crossing his legs facing Gremlin.

"Not yet. It is not time. I cannot give you the information you truly seek until we are back in The Dragon Realm. There is so much you have to learn, prejudices you have to leave behind, and thoughts on dragons you have to change," Gremlin instructed as he raised his head off the ground, eyes now wide open and piercing straight into the heart and soul of Muniath. "We are not beasts; we were not created for man to only ride on our backs and do their bidding. We are dragons. We are the dominant. Our servitude under humans was a gift, which has been abused by some."

"You can feel every dragon in every world, can't you?" The question was based on the suspicions Muniath had come to have.

"I can, and I communicate with them. The strongest of course is with my hatchling mates and my mother."

"Screamer knows you, can she talk to you?"

"Yes, and I to her. She is very fond of you, Muniath. She says you treat all dragons with respect and care. She has tried to reach out to Urmond, but she says his mind is closed. As ruler it should not be, that is one thing we need to change when we get back. There is one other we need to search for, though I have a feeling he will not be hard to find."

"Who is he?"

"A man who is lost. A man of no name—he believes. But his name shines brightly in the stars. Of all Dragon-Blood, he has the most of our blood in his veins. I am almost certain of its purity."

"If that is true, and from what you have told me about the rulers of The Dragon Realm, then he should be thought of as an heir to Urmond. I know Urmond's daughter Orlagh is not..." He hesitated to say the name, "Dragon-Blood."

"Is it so hard to come to terms with, that the red blood that runs through your veins is the same as mine, Muniath?" Gremlin asked curiously.

"I must admit that it is taking me a little while to get used to the idea."

"It will come with time and education. But you are right, Orlagh is not the heir and can never be. Now what can you tell me of what happens at court?"

"You can't see yourself?"

"I may have been born with knowledge, but it is not so complete that I can see everywhere," he said a little testily, to which Muniath gave a small chuckle.

"Urmond is a kind king, just and fair. Orlagh is more interested in becoming General, I think, than queen. The councilors all try to get their way, and Urmond is very good at brushing their suggestions away when they are too ridiculous. Orcades is the one that needs to be watched. He is power hungry and is using every method he can to gain the throne."

"Does he have the silver?"

"No, he does not."

"Then he will not rule."

"He is to marry my sister."

"*She is a different matter,*" Gremlin said, and he stretched out his wings further to catch more of the sun's rays.

"Ide? What has she got to do with this?"

"It is of no matter at the moment, only a detail you do not need to worry yourself over. I wish I could fly during the day." Gremlin stretched out his long neck towards the sky and looked longingly at the expanse of blue.

"When we get home, you will be able to, whenever you wish."

"That must be soon. We have an appointment to keep and one more person to collect." The large dragon sighed deeply.

"When are we to leave, because you keep saying soon?"

Gremlin lowered his head and brought it close to Muniath's. "When I say it is time. If you wish to mark the length, then in two days' time. I know you are in a hurry to get back, but you must spend this time to get to know Teagan and her father."

"I've spent time with her," Muniath said, a little frustrated.

"Yes, you have, but not in the way I wish you to. Let those feelings go, Muniath. Accept them. She is not a little girl any longer, but a full-grown woman."

"I know that." Muniath said uncomfortably and stood to move away from the dragon.

"So why are you so reluctant?"

"Because she sees me as old, as someone who betrayed not only her father, but herself. I was there when they went through the portal. I looked after her while her father was being charged."

"I think you might be a little surprised by how she feels, Muniath." Gremlin laughed at his discomfort with how the conversation had turned. "Go and think about what I have said. There are people I need to check in on and find out how things are going."

Muniath headed up the track with Gremlin's words still large in his mind. But not the ones the dragon had hoped he would be thinking on. Instead Muniath was fixated on the timeline of two days. Only a short while now and he would be home, where things were familiar to him and the overload of his senses could be relaxed and eased. There was so much complexity in this world; so much that a person had to learn and come to terms with. But from what he could see of his short visits out into the community around the house, these things came naturally to these people. The gadgets and mechanics that they had created had made their lives sedentary; they drove everywhere. If they wanted to talk to someone they picked up a flat instrument made of glass and inorganic material and talked. He had asked Teagan about letter writing after she had come into the house from clearing the letter box and her response astounded him. These people did not write to each other, the only mail they tended to receive were demands for payment of goods and services.

"I'll be happy to get away from this place," he shook his head in wonder. "Get back to a normal life, and to dragons."

Of all the things he missed—his parents, brother, sister, Meara, and her family—the most was dragons. They were his life. He was in a hurry to see how the two fledglings were developing, especially under Wick's care. Muniath knew that he was a capable lad and had been well trained in a work ethic by not only Meara, but by Taran as well. The boy was skilled, but not as much as Muniath had hoped he would be. His rudimentary contact with the dragons was hindering him. Muniath stopped in his tracks.

"Now with these new skills having been opened up in me, maybe I can train him a little more," he mused aloud. The only reply he got was from a bird who was hopping along a branch far above him. Muniath looked up as it warbled some more. "You're no help." He laughed at his own words and carried on to the house.

As he walked in the back door, in the front came Tharain, along with him he brought two large bags of meat. Muniath went to his assistance and helped to carry them out to the laundry.

"I think that lot will last Gremlin," Muniath told his former general.

"Why do you say that?" Tharain replied, going and washing his hands thoroughly.

"Gremlin let slip that it will only be a matter of days now until we leave."

"Days, as in one, two, three…?"

"Two days," Muniath confirmed.

"That soon." Tharain hung up the towel he had been wiping his hands on and then moved out into the kitchen.

"You will be coming with us, Urmond is expecting you. Also, Gremlin insists."

"Well then, if a beast insists that I go back to that place and live in poverty, then I must obey, mustn't I." He went to the fridge and pulled out a bottle of water, opened it and began to drink heavily from it.

"We would not allow that to happen, you know this. Mother and Father will take you in. They took Meara in when Taran lost his wife."

"You're a bit naïve, Muniath. They took little Meara in because she needed looking after, she was a child. I am a man, one who has disgraced himself and his family. I can't face going back to that."

"My parents care for their friends as much as their family. They will take you in. I am certain of it."

"I am a man who was once used to privilege and prosperity. I have found myself down in the dirt, scrubbing around on my hands and knees to make enough to clothe, feed and put a roof over my daughter's head. I cannot go back to starting over again. I have a good job, a place here; though it is not much, it's still mine. I will be better off staying." He jammed the lid back onto the bottle and put it down on the bench.

"Think of Teagan."

"Teagan is a grown woman. She need not worry herself over a broken-down old man."

"You are her father, of course she is going to worry about you. And every day she is in our world she will worry how you are doing. Tharain, please reconsider. Teagan will be happier with you near, her only family."

"Urmond is her family also."

"But not her father," Muniath said, his voice growing louder to re-emphasis the point.

"If it isn't going to be Urmond who takes my head, then it will be someone else! Everyone knows that I committed and admitted to the crime, there will be some who will see Urmond's assurances as weakness and will take the law into their own hands." Tharain's own voice was rising to match that of Muniath's.

"I have never met with a man more stubborn, more pig headed than you are. You are being offered immunity, a welcome back to your home world to be with your daughter and you refuse it!"

"Do not presume to tell me what I am or what my daughter needs or should do. You were still wet behind the ears when we left, and from what I can see you have not grown much as a man. Tell me, did you follow in your brother's footsteps when you came of age? Did you go out whoring and drinking with him? I remember what he used to get up to."

"You do not know me, sir. Do not presume to know what has happened to me or my brother since you left."

"I'm right, aren't I?" Tharain yelled nodding.

"You know nothing of what has happened to me since you left. Every time I start to bring up what has happened on our world you shut me down."

"So, tell me this, what was the great miracle that made you change your ways," he demanded with a face that was turning red, showing his rage.

"I got my master and the woman who loved me killed," Muniath shouted back.

Silence descended like a thick blanket between the two men. They stood toe to toe looking at each other, both breathing hard until the color returned to their cheeks.

"Now that it's out in the open, can you two please tell me what the hell is going on?" Teagan demanded from the lounge door.

Neither man had heard her car pulling up, nor the front door open as she had entered. But by the look on her face they could see that she had heard enough of their argument.

"Just a disagreement, Teagan, nothing to fret over," Tharain spoke first, trying to ease her temper.

"It didn't seem that way to me." Teagan moved into the room placing her bag she still held in her hands by the door.

"Your father is still refusing to come with us, even after I told him that Gremlin said it was necessary he does," Muniath informed her, running a hand through his thick hair.

"So, you decided to berate him?" she asked him.

"No, my temper got away from me."

"And what was that last bit about? The getting people killed part?" The hesitancy in bringing the subject up was in her voice and he noticed she had become wary of him. For some reason that hurt to think that she did not trust him.

"It was on a mission; we were going to collect the eggs from a large Black. Arcois, my master had discovered the pair high in the mountains, we went out searching and it all went wrong."

Tharain detected the still deep cut that it caused Muniath. He placed a hand on the younger man's shoulder. "You don't need to tell us, son. It must have been very painful. I am sorry I yelled at you."

"We thought the male had already left but he came at us from out of the sun. It was a bloody fight and I watched them both die."

"Who was she?" Teagan asked, stepping cautiously forward.

"Cara. She was young, just out of her Rider apprenticeship and wanting to prove herself—not only her metal to her superiors—but also to me. I knew she was only there because of me. She wanted me to see that she was worthy of my notice. Cara was in love with me, and being the idiot I was, I encouraged her. I felt flattered. My male ego was stroked, and it got her killed."

Muniath left the kitchen and headed to the couch, slumping down on it, and resting his head in his hands. The pain of the loss and the guilt of surviving was still real to him. He could see their deaths so clearly in his mind and he relived them over and over again.

"It sounds like it wasn't your fault, son," Tharain said as he sat down next to Muniath placing a fatherly hand on his shoulder. "I can't imagine what a loss that was to you, with your skill. It's no wonder you reacted the way you did. Again, I apologize."

"It is something I am coming to terms with. I am sorry also for losing my temper, Tharain." Muniath responded.

Muniath's training was steady and constant right up to the day of departure. Tharain was still insisting that he would not be going with them and nothing either Teagan or Muniath could say would change his mind. Saturday dawned and it was bucketing down with rain outside. Teagan looked around her room at all the things she had accumulated over the years. Books, stuffed animals, and the room itself. It was the longest she and her father had spent in one place since finding themselves in this world. It had become home, more than anywhere and she realized she would miss it.

Muniath had tried to give her a warning that things would be vastly different once they passed through the portal, she would have to give up her gadgets and electronic devices. She had laughed at him and reminded Muniath that she had done without them before they were exiled and she was sure she could do without them once more. She had also laughed because she had noticed that Muniath had become very used to things like the television and using the car to get around.

A thunderous bang from high above the house rattled the windowpanes and made Teagan jump. It brought her out of her reverie and back to what she should be doing. The backpack on the bed was now full of the things she wished to take, a few items of clothing, photographs of moments special to her, and a couple of books. Hooking her hand through the strap she lifted it up and shrugged it onto her shoulder. With a little sigh and a last look, she turned and headed through the doorway. With an action that was more habit than any really thought-out moment, Teagan shut the door on her room for the last time and she headed to the back door.

Tharain was there, going through the fridge and placing all the contents in the bin beside him.

"What on earth are you doing Papa?" Teagan asked, putting her bag down.

"Well, it will all spoil and I wouldn't want the next occupant to have to deal with it," he replied as he ducked back into the fridge.

"Does this mean that you are coming with us?" she asked in a whisper not even daring to believe, let alone hope.

"I can't take back the money I have sent the landlord as a payment to get us out of the lease, and I have asked the neighbors to finalize our bills when they come in and take the bin out on Tuesday." He stopped what he was doing and looked at his daughter. "I tried to imagine you not being here. Of you going through the next phase of your life without me to be there for you. I don't want to miss out on all your joys and pains," he told her a little embarrassed.

"Papa!" Teagan ran to her father and threw her arms around him.

"Alright, yes, I was being stubborn and very foolish," he said with a silly smile and patting her back. "Now, can you help me?"

With the final preparations done, the trio hefted their bags onto their shoulders and Teagan made one last check that the amulet was still around her neck. Reassured, she shut the back door, turned the key in the lock and then slipped it under the door, her father's were left sitting on the bench. She turned, smiled at Tharain, and took his outstretched hand, and together with Muniath they walked into the forest up the well-worn track.

The birds overhead called out in the late, wet afternoon weather, shaking out their damp feathers as they huddled on their perches. The wind shook the branches, dislodging a shower of droplets to land pattering down on the leaf littered ground, making it slick underfoot. A hazy mist crept along the ground around the trunks of the closely growing trees, making it all seem more mystical, heightening the anticipation of what was to come.

The clearing opened up before them and Gremlin was standing in the middle of it, his head held high and looking very regal. As they entered, he bowed to them, bending a knee, and flaring out his wings dramatically. As he rose, Teagan dropped into a bow of her own, in acknowledgement of his.

"Are you ready to take us home, Child of Dragons?" he asked her.

"*I am, Gremlin.*" Teagan walked forward with Tharain and Muniath following behind. She reached out a hand and placed it gently on Gremlin's nose and held it there for a moment.

"*You know what you must do,*" he said, blinking his silver eyes at her.

In the ground before them she used her foot to mark a line in the dirt. With Gremlin standing to her left and her father and Muniath to her right, she took out the amulet from under her shirt. Holding it firmly in her left, she extended her right arm pushing her hand out, palm facing forwards and fingers stretched like she was pressing against a wall. Teagan closed her eyes and thought of The Realm. Her childhood home.

The castle; the citadel; the streets, sights, and smells of the town; the shores of the lake that glinted and glistened like a jewel, so far down below the walls of the castle; all of which had been her home. She remembered the smells that went with it, the flowers she liked to fashion into garlands for her hair. The sound of her footsteps on the highly polished floors. Playing in the corridors and secret passages with her cousin, stealing little cakes and pastries from the kitchen when cook wasn't watching. The joy of receiving her puppy on her birthday, and lastly the memory of the last time she saw her mother. Every detail she could remember, she brought forward.

Gently she felt the hands of her father and Muniath placed on each shoulder and knew they were also thinking of their home. Willing and wanting to return. The family Muniath had left behind, the dragons he loved and cared for. For Tharain it was the memory of his wife, the woman who was his whole life. Each of them feeding Teagan their memories, the things they held dear.

Teagan pushed the images out of her thoughts and through her hand, believing with every fiber of her being that it would work. Her eyebrows knitted together with concentration, as she poured her whole self in next.

"Aperta portal," Teagan cried out when she felt at bursting point. Before her came a sudden gust of wind, which blew hot on her face. Teagan opened her eyes and stared at the shimmering portal which sat before them on the line she had drawn. It shimmered and wobbled a little, reflective like a mirror, it sent back distorted images of them all.

"It is done," Gremlin said quietly. "Take me home please, Teagan."

Without a look back at the others, Teagan stepped forward and entered the silvery material. It was warm as it surrounded her, and she unconsciously held her breath as she passed through. It did not take long for her to step out the other side and stumble down the small steps she forgot were there.

The room she found herself in was dimly lit, with only a couple of torches blazing away on either side of the ornately carved frame she had just come through. She turned as Tharain stepped through and helped him when he too stumbled. She could see that he felt dizzy from the jump between worlds. He was quickly followed by Muniath, who ushered them both away as the head of Gremlin appeared, to be quickly followed by his large body, with his wings carefully and tightly tucked against him. He only just fit through the frame. Once he was through Muniath took charge.

"I want you three to stay here. I need to go find King Urmond." He seemed nervous, but turned and strode down the hall, swallowed up in the darkness. A moment later they heard him thump on the doors and a crack of light appeared as it opened. The dark shape of Muniath disappeared through it and the light vanished as they heard the door shut behind him with a resounding thump, which echoed its way down to them.

The red car raced up the dirt driveway, the engine revving, and the occupant eager and anticipating the night ahead. The headlights blazed a way forward through the still thundering rain, and he stopped the car outside the gate. With a quick twist he shut the car off and stepped out, pushing the door shut and quickly making his way to the gate. It protested as it opened and slammed shut with a clang after him. He raced up the concrete path to the front door and knocked on the glass panel. Carefully he checked himself over, straightening his shirt and pushing his dark hair back off his face.

There was no response, so he knocked again a little harder. This time he noticed that there were no lights on inside. He tried to peer in through the mottled glass but could see no movement.

"Teagan?" he called out loudly but received no response. In great confusion he stepped off the porch and headed around the house. Each window was empty and staring out blankly. The backdoor was locked when he tried it. Pulling out his phone he squinted when it blazed brightly in the darkness. He flicked through his contacts and found her number. It rang and rang finally ending in an answering service.

"It's Mark, did you forget our date? Call me as soon as you get this," he said making his way back to the car and then finally noticed that her little white car was not there before jumping back into his car out of the rain.

"Eric?" he asked into the phone when it answered his next call.

"Mark, what's up?" his boss responded.

"Is Teagan away in the forest?" he asked.

"No, actually Teagan doesn't work for DOC anymore. She tendered her notice in the middle of the week. She didn't want to make a fuss. Why are you asking?"

"We were supposed to be on a date. There is no one here, not even her father."

"She did say it was a family emergency. That they were going home. She seemed very nervous about it."

"I wish she had told me," Mark said, a little hurt and becoming angry as he hung up on his boss rudely. Pushing the key into the ignition with some force he started the car and revved the engine as it roared to life. Thrusting it into gear he released the brake and swung the car around to race down the drive, the tires slipping slightly on the wet gravel as he sped away.

Fear

Scetis sat back in the comfy chair, a book open on his lap and his long legs stretched out before him. The fire was doing something to take the damp chill out of the air, but not much. His eyes were closing slightly, and his head began to nod onto his chest. For two days he had been there waiting for word from Etain, and only that morning had he convinced his hostess to wait, before leaving the safety of the house and making the journey to The Realm. Now he had settled himself in and was enjoying the benefits of the vast library the old lord had accumulated. Most of it was to do with dragons and he found the subject interested him greatly now.

The large door opened, bringing with it a gust of a cold draft and Scetis stirred as Gant entered.

"Dinner is ready, Scetis," the old man informed him.

That was another thing he had managed to do; stop Gant from referring to him as Physician or Sir, at least while they were not in the presence of his mistress.

"Thank you, Gant," he replied and rose from the chair, placing the book down on the table beside it, then following the butler.

"Just a little warning, the Mistress has guests," Gant told him.

"I'll be on my best behavior then. Thank you for the warning, who are they?" he asked curiously. From what he had come to understand, Lady Nora had not had any visitors before him for some time.

"I am not allowed to say. My Mistress said she wanted them to be a surprise. I can only say they are relatives of my Mistress." Gant replied.

Grant led him to the large formal dining room, instead of Lady Nora's personal sitting room. A large and very long table ran the length of the dim room, with chairs all placed at carefully measured spaces along each side. Enormous and elaborate decorations lined the center between the candelabras which were unlit, except for the last two. Only four places had been set at the other end of the table.

Lady Nora sat at the head and waved and smiled at him. Her guests were hidden from view by the display of wealth and as he neared, they became visible. To Lady Nora's immediate right sat Wradech Foghladh. He was sat back in his chair idly playing with the silverware before him. He looked up at Scetis and smiled broadly as he recognized him.

"Grandmother, you did not say your guest was an old apprentice of my Master's. Scetis, it has been a very long time." Wradech stood up as Scetis made his seat and extended a hand across the table. For the sake of his hostess, Scetis took the offered hand of his enemy and the man who wished him dead.

"Wradech, this is a surprise." Scetis replied, then looked at the young man that sat beside him.

"Oh yes, you know Loxa don't you, he was your apprentice just a short time ago. He is now following his true calling and is apprenticed to me. Did you also know he is my cousin?"

Scetis looked at Loxa again; this piece of news was definitely a surprise. The young man made no sign that he felt guilty at Scetis finding out.

"No, I had no idea. The world is a very small place," Scetis said sitting down. "Are you enjoying learning about being a Physician?"

"I am. I'm learning a great deal," Loxa answered.

"And not once in all the time we were together did you even let on that you were his cousin. I could have told you some stories of him, but then again, I guess you could have told me a few of your own." Scetis said feeling anger swell inside him.

Gant and Keira entered then with food and the conversation halted.

"Gant, you will never believe it. Scetis knows Wradech and it appears that Loxa was once his apprentice," Lady Nora gushed.

"Is that so, Mistress?" Gant gave Scetis a quick startled look at that moment, which gave him pause in his thoughts.

"Yes, it seems our guest is greatly attached to this family. Do you know of the disturbing troubles in The Convocation at the moment?" she asked, turning her attention to her grandsons.

"No, Grandmother. I am just a humble physician and not high in The Convocation or it's politics," Wradech lied, as he placed a hand over his grandmother's.

"You are going to have to give that all up when I go, so you can take over the family seat," the old lady said, removing her hand from his and helping herself from the platters of food Gant now held out for her.

"And I pray that that day will be a very long time away, Grandmother." Wradech only stared at Scetis while he spoke. He knew him well enough to know that Wradech could not wait to get his hands on the prestige and gold that came with such an old house.

The meal continued; it seemed the cook had outdone herself once she had heard the heir was visiting. Each dish was turned out with perfection and flair. It was richer than the simple fair that had been produced for Lady Nora and himself over the last couple of days.

After the meal they lingered at the table, each sipping from hot cups of taraxacum tea, while Lady Nora dozed into her chest, snoring softly.

"How is your health these days, Scetis? I had heard that you reacted badly to the little surprise I left for you. By the way, Aunt Etain sends her regards, and reminds you that you need to take your medicine soon." Wradech arched his eyebrow.

Scetis guessed that Loxa had told him the effects of the elixir that kept him alive. When he looked at his former apprentice, he found him staring back, with an almost blank expression. The appearance of a little boy taken from his family was gone, replaced by a person who seemed far older and more comfortable with privilege and wealth. His guard was well and truly up now. These two had been part of this plot from the beginning.

"Etain seemed very concerned for your health," Loxa told him.

"As she always was," Scetis replied toying with the handle of his cup. "So, the whole background story was a way to get me to be open and more comfortable with you?" He raised his cup to his lips and drank deeply of the hot dark liquid.

"Etain thought you would be more receptive to it, given your own unfortunate background," Loxa replied.

"Is anything you told me true?"

"I'm sorry to disappoint you, Scetis, but no. Except for my name. There was no farm, no desperately poor parents, or Apothecary. In fact there is no apprenticeship, with either you or my cousin here. I have dedicated my life to a secret order." Loxa pulled up the sleeve of his shirt and revealed a dark tattoo. The ink had penetrated deeply into the skin and Scetis could see that scarring would occur because of it. It was still red and inflamed. The image was a dagger. A fairly common design for any back-alley tattooist in any town or village. It was the design on the curved blade that caught Scetis' eye. It was a representation of a Taxus Baccata or Graveyard Tree. The whole tree was toxic and had many uses, medicinally as well as lethally. It was the seeds of the red berries that were the most toxic, it was also these seeds which had been used on Scetis. The image etched on Loxa's skin sent a shiver down Scetis spine.

"An assassin," he let out a breath and noticed the cousins shooting looks at their grandmother. "It's fresh, so you have only just finished your apprenticeship."

"My last task was performed the day before my ceremony." Loxa tugged down his sleeve, wincing at the pain it caused him.

"Who was your victim?" Scetis asked quietly, fearing for Tavae.

"One of the last to voice their objections to our plans," Wradech said with an evil grin, enjoying watching Scetis squirm. "I believe he was once your master in Medicine."

"Master Picti Ómuireadhaigh?" Scetis exclaimed, both horrified and relieved.

"Yes," Wradech nodded, his grin stretching further.

"Tavae will never let you get away with this."

Wradech began to laugh. "Loxa, tell him how old Picti died."

"He was invited to a private audience with Tavae. When he entered the office, he found not only our Regulator, but also three other persons. My cousin Wradech, myself and my mother."

Scetis asked the question, hoping against his sick, sinking stomach that he was wrong. "Who is your mother?"

Loxa grinned. "Why, Etain of course. My mother and my father have both been so kind to me and guided my life and skills."

"You killed Picti in front of Tavae?" Scetis demanded quietly through teeth that were clenched, not only in anger but to keep the dinner he had consumed from coming back up.

"Of course, no death is ever ordered without the say so of the Regulator. It was such a fortuitous day when they placed the seemingly meek and humble Tavae on the seat of Regulator. My father was so pleased when he gained the nomination. We celebrated long into the night as a family."

"Tavae is your father?" Scetis could not quite believe what he was hearing.

"How does it feel, Scetis? To find out everything you hold dear and true is a complete fabrication? That the whole purpose of your life was to be used; not only as a tool, but also as a scapegoat?" Wradech leaned forward in his seat while he spoke quietly. "Oh, I must thank you by the way, for being our test subject for the elixir. Now we know that it works and what the side effects are, so we can keep our Regulator safe once his part becomes known in our plan." Wradech laughed loudly enough to awaken the old lady. She sat up with a start.

"Oh dear me, all that rich food is too much for me at my age. I have told Bridei to only serve plain food at my table." She adjusted herself in her seat and blinked sleepily at the three men.

"But you know how she likes to spoil your grandchildren," Wradech said reaching across and once more taking up her arthritic hand.

"She does indeed. I believe she still thinks of you all as children." As Lady Nora took back her hand and started to rise, Wradech was there to solicitously help her stand. "I'm going to say goodnight to you all. You young ones have more stamina to stay awake late into the night."

Wradech dutifully kissed her cheek, quickly followed by Loxa to say goodnight, then she turned to Scetis.

"Good night, Lady Nora. And may I say thank you for your hospitality once more. It gladdens my heart to know that there are still kind and decent people within the nobility." Scetis gave her a formal bow over her hand and kissed her ring of house.

"It is the duty of those in the positions of power and wealth to aid those in need." The old lady smiled at him then made her way out of the dining room, heading back to her apartment close by.

Once he was sure that she was out of earshot, Scetis turned to the cousins. They were both on the other side of the table eyeing him up, waiting to see how he would act now that his protector was not there.

"Shall I expect a visitor during the night? Or will you kill your grandmother and incriminate me in her murder? Or," he said as he started to head to the door, "should I go make as many antidotes as I can to prevent whatever poison you managed to slip me tonight?" He kept his eyes on Loxa.

"With what is already in your system, any poison I may have used would have no effect. No, in fact it is the second option. Grandmother has almost lost her mind as it is. Do you know that she believes you have dragon blood in your veins? She has herself believing fairy stories," Loxa told him.

"So, if I run now, I will be hunted?"

"Scetis, believe me when I say, I truly wish my cousin would slip one of the numerous daggers he has secreted around his person in between your ribs, but I faithfully promised that I would not. I would, however, suggest you do not tarry too long in these halls tonight. If you are still here by midnight, I will not hesitate to do the deed myself," Wradech told him darkly.

"Why have you always hated me? What did I ever do to you?" Scetis continued to move to the door and the cousins matched him stride for stride on the other side of the long table.

He gave Scetis a tight smile, which turned to confusion and then to a sneer. "You don't know your parentage? Well, there is a fine thing. Tavae kept you well and truly in the dark. I wonder why he would do that? But if you don't know then I am not going to enlighten you anymore." He gave out a ringing laugh that seemed to fill the large room. "Run along, Scetis. If the guard we brought with us does not catch up with you, then these mountains will do our job for us."

Scetis did not wait for any more words from either one, and made the door, dragging it open and slamming it shut behind him. From the grand entrance the clock chimed out the eleventh hour in long mournful tolling. He made the bottom of the stairs and found Gant coming down them as quickly as he could hobble. In his hands he clasped both of Scetis bags and some warm garments.

"Gant," Scetis cried out and took the steps two at a time to meet him.

"Sir, quickly. My mistress gave me warning and begged me to help you." The old man gasped and came to a stop.

"Lady Nora knows?"

"Her suspicions were confirmed tonight, when they thought her asleep. They think her feeble and that is what she wants. Do not fear for her, she will be safely hidden away, and they will not harm her this night. I will die to protect her," he said bravely standing up as straight as he could and thrusting the bags and coat into Scetis' arms.

"You have my thanks, and please pass them onto Lady Nora."

"You best be going. In the pocket of the mountain coat is a map. It will guide you through the passes, I just hope it is not too late in the season for you to get through and that nothing major has changed up there. The map was made when I was but a lad."

Scetis took the items and shook Gant's hand firmly. "Go look after your mistress and get your family safely away."

"They already are, Scetis. Good luck." Gant turned and hurried back up the steps as fast as he could climb them.

Scetis watched him for a moment before turning and racing down the stairs as he had mounted them. When he reached the bottom, he did not head to the front door, instead he disappeared through another that led to a disused wing. He had not just been idly reading away the hours since he had arrived. He had explored the whole castle on his first night. A habit from his childhood, it had always comforted him to know where all the escape routes were.

Rushing now down the dark corridors he knew exactly where to go. The darkness was not really all that much of an issue for him. Rays of moonlight pierced through the dust encrusted windows that had not been cleaned for so long, lighting the way a little for him. But he had always had good eyesight in the dark. Scetis counted the doors to the right and found the large richly decorated double doors he wanted and opened one side, the door creaking loudly its protest of moving. He slipped through the narrow gap and closed it carefully behind him with a barely audible click.

The room he found himself in was cavernous. A ballroom at one point in time, with large chandeliers hanging ponderously above and an entire wall of windows, with a set of glass doors in the center. This was his escape. Beyond the doors was a large terrace that jutted out over the side of the mountain perch. The large, curved balustrade keeping the guests and family safe from the sudden drop, also had a path leading down one side. The steps had been carefully carved out of the solid rock of the mountain. They wound down steeply to a small overgrown and largely forgotten garden. The pond was choked with water weed and stunk of rotten things.

Running round the edge of the pond he found the gate the gardeners would have used as access to do their work. Squeezing his way passed the metal gate which was frozen into position with the passage of time and rust, he continued to run along the path until he made it to the protective wall of the castle. The spot he had found had crumbled at some point, large stones had tumbled from the top, giving him aid to climb over it. As he mounted the top of the pile he looked back at the towering castle with its many turrets, and the flag still blowing in the wind. Some faint lights could be seen in a few windows. Then he heard it. The alarm call. Blaring and echoing out, proclaiming trouble to those around.

Without a second look he finished scaling the fallen wall and dropped down the other side. As soon as his feet hit the ground he ran.

The first blush of morning began to lighten the sky and Scetis had not stopped all night, climbing further and higher into the mountains. His steps were stumbling as fatigue started to settle into his limbs. The shaking of his legs finally got the better of him and he felt himself sliding sideways between two large boulders. Through the cold that had seeped deep down into his bones, he could feel the first onset of the poison once more invading his system.

"I have to make it," Scetis said out loud, noticing for the first time how his breath condensed as it left his body.

The jacket Gant had pressed in his hands as he left, he now donned with fumbling fingers and hands. He pulled the deep hood up over his head, immediately feeling the benefits of the fur lining, and tucked the face covering into the hood beside his head. He pulled the sleeves down over his hands and wrapped them about his body, shivering and desperate for some rest, hoping that Wradech would believe he had perished in the cold, desolate, and dangerous mountains.

Scetis slept.

It was his own body shivering that woke him. It was still daylight, but the light was wrong. He wiped at his eyes to clear his vision and found everything was white. Large flakes fell from the sky landing wetly on the dark bare rock. An already thick layer of crisp white snow lay about him, and for a moment he could only stare at the drifting clouds as they floated down. He reached out a hand and like a child delighted in catching a few flakes in his palm. Until his body betrayed him once more.

It shook and spasmed in the cold. His muscles tensed and he clenched his jaw together to stop his teeth chattering inside his mouth, also to stop him from biting his tongue. Closing his eyes, he grimaced at the pain that was shooting through his limbs. It hadn't been this bad for some time. He had always taken the elixir before these symptoms took hold. But he could not afford to stop now and dose himself with the antidote. He was too exposed on the side of the mountain and it seemed that winter was coming early at these heights. If he were to take it and slip into the sleep it induced, he would freeze to death. He would have to wait.

The tremors began to lesson somewhat, and he pulled himself up out of the shelter he had inadvertently found. His head swam as he made it to his feet, and he held onto one of the boulders for support until it cleared. Breathing deeply he shouldered his bags and headed out into the gathering blizzard. Each step sunk into the soft snow, it was dry and powdery, but still the cold seeped through the leather. His arms were wrapped tightly around him, trying to keep the freezing air from invading the warm layer, but still he shivered.

On and on Scetis trekked, following the mountain path that was steadily getting steeper and steeper. His hands grasped the rock beside him, to stop him from slipping off the now plunging side to his left, which he steadily kept his eyes away from. As the day went on the wind increased. The snow, which was thick and falling lazily when he woke, was now flung at him by the howling wind. It sought out all his exposed skin and stung. He leaned up against the wall beside him and with fumbling and stiff fingers managed to pull off the face covering attached to the hood. The short soft fur of the flap fit snugly across his mouth and nose, leaving only the eyes to the elements, and these were squinted. Scetis breathed deeply for a moment, trying to gain some strength to carry on, knowing he would need to find some sort of shelter to ride out the storm soon.

Pushing off the wall behind him he carried on, unaware of his surroundings or the storm that was increasing. All he could think was one foot in front of the other and keep away from the edge. The wall suddenly was not there, and he fell, groping as he did for something to stop him, only to land heavily on the snow which was now deeper and up to his calves. Pushing himself up he looked around. The sudden stop of the wall was disconcerting, he could not see in front of him, it was a blanket of white streaks as the wind eddied and swirled the large snowflakes. Leaning back on his heels he remembered the map and carefully searched the pockets, finding it at last.

The paper was old and there were already some tears in it. Putting his back to the wind he hunched over as his stiff fingers unfolded the map. Dark lines wandered over the page, and he wiped his eyes to see more clearly. The route he was on came into focus and he followed it carefully. It ended in a divergent. Where there was one, now there were two paths. The page wavered and he held it fast, trying to trace where each route would take him. Looking around he made his decision. The only way he could go was up, following the right-hand bend. Scetis folded the map carefully and tucked it away again in his coat.

The wind tugged at the fur outer edge as it sought to tear the snug fitting hood from his head. Scetis made sure the mouth and nose flap was securely in place as he squinted into the raging blizzard. His only thought was up. As long as he could still feel himself climbing, he knew he was going the right way. He lifted his foot out of the newly fallen soft snow and stepped forwards, only for it to sink down now to his knee. Pulling at his other he kept moving higher and higher.

A cold chill went up his spine, one that had nothing to do with the bad weather around him. Scetis stumbled a little, feeling his legs go numb and pains race through his chest. He felt like the air was leaving his body and ripped the covering from his face. The freezing air raced into his lungs and chilled him to the bone. Driven down onto his knees he sank into the snow, it gripped at him, almost welcoming him into its embrace. Still gasping for breath, he fumbled with the straps of his bag, hoping to get to the elixir, trying to stop the pain that now ravaged his body as the poison took over. His mind raced, his hands shook, and he could not get the buckles undone. A cry escaped his lips and he pitched forward into the snow. Then all was dark.

Home

The wait in near darkness seemed to be long, but Teagan knew it was not really. She sat on the cold step beside the mirror and held her head in her hands. Tharain stood nearby almost at attention, with his hands clasped behind his straight back, and she realized her father was steeling himself to face Urmond. His old training coming back to him automatically, hoping to not show any disrespect to his Lord King. Her eyes then went to Gremlin, his emerald-green scales almost seemed black, but glinted as brilliantly as jewels in the wavering torchlight. He was inspecting the mirrors, looking at each dragon that had been carved on the frames and sighing a little.

"What's wrong, Gremlin?" Her voice, even though it was sent from her mind, sounded loud in the silence.

"My brethren. Each a carved replica of the originals," he sighed again as he moved to the next, his tail hissing on the polished marble floor as it swished. *"Almost all gone."*

"How many were there?" Teagan asked standing and walking over to his side. Without realizing he lowered his wing protectively around her.

"There were twenty original races, each making twenty different worlds their homes. Of those twenty, sadly only eight still have dragons existing on them. We are a dying breed, but on this world, we cannot die out; we must not die out. Already I feel a change in the dragons here. Those that are held in captivity are meeker, and almost have no will of their own. There are some out in the wild who are still strong, but even out there changes are happening to my kin." He walked on to the next mirror, the darkness of wood almost lost in the shadows of the little light that managed to penetrate the darkness, Teagan followed.

"Is there anything that can be done?" she asked him, her hand going to his neck.

"Yes, there is much that can be done. Much both you and I will hopefully do, Teagan," he said softly to her.

"What is taking him so long?" Tharain called out. Teagan could hear the nerves in his voice and was suddenly anxious for her father.

"I'm sure they won't be long," she said going to his side and holding onto his arm.

"Long enough to bring the guard," he muttered.

"Muniath said that Urmond promised there will be no guard," she tried to reassure him and hoped that they both had not been misled.

A shaft of bright light broke through to them as the large doors opened at the end of the hall. Both doors swung wide and two shadowy figures filled the void as they walked towards them. Teagan immediately recognized Muniath and stood holding onto her father's arm as she stared at the other. As they neared their features became more apparent, Muniath was smiling, and Urmond only had eyes for Tharain and Teagan, until Gremlin came to stand behind the father and daughter. His step for a moment halted, but quickly he recovered and walked on.

"Tharain, my old friend." Urmond smiled broadly and held out a hand for Tharain to take.

"My Lord King." Tharain dropped to one knee, his head bowing in supplication.

"Get up, we're cousins in a way, and we were friends long before that." Urmond reached down and grasped Tharain's shoulders, pulling him to his feet and staring into the aged face, before embracing him. "Welcome home."

Teagan heard the slight gasp and sob that almost betrayed her father's feelings and noticed the other two men did also. Tharain released Urmond and stepped aside.

"My Lord King, may I present my daughter, Teagan Loinsigh," Tharain said, taking up his daughter's hand and presenting it to Urmond.

"Lady Teagan it is so good to have you home with us once more," Urmond said, bending over her hand and kissing her fingers lightly.

Teagan was not used to such a gesture and blushed. As she looked around her in embarrassment, she noticed a slight scowl come over Muniath for a moment before he recollected himself and shifted uncomfortably on his feet.

"My Lord King, I am eager to see the home of my childhood once more, but there is someone I need to present to you," she said, still perplexed at Muniath's reaction, but pushing it aside for the moment. "This is, Gremlin." She indicated the dragon standing behind her.

"I have been very excited to meet you, Dragon King." Urmond bowed to the large green dragon.

"Teagan can you please tell Urmond that I am grateful for the welcome," Gremlin spoke in her mind.

"He cannot understand you?" She was surprised by this.

"He cannot, otherwise I would have spoken to him before now. He has some awareness, and has enough dragon blood to rule, but his skills are stunted. Now please let him know what I wish."

"My Lord King, Gremlin wishes you to know that he is grateful for the welcome," Teagan relayed to Urmond, who returned stunned eyes to her.

"You can understand him?" he stepped up close to Teagan and gently took her chin in his large hand, turning her face to the light, then nodded. "You are what I thought you were. Your blood is almost pure dragon. I can see it in your eyes. There is hope." Urmond let Teagan go as he remembered himself and gave a small smile. "The halls of the citadel have been cleared and there will be no one who will see you pass." Urmond reassured them.

"Tell him that I will not be staying in the Eyrie, I will be going to my home in the mountains, there is something I need to attend to there," Gremlin asked Teagan and she relayed the message.

"It will soon be dark, you can leave in relative secret under its cover," Urmond said, giving the dragon a slight bow.

"And where am I to go?" Tharain asked quietly, stepping forward.

"You, my friend, will be staying in your old quarters for now and then you will be travelling to your home, where you grew up. The lands reverted back to the crown when you were exiled, but I have seen to it that your home farm is once more yours. It has been worked and the land is still fertile and productive. I knew you would return home, that is why I gave Lady Teagan the amulet."

"I thank you, my Lord King." There was a catch in his vice as he bowed. "It is far more than I deserve."

"I should have seen the signs. You, Gael, and I were so close once. We knew each other so well, and when my cousin died, I did not take care of you. You made sure I was still functioning after my own wife passed."

"There is nothing to be done. Your responsibilities for the Realm takes precedence over everything else. It was not your responsibility, but my own."

"Enough said on the matter now. I'll come visit you tonight and we can talk over old times together."

"I would like that, Urmond," Tharain said humbly.

"Now, Lady Teagan. You will stay with your father tonight, and in the morning we will all get together with Galanan and Domnall to discuss what is to be done about this threat. Also, I know that Orlagh will like to get to know her cousin again. And she can advise you regarding clothing and other things that concern young ladies."

"Thank you," Teagan said, unsure how to address the king and felt awkward.

"Muniath, your parents will be eager to see you. Also, there is news regarding your sister, Ide. It seems her suitor is eager to move up their nuptials and with you home now, she will have no objections to it."

"I'll make my way there now." A frown clouded Muniath's features for a moment and he automatically turned to leave.

"Don't be in too much of a hurry. You still need to guide our friend here to the Flyway," Urmond instructed.

"Yes, my King." Muniath stopped, his eyes flicked to the open doors at the end of the hall.

"I think my orders should have been carried out by now. It should be safe enough for you to lead the way." Urmond then turned to Gremlin. "It is a great honor to have you home with us." The king bowed before the Dragon who returned the gesture.

Gremlin then turned to Teagan. *"I will still be able to communicate with you. I will be back soon."* He brought his face close to hers. Teagan placed a hand on the side of his large head and leaned her forehead against his smooth cheek.

"Take care," she told him.

"I am home. I will be more now," he said cryptically and pulled away. "Lead on Muniath."

The pair headed out of the Hall of Secrets and Teagan watched them go. It was the first time they would be so far apart. It gave her a moment of panic as she thought about it when his voice came back to her.

"Peace," he soothed.

The hallways and even the rooms off from them were empty. Only once before had Muniath seen the citadel so devoid of all humans. Even the guard posts were deserted. There were no ambient sounds, no feeling that someone was watching them pass. The only sound was his own boots and the long claws of Gremlin's feet clipping on the marble floor.

Now they were back in the world where they both belonged, Gremlin not only appeared physically to have changed, but also mentally. There was a presence about him that almost filled up Muniath's mind. He could feel Gremlin asserting himself, pushing his thoughts out to the world hungrily. Muniath stopped mid stride, voices were calling back, most distant, but some very close.

Gremlin stopped and looked back at Muniath. *"How else did you think we would communicate?"* There was a humorous tone to his thought.

"I don't know. We always assumed it was the cries, the roar and other vocalizations, along with the images, I used to receive."

"They all play their part but are not necessary. My mother and siblings are excited that I am home. I would like to see them before I go where I am needed."

"I'll meet you up at the Eyrie."

"No, you will ride on my back. I get a sense that you do not fully trust me, Muniath, and that cannot be. Especially if you wish to be Teagan's mate."

"Teagan's what?" Muniath spluttered and stopped in shock at what Gremlin had said.

"I have seen how you are with her, the way your eyes seek her out. It is to be, that is why I sent those dreams to you." Gremlin chuckled a little and carried on down the hall towards the large double doors and the terrace beyond.

Muniath stood stunned at the dragon. It was true, he had had dreams of Teagan even well before meeting her.

"How long have you been aware of me?" He hurried to catch up to Gremlin.

"Even while I was in the egg. I was not happy that you had fallen into such a state. By the way, my egg being stolen and by who did the deed, was no mistake. I needed to get Teagan back to this Realm, so I put it all into motion. It is only with both of you that the threat will be abated."

"Who was it?" Muniath asked.

"You and he will meet, all in good time." Gremlin stopped at the open doors and looked out at the mountains beyond the lake, their white caps gleaming brightly under the waning crescents of each moon. *"These are thoughts for another day,"* he sighed.

Gremlin stepped out of the doors into the night air and breathed deeply. Below, the lake sparkled in the night and the noise of the town filtered up to them, along with the lamp light of the streets. He moved his large head to see Muniath still standing in the doorway.

"Come. We do not have much time left," he commanded.

Muniath quickly settled himself onto the dragon's back, finding the natural seat between the shoulders and neck. Gremlin flared his magnificent wings out and drew them high into the air. Muniath could feel the muscles bunch and release as Gremlin made the first downward stroke. The pressure of the wind immediately drew them off the ground and with another mighty flap of the wings they went higher. Muniath marveled at how strong Gremlin was. It seemed to the Dragon Master that it took him very little effort to get airborne. Soon they were out over the lake. Gremlin banked to the right and made the turn before reaching the cliff face on the far shore. Using the slight wind that was blowing and marring the mirror surface of the lake and the very air around them, he began to climb in long lazy circles. Far below now was the castle and citadel, with the town nestled close by. Below even that on the shore, Muniath's childhood home. The lights on and gleaming brightly and standing looking out at the lake a lone figure. His sister.

Ide was soon lost in the shadows as Gremlin made his way to the Eyrie. Muniath saw the entrance fall below them as Gremlin sought out the dragons' entrances. Great natural holes in the top, wide enough for even Gremlin to lower himself down into the cavernous walkway below. His wings flared and fluttered, controlling the descent slowly until finally Muniath heard his claws touch the solid stone of the cave floor.

The sudden roar as they entered the caverns hit him as did the cries of *'Vojin'*. Gremlin had earlier alluded to the fact he had a true name and Muniath now wondered if this was it.

From the dimness, not only running footsteps could be heard, but also the click of talons on the rock floor. From out of the gloom came the small red and gold dragon, which was attached to Muniath, with her wings spread wide and flapping, taking short hops of flight in her excitement. Coming up behind was a harassed looking Wick. His running step slowed only slightly when he saw the large strange green dragon that stepped into a shaft of light from one of the flickering torches embedded into the wall. He quickened to stop Fleet from approaching this new-comer and then he saw Muniath.

"You're back!" Wick cried out, still eyeing the imposing dragon beside Muniath.

The smaller dragon launched herself at Muniath, her wings enfolding him in a very human-like gesture of a hug. The force of her enthusiasm knocked not only Muniath over physically, but also the wind from his lungs.

"You found him, you found him!" her voice cried out through his mind with great exuberance.

Carefully Muniath extracted himself to find Wick before him, a hand stretched out to help him up.

"Where've you been?" the young man asked him.

"On a mission for the King," Muniath answered as soon as he caught his breath.

"The dragons, they knew you were back. This one here kept saying your name," Wick indicated Fleet.

"Wick, this is Gremlin, though by the noise of the dragons it seems his name is really Vojin," Muniath introduced him. Wick turned now to Gremlin and bowed deeply; Gremlin returned the gesture.

"It is indeed. It is my pleasure to meet you, Wick," Gremlin greeted him.

Wick stepped back a moment. "I don't... I'm...," he stammered.

Muniath laughed lightly and placed a reassuring hand on Wick's shoulder. "Don't panic son, it will take a little to get used to. I know I fought it, better to just allow your mind to accept his thoughts for now."

Meanwhile the small dragon, who was considerably larger than the last time Muniath had seen her was approaching her sibling. *"Vojin,"* she greeted him with awe.

"Fleet," he responded, stretching out his long neck so that their noses touched gently, each breathing in the other's breath and connecting as they should have after hatching.

"Come, Mother is waiting," Fleet told her brother eagerly, then turned and raced back the way she had come.

The large dragon and the two men moved after her. Muniath could feel the expectation and surprisingly, Gremlin's nerves as he approached Screamer's cavern. They rounded the corner and sitting majestically was his mother. Her head held proudly erect and her gold wings tucked close to her body of red scales. At her side stood her other two children. Fleet was looking between her mother and her brother, while the third of the siblings, Sting—a green and gold—stood staring at the brother he had only felt a small connection to.

Gremlin approached his mother with caution, his head down in an almost submissive gesture. A slight perspective nod on her side was encouragement enough for Gremlin to proceed. He once more stretched his neck and greeted Screamer, who immediately began to purr deeply in her throat. She finally had all her children with her. Screamer moved her head and wrapped her sinuous neck around his, pulling him closer to her. His eyes closed and leaned into the mother he had been only linked to in the mind.

From beside the reunion a slight growl could be heard from Sting. Muniath looked closely at the green and gold who was attached to Wick and could see him puffing out his chest. Not as big as his brother and still growing, Muniath recognized the first signs of competition and jealousy.

Gremlin removed himself from his mother's embrace and turned to his brother. As he reached to share the breath and create the bond of family, Sting once more gave a low growl. Screamer huffed a little at her child. He looked up at her with stubborn and steely eyes, then mirrored the gesture, making the physical and spiritual connection with his brother. Sting's eyes closed as they shared the breath, and as he pulled away, he opened them and stared at Gremlin.

"My brother, welcome home," the smaller dragon greeted him.

"My brother, I thank you, it is good to be back."

Wick tugged Muniath's sleeve, and the pair walked out of the cavern, leaving the family group to get used to each other.

"How've things been since I've been gone?" Muniath asked getting down to business straight away.

Wick stood with his legs slightly apart, his hands clasped behind his back and in a relaxed posture. "All has been well, Sting and Fleet's progress is growing, they should be ready for their first flight soon. Fleet has been a bit preoccupied since you've been gone. She gets very excited and playful at the oddest of moments, while Sting seems to have slipped into a sort of grumpiness. Screamer is showing signs of wanting her offspring out of the nest. While Scorcher is still being amorous towards Rain."

"I had hoped he would've gotten over that by now. I think it might be time for a little experimenting. Have you noticed how Rain reacts to Scorcher?"

"She notices him, but it's not with an all-consuming interest," Wick replied.

"Good. Is there anything else I should be aware of?"

"No sir, everything is as it should be, but I will be happy to hear your feedback after your inspection."

"Well done, Wick," Muniath gave a little chuckle. "That'll have to wait until tomorrow, there are a few things I need to do tonight. Why don't you head home."

"I will. Thank you, sir." Wick stood to attention and gave Muniath a salute, who returned it with a nod. "Welcome back Uncle Mun, you've come back at the right time. Where did you go anyway?"

"None of your concern at the moment. Why is it the right time?"

"I overheard Ma and Pop talking; it seems there are some concerns about Ide. I couldn't work out what they might be." Wick's face turned to a frown. Muniath, his sister and brother were as close as real aunt and uncles to the boy. They had been there for him when his father had died and had been there for his mother even before he was born.

"I'll go down and see her soon."

"Muniath. This dragon. Is it really the lost one?" Wick asked, concerned.

"He is."

"But he is so much bigger and older in appearance than his two siblings."

"There is a reason for it, and I am not going to go into it right now. Gremlin—or Vojin— is very special and I promise as soon as I am able to, I'll explain it all. Right now, I think it is time we go back into Screamer's cavern." Muniath placed a guiding hand on Wick's shoulder, gently steering him through the entrance to Screamer's cave.

The pair found Gremlin saying his goodbyes. Screamer cooed softly at him and inside his mind Muniath could hear her voice rumbling full of love and joy but tinged with sadness. He could almost work out the words she was saying, until it was shut off and he was pushed to one side.

"It is time for me to go, there is someone I have to find before the sun rises," Gremlin said as he turned. Muniath and Gremlin walked to the great

walkway with its large gaps overhead. They reached the last opening before the human entrance and Gremlin turned to him.

"Now I am home things will work out. It will all be the way it is supposed to be," Gremlin said gently meaning to comfort Muniath.

"I thank you my friend. When will you be back?"

"As soon as I can. The one I seek is even more stubborn than you, Muniath Dragon-Blood." Gremlin chuckled.

Spreading his wings wide he lifted them high, as Muniath stepped back out of the way. The wind generated by the massive wings being beaten buffeted him and he headed to the barricaded entrance. Reaching it, he watched as Gremlin took to his wings and headed off into the dark of the night. His wings stretched majestically, and he saw the great belch of fire as he finally felt free enough to enjoy it. Muniath also heard the call he put out to the world. A cry of joy, of freedom, and reunion. He stood there until he could not see him anymore, then turned and headed down the steep steps for home.

His steps quickened as he raced down the walkway set into the side of the mountain behind the castle and citadel. His mind on getting home and trying to convince his sister to not marry Orcades.

It was a long climb down, and for once Muniath did not pay attention to the sights along the way. He made it to the front steps of the house and stopped, his foot on the bottom stair that led to the main doors. He cleared his mind and sent out a thought as Gremlin had taught him. The search was for Ide. He did not want to see her if Orcades was nearby. His own feelings for the man would take over and be uncontrolled.

Muniath found Ide on the other side of the house, in the same spot he had seen her earlier from the back of Gremlin. She was alone. Changing direction, he headed around the large house, making sure he would not be seen from the lit windows on the ground floor, feeling the presence of his mother and father inside. It was Ide he needed to see first.

Heading through the gardens he found the steps to the large terrace that looked out over the lake and found her still there. Arms crossed in front of her, leaning against the balustrade, staring at the water shimmering under the moons.

"About time you got back," she said quietly then giving a little chuckle that belied the tone in her voice.

"How are you?" he asked, not surprised that she had sensed him before making himself known.

"Where have you been?" she countered, turning now to face him.

"On a mission; one I cannot talk about."

"Why can't you talk about it?" she asked, stepping towards him.

"You should know that reason, Ide," he chuckled softly. "And you did not respond to my first question; how are you?" he repeated.

"Fine. Orcades wants to move the ceremony up," she told him, her tone was one of regret and dread.

Muniath heard the catch in her voice and could tell immediately that she had changed her mind about her intended. He rethought the situation and found all the possible ways he could extract his sister from the situation she found herself in.

"You don't wish for the union anymore," he stated the obvious.

"No, Mun. I've discovered something," she told him.

Muniath drew his sister in a comforting hug. "I know what it is. It was because of your discovery that I went on my mission."

Ide held onto her younger brother. "But it is not only because of that. I don't love him. I realize that now. I felt flattered he had noticed me; had told me he could not live without me. He said all the right things to cajole and make me feel special; to turn my head to think that I loved him. Why do men do that, Mun?"

Muniath kissed the top of her head. "To do just as you have said, so they get their own way and also to flatter their own ego. I've been guilty of it myself," he admitted to her.

"There is another reason," Ide told him, breaking his hold, and moving back to the spot he had found her. Her arms once more hugging her body. Muniath came to stand with her, looking down on his older sister.

"What is it?"

"I don't know if I can explain it," she said, shaking her head.

"Try me. Ide, I can't help you if you don't open up to me. You're always there for me, let me help you." He placed a caring hand on her shoulder. With a sudden insight his eyes went wide. "There's another?" he asked quietly. He saw her nod slowly. "He appears in your dreams?" Again, a nod.

"They are plagued by them, Mun."

"Is it the man who took you?"

"It is," she said plainly. "That journey down the gorge changed me. He opened my eyes. It was he who told me of the plot, of who Orcades is and what he wants. Scetis is not the man you think he is." She tilted her face up to meet his eyes, pleading with him to understand.

"Tell me of his eyes?" Muniath asked her.

"His eyes? Why do you want to know about his eyes?"

"Just describe them for me."

"Blue; a bright vivid blue."

"Is there anything else?"

"He has a silver ring around the iris, just like you do, and I could have sworn that they glowed at one point. Why?"

"So that is who Gremlin has gone to find," Muniath murmured and from the depths of his mind he heard the dragon chuckle.

"Muniath, explain to me now why you wanted to know about Scetis' eyes." Ide demanded, her voice rising.

"You have the silver in your eyes as well, sister dearest. It marks us as being a little bit different."

"Different, how?"

"*She is not ready yet,*" Gremlin broke through into Muniath's mind and left just as quickly.

When he had not answered her quickly enough, Ide demanded the same question. "Different, how, Muniath?"

"I can't tell you just yet, but you'll know soon. I promise."

"Muniath, you are all about secrets tonight." Ide started to head inside the house behind them. "The only one who has been straight with me is Scetis."

"Ide, don't be like that. I've already told you that I can't tell you. It all has to do with why I had to go away for a bit." He reached out to hold her back.

"Tell me, Muniath, who knows you are back?" she asked, stopping short of the house.

"Only King Urmond and Wick."

"Don't go inside. Don't let anyone know you're home, please. I made Orcades a promise that we would wed when you got home. I need more time. Please, Mun." Her voice broke and a tear fell from her eye, glinting in the moonlight as it rolled down her cheek, leaving an almost glowing trail in its wake. Muniath reached out and wiped the tear gently from his sister's face then pulled her into his arms once more to comfort her.

"I'll go beg a room from Mae. She and Taran won't let on that I'm back to anyone. I promise Ide, you will not be marrying Orcades anytime soon, not if I have anything to do with it," he told her.

Teagan wandered the opulently decorated suit of rooms, trying to remember her time there before being exiled with her father, but it was hard. She searched for the memories of her mother but found them difficult to grasp. A tinkling and quick laugh, eyes bright and twinkling, but the sound of her voice was gone. Teagan went to the window and looked out. The rooms faced the town. The light was muted from the streetlamps which shone a golden glow rather than the bright white or orange she was used to. The streets were empty except for some walking in twos or threes. One caught her attention. A lone figure striding along, ducking into shadows when anyone neared. She lost him behind a building, but when he re-emerged, she could tell he was being furtive. He stopped for a moment and looked up at the castle. Teagan gasped as she recognized Muniath, not only physically and visually, but found him with her mind also. She could not see his expression but recognized he had felt her watching. Reaching out as she did with Gremlin she found a connection and grasped it like a child with a new toy.

"*Easy,*" Muniath instructed her. "*But now is not really the time.*" He gently pushed her away.

Teagan stumbled back from the window and the break, as she continued to stare out at the dark night and her own illuminated reflection.

"*All in good time, Child of Dragons,*" Gremlin said and then his chuckle faded.

The room around her suddenly felt empty and almost oppressive, and she left her childhood bedroom in search of her father. Teagan found him sitting by the large fireplace and the image of when she had last seen him there came back to her. He looked up at his daughter with a smile, which she returned.

"It's good to be home," he told her.

"It is, Papa." She sat down on the chair on the other side of the fireplace.

"We need to talk, before Urmond joins us," he told her.

"What about?" she asked curiously.

"Tomorrow we will be parted," Tharain started.

"Yes, we will. But you said the farm was not far from here." Teagan moved in her chair, now sitting on the edge of the soft cushioned seat.

"It's not, but I'm worried about leaving you here on your own. Things are very different here. Everyone knows everyone and their business. It's not like Earth, where we barely saw our neighbors."

"I think I can handle things, Papa." Teagan said confidently, deliberately sitting back.

"I know you're capable of handling yourself, Teagan, but there are people who will want to use you, due to your position and relationship with the king. They will try to get to the king through you." His whole manner and expression were serious and concerned.

A knock at the door broke their conversation and Tharain leapt from his seat to go answer it. Opening the door wide he admitted Urmond and one other. A woman with hair that was the color of straw, dressed in close fitting leather trousers and an over dress that was synched at the waist and was longer in the back than the front. Her boots were calf length and were tied with crossing laces.

"I hope we're not interrupting," Urmond said as he entered the room.

"My King, you don't disturb us in the slightest." Tharain bowed.

"May I reintroduce you to my daughter, Orlagh," Urmond brought her forward to stand beside him.

"You have grown, Princess," Tharain said stupidly, bowing to her.

"Please, Cousin Tharain, just Orlagh will do." She then turned her gaze to Teagan. "Do you remember me?" she asked shyly.

"I do," Teagan said, walking towards her.

Just as Tharain was about to shut the door, Urmond stopped him. "There is one more who wishes to say hello," he said with a wink.

Urmond whistled and a large caramel colored, brindled dog came through the door, with grey on his muzzle. He bound up to Teagan, his tail wagging madly. The dog jumped up, his front paws landing on her stomach, his tongue hanging out and his eyes bright.

"Bili?" she asked, her hands going to his head and scratching the dog's ears.

"The closer we got to these rooms the more excited he became," Urmond told her. "He still remembers you, Teagan, and he is yours once more. A little older maybe, but still loyal to you," he said kindly.

"I can't believe he's still alive," she said in wonder, sinking to her knees and wrapping arms around the dog's neck. Bili in turn licked her face over and over.

"He is old for a dog. I believe he's been waiting for you to come home,"

"Thank you for looking after him," she said into the short fur.

The others stood around watching the tender reunion with smiles on their faces.

Urmond cleared his throat. "Why don't you and Orlagh go get acquainted again, take Bili with you. I need to talk with your father."

Teagan let the dog go and stood to face her cousin, who was smiling at her. "Will you be alright, Papa?" she asked, concern for her father welling up.

"I'll be fine, go and have fun," Tharain reassured her.

"I'll be back soon," she told him and then turned to Orlagh. The two women left, and Teagan looked back at Bili who was now sat beside Urmond, staring at her. She smiled a little. "He may remember me, but he appears to be more loyal to you, My Lord King," she stumbled over the words.

"He does, and Teagan we are family, please call me Urmond."

Teagan nodded her agreement and followed Orlagh down the hall, hearing the door close behind them.

Orlagh linked her arm with Teagan as they walked. "Do you remember the secret passage to the pastry kitchen?"

"It's been a very long time since I've been here."

"Well then, let me reacquaint you with it. The old cook is still there, and she remembers you. When I told her you were home she lit up and has made something special for you." Orlagh laughed lightly.

"So much of my childhood has gone," Teagan told her.

"It'll come back now you are home. Once we're finished in the kitchen, then I have been instructed to help you with a new wardrobe. And I want you to meet someone. Teagan, I am so happy you are home. I cried for a whole month after you left. I wouldn't talk to my father for three. I blamed him for you leaving us."

"But it wasn't his fault."

"I know that now. I remember when your father would take us up to the Eyrie to see the dragons. I fell in love with them then, and your mother—"

"You remember my mother?" she interrupted, stopping for a moment.

"I do. So very clearly. She was one of the best riders. You don't remember?"

"No," Teagan said sadly.

"Then we have a lot to talk about."

Information

Something cold dripped onto Scetis' face. He was barely aware of it at first and imagined it was part of the confused dream he was having. A dream he believed was all part of the poison that was once more overtaking his body. He wondered how long it would be until it finally saturated his blood and stopped his heart. The curious thoughts seemed so remote from what his mind was seeing, and it struck him as being funny.

The dream that surrounded him was vivid and bright. Once more he felt like he was flying high through pure white clouds, so far above the earth. He could feel the slight up lift as the mighty wings beat through the air and the cold wind brushed over his face. He could feel the roar build in his throat and willed it to release. It welled up until he felt his chest would burst if it were not let go. It started as a low rumble barely audible but rattled in his chest. It bellowed out, until his ears hurt. The heat that came with it boiled away inside. It crept up his throat, burning, until it escaped his lips. A jet of flame belched out in a strong steady stream, bright white and orange flames rolled over themselves as they instantly burned away the cloud around him.

A dark shape suddenly rose in front of him. Large wings wide, dark scales of matte black absorbed the light from around it. The new dragon's head festooned with small glossy spikes, glistened in the dimmed light. The large male black dragon worked hard with his leathery wings to hold himself in place. His tail whipping around behind him.

"Vojin." The dragon bowed his head in reverence to Scetis. It was a name he had never heard before.

"Tell our brethren that I have come home. Tell them that a new ruler will soon sit on the Throne of Dragons. Let them know they will no longer be hunted," a growl came from his lips, but the words were not his.

The great black took to wing again and swooped away through the clouds and out of sight. Scetis felt himself climb higher into the sky. The air thinned, but he still breathed deeply. The clouds fell far below, and he basked in the full sun that beat down, even though the air around him was cool, it warmed him.

"Wake Scetis," the deep voice called out to him. Again, he felt what seemed like rain on his face and stirred with the words. "You must wake, Scetis. Your time to die is not yet come," it barked at him.

Scetis pried opened his crusty, red-rimmed eyes to look out at the dim room of rock. He lay there for a moment, trying to get his bearings, unsure if he was still dreaming or not. Droplets of water once more rained down on his face, making him blink. He looked up to the rugged roof which was only just discernible in the dim flickering light but could not see the source of the droplets.

"Are you awake?" a high-pitched voice called out.

Scetis heard water splashing about before another drenching of droplets fell on his face. He turned his head and peered through the gloom. A small lake lay beside him, with tendrils of steam rising from it, swirling, and eddying as something moved in its depths. Slowly a creature rose from the water, rivulets streamed from its long red, serpentine body. Wings spread out behind the creature and flapped, shaking the water from the membrane. The face of the creature was long and pointed. It's eyes were set high on its head and the nostrils set at the end, just above the mouth, which was filled with sharp, needle-like teeth. The small arms ended in what looked more like fingers than the claws of a normal one of its kind. Each finger was adorned with a sharpened nail of glistening red, which matched that of its body. The underbelly was a lighter shade to that of its back. The small dragon waded out of the water, holding itself up on hind legs, walking like a human and standing just taller by a foot or two than the average man. He shambled closer to Scetis and peered at him, bringing his nose close.

"You are awake. Your eyes are open," it cooed, the voice did not come directly from the creature, but sounded loud in Scetis' mind.

Coming to his senses he scrambled away from the dragon. The sudden movement set off waves of pain through his body, making his muscles spasm. Scetis ground and clenched his teeth as he tried to control it and not show any weakness before the dragon that was staring at him. Scetis searched around him for his bag, desperate to take the potion to ease his symptoms.

"Oh, no, no, no," the creature said, rushing over to the bag by the wall. "He said that you were not to take it. You have to burn what ails you from your blood. You will not die. He told me, he assured me that you would not" the dragon said, picking up the bags and clutching them, protectively. His tail, which ended in an arrow looking point, swished around him in agitation.

"I need it," Scetis said aloud weakly. The shaking was becoming worse as it felt like ice was flowing through his veins.

"You were fine while you slept. You had no trembling or shaking then," the dragon said curiously, as it took a hesitant step closer.

"Please, I will die," Scetis whispered.

"No, you won't. Your blood is that of a dragon." The small dragon came over to Scetis and laid a hand on his head. *"It's fighting, yes. I can feel it."* He placed the bags down and as soon as they were released, Scetis grabbed them.

With numb and fumbling fingers, he tried to open the buckles on the bag. Before they were released it was snatched from his failing hands.

"You are not to, he commanded it," the dragon said emphatically. With small running steps he moved to the wall and placed the bags back down. *"You need the water,"* he said, turning back to Scetis.

"Water?"

"The mineral spring is hot. You must burn the poison from your body," he said, quickly coming back. He leaned down and his human like hands began to pull at the jacket Scetis still wore.

"Get off me!" Scetis demanded trying to fend him off.

The dragon huffed in frustration and stepped back. "Vojin, what am I to do? You charge me to find him, to go out in the cold and bring him here. I did that. You told me to help him, but he will not listen. What am I to do?" His arms were crossed in front of him, and his foot tapped irritably on the smooth stone floor.

"Audel, he will listen," the booming voice spoke. "Scetis, you must follow his instructions. The poison which flows through your veins is attacking your human side. Your dragon side will dispel it, but you have to let it."

"Who are you?" Scetis cried out loud as well in his mind.

"We will meet soon. I'm almost there. Follow Audel's instructions, I sent him to help you," the voice said and was gone.

"Now will you do as you're told?" the dragon at his side said huffily.

Scetis stared at the small dragon, who stared back with his bright green reptilian eyes.

"I don't understand," Scetis said quietly.

"What is there to understand? If you want to live, then do as you are told."

"What is dragon blood?"

"Just undress and get into the water. I'll explain once you do," he said smugly. "And my name is Squirt, not Audel. No matter what Vojin says."

With difficulty Scetis sat and started to undo the jacket or attempted to. His fingers shook so much that he gave up with a grunt. The red dragon was there and quickly stripping Scetis of the clothing that stuck to him with the sweat from his body. Scetis noticed Squirt turn his head with the stench that was leaching from his pores and he had to agree that he was rank.

The small dragon was definitely stronger than his size led Scetis to believe. Squirt helped to move Scetis to the water with ease. The water from the natural spring seeped over his bare feet and crept up his body the further they moved into it. When the water reached his knees, he sunk down into it, lying down, and immersing all his body in the water that drew its heat from the center of the earth. Scetis closed his eyes, letting the soothing water relax his muscles. A splash beside him indicated that the small dragon had joined him.

"Right, you wish to know, and I can explain a little," Squirt began. "You are mostly dragon if what Vojin has to say about it is true. The story of how your kind came about is long and tedious, but they were created to deal with the humans who were afraid of us. Isn't that ridiculous? So there you have it, you are dragon, like me," he said proudly.

Scetis watched as the small dragon floated on his back, using his wings to move him about in the water. Squirt turned his head and sucked in the water through pursed lips, then looked up to the ceiling. A long stream of the steaming water erupted from his mouth before it fell, tinkling back into the water around his head. Scetis decided at that point he must still be in the midst of delirium and closed his eyes. He heard the creature chuckle a little before another round of tinkling water.

More drops of water fell over Scetis' face, waking him from a deep, dreamless sleep. He shook them from his face and looked about him blearily. Realizing he was naked floating in hot water brought back what he thought had been a dream,

"Time to wake. Vojin will be here soon. He will help you harness your dragon blood to burn the rest of the poison from you," Squirt told him.

The small dragon stood and walked out of the water then rushed to the entrance of the cave, which still showed it to be dark outside. Soft white snow fell, glistening in the flickering firelight.

"Who is he?" Scetis asked sitting up and immediately feeling the cold that was in the air.

"Who is he? Who is he?" Squirt spluttered from the entrance. "HE is only the most important dragon ever to have existed. HE is the reason you exist!"

Scetis stared at the small dragon and when he did not say anything further Squirt continued.

"Vojin was one of the High Dragons, one of the very first. They ruled over this world and many others before man came to our world. The High Dragons sacrificed themselves so that your kind, Dragon Blood, may be born and continue the dragon's rule." Squirt moved away from the large entrance and splashed his way back into the pool. "If there's not one of Dragon Blood on the throne in the Dragon Realm, then dragons will be no more." Squirt shivered and Scetis could not tell if it was because of the cold or from the prospect of there being no dragons.

"Look at me!" Squirt cried, looking at himself in the swirling water. "I am a runt, an irregularity in the world of Dragons. I am stunted and small. Weak, my mother called me before tossing me out of the nest. I have been shunned by my kind all my life, even hunted in some instances. My own sire decided he did not want it known that I was his off-spring and tried to kill me. But I was too quick for them. They like the hot lands, so I went cold. I came up here and found this cave. Nice and warm. Is it my fault I was born this way? But I am fast, and smart, and Vojin is my friend." Squirt lay back and began his slow swimming, using his stunted wings to propel him around.

"You're a Red; a fire breather?" Scetis asked, finally finding his voice.

"I am. But I wish I had been born a white or a blue, as you people call us."

"What do you call your breeds?" Scetis asked, laying back down into the thermal pool to soak up the warmth once more.

"Well I am not just a Red, I am an Ignis. And before you ask; yes, I can still produce a flame." To prove his point a little jet of flame erupted from his mouth followed by a puff of smoke.

"But other breeds produce fire," Scetis was curious now.

"Yes they can, but an Ignis can withstand flames and other heat sources. We were born from the very bowels of this world, deep in its molten core," he said proudly, his chest puffing out.

"If you've been hunted and shunned how do you know all this?"

"I woke up one morning a few weeks ago and Vojin spoke to me. He explained and taught me everything."

From the jagged opening of the cave, a cry called out in the snowstorm that raged and fell outside. Squirt sat up and quickly left the pool.

"He's here! Vojin is here!" he cried excitedly, clapping his hand like paws, and jumping up and down like an excited child. He turned elated

eyes to Scetis and started running his hands over his head and body, stripping the rivulets of water from his scales. *"Do I look alright?"*

"I do not care what you look like, Audel," a deep voice said from the entrance. Out of the gloom and shifting white of the snow a head appeared quickly, followed by an enormous body of the deepest of emerald-green. Large wings were tucked to the sides as he squeezed his way into the cave, taking up most of the room. Squirt bowed low to the newcomer, his elongated nose just about scraping the ground.

"Vojin, welcome. I hope I have served you well and have done all you asked of me," Squirt said eloquently.

"Get up, Audel. You have done well." The large dragon turned his silver eyes to Scetis. *"We meet at last Scetis."* He nodded his head to Scetis.

"You. It was your voice I've been hearing?" Scetis tried to scrabble out of the water, but stumbled, his legs feeling weak and numb from the poison. He pitched forwards and landed face first into the water, a great splash erupting around him. Squirt was at his side in only a moment, pulling him to shallower depths and rolling him onto his back.

"He's burning up, Vojin, his body is shutting down," Squirt called out.

"Scetis will not die. Bring him to the fire," Vojin instructed.

Placing his clawed hands under Scetis' shoulders, Squirt dragged the now unconscious form of the man to the small fire, which was only used for light, rather than warmth. Lying him down gently, Squirt then retrieved his jacket and placed it under the man's head before stepping back to leave room for Vojin. The large dragon placed his head close to the fevered brow of Scetis and closed his eyes.

Deep within his mind Scetis found himself. A voice was gently calling to him. *"Awaken, Scetis. Open that part of your mind which has been closed. Awaken your dragon side,"* it cooed to him.

"How? I don't understand," Scetis called out in fright.

"Just relax and calm yourself. It will come to you," the voice said gently and patiently.

Scetis clung to that voice, as he had to his mother's hand when he was a child. A light appeared before him. It grew in intensity and size until it enveloped him. With it came an awareness that he was not alone.

For the first time in his life, he felt he belonged to something more; something larger. He desired that, craved, and wanted it greedily. Closing his eyes, he pushed his head back, exposing his vulnerable throat and spread his arms wide.

"I am Blood of Dragon. I was born from dragons and wish to be one of the Draconem!" he cried out, feeling the call leave his mind and spread far into the world.

The light enveloped him and from far and near distances a collective roar went up from many voices. Voices rejoicing in his acceptance. The minds of others crowded in on his own. They were many, yet each individual distinct from the others. The rush of acceptance was overwhelming, and he felt a lump grow in his throat. Tears streamed from his eyes leaving rapidly cooling trails down his cheeks. But he ignored them, ignored the feeling of them freezing in place.

"Breathe, Scetis," Vojin said gently and waited for the feeling of euphoria to ebb.

Drawing in a great breath, Scetis' vision cleared, and he was back in the cave, standing before the greatest dragon to have ever lived. He drew in another great breath and let it out shuddering as he did so, the emotions threatening to envelope him. He bent over double and wiped the freezing tears from his face. When he stood, he was more composed and in control on the outside, though his insides were still racing and feeling like they had turned to liquid. Once more he took in a lungful of air and expelled it this time in a great rush.

"You said I could burn the poison from my blood. How?" he asked, looking Vojin in his silvery eyes.

"Concentrate on the fire in the corner. Look into its flames," Vojin instructed.

Scetis walked to the fire and felt the welcoming heat from the dancing tongues of flame. He crouched down and rested his arms on his knees, while he peered into the depths of the fire. It crackled and flickered in the draft from the opening of the cave and then it went still. The flames were straight, like the flame on a candle in a still room. He continued to stare and drew in the heat from the fire, feeling it absorb through his skin and into his very flesh.

He felt the burning reach his veins and the blood that pumped through them. Finally, the heat which was growing hotter by the moment reached his heart. Scetis felt it swell and stumble in its beat. He wobbled where he was crouched and finally went to one knee. The irregular beat continued, but he did not break his stare or concentration of the flames. Finally, on both knees he placed his hands on the ground before him.

His heart began to sprint and Scetis felt the invading heat race through his body, to the very tips of his toes and the roots of his hair. A burning, cleansing heat. There was no pain like he thought there would be, only a gentleness like a caress. The poison was gathering and collecting in a pocket. Somehow it leached from every part of his body and collected in his stomach. With a heaving lurch it fought its way out of him. He gagged on it and felt it move up from his stomach to his mouth. The emptiness of his stomach did not help the matter. The poison when it was finally expelled lay in a puddle by the fire, green and gelatinous. It smelled terrible. Scetis wiped his mouth with the back of his hand. His canteen was held out in front of him in a clawed hand. He took it and drank greedily from the overly long stored water.

Scetis sat back on his heels, sweat dripping down his face from the purging. He breathed deeply, his eyes closed, and he wiped his face with a hand and sighed. For a moment he just sat. For the first time since he had been poisoned, he felt good. Not just good, but amazing. His heart beating a little fast in his chest still from the exertion, but it was strong. He did not feel the tremors which always seemed to be threatening.

Taking in another deep breath, he finally registered the pile of poisonous gunk he had expelled. He wrinkled his nose at the smell and went to toss dirt from the floor over the top of it.

"Leave it, Scetis. Audel will deal with it," Vojin said gently.

Squirt was soon there beside him, his clawed hands moved Scetis out of the way and then the small dragon stood straight. His head was thrown back a little, then he thrust it forward. His mouth opened and a jet of liquid flame shot out, spreading out over the mess. The concoction caught fire and it rankled and boiled away as Squirt continued to shoot the jet at it. The smoke from the burning poison rose in boiling black clouds and hung in the air. A gentle wind fanned by Vojin's large wings dispersed the toxic fumes out of the cave mouth.

Finally out of breath, Squirt stepped back from the charred mess. It was dry and flaky now and Squirt began to pick up the pieces, then took them outside.

"There is more I need to know; isn't there?" Scetis asked, taking another sip of the water.

'There is much you need to know. Some I will leave to Audel to instruct you on. Do not dismiss him offhand due to his size. He is strong and smarter than he appears," Vojin replied.

"I will not, I assure you." Scetis got to his feet slowly, feeling slightly light-headed, while Vojin regarded the half dragon before him.

"The change is complete. I will stay with you for a few days. It is important that we get to know each other. We will be working closely together." Vojin moved closer to the small fire.

"What is there that I must learn?"

"How to be a king for a start. But that will come later. Firstly, you must learn our history and yours, Scetis. You were born to rule."

"I come from the wrong side of anyone's sheets to rule. I'm an orphan, and a nobody."

"That is where you are wrong. Dragons do not hold to the conventions of man. It does not matter that you are illegitimate in their eyes. You were born from a great love. A first love."

Squirt came bustling in at that point. He flew through the entrance, with both arms and hind legs occupied with a large and heavy amount of wood. He deposited his bundle down beside the fire. Scetis watched the curious creature. Small he may be, but he was quick and strong. His eyes darted everywhere, taking in everything and where everyone was. He bustled away to the packs that were laying on the ground and tidied them against the wall. Scetis also saw that the small dragon's curious eyes lingered on the small one that contained the medicines, and his hands twitched as if he were wanting to investigate what lay within.

"You'll be hungry," Squirt said, moving over to the dark corner of the cave. When he came back he was dragging along behind him a large frozen animal.

With a sudden revulsion that he might be expected to eat the animal raw along with these two dragons, Scetis began to protest. Until Squirt passed him and headed outside. A deep chuckle from behind him made Scetis turn.

"You will not be subjected to that. You are not a full dragon. Squirt will prepare a portion for you; he feels that your sensibilities will be offended if he cut it up in here." As he spoke Vojin moved even closer to the small fire.

Scetis jumped up, went to the wood pile, and started to feed the flames. They bloomed upwards, reaching high towards the roof of the cave. He looked around and found a dazzling display of crystals embedded in the dark rock. The light they threw back glittered and sparkled and in amongst them a thick vein of gold branched out in long ropey fingers.

"This cave has been used for many centuries. Since the dawn of this world, when the first dragons emerged from the fires within this mountain." Vojin sighed deeply and rested his head on his fore paws. "But we will begin your education in the morning. You need rest and food first."

A rustling by his head roused Scetis. The distinctive sound of the clasp opening on his potion box made his eyes fly open and he was reaching out to take it from Squirt's hands.

"No!" he cried out as if to a small child. The box now in his hands, Scetis held it and saw the small dragon look at him, with a mix of astonishment and hurt in his eyes.

"I just wanted to see," Squirt told him.

"There are some very dangerous and deadly potions and powders in here. I did not mean to speak so sharply, just to keep you safe."

"So show him," Vojin yawned from beside the fire.

"In the morning?" Squirt asked eagerly.

"The morning." Scetis agreed and carefully placed the book like box back into his pack and drew both to him, noticing each had been opened and searched.

Settling back down on the opposite side of the fire to Vojin, Scetis stared into the flames. He watched as Squirt tended the fire, building it up against the invading cold. The dragon sat hunched beside it, not looking like he would settle for sleep. His hands hugged his knees, and he drew his wings around him. His eyes never left the fire, and the dragon began to hum. The tune at first sounded droning, but soon it changed. It soared into high notes and cooed in the low.

The Squirt's song lulled Scetis' eyes to close and his breathing to deepen without realizing it. The song soon had Scetis asleep, but it invaded there also. It wove itself through the dream, a dream of soaring through clouds, then plunging with the music, down low over fields. Before him loomed a large mountain. Tall and steep it towered, surrounded by water of a deep lake.

The dream took him to that mountain. The steep cliff loomed large before him. He felt himself moving up, his wings beating and climbing. He knew where he was going; was looking for the opening that was only just a few wing beats away. What looked like the ever-approaching tip of the mountain zoomed passed him and spread out in the form of a large ledge. Flat and even. At the back of this platform was a gaping opening. It yawned wide and dark before Scetis as he landed on the ledge. He looked down at the flat rock at his feet and found he was in human form, and for a moment regretted it, reviled it.

Walking towards the cave mouth he saw shadows moving, large and fleeting glimpses of something moving around in another time. Shadows of past dragons that had used this space. Standing at the entrance he waited. He could feel the pull to enter, but he felt he should wait. He was not sure for what, but it held him back.

"Enter Scetis," the deep booming voice he now knew called out to him. *"Enter and start your education."*

With a step he crossed the invisible threshold and entered a world of darkness. He blinked his eyes and soon became accustomed to the inky black interior. His footsteps, sure and unfaltering, moved him into the large space. A wide corridor led further into the mountain, the wind from outside whipped around him, funneling into the cave. On he went, it seemed to never end, and the echoic footsteps of the shadowy dragons were soft in his ears, as they accompanied him on his journey.

A glow made itself known to him by way of flickering shadows that had nothing to do with his companions. They gave the walls, roof, and floor an undulating feeling, like the mountain itself was breathing. There was also another noise. A rushing sound that irritatingly merged with the cool wind from outside, it was not quite a roar, but he felt the vibration from it.

The more he walked the brighter the glow became. It burned brightly now, a white light and then he felt the heat. A rush from in front was warm and it seeped into his bones. Scetis found himself walking quicker, eager to get to the source of the light and the heat, until he was running. Now he could see the great arch, silhouetted against the light. He could see another platform stretching out before it suddenly stopped. He burst out onto that ledge and stopped at the edge. He stared out into the largest cavern he could ever imagine. His eyes wide as he took it all in. The opposite side was just visible.

Rows upon rows of ledges like the one he stood on ringed the circular cavern. They stepped down like a giant funnel. He looked down into the depths and found the source of the light. Far below was a large pool. The edges carved intricately in swirling patterns. The pool was not filled with water but boiling fiery liquid. The heat that rose from the liquid fire was immense and the smell of sulfur hung in the air.

'This is our birthplace,' the voice of Vojin spoke to him. The rumble of his voice almost lost in the sounds from below. 'This is where we emerged, from the liquid fire of the earth. The first were formed from the very center of this world, from the very stone of the core that remains there. They emerged, climbing out of the pit below into this volcano. Their wings did not exist, their bellies did not have the fire, but they were strong, and they survived. The Firsts clawed their way out, they found this cave and dug it out. When they beheld the land beyond they roared. It was cold and the heat from the world still sped through their veins. They came back in here and settled. They made this their home, but hunger soon caught at them. On the winds that filtered in were the scents of game, of vegetation, and they longed to taste it.

"Within their structure was the stuff of the world. A magical essence that they had in abundance. Using that essence they changed themselves. They molded their forms, became bigger and stronger. Each time they changed, they would swim within the liquid fire, the source regenerating their magic. With these new forms they left the cave and hunted. The land beyond held an abundance of food and they feasted long. Our ancestors mated and the offspring were prodigious, they spread wide until the world was groaning at their number. Again the Firsts turned to their magic. They returned to the caves, the ledges they dug out so they could rest in comfort, while discussing what needed to be done.

"A solution of discovering new worlds was proposed and studied. With the use of the pit below they discovered where our world and others were close, where the veil of time and space between them was thin and they managed to open up a tear. The openings were unstable and prone to collapse. A liquid metal was found to hold them open. The large mirrors used to be held here, in this very cave.

"With the opening of worlds, we spread. Moved out into other lands and dimensions. They populated the worlds, some flourished while others died out. It was through the portals the humankind came; they were afraid and did the only thing they knew. They hunted and killed our kind. When we discovered that they would stay, we had to find a way to live with their kind. We had to change. We drew all we could from the center of the world, we sacrificed ourselves one by one, the originals, until there was only one. Me.

"A young dragon was chosen and was brought before me, down by the pit. He was a fierce and brave youngling. Not once did he cry out as I changed his form. Made him into the image of a human. But I left one particular detail. The eyes. The silver in his eyes was deep and dark.

"My time had come, my energy spent. I waded into the pool and sunk beneath the surface of fire, never to wake again, or so I thought. Our young dragon did as we hoped, he mated with a human woman, a chief's daughter, and their children carried the dragon blood. As long as one of the Blood of Dragons rules this land, then the dragons will survive. I found my spirit would return every now and then when the line is in peril. And once more, now is one of those times."

While Vojin had been talking, the shades of the old dragons moved around them, playing out the story. Scetis now stood in the quiet.

"What now? Why is this important to me?" he asked, his voice a whisper in the large space.

"I will explain that soon. For now you need rest," Vojin told him and the vision of the cave slipped away into darkness.

Scetis stood in an empty void with nothing around him. The sound of Squirt's song had changed, it was different, lighter, softer. Movement before him caught his eye. A figure emerged and stood before him. The figure of a woman who caught at his heart and made his breath freeze in his lungs. Ide.

Her long dark hair was loose around her bare shoulders. Dressed only in a filmy slip, the sight of her body excited him. He forced his eyes away from her curves to her eyes. They were confused and questioning. The silver around the iris of her eyes sparkled and shone brightly.

"Scetis?" she questioned softly. His name sounded sweet from her red lips.

"Ide," he greeted her back.

A few drops of water dripped onto Scetis' face and he twitched. A few more joined the others and slid down his face. Still half asleep he wiped them away with some irritation and rolled over onto his side, pulling his jacket up to his chin. His eyes never opened, and he just wished to go back to the dream he had been having. Ide. He sighed as he remembered how she felt in his arms.

She had walked into them without hesitation, had offered him her soft lips without question. They had accepted each other without words. Scetis sighed again, regretting it was just a dream, one he hoped to go back to.

A torrent of water spilled over his head. It invaded his nose and mouth, making him splutter and curse. Sitting up suddenly he wiped the dripping water from his face and short cropped hair, while hearing the chortle of laughter and water splashing from the hot spring.

"A good morning to you Scetis," Squirt greeted him from the pool as he pushed himself around with his bat like wings.

"Don't do that again," Scetis growled at him, pushing the wet jacket from him, feeling the water cool quickly on his exposed skin from the wind.

"Do what?" Squirt chuckled as innocently as he could.

Scetis turned his back on the small dragon. It was a mistake. Another jet of water streamed over his head, this time Squirt did nothing to hide his mirth. With eyes flashing with silver, Scetis turned back to him. His mouth opened to yell at the still laughing small dragon when Vojin stepped between them.

"Leave him. It is his idea of a jest. I asked him to wake you, but I should have specified how and how not to." Vojin moved his bulky form closer to the fire, leaving a trail of snow from his large feet. He curled his tail around him tightly as he lay beside the dancing flames.

"But—"

"Scetis, he will not change because you tell him off. Let him be, he will grow bored with it soon enough."

Scetis moved closer to the fire as his stomach growled loudly. Pulling his bags near him he searched through them, finding the small amount of provisions Gant had provided the night he had fled. Quickly he ate and cleaned up after himself, all the while conscious of the fact that the large dragon was watching with his glittering eyes, but also with the connection in their minds. Sitting back after putting his bags back against the wall, he turned his attention to the dragon.

"Last night," he began. "You showed me a vision. It was no dream was it?"

"It was not," Vojin said, his eyes blinking slowly.

"So does that mean that the second dream was just a dream?"

"It was not," the large dragon said again, resting his head on his front feet. *"Did it displease you?"*

"No; it did not." Scetis blushed slightly.

The education of Scetis continued for the next day and night. Once more he was rewarded for his efforts with a visit from Ide. Throughout the day he would catch Squirt trying to sneak a peak in his bags, curious to know what this human hybrid had stored there.

The things Scetis was shown at first had him disbelieving. It was hard for him to reorganize his thinking. He felt the changes happen slowly, not only mentally, but physically. Always a fit man, the changes to his body were noticeable the second morning. The sleeves on his shirt were starting to creep up his arms, also the cuffs of his leather pants. His body was elongating, becoming leaner and more muscular. When he commented on these changes, Vojin only said they were necessary.

"More dragon-like," Squirt commented from his reclining pose in the pool.

Scetis stared at the little dragon as he propelled himself lazily through the spring fed water. "You're a fire-breather are you not?" he asked.

"I am, we have discussed this already," Squirt replied, shooting a jet of water up into the air above him.

"So, should you be doing that?" Scetis had risen from his spot by the fire, feeling Vojin's eyes watching him carefully.

"Why not?" Squirt responded with a chortle.

"Aren't you afraid of putting your fire out?"

"You have a lot to learn, human. The fire cannot be put out, but only tempered."

"So you can still breathe fire?"

"What a silly question! Of course I can't breathe fire. If I breathed it, then my lungs would be scorched. Then I would be dead," he said before sending another spray of water droplets up into the air, to fall back with a musical tinkling sound.

"So where does the fire come from?" Scetis asked, now crouching beside the edge of the pool.

"All these questions and concerns. Oh my, Scetis, you are a curious one." Squirt propelled himself across the pool, causing waves to lap at Scetis' feet.

"If he does not ask the questions, then he cannot learn, Audel. Tell him the answers he seeks," Vojin called from beside the fire.

The small red dragon sighed dramatically and turned, heading back to the shore.

"Very well. The fire—as you call it—does not come from our bellies, as the humans like to believe, and we do not regurgitate it like some feel we do. It comes from a gland in our throats, down here." Squirt indicated a spot right at the base of his long neck where it connected with his body. "Just above where our windpipe splits to our lungs. A little higher sits two hard spots, like the flint that humans need to make fire with. As the mucus is expelled from the gland, these two stones strike and cause a spark, igniting the flammable excrement, sending it out as a jet of flame, this mucus sticks to things and keeps the flame going, until it has been burned away." He turned his little eyes to Scetis. 'There, is that enough information?" Squirt asked.

"It is and I thank you." Scetis went to stand, but a word from Squirt had him pausing.

"So information for information." The dragon sat up in the pool. His head, chest, and part of his stomach were exposed, and his hands still moved in the water.

"Information?"

"Yes; I gave you something, so now it's your turn. What is it you have hiding in your bags?" Squirt narrowed his reptilian eyes at Scetis.

"My personal belongings and medicinal equipment," Scetis replied.

"I would like to see," Squirt told him as eagerly as a child wanting a sweet.

"Then I would like more information."

"What would you like to know?" Squirt stood and waded towards Scetis. He sat down at the edge of the pool with a splash in the water, happy they had a bargain.

"Everything."

"That is a lot of information. Shall we start with something simple or would you like to jump straight to the complex explanations."

"I'm happy with simple just now," Scetis told him, getting up to retrieve his bags. "For a start, do you remember what it was like being in the egg?"

"A very unusual question. Yes, is the simple answer. It was warm and comfortable, and I remember my mother turning the egg, I could feel her mind touch mine. The barest brush to check I was still alive. Thankfully, she did not see how deformed and mutated I was." Squirt looked down at his diminutive form.

"You are what I wanted you to be," Vojin called to him.

Scetis opened the first bag and pulled out a set of clothes, holding them up for Squirt to see.

"Bah, human things," he snorted. "Next question."

This continued on and Squirt was very curious when Scetis pulled out the medicinal compounds and herbs. He clambered out of the warm water and padded over to Scetis. Picking the jars up carefully he opened them, inspecting each and giving his opinion on them.

Scetis was impressed with his knowledge and chided himself for presuming, just because this dragon was small did not mean he was not intelligent. They carried on with this exchange until there was only one item remaining in the second bag. Scetis' secret case. The case that appeared to be a book on anatomy by the skeleton etched on the front. He could see the gleam in Squirt's eye and his fingers actually twitching with his eagerness to get his hands on the case. The dragon reached out, but Scetis was reluctant to hand it over. He knew what was inside and the potency of some of the potions.

"You must be careful how you handle this," he warned the dragon.

"*Yes, yes; I will,*" Squirt replied, not taking his eyes off the fake book and reaching out.

With a final hesitation, Scetis handed it over to the dragon. Squirt took it carefully from the man and stared at it, taking in all the details that were etched on the thick leather cover, a taloned finger tracing the decorations. The complex silver lock was soon unclasped, and the cover opened, revealing the secret drawers and compartments holding their vials and jars. Very gently and using the talons of two fingers, Squirt pulled out the stoppered bottles one by one, easing off the small cork stoppers and smelling each. With incredible accuracy he named each component that made up the ointments and liquids. Then he came to the secured one. Scetis almost cried out a warning about the contents when Squirt pulled his fingers away.

"I will not touch this one, but you need to dispose of it. It will do harm to those who do not have dragon blood. It helped you because your blood is different to a human. It sustained you until we could deal with the poison the first night. But, if you were to touch it without the poison, then it would harm you."

Squirt made sure everything was back in place, then closed the lid, securing the lock. Handing it back with two hands he bowed his head slightly.

"I'll take care of it," Scetis promised. A thought then occurred to him. "That elixir, what exactly would it do to a normal man?"

Squirt looked him hard in the eye, his whole body tensed. *"What were the side effects for you?"* he responded.

"Cold sweats, deep sleep for a couple of days, sleep talking, confusion, extreme weakness," Scetis listed them off.

"For one such as yourself, they are mild. For a human, I am afraid the deep sleep you mentioned, they would not wake from. Even a few drops would have them in an ever-lasting sleep. A few more and they will die,' Squirt said almost matter-of-factly.

"So they would have known of the effects," Scetis mused to himself.

"They may not. The ingredients for that elixir separately are harmless enough, but together and with the inclusion of one particular plant, it becomes deadly. Those in the Convocation are knowledgeable, but they do not know everything. I believe they managed to save you by accident."

"I was in no condition at the time to take note of their process," Scetis placed the chest back into his bag.

The conversation at an end, Squirt stood and scampered back to the warm water. With a splash he continued with his lazy swimming. Feeling the need for more warmth and to wash away the last couple of strange days, Scetis undressed and headed into the water. The warmth of it seeped into his body, relaxing his muscles.

Thinking over everything started to confuse him. His life had taken a strange turn. It had been so straight. He saw where he was going, enjoyed the work he had been doing. Further back he went; further until when Tavae took him on as an apprentice. How happy he felt to be taken from the slave levels to the Apothecary Circle. Tavae had opened a whole new world to Scetis. He had been so kind and gentle with him, not in the way some of the members had been before that. That part of his life he skipped over. It was hard to think about how those in the positions of power thought they could use a young vulnerable boy.

His thoughts turned to before he had been brought to The Convocation. To the moment his mother had sold him. He remembered the smell of her skin and hair as she hugged him close for the final time. Her long, dark hair caught at the nape of her neck in a simple leather cord. That clean pleasant smell of homemade soap. He remembered the sadness that dripped from her dark eyes and lashes. His child hands wiping those tears, not understanding what was making her so sad.

The face of the man who had placed one silver piece into her hand, who had taken him from her was clear in his mind. He recognized him. Tavae Stiobhard. His old master who had treated him so kindly as he trained him. Scetis saw in the memory Tavae only looked upon him as a possession and treated him as such as they made the journey to The Convocation.

Dispelling his dark thoughts, he tried to push further back. The short time he had been with his mother was bright in his mind. The memory rose and was clear. The simple life they had led, the shelter they slept in, their meagre possessions and the love his mother had for him. Scetis understood she thought he would have a better life, did not know what lay ahead of him. She had loved him. With his adult mind and understanding he could see through his child eyes, and see the pity and disapproval of the people in their village. Some had pressed food into his mother's hands and when she wouldn't take it, into his own. Some had spat at her and called her vile names. Scetis fixed those faces in his mind, he was not sure what he would do if he saw them again.

Back further still, being held in her arms. A man in a uniform standing before her. The building behind he recognized. It was the citadel. The man looked official. He seemed stern and angry with his mother. The man handed her a pouch that jingled and told her to go.

"Enough with the self-pity Scetis. Time for us to leave," Vojin told him gently.

Scetis sat up and looked out the cave mouth. The flakes of snow drifted down slowly, but the blizzard was abating. A shaft of sunlight broke through the clouds and shone through the entrance. Bright and yellow, like the dawning of a new day.

"It is, but I still have questions," he told Vojin.

"There will always be questions. But you are not ready for the answers. You are like a newly hatched youngling. You need to learn to find your feet and what you are capable of. Be grateful that you are starting a new life, full of promise and hope."

"I am grateful, Vojin," he said. "We will leave when you are ready."

"An hour it is," Vojin agreed.

Meeting

Muniath entered Mae's inn, shutting the door carefully behind him. As a precaution, he kept to the shadows and skirted around the large building to the back entrance. The smell from the stove top and the roasting meat in the oven made him feel very hungry. Going straight to a fresh loaf of bread on the table, he pulled a crusty hunk off and dipped it into the stew, blowing on it as he raised it to his mouth.

"If you wanted to eat, all you had to do was ask," Mae said from behind him. "When did you get back?" Going to the freshwater bucket, she dipped in a clean cup and drank deeply from it.

Muniath answered from around the bread and dripping gravy. "About an hour ago." He hugged his foster sister and swallowed the rest, licking his fingers loudly.

"Dad'll be happy. He's been limping up to the citadel every day to check," she told him as he released her so she could check on the stew.

"Where is he?"

"Sit," she told him, pushing him to the table. Pulling a bowl from a stack beside the stove, she ladled some of the stew into it, picked up the bread Muniath had torn into and brought it over to the table, placing it in front of him.

"I've missed your cooking," he said as he picked up the bread and tore into it again to dip it.

"Use a spoon," Mae said, making a face. "You may not be out there in the public room but have some manners." She placed a spoon firmly down on the table beside him. Muniath picked it up and began eating.

"Dad's down by the lake, trying to fish."

"Since when did Taran start fishing?"

"You really weren't aware of anything when you were off in your self-pity world." Mae sat down opposite him. "He couldn't stand the sight of your self-destruction. So he took himself off to the lake. He met some men down there and now they meet up every couple of days to fish. I have had to find some new ways to cook what he catches."

"So he does quite well then?" Muniath broke off another hunk of bread.

"He does. He should be back soon. I presume that's why you are here?"

"Actually, I am here to beg for a room."

"You still have credit from your last payment, and that room has finally lost the stench you left in it." She grinned at him. "Of course you can, you know you know that, Mun." She stood to go get the room ready, but Muniath waived her back.

"No one must know I am here, Mae," he told her as she sat back down.

"Is this to do with why you left or for some other reason?" Mae's curiosity got the better of her.

"Ide doesn't want Orcades to know I am back."

"Ahhh; she wants to delay the wedding. About time she woke up to that asshole. He doesn't dare show his face in here. So why doesn't she just tell him she doesn't want to marry him?"

"Because there are reasons, so don't go trying to find them out. Not yet anyway."

"All right, I won't. I'll go get your room ready." Mae stood, just as a bell rang from the main room.

"Go. I know where everything is," Muniath told her.

Mae gave him a smile and headed to the front. Muniath finished his meal scraping the bowl with the remaining bread. He washed up and was wiping down the table when Taran came in the back door with a large fish in his hands.

"Well look what the dragon dragged in!" He placed the fish on the bench. "When did you get back?"

"A little while ago," Muniath said clutching the older man's hand.

"And did you succeed?" Taran asked, still holding on to Muniath's hand.

"I did. Tharain, Teagan, and the dragon have all returned."

"Excellent." Taran slapped Muniath's shoulder good naturedly and then let the handshake drop. "Is the dragon all you hoped for?"

"More. So much more."

"Is he up at the Eyrie?" Taran leaned against the bench.

"He's not."

"What?"

"The dragon has gone to find someone."

"And you let him?"

"There is no restraining this dragon. Taran, the lore of dragons is more than we thought. So much has been lost to us. But it can wait until we meet tomorrow."

"How is Tharain?"

"Jaded. It took a lot to convince him to come back."

"And young Teagan?"

"All grown up." Muniath couldn't look him in the eye and instead looked at the fish. "Good fish."

Taran looked at Muniath and chuckled. "She's that good looking? It wouldn't surprise me; her mother was a beauty."

"What the fish?" Muniath asked, still trying to cover his embarrassment.

Taran clapped him on the shoulder and laughed a little more. "It put up a good fight."

Teagan and her father were escorted to Urmond's private study the next morning. Tharain was chatting to their guide, reminiscing on happier times. General Domnall Gerarailt of the Foot was how he was introduced to her, and she vaguely remembered him. As she walked through the halls the sound of his footfalls echoing off the highly polished floors brought back the fear and confusion of a little girl with flowers through her hair. Slowly, Teagan began to feel nervous at what lay ahead.

They were taken up numerous stairs and through long corridors until they reached a large set of double doors. Standing outside was another man in uniform, about the same age as her father. He looked stern for a moment before breaking out into a large grin.

"Tharain, you old goat! Welcome home, my friend. You've been greatly missed," the man called out now stepping closer with his arms extended. He enfolded her father in a warm embrace, slapping each other's backs.

"Galanan! Or should I say, General Magaoidh," Tharain said stepping back and saluting.

"Put that away, my old friend." The manner of his speech and the way he looked reminded Teagan of someone.

"Do you remember my daughter?" Tharain said now bringing her forward.

"Lady Teagan. You look just like your mother. Welcome home, my lady." Galanan gave a little bow to her and she felt confused.

"Thank you," she replied hesitantly and with a slight blush.

"It will take a little while for you to get used to our ways again, my lady. But then no one has ever come back from that world," Galanan said with a smile that reached his dark eyes.

"Is our King here already?" Domnall asked.

"Not yet. He and Princess Orlagh will be along shortly," Galanan responded. "We're also waiting for Venicones and Muniath."

With the speaking of his name, Teagan felt a rush through her. And also a recognition. Galanan reminded her of Muniath. She could see certain mannerisms that were the same, but it was the eyes that the similarity was the most notable.

"He's changed much," her father spoke.

"A man grows or perishes after an event such as he went through."

"He told us the story. How is your other son?"

"Venicones is as much the same as always."

The sound of footsteps down the hall caught Teagan's attention. She turned to see three figures approaching and Teagan had to take a second look at one of the men. If it weren't for the fact that this man had short hair, she would have mistaken him for Muniath. It was also not lost on Teagan that she was looking out for him. It was a fact she really did not want to acknowledge.

Urmond, with his daughter at his side, smiled at the gathering. "Why are you not inside already? Please enter, don't stand on ceremony on this occasion."

Orlagh left her father's side and took Teagan's arm. "Do you know what this is all about?"

"No; well, not really. I just know that it's important and to do with Gremlin."

"Father—as usual—has not told me anything," she pouted. "He thinks I'm still a child and forgets that at some stage I will be taking over from him, unfortunately."

"Don't you wish to be queen?" Teagan asked quietly, amazed at her cousin's words.

"I do not! I would much rather spend my time defending the Realm on the back of Storm, with Feth at my side. If I became queen it would be expected that I produce an heir, which means a man." Orlagh pulled a face of disgust.

The two women entered the room and the doors shut behind them with a soft click.

The private study of the king was airy and light with a view of the mountain beyond. Tharain, the previous night, had reminded Teagan that the steps attached to the steep cliff went up to the Eyrie, where the mounts of the Rider Guard were housed. Her gaze rose to where the steps ended, and she longed to see it.

"Where is that errant son of yours?" Urmond called out as the others took their seats.

"He should be along shortly," Galanan informed his king.

Teagan tore her attention away from the prospect of seeing the great creatures of her childhood, to the room around her. Urmond saw her turn and indicated a seat on the small couch. As she sat down a silence descended on the room. Each looking at the others awkwardly. This silence was broken up by the sudden knock at the door.

Urmond himself opened it and Teagan's eyes widened at the sight of Muniath on the other side. He was freshly combed and wore a pristine formal uniform, of a white shirt, caught at the neck with an emerald-green tie, adorned with a gold pin in the shape of a soaring dragon. Over the shirt was a surcoat, buttoned down to the waist with gold buttons, each impressed with the insignia of the Realm. The coat then draped over his hips and was longer at the back, worn over a pair of tight-fitting breeches and highly polished calf length boots. His long hair was caught at the nape of his neck and his beard looked freshly trimmed.

Teagan felt herself blushing and looked away from Muniath to the man who was limping in beside him. He wore his pain well, only the smallest of grimaces crossing his weathered features as he entered the room. His dress was of a plainer cut, like those Muniath had worn when they had first met. This man walked up to her father and embraced him fondly.

"Tharain," the man said as he slapped her father's back.

"Taran," Tharain responded.

"Right, we are all here," Urmond said, clapping his hands together. He stood beside the fireplace which was unlit. "Now, down to the reason why I have asked you all to meet. A plot has been discovered that threatens the very crown I usually wear on my head. But that is not the only problem that the Realm faces. But we will get to that in a little bit."

"Plot? What plot?" Galanan called out.

"The plot for the moment is linked to the first item we must discuss."

"What could be more important than someone trying to overthrow the throne?"

"The question of succession, Galanan, that is what. It doesn't matter that there is a plot, but if there is no clear heir then it will make their job a lot easier."

"But you have an heir, Urmond; Orlagh," Domnall insisted, then added, "Also Orcades.

Urmond came to stand behind his daughter, placing his hands on her shoulders lightly. "My daughter has no wish to rule. I have known this for some time. Also, she is unable to, she lacks a certain quality to sit on the throne of the Dragon Realm."

"But Father—" Orlagh started.

"Orlagh, I have long known that you could never sit on the throne. Not only because of your own personal preferences, but because you do not have the silver in your eyes that you require."

"What does that have to do with it? Princess Orlagh has long been recognized as the only heir you have. She has been groomed to rule since she was born," Domnall joined in the argument.

"But she cannot." Urmond lifted his hands from his daughter's shoulders. "Taran you have studied it along with me, will you please explain?"

"It would be my honor, my Lord King." Taran said and as he moved in his seat, he cleared his throat and started. "The Dragon Realm was founded by the first humans to inhabit this world and by the union with a dragon hybrid. We have scoured every book in this library and those in other lands. They have revealed that only those with the mark of one with dragon blood may sit on the throne."

"What mark?" Orlagh asked before either of the generals.

"The mark is a ring of silver around the pupil. The more pronounced this ring is, the purer the dragon blood."

Orlagh looked to her father, but her response was not what he had expected. "Thank the heavens I have no silver! So it will be as Domnall has pointed out, Orcades."

"You are not even a little disappointed?" Urmond asked with some bemusement.

"No, I am not, Father. For the first time in my life I feel free."

"Well, I was not sure how you would react to the news. And it will not be Orcades. Even though he is my sister's son, he does not possess the silver either."

While the father and daughter were talking, the two generals looked at not only each other, but all those gathered, and their eyes fell on Teagan. She was the closest relative to the king, via his cousin, her mother, and they both noticed she had a strong ring around the pupil. Teagan began to become aware of their scrutiny and shifted uncomfortably under their stares. Tharain from across the room also gazed at his daughter. She turned pleading eyes to her father in order to stop any declaration from the pair.

"My King, there is one here of royal blood and also has the silver ring," Galanan ventured slowly before Tharain could utter a word. Urmond turned to him. "She is your cousin's daughter."

"No!" Tharain interrupted, leaping from his seat. "No, My Lord King, there is another, you know who I speak of."

"But he has been lost to this citadel and castle, let alone the throne from the moment he was born. I would have no idea where in this world he may be, or even if he still lives." Urmond said, shaking his head.

"But you know where she lived. You still remember her, I believe you even still love her," Tharain insisted.

"It was too long ago. She would have cursed me many times over."

"Who does Uncle Tharain speak of, Father?" Orlagh demanded.

"This does not concern you, Orlagh." Urmond said softly.

"I think it does. If I cannot rule, then I have the right to know who usurps my place." Urmond turned hurt eyes to his daughter. "Who, Father?" she asked again quietly.

"My Princess," Tharain started. Orlagh whipped her head around to face him. "It happened a very long time ago. Before your father met your mother. We were posted to a border patrol. Your father, my Gael, and I."

"She lived in the village that was located on the other side. Aelwen was her name." Urmond said, taking up the story. "I loved her deeply. We had a relationship and I promised that I would go back for her, but my father forbade it. My wife, your mother, had already been chosen for me. It was not until many years later that I learned she had come to the citadel to find me, with a child in her arms. I sent Tharain to find her, to look at the child." Urmond said sinking into a chair.

"I went back to that village. I searched and talked to all I knew who were still there." Tharain told the room.

"And what did you find?" Orlagh asked quietly.

"Aelwen had had a boy. A child who was the apple of her eye. When she returned from searching for your father, she was not the same woman. She refused help from everyone, instead insisting she would care for the boy herself. It sent her mad. A friend who had tried to help, told me that one day the boy wasn't there. She had asked Aelwen what had happened, and she broke down saying that the boy had been sold. She threw the silver piece at her friend and ran off. They found her a couple of days later at the bottom of a cliff."

"But what of her boy?"

"We don't know. She never told who she sold the child to." Tharain shrugged his shoulders.

"There must have been some clue? Someone would have seen a stranger?" Orlagh demanded.

Teagan sat on her chair watching the whole story play out. She was grateful that her father's tale had drawn the attention away from her. *'There would be no way I would be fit to rule,'* she thought to herself.

"But a magnificent Queen you would be, Child of Dragons," Gremlin's voice broke through.

"Where are you?" she asked, trying to not let her excitement show to the room.

"I have been with you this whole time. I never left."

"Gremlin?"

"I am up in the clouds heading back to the cave of my mother."

"Where have you been?"

"Searching."

"I'm becoming so frustrated with you. Will you please answer me plainly."

"Just tell Muniath and your father to meet us up at the Eyrie. It is important that your father is there." Gremlin said in a tone that left no doubt in her mind that this was not a request to be taken lightly.

Looking up at the room she could see that the revelation of an illegitimate heir was still being discussed. Her eyes turned to Muniath and he was staring back at her. His whole expression made her realize that he had received the same instruction.

"My King?" Muniath started, realizing that Teagan felt overwhelmed at breaking into the conversation.

"Muniath, you have something you wish to add to this mad conversation?" Urmond said, looking almost defeated.

"No, my King. I just thought that this conversation will be a long one and maybe Teagan would like to see the dragon eyrie. I need to check on one of my charges and the discussion does not really involve either of us."

"Does not involve her?" Galanan called out. "Lady Teagan is quite possibly the only heir we have. You may go about your duties Captain, but I believe the girl needs to stay here."

Teagan saw a little tension between father and son and found her voice. "Please, I would like to go and see it for myself. Muniath has described it to me so vividly, and I don't feel that I would make a good ruler of these lands. I have lived too long away from them to understand it anymore."

"You may go of course, Teagan. There'll be nothing decided today that you cannot be informed of later." Urmond said kindly, understanding how ill at ease she was.

"Tharain, will you join us? I'm sure some of the older dragons would like to see you one more time," Muniath asked seamlessly.

Tharain looked around him, there was clearly a conflict going on inside. Wanting to stay and feel useful as a part of history, competed with the desire to see where he had once commanded. A barely imperceptible nod of the head from Urmond made up his mind. He had played his part in the telling of the tale, now he must go.

"It would be a pleasure, Muniath," he said rising to his feet.

The three left a quiet room behind them and made their way out of the castle. They spoke no words to each other, just the sound of their feet on the floor accompanied them. The boots she wore dug in just above the heel, the leather was still stiff and unworked. Teagan tried to forget about the pain it was causing her as she walked a little behind both. Her mind was fixed on the problem with which she now faced. Thrown into a world she barely remembered and caught up in a situation of turmoil. So fixed on the cryptic message that Gremlin had sent, she did not see the officious man step out in front of the trio, she did bump into her father's shoulder and felt the steadying hands of Muniath.

The man that stood in front of them was tall and full of his own self-importance. He was dressed immaculately in a similar uniform to Domnall, but his seemed to have been tailored to fit and show off his muscular frame. His hand rested on the pommel of a sword strapped to his waist and he started at Tharain, dismissing him because of his age, before turning dark and threatening eyes to Muniath.

"So the rumors are true, you're back." His tone was superior and there was almost a hit of triumph to it.

"Orcades," Muniath responded curtly. "Yes, as you can see, I am back."

"Excellent. Ide and I can now continue with our plans."

"I think you'd better talk to my sister about that. Now excuse me, we have business to attend to." Muniath went to move past Orcades, but he held out a hand to stop them.

"Not so fast. Where did you go to?" he demanded.

"It was a mission, directed by our King. If you wish to know the details, I suggest that you speak directly to him. Neither my father nor General Gerarailt knew of it, so I don't like your chances of getting the details from him."

This news did not sit well with Orcades. Teagan could see that he was trying hard to find a way around it and make Muniath tell him. He looked up and caught her eye. His hard, cold, blue eyes bore into hers for a moment.

"Who are these two? I've not seen them before?" Orcades pulled himself up to his full height, puffing out his chest, as he tried to make himself more domineering.

"Who they are does not concern you."

"As Captain of the Foot I think it does concern me," he responded, taking a small step closer to Muniath and giving his voice an edge to it.

"Yes, but under General Gerarailt's orders, they are to remain anonymous for now," Muniath responded, facing up to Orcades, almost toe to toe now.

"I've heard of no such orders."

"He is currently in a meeting with my father, Taran and the King himself in the king's private study, along with Princess Orlagh, if you wish to get confirmation."

Teagan could immediately see that this news was not welcome to Orcades. She watched him closely. He took a small step backwards and his eyes darted back the way the trio had walked from. He seemed to start to say something then stopped, before attempting again.

"Well, I will inform Ide that you have returned. She'll be pleased that our plans can now continue." He turned on his heel and hurried down the corridor he had stepped from.

"He seemed a bit off. Who is he?" Tharain asked.

"Orcades Braonáin, the king's nephew," Muniath told the pair as they carried on.

"That's young Orcades? And he's marrying Ide?" Tharain began to chuckle. "If she hasn't changed from when she was a child, then that jumped up little shit will have his hands full."

"Over my dead body will he marry my sister." Muniath's pace had quickened as they headed towards a large set of double doors at the end of the corridor.

"Ah, like that." Tharain knew when to keep quiet and Teagan was grateful he did.

Outside finally the three stood at the base of a long, steep set of steps, the same ones Teagan had seen from Urmond's study. Muniath had no hesitation in mounting the first series of steps, and he was quickly followed by Tharain who—he noticed—was becoming more child-like in his eagerness for their destination. Teagan held onto the rail beside her and started up behind them.

Every now and then Muniath gave a quick look behind to see how she was faring. He was pleased to see that she was fairly fit and managed the first two sections easily enough. But her father was finding it rather tough going. His breathing was labored, and his face was going red with the exertion. Tharain stopped at the next landing in an attempt to catch his breath. Muniath could see him looking out over the wide expanse of the valley filled mostly with the deep lake, sparkling far below them in the sun.

Muniath clapped him on the shoulder. "Do you want a lift?"

"No, I am not that old!" he insisted and began his climb once more. Teagan looked around as she slowly climbed behind her father but could not see how they could lift her father up the side of the steep mountain, with a complete solid sheer face. Muniath saw her looking and worked out what she was thinking.

"On the handrail you'll see a rope, it doesn't serve any other function than to be pulled on. A bell rings at both ends and a chair is secured into a rope and pulley system. It allows those who cannot make it up to the Eyrie by normal means, a way to visit," he explained, stepping up sideways beside Tharain.

"And there will never be a day when there will be cause for me to use it!" Tharain puffed beside them.

Muniath grinned down at Teagan and noticed she quickly looked away out at the scenery. A faint red blush crept over her cheeks and long neck, making the freckles that kissed her skin fade slightly. Her rich auburn hair was caught back in a ponytail as was her preferred style. The clothing of the land suited her, and she wore the tight-fitting leather riding pants and vest without self-consciousness. He continued to watch her, her green eyes flecked with the silver were stunning and were framed with lashes of the same fiery hue as her hair. Her eyes had captivated him the first moment he had seen her. The silver around the pupal only heighted the deep shade of green. Those same eyes now flicked back to see him still staring and quickly looked away again.

"Calm, Muniath. Not yet. She must still accept that all this is happening. She is like a startled deer and will need patience," Gremlin said in his mind.

"Does she feel the same as I do?" he asked, now turning and climbing.

"I will not tell you. She is not sure of her feelings herself. Be there to support her and show you care," Gremlin advised and soon he was gone.

The top of the stairs was soon reached and Tharain stared out of the guard rail in an attempt to hide the fact he was no longer as young as he had once been, embarrassed by how much he had let himself go. Teagan stood at his side and Muniath compared the father and daughter. They were of equal height, but that is where the physical similarities finished. He had met her mother a few times before her death and his memory was sketchy. But Teagan did have her mother's hair and eyes. Of her temperament and personality—he decided— were a direct copy of her father. He watched as Tharain turned to his daughter. The pair exchanged a look and a slight nod to the head, a silent and unconscious communication between the pair.

Turning and entering the dark cavern he heard them follow. The two guards at the barricade snapped to attention as Muniath entered.

"Is Wick in?" he asked the guard to the left.

"Yes sir. At first light as he is supposed to," the man said giving Muniath a slight wink.

"Good. He's young and may wake up to the fact that he isn't required to be here before breakfast one day." Muniath laughed with the guard, who opened the locked gate to allow the three to enter.

"How many Riders now?" Tharain asked as He walked beside Muniath with his hands clasped behind his back.

"A company of only 100 now, Tharain." Muniath answered. "And not all of those have mounts."

"Only 100. Have I been gone that long?"

"No, sir. It has been a case of not taking on only a limited number of new recruits until the number of dragons increases. Unfortunately, that is not going to happen soon."

"It will if what Gremlin says is true," Teagan spoke up quietly.

"What was that, Teagan?" Tharain asked.

"I said, that the numbers will increase once more, if what Gremlin says is true." Her eyes darted between the two men and Muniath could see how shy she actually was as she averted her gaze from both.

"This is all tied up with the heir thing isn't it?" Muniath asked.

"It is to do with all that is going on," a voice spoke from the shadows.

The man that belonged to that voice stepped out. His head had a short growth of dark stubble, the same shade as on his chin. He wore the common leather trousers that most men wore, a dark black shirt, buttoned to the neck, and a dark vest, made of a brocaded material.

Muniath immediately became defensive at the sight of the man. He knew who he was the moment he laid eyes on him. Scetis. The man who had almost killed Ide, his sister. The man who had stolen the dragon eggs. But also the man his sister loved.

"Scetis," Muniath said quietly in an almost growl.

"You know him?" Tharain asked as he stepped slightly in front of Teagan.

"In a manner of speaking."

"You must be Muniath, and you," Scetis said, looking at Teagan over Tharain's shoulder. "Must be Teagan. Vojin asked me to wait here for you." He gave a slight smile which pulled across his slightly crooked teeth. "He's waiting for us with his mother and siblings. Shall we?" he stepped aside and waited for them to pass.

Muniath quickly looked to Teagan and could see that she found this stranger to be very intriguing. Scetis seemed very self-assured and even a little cocky. But underneath he sensed this man was just as confused as they were. As they passed Scetis, Muniath noticed him give Teagan a sideways look. The light from the flicker torch nearby highlighted the silver in Teagan's eyes and made them appear to be almost golden. Something deep inside acknowledged that golden flicker as something special and he could see that Scetis had a similar reaction.

"Shall we go?" Muniath asked abruptly.

His words drew Teagan's eyes to him, but he was still staring at the newcomer, a feeling deep inside was growing and he didn't like it. Jealousy. When he did look at her, she gave him a small smile. Her smile seemed to calm him and give him some reassurance. She had seen his jealousy.

They walked down the wide cavern until they reached an opening in the side. Teagan noted the coat of arms which she had seen in the castle and citadel, was displayed to one side of the entrance. Further beyond the opening, the flickering torches illuminated four dragons inside. The largest of all was Gremlin. The sight of the dragon Teagan had cared for from just a fledgling, put her at ease for his welfare and she rushed to him, wrapping her arms around his thick sinuously long neck. She placed her head on his cheek and closed her eyes.

"You're safe," she said with her voice as well as her mind.

"I was never in danger, Child of Dragons," he intoned, leaning into her embrace. "Come, meet my siblings and my mother."

Teagan pulled away and found three dragons staring at her. One of the smaller dragons moved from her mother's side and ran straight to Muniath. She cooed and Teagan could quite clearly hear her words.

"You're back! I'm almost ready to fly!" The excitement of her greeting very nearly drove Muniath off his feet.

"Calm, Fleet. I know how eager you are, but your wing muscles have not developed properly yet." He caressed her neck and she purred at his touch.

Teagan then looked to the other small dragon. He was green and gold, and held himself aloof and proudly, unlike his sister. His reptilian eyes blinked at her, staring openly at this woman. She could see he was trying to be serious, already taking on the persona of an adult male dragon. He sat near his still caring mother, but not close enough for everyone to see that he still depended on her for many things.

As he continued to stare, she could feel him pushing out with his mind. Teagan could also feel Gremlin carefully and gently guiding him.

"I am bonded with Wick," she heard him say.

"You are, Brother, but she is special. She has been bonded to me and is the Child of Dragons." Gremlin's words came to her.

The smaller dragon turned his eyes back to Teagan once more and they widened as he looked deeply into hers. He stood to his four feet that appeared overly large for his body, spread his wings up behind him and stepped closer to Teagan. His head lowered and he bent a knee to her.

"I am privileged to greet the Child of Dragons. I am called Sting." Behind him his mother echoed the same gesture.

Teagan turned to Gremlin.

"Why do you keep calling me, Child of Dragons, what does that mean?"

"Scetis can tell you." Gremlin told her.

The assembled group turned to the stranger. He was still standing by the opening, leaning up against the smoothed rock wall. He looked at the three humans and the four dragons, then turned his eyes back to Teagan.

"Child of Dragons." He gave her a low bow. "The highest of the high. The Leader. A direct descendant of the first." The silence that greeted his words was great.

Tharain was the first to move and speak. "So it is Teagan who will rule?" he asked hesitantly. He turned to his daughter and she saw the gleam of power that used to be there before their exile.

"You misheard me, sir. The Child of Dragons is not a ruler of men. That position is taken by someone else, which by the way, came as a complete surprise to that person," he said with a crooked smile. "The role of the Child of Dragons is to lead the Dragons, a general of sorts. That role does not necessarily have to be filled by a full dragon. The Child of Dragons can be identified by a special feature. We who are descendants of the first human dragon hybrid all have silver in our eyes. But the Child," he said stepping closer to Teagan. He reached out and took her chin in his warm hand and turned her face to the torch light. "The silver will still be in the Child's eye, but also in these special eyes is the fire from the center of the world."

Muniath and Tharain both saw the flash of gold, almost like the flash of a flame. Scetis stepped aside as Tharain came to inspect her eyes. He marveled at the change from silver to gold. Muniath stayed where he was.

"She is great and the feelings you have for her are evident, but do not lose hope," the young dragon said softly and quietly not only in his mind, but also open for Teagan's.

"How do you know this?" he asked a little stunned.

"Vojin told me. A magnificent pair you will make. With her on Vojin's back and you on mine, there will be no end to all we will do and see." she said with some wonder.

"I will not give up hope then, but neither will I put all my hope into it coming true." Muniath said sadly and turned his attention to what was going on before them, only to find Teagan staring at him.

Scetis bowed a little to Muniath. "I wish to give my apologies to you, sir. I believe I caused a rather lot of bother after my last visit. Screamer here has kindly forgiven me, along with Fleet and Sting. I would like to have yours, as Dragon Master."

Muniath looked deeply into the blue eyes of this stranger then took a step towards Scetis and held out his hand to the man. "From what I have figured out, you didn't exactly have a choice in the matter; in fact, none of us do."

Scetis grasped his hand firmly and shook it. All the while this apology was going on Tharain was studying the young intruder.

"You stole the eggs? It was you who forced the young egg through the portal?" Tharain demanded.

"Yes, I did, sir, and I sincerely apologize for it. It was done on the orders of my hierarchy; one I now know to be corrupt and attempting to pervert international treaties. There is a plot afoot to damage relations between this Realm and the lands controlled by The Convocation, and it is not the first time they have tried it They mean to have the Realm under their control. The true hierarchy does not know what the few are trying to do. Unfortunately, I believe that those involved will have much support from within the Council of The Realm. They must be stopped."

"I agree with you, young man. We need to take you to see Generals Magaoidh and Gerarailt."

"No. My business first must be with the king. There are other matters I must discuss with him."

Teagan saw her father study the young man closely, before the look of recognition hit him.

"Where do you come from?" he asked quietly.

"That is of no importance at the moment," Scetis responded with some defense.

"I think it does." Tharain turned to Teagan. "Ask Gremlin who this man is and where he comes from, especially his parentage."

"There is no need," Scetis said quickly before Teagan could turn to the large dragon. "I am, Scetis Mordha. I have no real surname, this one I bear was given to me by the Convocation, a slur that means majestic. It was given to me when I was sold into slavery by my mother. Raised up from the slave pens to become an Apothecary, Practitioner, and Trader in the Convocation of Mystical Medicine. I am my own man. Free and alone."

"But you have a true surname. You have connections," Tharain said pressing on. "Who was your mother?"

Scetis stared at this old man, his jaw tightening visibly.

"Let go and finally speak who you are," Vojin guided him. But still Scetis hesitated.

"Who was your mother?" Tharain repeated.

"My mother was Aelwen. I understand she died shortly after selling me. She lived in a small village in the mountains near a border crossing between the Realm and those lands. I was born a bastard." He made himself stand taller and tried to put as much conviction in his voice as he could.

"Aelwen Omaolomhnaigh! You were born from a great love. One that still survives in your father's heart. He did not know you existed until much later, after he was reposted. Your existence was kept from him until it was too late. He did not know your mother had died until years after the fact. He sent me to find you both. No one in the village knew where you were. I tried to trace you, your highness." Tharain bowed to the young man.

"You are Urmond's son?" Muniath asked. "Are you sure, Tharain?"

"I am as sure of his parentage as I am as sure of yours. You cannot deny it. You must know who you are?" Tharain asked Scetis.

"I do, sir. It has been shown to me," Scetis replied.

"Then we must go back." Tharain started to move towards the entrance.

"We will, soon. But first I have a need to tell you something. It is the reason Vojin requested the three of you come here."

"Then speak quickly," Tharain said excitedly.

"The plot has reached the Realm. There are people in the citadel that are part of it. They need to be neutralized, and soon before it goes much further."

"Who?" Muniath demanded.

"The man your sister is supposed to marry."

"Yes, I know, she has spoken to me already."

"And another who has control of one of the military arms," Scetis said quietly.

"Not my father?" Muniath growled.

"No, not the Riders. But the Foot."

"Gerarailt? No I cannot believe that!" Tharain burst out.

"I'm afraid it is true."

"Do you have proof?" Muniath demanded looking equally as shocked as Teagan's father.

"I have seen them meeting in secret," Scetis confirmed. "Vojin brought me here yesterday and I have been trailing Orcades. He is a cousin to the family at the heart of the plot. He and Gerarailt have been meeting in some strange places. Far stranger than a Captain should be meeting his General. I believe Gerarailt is part of this. Is he related to Orcades?"

"He is. Orcades' mother is sister to the king, but his father was cousin to Gerarailt. That part of the family has many relations in the neighboring land," Tharain confirmed for him.

"Including relations within the House Planirana?" Scetis asked.

Tharain thought for a moment, trying to remember the connections of the families. "Yes. Orcade's father was the son of the current ruling lady."

"So a direct cousin of Wradech Foghladh, the heir of that house, and of Loxa," Scetis mused out loud to himself. He looked at the gathered group whose eyes were all set on him. "This confirms it for me. It's time this information reached King Urmond." Scetis drew himself up, almost like he was stealing himself for the confrontation with a father he had never known.

Scetis stood before the large doors. They had a white veneer and were decorated in scrolls and gold flowers. His heart was racing, and his palms were becoming sweaty. This meeting was one he would quite happily put off if he could, but the need and urgency was great. The door swung open and the man on the other side stared back at him with eyes that were the same as Scetis' own. Urmond held the door in his hand. There was no mistaking the features of the young man, they were of his own. But there was also the hint of the face that haunted his dreams still. The woman he had loved above all others.

"You had better come in," Urmond invited the group and stepped aside to let them pass.

Entering the room Scetis took in everything and everyone inside. Three older men, two in uniforms stood by the fireside while a woman with golden hair was beside the large simple desk. A man with similar features as Muniath was lounging in a chair with his ankle casually resting on a knee.

"I think introductions are in order," Galanan said to his son who was entering behind Scetis.

"This is of a delicate nature," Muniath replied. "But it seems our need has just been filled." Muniath responded while looking not at his father, but Urmond.

"Gentlemen, I think our meeting is over. I will call you when I am ready, so do not go far from the citadel," Urmond instructed the group. "Tharain I thank you and your daughter, and also you Muniath, for your assistance. But this is a meeting that should take place alone."

"As you wish, my Lord King," Muniath said bowing and starting to usher everyone out.

"Not you, Orlagh." Urmond commanded his daughter.

Once the doors were shut, Urmond turned to Scetis. "There is no mistaking who you are. Your mother was Aelwen?"

"I believe you know that answer," Scetis said quietly.

"Orlagh, this is your brother." Urmond said slowly.

"You know who I am?" Scetis asked, swallowing hard.

"It is unmistakable as to who you are. You have your mother's eyes. Please sit," Urmond offered.

Scetis rubbed his sweaty palms on his legs and took the seat offered by the king. This was not a moment he had thought would ever happen, or even imagined would happen. Family had been lost to him and he was finding this hard to comprehend. He looked about the room, feeling tongue tied and unable to think. His eyes caught that of the blond woman now sitting opposite him. She stared at him intently and he grew self-conscious under that gaze.

"Well, I can honestly say that I welcome your sudden arrival," she said and smiled with genuine warmth.

"It is not my place to take yours," he started.

"Oh it is, and I think you already know this," Orlagh stated with a slight laugh.

"That is a matter for another time. Firstly, I would like to know the name you were given." Urmond asked, sitting down beside his daughter.

"Scetis."

Urmond nodded and a small smile played on his lips. "My middle name."

Quiet descended between the three for a moment, before Urmond recovered himself from memories that quite obviously seemed to swamp him.

"Muniath mentioned you knowing something important?" Urmond asked.

Glad to be talking on a more urgent and less personal subject, Scetis nodded and began quickly. "I believe you are aware of the plot to overthrow your crown?"

"We are."

"Do you know who is involved?"

"I have the name of one person. I think that is thanks to you giving Ide the warning."

"Orcades is one. He is power hungry and that is being fed by his relatives in the next lands. His connections run deep, far deeper than I knew before that incident." He blushed a little at the thought of Ide and knowing she was close, possibly even in the same building.

"Just how deep does this conspiracy run?" Urmond asked.

"To the top," Scetis said quietly. "To some I had almost counted as family. The Regulator, himself. His secret wife, their son, her nephew, and I am not sure how many more. The whole hierarchy is not aware of it, of that I am certain. They would've taken steps against such a threat by now."

"Why did you not make them aware?" Urmond asked.

"The Regulator had me so held fast in his grip that I did not know what the truth was. I only found out his involvement as I was making my escape. The nephew, Wradech Foghladh, took great delight in destroying my world when he told me. All my life I have been lied to."

"Do you think that they knew who you are? Your connection to me?" Urmond sat forward in his seat.

"I really cannot tell you."

"I think they did. Somehow they became aware of you and your parentage." Urmond stood quickly and went to his desk. Opening a drawer, he rummaged around for a moment and pulled out an object. He came back and held out the small pin to Scetis who looked at it. A small dragon pin with a stone set in the middle, the same color blue as his eyes. "Please take it," Urmond urged.

"What is this?" Scetis asked warily.

"The pin I gave your mother. It was supposed to gain her access to me when she came to the citadel. It was taken from her and she was sent away without seeing me," he said sadly

"She was sent away with a bag of coins," Scetis said quietly.

"Yes, she was. You were but a babe in her arms, how could you know this? Did she tell you?"

"My mother did not tell me. My memory is a recently discovered one. Dragons, it seems, are able to remember from before they are hatched. I am only grateful that I do not remember that far back." He gave a nervous little laugh. "My training with Vojin was extensive."

"So he brought you to us."

"He did."

"When we have the time I would greatly like to hear about it."

"Time, I feel, is something we do not have much of at the moment."

"Please, take the pin. It is yours by right." Urmond offered it again to Scetis.

Reaching out a hand he took the silver object. He held it in his hand and looked at it closely. A flickering memory of his mother and her wearing the jewel on her cloak, her hands gently prying his chubby baby fingers away from it. Scetis closed a fist around it. Holding it tightly until he could feel it biting into the flesh of the palm of his hand.

"Thank you," he said quietly, realizing he finally had a connection to the mother he had lost. A tear sprang to his eye and he blinked it away quickly. Sniffing he drew in a long breath.

"Yes, we can reminisce more later," Urmond told him quietly. "I believe someone in the citadel was involved. The only four people who knew of your existence apart from your mother, were the Captain who did my father's bidding, my father, and the guard at the gate."

"Was one of those men Domnall Gerarailt?" Scetis asked.

"Do you know him?."

"I recognized him. I must confess that I've been within these walls for the last day. I've been watching your nephew Orcades, as he walks about knowing it will be all his soon. I saw him meet with General Gerarailt on a couple of occasions. They looked like they did not want to be overheard or seen together."

"That is very interesting. It would make sense; he passes the information onto those that have influence and can raise him further. The information of your birth would interest a lot of the border families, where the ties are strong. Can I ask why you did not make yourself known to us earlier? Why wait?"

"I was instructed to. Vojin thought it best that I learn a little more of the layout."

"But you know it already. It was you who stole the eggs," Urmond said with a slight grin.

"What?" Orlagh exclaimed getting to her feet. "That is a great crime."

"I know it is, Orlagh, please sit and be patient. It's also a crime that he has been absolved of already. I believe the Regulator had a great need of keeping you alive. It was part of the agreement that we came to. Though I did not know his true reasons for it."

"But Papa—"

"No! The matter has been sorted and you are not to mention it again," Urmond raised his voice to his daughter. "It was necessary as it turns out. Vojin needed to find Teagan and bring her home. His reach is far. It was he who set the course for his own removal into the lost world."

"But he's just a dragon, a beast," Orlagh argued.

"Not just a beast, my child. But the greatest of dragons. You know the history." Urmond then turned to Scetis. "Now tell me, why did he need to find Teagan?"

"She is my counterpart. I am to rule, and she is to lead. We both have more dragon blood running through our veins than anyone else. Teagan is special. She is the Child of Dragons. A role she needs to accept and take on. She is to lead the Flight of Dragons in the coming war."

"War? What war? This plot is just in its infancy," Urmond exclaimed.

"I'm afraid you're very mistaken. They have infiltrated the Foot here in the citadel and they have been moving troops, both recruited and mercenary, over the border for some time. This is only an extension to that which started with the downfall of Tharain Loinsigh. My king, the plot is about to explode. You need to prepare, and Teagan needs to learn warfare. On the back of Vojin she will call up all dragons, not just those in the eyrie. They will come to her call and they will fight to defend this realm."

"But dragons are in the decline," Orlagh told him.

"They will come and in numbers greater than you think."

Urmond sat back and was quiet for a moment, his eyes never leaving the face of the younger man in front of him. The son he thought he had lost. "I will have rooms made up for you."

"I thank you, but no. If Orcades and Gerarailt know I am here, then all could be lost. I'll go back to where I was hiding."

"But if we need you, how will I find you?" Urmond asked, not wanting to let Scetis out of his sight.

"Just think of my name." Reaching out with his mind as Vojin taught him he found the tiniest glimmer of the collective mind in Urmond. Working his way in he expanded it and opened up that which had been silent in the rulers of the Dragon Realm for centuries.

Urmond gasped as he heard the murmur of the voices of dragons for the first time. He looked closely at Scetis.

"*Can you hear me?*" Scetis asked through the link.

"I do!" Urmond spoke out loud in surprise.

"This is how you find me." Scetis instructed.

Flight

Darkness cloaked the cave, broken up by the intermittent and flickering light from the torches placed along the long walkway. Quietness had descended on the Eyrie some hours after dark and only two Riders stood guarding the entrance at the top of the stairway. They leaned heavily on the long spears they held, shifting every so often on tired feet, and softly spoke between them, yawning often in the late hour. Soft clicking could barely be heard further in the cave system. A sound that was expected and the two Riders were used to, as their own mounts had the habit of visiting them by the barrier in the middle of the night. The taller of the two looked back into the gloom but saw no dragons in the long gallery. He shrugged to his friend and they resumed their quiet conversation.

Further in, a small dragon crouched low over the smooth rock and kept to the dancing shadows of the torches. His tail snaked out behind him, held just above the rock under his feet, and his wings held close to his body. He paused a moment and sniffed the air. He caught the torch light and his scales glistened brightly in the dimness, as he moved towards the dragon caverns cautiously and deliberately, so as not to draw attention to himself. His smallness worked in his favor.

A sound from in front of him froze him in place and he waited to see who or what it was. A large shadowy figure walked towards him and darting behind was a juvenile, almost fully grown and full of curiosity. Fleet was curious about this stranger her brother was going to meet.

"You gave me a fright," Squirt said standing up on his hind legs and placing his front hand like feet on his sides. He was more human-like than any other dragon Fleet had ever seen, and she stared at him.

"Is he really fully grown?" Fleet asked without thinking to her brother.

"Yes, he is indeed, and smarter than most too," Vojin told her with a chuckle.

"Those humans that guard this place are not up to much. I sneaked in without even one of them coming to investigate, even when I deliberately made a noise," Squirt told them with some disgust.

"That will change. Let's go further in just in case. Sister, please go back to Mother." Vojin instructed Fleet.

"No. If I am to carry Muniath on my back then I need to know what is going on," Fleet said stubbornly and standing straighter. Her wings ruffled a little as she lifted her head with pride.

"Impudent little dragon," Squirt said, giving a little chuckle.

Vojin turned around and a small laugh escaped his throat while he moved further into the cave system, back towards the deeper reaches where dragons had once been held. With so few in the service of the Realm, these tunnels and caverns had been long abandoned to time, but Fleet knew they were still occupied. The shades and echoes called to her brother in acknowledgment from down the ages as he passed. Their lives imprinted in the very rock that surrounded them. The sense of history that enveloped the trio was not only projected to Vojin. Fleet became more subdued and less flighty, walking closer to her considerably larger brother.

She looked towards the newcomer, Squirt and felt the malevolence that was directed at the small dragon. The past lives were passing harsh judgement and did not hold back the abhorrence at his differences. It pleased Fleet to see that he was not cowering from the perceived hatred of his kind from the past. Squirt pulled himself up and held his head high. They could not hurt him. They were of the past and only shadows.

"Why do they do that?" Fleet asked quietly, unable to hold back the question as she watched the shifting shadows from beside her brother.

"They are just shadows, Sister," Vojin tried to tell her carefully and gently.

"But they don't like Audel. I can feel it," she said, taking a quick peek at the dragon who was only just taller than herself.

"It is because I am deformed," Squirt told her.

"You are who you are meant to be. Because that is how I need you. Scetis is going to need your advice and you will not fit in the citadel if you are of normal stature." Vojin paused a moment and looked at the shifting shadows, and he snorted his disgust to them. "And like the humanoids, these memories have forgotten that dragons of your size were once common. They moved about the citadel and were part of the everyday life of this Realm, and I mean for them to be so again, starting with you, my friend."

"Is that why you filled my head with all that—stuff?" Squirt asked with some curiosity.

"Yes, that stuff as you call it will be needed. Scetis needs to rule as a dragon hybrid and it will be your job to see that he does."

Squirt drew himself up, standing now on his rear legs, to meet Vojin's gaze eye to eye. He nodded to the large dragon and then looked around at the shades of dragons gone by. The fierceness of his glare had some recede further into the gloom, but others stood their ground.

"*Away!*" Vojin growled beside him and like tendrils of mist they dissipated into the rock. Vojin then turned to Squirt. "*What have you found out?*"

"It is as you had feared, more men pour over the border each night. They are hiding in the mountains like pack rats. The Riders on the Rostra have become lax in their comfort and peace. They do not patrol very much and when they do, it is more to amuse themselves than to protect these lands. The dragons there are frustrated with their bond Riders. They cannot make their warnings be heard. They are also punished when the humans perceive them to be rebellious or do something wrong."

"This is dire news. Humans and dragons have become separated too much," Vojin said, pondering Squirt's report.

"*Why do they not hear us now?*" Fleet asked, her curiosity brimming once more.

"Because it has been lost to them. Either the amount of dragon blood has diminished to such low levels that it is barely there, or the knowledge of it has been lost," Squirt replied before Vojin could answer.

"But I can hear them, and I can understand. When it's quiet in the dark of the night, I hear their dreams."

"It is not surprising, Sister, that you can. You are bonded to Muniath and in some small way with Wick," Vojin told her.

"I don't think she means just those two, Vojin," Squirt said, shuffling closer to Fleet. "There are more aren't there, little one?"

Fleet took a step back from the stunted dragon, suddenly afraid to speak of the dreams she has each night. *"I... um... there are more,"* she stuttered and sought the comfort from Vojin under the scrutiny of Squirt.

"Yes, more. Your gift will be valuable. With Muniath and you, Scetis can bring the hybrids back," Squirt said eagerly. He looked up to Vojin. "Was this your doing?"

"No, this goes deeper than my influence. Are you sure you are not just tapping into the dragon mind, Sister?"

"I dream of many in the Realm, not just Muniath and Wick; the full dragon dreams are different to the hybrids; they dream of different things; but we both dream of flying, isn't that funny; I mean, because we can, well, I can't at the moment, but Muniath says I will soon, but humans can't, because they don't have wings." Fleet drew in a deep breath as she finished her train of thought.

Squirt stared at her amazed and with some amusement. "With that ability to pick out the human minds, we could have Fleet open them up. It would advance our cause greatly."

Vojin looked hard at his sister then shook his head. "It would only sow discord between those of our blood and those that do not. There is already this situation to deal with. I don't need to have to suddenly turn around and control civil unrest within the Realm." He turned his gaze back to Squirt. "Did you find anything else out about the troops they are bringing through the border?"

"Filthy mercenaries mainly, but professional bands, not just those that are sell-swords. They are also bringing wagons with them."

"Probably supplies."

"I couldn't see, they were well guarded and covered."

"You have done well, Audel. I want you back at the border and keeping an eye on things. If you see anything that worries you, report back immediately. In the meantime, rest, stay here and sleep," Vojin advised him.

"Here? You have to be joking! I am not staying where the long dead can judge me in my sleep. I found a nice spot on the way back, so I'll go there and warm my bones," Squirt scoffed. He turned then stopped before heading back the way they had come, faced Fleet and gave her a gracious bow. "Until we meet again, Fleet."

Fleet giggled a little at his manner and looked sideways at her brother, who only rolled his eyes at the diminutive dragon. There was something about Squirt that Fleet liked, he did not talk down to her like other older dragons, in fact he was not like any other dragon she had met before. They both watched as he left them in the gloom of the deep caverns. Vojin began to follow Squirt to return to the cavern of his mother, as he did another dragon stepped in front of the brother and sister, barring their way back.

"Brother?" Vojin asked, surprised at his appearance.

"Brother," Sting replied flatly, ignoring their sister. "Do you deliberately leave me out of the planning? Do you not trust me to help? Do you think I am too young, too weak?" His voice had dropped to a whisper and it growled in his throat.

Vojin let out a sigh before answering. "I do not, Brother, to any of those questions."

"Yet here you are, meeting with a deformed and with our sister at your side." Sting stepped closer; anger burning in his eyes. Fleet had often felt his anger and had long deduced it was because his egg was the one to be left behind with their mother, while her own and Vojin's had gone on adventures.

"Yes, I was meeting Audel, he has an important role to play in the coming events and what happens after. I did not invite our sister along, she invited herself. As did you by the looks of it. You are destined, Brother, to play your part. Have no fear, it will be harrowing and bloody. I had hoped to save you from what is to come for a little longer," Vojin growled back.

"I am more than ready to face what is to come!" Sting insisted, pulling himself up to his full height and flaring out his ever-growing wings.

"But can you fly?" Vojin asked him quietly.

"It will not be long. Before our sister, I think," he said arrogantly.

"That is not true!" Fleet exclaimed standing up to her nest-mate, anger suddenly flaring at his suggestion. *"I will be flying before you, you just watch!"*

Fleet pushed past both of her brothers and hurried down the tunnel. She was muttering under her breath as she went and was unaware that both Vojin and Sting had followed. Her claws gripped the rock at her feet as she gained speed and turned into the main cavern. The flare of the torches made her squint a little after being in the near darkness.

Making her way to the launch zone she spread her wings fully and started to flap. The golden wings stretched to their full potential and as she reached the first opening in the roof she deliberately began to work them in earnest. The air billowed under the membrane, while the gold caught and reflected the torch light as they moved up and down furiously.

"Sister, wait!" Vojin called out to her in a great bellow which echoed down the cavern and caught the attention of the sleepy guards, making them turn where they stood.

"No! I know what you think. That my mind was affected when my egg was stolen, that it was left to go cold and shaken too many times!" Fleet bellowed back, her voice a match for Vojin's. "But I am strong!"

As one of the guards entered the cavern to investigate, the other was raising the alarm, hoping to rouse either Muniath or Wick. The sight that greeted the Rider as he neared the three dragons was one he had never seen before. A youngling beating her wings and being faced down by two others. The sounds of their bellows shook his insides and he stopped to watch the confrontation. His spear held ready before him; in case he was forced to act.

The youngling roared once more before forcing her wings down, her feet lifting a few inches off the ground. Again with another mighty effort she forced her wings down and rose higher. With each large push the red and gold dragon lifted higher into the air, getting closer and closer to the opening above her. The Rider gaped as his fellow guard reached his side.

"What's happening?" he gasped.

"She's trying to fly," the first said quietly.

"The alarm has been responded to, Muniath is on his way."

The pair watched as the young dragon lifted herself out of the opening and into the night beyond. The two turned as one and ran to the platform out the front of the cave system, trying to see where the young dragon was heading. Behind them the largest of the two remaining dragons lifted off and gave chase.

Muniath stirred as the hand once more shook his shoulder. He pried his eyes apart and struggled to rise from the perfect dream he was having.

"Uncle Mun, there's something going on in the eyrie," Wick's voice said beside him.

Muniath rose to one elbow, wiping his face with a weary hand. "What?" he asked groggily, only wishing to go back to sleep again.

"There's something happening with the younglings," Wick told him, throwing the pants Muniath had discarded when he went to sleep.

This news woke him fully. "What about them?" he asked, hurriedly pushing the covers off his legs, and dragging his clothes on.

"The guard said that one is attempting to fly. It's too soon for either of them." The worry that carried in Wick's voice made Muniath proud of his apprentice.

Muniath grabbed his shirt and jacket after pulling on his boots. "Well, let's go find out." He headed for the door pulling the white shirt over his head. By the time they reached the front door of his parent's house his jacket was on and the pair broke into a run.

Mounting the never-ending steps two at a time, he called out in his mind to Gremlin. *"What's going on?"* He felt the large dragon react to his call and waited as he continued to climb.

"My sister is being a fool!" Gremlin replied, his words and tone were one Muniath had not had from Gremlin before and that had him worried.

"Where is she?" he cried out hoping for some direction.

"Above the caverns. She is gaining height. Her fear is growing, and I am trying to coax her down," Gremlin told him.

"Keep trying, I'm on my way." Muniath turned the corner to head up yet another flight, when a large Red and Gold dragon landed before them.

"Hurry, climb on!" Screamer said quickly.

Muniath glanced at Wick. "Follow after and make sure the other dragons are alright," he instructed his apprentice, who nodded and waited until the way was clear.

Muniath climbed onto Screamer's back and sat himself as comfortably as possible without the aid of a saddle or guide straps. He gripped her scales as she rose into the air and glided off the side of the steep mountain. He looked up at the shear face that rose above them and felt her muscles working beneath his knees. Those muscles controlled their speed, and the lift under the wings as they beat and clawed through the air. Climbing higher and higher, leaving Wick far behind.

"There!" she cried out to him.

Looking up he could see the daughter that resembled the mother in all but sense. Her weak wings beating rapidly, and he could see she was tiring fast. Hovering just below, Gremlin was trying to get through to the now terrified youngling. Muniath watched as he positioned his large bulky body directly below Fleet. It was not a moment too soon as she dropped down. Gremlin rose high to meet her; her talons scraped the scales of his back and he heard him quietly talking to her.

"I've got you, Sister. Slowly now, we'll descend." His voice was soothing and calm.

The pair began to lower, her feet just barely touching his back as he helped her to descend. Muniath and Screamer followed them back to the Eyrie. Down they drifted through the sky portals and back onto the safe and solid rock of the mountain cavern. As Screamer touched down Muniath slid off her back and ran to Fleet. His expert hands immediately going over her wing muscles and checking for any strains.

Wick was soon with them, puffing heavily from his hurried climb. He took the other side of Fleet and helped check her over. Soon the two men pronounced her unharmed, to which she immediately collapsed to the ground, still gasping for air, and trembling slightly.

Muniath lifted her head, now so much larger than his own and stroked it. *"What were you thinking?"* he asked gently.

"I wasn't," she replied, a bit ashamed by her actions.

"You could have hurt yourself."

"I realize that, now," she said and laid her head on his shoulder, seeking comfort from her fear.

"But you flew, Sister!" Sting said with some wonder, coming up and rubbing his head against hers. "You flew! And I am sorry I goaded you. It was very wrong of me."

"Sister, it was a very dangerous action. Flight must be taken slowly and with guidance." Gremlin said, coming to stand with his siblings. "And, Brother, you were not left out. You are both going to play major roles to come, this bickering and jealousy between you must stop. It does neither of you any good, but only to push a wedge between all of us. We must stand together. We must work together."

"I felt left out. You and our sister seem to spend so much time together, that it feels like you exclude me deliberately. I know that I was left behind when your eggs were stolen, I was left behind, and it feels like you leave me behind still." Sting told him as he stared his brother in the eye.

"It is unintentional, Brother. I need you both to concentrate on growing and learning all you can." Gremlin paused and turned to Wick who was standing back with the two guards. "Brother, it is time to bring Wick into the understanding."

"About time!" Sting said eagerly and left his siblings to stand before his bonded Rider.

Wick looked confused and turned to Muniath for guidance. Muniath, having heard the three dragons talking, walked over to where his apprentice stood and then called to the two guards. "Cal and Dren, go back to your posts, everything is in hand now."

Reluctantly they saluted their superior officer and headed back towards the gate. They muttered between them about the night's strange events, but neither could give the other an explanation of what had happened or what was still to occur.

"Wick, I need you to keep your mind open. I know you have that special talent of understanding dragons, but that is only the beginning of it. Last night you had a taste of a real connection when Gremlin spoke to you. Now, I want you to open your mind to Sting," Muniath instructed and then nodded to the near grown dragon.

Sting stared straight into Wick's eyes, sending out his wishes to the young man. Muniath felt Wick reaching, desperate to grasp onto the thoughts and he called louder and stronger to Wick. Finally the connection was made. Wick's eyes widened as he understood the call.

"Hear me, Wick. Welcome to the dragon mind, where you belong. Join us and take up your position with us," Sting called to him.

"I hear you!" Wick told him out loud, his voice full of wonder.

"Use your mind," Muniath said, placing a fatherly hand on Wick's shoulder.

Wick nodded and tried again. *'I hear you,'* he repeated, pushing out the thought.

Sting did something unusual for him. He laid his head on Wick's shoulder and accepted the touch. He had not been this close to Wick since he was just hatched. All his pretensions and misgivings were swept away with that touch and the bond was finally cemented between the two.

'Now, when can I fly?' the young dragon asked eagerly.

Scetis watched from the shadows. This was not part of his story, and was nothing to do with him, but it did not stop him from feeling left out and excluded. He understood how the young green had felt as he watched the world of the dragons be opened up to the teenager.

"For a dragon you are dim," a familiar voice spoke to him.

"Squirt, I thought Gremlin had sent you back to the border?"

"He had, but then I heard all the commotion, so I came back," Squirt told him, coming to stand next to Scetis. *"But I sense that your mood is more than what is happening here."* Squirt nodded to the large flight deck cavern and the figures that still stood there.

"It is," Scetis nodded in agreement.

"If I am to be your advisor, I need to know all the particulars before advising you," he said as he stood upright, towering over Scetis by about three feet.

"It is a matter you cannot help with," Scetis told him with a sad smile.

"Can Muniath help you? You and he are of the same species and have a similar look about you. You both have a longing in your spirits."

Scetis looked at the long-haired man, who was talking to the boy. *"I wonder who he longs for?"* he mused softly.

"Ahh, I understand now. The longing you feel is for a female."

"That is none of your business, Squirt," Scetis said, pushing himself away from the wall with some agitation.

"But it is true, why don't you go see her, it will help to settle you. Your mind will be then focused on what needs to be done," Squirt advised.

"It doesn't work that way with humans. In fact, from what I understand of the matter, it's the opposite," Scetis said quietly with a sigh.

"You know where she is?" Squirt asked eagerly, warming to the subject.

"Not really," Scetis replied, still staring at Muniath, the only physical link to Ide nearby.

Squirt followed his gaze. *"Ahh, is the one you think of tied to him?"* Squirt stepped closer to the edge to get a closer look at the man amongst the dragons.

"In a way. She is his sister."

"Then ask him to take you to her."

"I don't need him to know where she is. I can see her. She dreams and I would not disturb such beautiful dreams."

"You see her dreams while you are awake? The bond between you must be very strong." Squirt paused for a moment. "Do you want to see her?"

"With all my being."

"Then I shall take you." Squirt drew himself up with purpose.

"You? But can you take my weight?" Scetis asked with some skepticism.

"My wings are strong. I'm sure I can carry you," he said indignantly. "When this lot disperses, I'll show you," he huffed.

Out in the main cavern the occupants were doing just that. Wick and Muniath were moving back to the entrance. Muniath's fatherly hand rested on the younger man's shoulder as they talked. A pang of jealousy and loss for something he had never known sped through Scetis. For a brief moment he hated Muniath for a wrong never done by him.

As soon as it was clear, Squirt scampered out of the cave they were hidden in and out into the flickering light of the torches. He stopped and turned back to Scetis. *"Come, we won't be going anywhere if you remain there."*

Scetis took a step unsure as to why he was following the dragon. But he now was eager to see Ide again. He followed Squirt out under one of the sky portals. A beam from one of the large full moons spilled down from above creating a blueish puddle of light. Squirt stood in the middle of it and crouched lower, waiting for Scetis to mount him.

Scetis looked at the diminutive dragon and his reservations once more kicked in. He approached slowly.

"Before I get on, you must promise that if I am too heavy for you, you do not struggle on stubbornly to carry me." Scetis waited for Squirt to answer.

"I promise. Anyway if you are too heavy I shall just tip you off." Squirt said with a chortle.

Scetis shook his head at the dragon's words and carefully climbed onto his back. The scales were smooth to the touch and tightly fitted together. The part he sat on was devoid of the sharp and jagged points which ran down the length of Squirt's neck and back, finishing at the arrow shaped pointed tail. Looking around there was nothing for his hands to hold onto and he tried to get a grip on the long sinewy neck, while his knees pressed tightly against the red scales.

"Are you comfortable?" Squirt asked looking back at Scetis.

"I think so," he told Squirt nervously.

"Hold on then." The leather wings of the dragon spread out either side of his thin body and they seemed to shiver with anticipation. Squirt raised them up high and pushed them down with great force and speed.

At first it felt like no change in their position, but the more they gathered air under the membrane, they began to move more. Slowly they rose to the sky portal and then through the rock opening, into the night air beyond. The clear starry sky stretched over them.

Squirt banked a bit and started a gentle and controlled spiral down the side of the mountain, away from the sight of the main gate. To Scetis, it was not like riding on the back of Gremlin. On his back, Scetis could feel the power of the large dragon. His legs and feet had grip and he felt confident in the dragon's ability in flight. On Squirt's it was very different. He gripped around Squirt's narrow neck, and his feet dangled on either side of his body.

"Are you going to tell me where we are going or do I just land in the lake?" Squirt called to him.

"Down by the shore, below the citadel. There is a large house." Scetis told him, looking below and the ever-approaching water. He saw the roof of the house; saw the terrace he had seen her on in his dreams and he felt his heart start to race.

"I'll put you down beyond the house, just in case we are seen. Muniath is on his way back, remember?"

"I remember. But thank you for the warning and the ride, Squirt."

The landing was gentle and smooth and Scetis slid off Squirt's back as carefully as he could, not wanting to hurt the dragon.

"I shall leave you. You do not need me around; she may prefer my superior good looks and charm." Squirt chuckled and then took to wing, rising up easier than he had with Scetis on his back.

Scetis watched him go and then turned to the house. The dreams of Ide which were constantly with him, he now concentrated on fully. Her flickering dream he inserted himself in and saw her turn to him with a smile.

"I've been waiting," she told him simply. Before him she stood with her dark lustrous hair down and floating on some undetected breeze. She wore a simple white gown that hugged her figure and clung in all the right places.

"It's been a busy night," he replied. "Wake for me, Ide. I'm outside now. I want you in my arms, I want to hold you in the real world."

For a moment, Ide looked puzzled at his words. "But this is just a dream. You keep telling me that it is."

"I am here, outside by the lake. Please Ide, wake up and come meet me," he pleaded, reaching for her hand. With that touch he passed on the location and the image of looking up at the house she slept in.

Ide's eyes opened wide. "You're here!" She let go of his hand and the dream splintered into fragments.

The sudden loss of it left Scetis feeling a little dizzy for a moment and he stumbled. Righting himself, he searched out for Ide. He could see her leave her bed, throw on a loose, long gown and head out of her room. He followed her down the steps and watched as she came to a sudden stop at the bottom as the main door opened. He watched Muniath enter through that door and hear them speak in whispers.

"Where have you been?" she asked, her hand resting on the balustrade.

"Up at the Eyrie. There was a problem with one of the dragons. What are you doing out of bed?" He shut the door quietly behind him and stepped closer to her.

Ide looked towards the back of the house, Scetis could feel her longing, wanting to hide their meeting from her brother. "I was just—" she trailed away.

"Ide? Are you all right?" The concern was very evident in his voice. Scetis felt Muniath reach out for his sister with his mind, and he understood where she was going. "Go, but be careful."

Ide looked at her brother and then kissed his cheek. She left him and Scetis looked up at the terrace in time to see her running quietly towards him. She stopped just as she reached him, only a few small steps away, a look of longing and love on her face.

"Are you really here, or is this still a dream?" she whispered as she hesitated to take those last few steps, so Scetis made them for her.

The back of his fingers brushed her cheek, and he brought his lips to meet hers. Softly and barely touching, he drew in a breath and drank in the scent of her, the taste of her lips. Her arms went around his neck and pulled him in closer. The kiss became ardent and fierce, not wanting to stop and break the spell of the moment. It was far different from their last as he had left her by the cold lake so many moons prior. His arms went around her stroking her back and remembering holding her in the water of the river. Their bodies pressed against each other, both lost in the other, before they broke the kiss and just held each other.

Becoming

Teagan mounted the steps up to the Eyrie with great eagerness. The sun was still to make its face fully known from behind the large mountain across the lake at the bottom of the valley. The sky above her was a pale blue in the early morning light, while the tops of the mountains were hiding their permanently snowy caps under thin wispy clouds that lay over them like a lacy cap. The air was sweet and chill, making the steps slick with the heavy dew that had fallen in the night.

The previous afternoon had been one of wonder and discovery, laced with sadness. Exploring the Eyrie again with her father brought back some of the lost memories she had, including a few of her mother. But it was not the cause of her sadness. When they had returned to the castle she had to say goodbye to her father. He had been seen off by a small group, including the King, General Magaoidh and Muniath. But she would see him again, the farm, she had been reassured, was not far from the town.

Teagan stopped on one of the many landings, resting a hand on the railing, and looking out at the magnificent vista. She breathed deeply of the crisp fresh air and let it out in a long breath to dispel the feelings. She felt at peace. A calmness she had never experienced on Earth. She smiled at that thought. To think she had now lived on two worlds. Had experienced two totally different cultures and now she knew which she preferred.

"Come on, Teagan," Orlagh called to her. Beside her cousin was Feth, a woman of equal height to Orlagh with dark hair and piercing blue eyes. Teagan had noted the silver flecks in them when she had been introduced to her over breakfast.

Feth had quietly contemplated Teagan over their meal while Orlagh had laid out the plans for the day. She had continued scrutinizing Teagan while Orlagh was outfitting her cousin in the garb of a Rider. It wasn't until the three had mounted the steps to the Eyrie that Feth had actually spoken to her.

"Are the rumors true?" Feth's voice was like silk, smooth, rich, and deep for a woman.

"Which rumors?" The news that there was already idle gossip about her was a little disconcerting to Teagan.

"You and Muniath?" They carried on up the steps slowly.

"I'm not sure what you mean?" Teagan said blushing.

"Stop teasing her," Orlagh said with a slight smile and blush which made Teagan believe it was her cousin who was the source of the rumors.

"There's nothing between Muniath and me," Teagan told them and forged ahead of the other two, her face going very red. From behind she heard Orlagh hit her girlfriend and telling her to shh.

"But you said—" Feth started to protest in a whisper.

"I know what I said," Orlagh spoke hurriedly. "But I said not to say anything."

There was quiet after her cousin's words, but it just reminded Teagan why she had never really got on with girls very much. The gossiping behind had always made her feel uncomfortable. But then she had always been awkward around boys as well. When she had first arrived on Earth and had finally figured out how things work, she had been teased on her first day of school for her accent by many. Mostly girls, but some boys. That was when she had turned quiet and introspective. She had kept to herself and had not made friends. Her father and her had moved so often that it was hard to keep count. Keeping friends had been impossible for the child Teagan.

Finally reaching the top of the stairs the group of three women were waved through the gates by guards who were still yawning and just taken over from the night shift. Orlagh led the way in and down the long landing cave, into the interior of the mountain. The sounds of dragons moving and eating echoed around them. The sound of scampering feet neared and Teagan recognized the nearly fully grown female dragon that was bonded to Muniath. Fleet bypassed both Orlagh and Feth to come to an enthusiastic and sudden stop in front of Teagan.

"Good morning, Child of Dragons." Fleet greeted her.

Teagan reached out and laid her hand on the side of Fleet's face as she would to Gremlin. *"Good morning, Fleet."*

"My brother awaits, will you join us?" Fleet asked, trying to be calm.

"I am supposed to be with Orlagh and Feth this morning," she said and looked up at her cousin and her girlfriend, only to find them both staring at her strangely. It was the same look most girls got when she tried to show them a lizard. That mixture of incredulousness and shock. *"You best go back to your mother, young one,"* Teagan said to Fleet and watched her go. Taking a deep breath waiting for the ridicule and jibes that would come at her expense.

"You can understand the dragons?" Orlagh asked.

"Yes, I can," Teagan said, steeling herself for the next words from Orlagh.

"But how?" Orlagh asked, stepping towards her.

"I don't know. Gremlin and I have always been able to understand each other and now I can understand the others," she said a little shyly.

"Can you teach me?" Feth asked eagerly.

"I'm not sure I can." Teagan said hesitantly.

"Teach her." Gremlin's voice said in her mind.

"How?"

"Bring her to me." He commanded.

"Follow me." Teagan said to the two women and then headed to the cavern that housed the Red and Gold dragon.

Inside the two nearly grown dragons both greeted Teagan and their mother bowed her head to her. Teagan went and greeted Gremlin with a tender stroke and hugging his large neck.

"Tell Feth to not move," Gremlin instructed her, and Teagan relayed the instruction.

Feth stayed where she was and soon her gaze was locked onto Gremlin's. Teagan watched as her eyes seemed to deepen and the silver glowed in the torch light. She saw the look of wonder as the world of dragon's was opened up to her. The collective mind that all dragons shared. As Teagan felt closer to that connection, she found one that felt familiar. Carefully she searched more for than one and felt the return recognition. Teagan pulled away from it quickly, but not before she felt the disappointment at her actions.

"He wants you," Fleet said quietly in her mind. *"He likes you."*

"I don't—" she started to say, but unable to finish.

"Make the connection Child of Dragons. He and you were meant for each other." This voice was different. It was more mature than Fleet's. Teagan looked up at the Red and Gold and the dragon nodded.

"But mother of my friend, I'm scared." She admitted to the large dragon.

"You are afraid of getting hurt, of being rejected. Muniath will not do this. He does not realize his feelings for you are being sent out. That we can all feel that he wants you as his mate and claiming that right to do so before all others. You both are like fledglings; your thoughts are scattered and out on display for the world. My son has not taught you to reign them in and control them."

"He truly likes me in that way?" Teagan asked quietly.

"Look for yourself. Connect with his heart as well as his mind and you will see his true feelings for you."

Teagan felt the older dragon pulling away from her thoughts, leaving her in the silence of her mind. Tentatively she searched again and was surprised how quickly she found him. She felt him stop walking and wait for her to be comfortable and not scare her away. Teagan took a deep breath and pressed forward.

"I feel what you feel." Teagan whispered to him.

"Are you sure you do?" he asked her equally as quiet, she could hear the fear in his own voice.

"I am sure." She told him and felt the immense joy that emanated from him.

"Stay where you are. I'll be there shortly," he said quickly.

Their connection remained strong and she felt him get nearer and nearer. But he was not alone. His apprentice was with him and she felt the change in the boy. She sensed he could understand, had heard their conversation.

She stood transfixed as she saw Muniath round the corner. He stopped in his tracks when he saw her. A brief smile played on his lips and his eyes widened slightly. She let go of the breath she was holding slowly. He made to step towards her when Feth greeted him. Teagan had almost forgotten that Orlagh and her girlfriend were still there, let alone the four dragons.

"Muniath!" Feth called out then also turning to Wick "You too?" she asked the apprentice.

"Yes. It's amazing isn't it?" Wick asked with a wide smile.

"What is?" Orlagh asked confusion written all over her.

"The dragons. I can understand them," Feth said in some awe. "Rain!"
 she said excitedly and rushed out of the cavern, Orlagh chasing after calling her name.

"Good morning, Sting." Wick said greeting the juvenile dragon who had moved closer.

"Time I learned to fly. I cannot be outdone by my sister," Sting said with some enthusiasm.

"Then we need to ask Muniath for help." Wick looked up eagerly to the Dragon Master, stopped before speaking again and then looked between both the man who had become a father figure and Teagan, the strange woman he had only the briefest of explanations on where she had come from. *"I think Sting, we should consult with your mother on this one."* He smiled.

Muniath almost shook himself awake. He grinned a little as Wick passed him with a wink and a smile of his own. Turning back to Teagan, Muniath stepped closer and then took her hand. They matched almost in height. He raised her hand to his lips and kissed the back of them gently. He never once took his eyes off hers.

"I hoped," he whispered. "But I didn't dare dream."

"Why?"

"You are—" he paused searching for the right words. "You are beyond me. I am not the right man for you."

"Can I be the judge of that?" she asked with a smile and her cheeks reddened.

"Why you?"

"I'm not sure I understand?" she said with a nervous laugh. "Why do you feel what you feel for me?"

"No. Why do you…you know," Muniath said, still stumbling over his words.

"I don't know," she told him simply. "I just do." Teagan lowered her gaze for the first time.

"What brought you to the Eyrie?" he asked her, completely forgetting anyone else had been there with her.

"I came with Orlagh. We were going to go flying. She and Feth wanted to introduce me to their mounts."

Muniath looked around them at the near empty cavern. Only Gremlin and Fleet along with their mother were still there. All of the dragons looked at the couple, with a seemingly similar expression of satisfaction that something momentous had occurred.

"We could go flying. I need to give Fleet a lesson, now she has spread her wings and I am sure Gremlin could use a little exercise." Muniath suggested, his words tumbling after each other.

"*Would you like to fly, Gremlin?*" Teagan asked eagerly, happy to be talking of something else now and the prospect of being out in the air on his back.

"*It would be my pleasure Teagan,*" Gremlin said bowing his head with some amusement.

"*Please, Muniath, please,*" Fleet began at the prospect of flying.

"Yes, young one," he said amused.

The couple led the way of the cavern hand in hand and the two dragons followed on the way to the wyvern training gate. Muniath picked up a saddle and placed it on Gremlin's back, then went to put on a halter and reins.

"No, I don't think so," Teagan stopped him.

"But he has to have it on so you will be safe on his back," Muniath protested.

"We have managed quite well without those. The saddle is one thing, but he does not need my hands guiding his head. We know together where to go, it's a mutual decision."

"If you insist." He then turned to place it on Fleet, who took a step back.

"If my brother does not need it, then neither do I," she protested holding herself up to her full height and puffing out her chest. Her wings fluttered in agitation and she snorted a little. A puff of steaming smoke escaped her nostrils.

"Ok, but you will need to listen very carefully to what I say, otherwise I will be insisting that it goes on." He hung up the leather reigns back onto the stand and then picked up a saddle. Gently he introduced it to her back, and he stood back waiting to see how she would react to the weight and pressure.

"Are you going to stand there all day?" Fleet asked him.

Muniath gave her a wry smile and then tightened up the straps to hold the saddle in place. Once he was finished, he ran his hand up her long neck and she purred a little at the gentle touch. *"Shall we go?"* he asked her and then led the way out of the saddlery and passed the main wyvern gate into another corridor and out onto a wide platform where they found Wick, Sting, and Screamer watching.

Sting was connected with a lead reign, while Screamer hovered nearby watching. When Sting saw both Fleet and Gremlin were without reigns he huffed his displeasure. *"Take it off,"* he demanded with some indignation.

"But—" Wick started turning to Muniath.

"Take it off Wick. It will do no harm. Things need to change I think."

Wick quickly did as he was instructed. While he did Teagan mounted the saddle on Gremlin's back and settled herself in. Gremlin lifted his wings and was soon in the air swooping away down the sheer drop off. Teagan felt free for the first time since coming back to the Dragon Realm. The air was cool at that height and Gremlin beat his wings harder, clawing at the air to climb higher.

"Where are we going?" Teagan asked him, coming to the realization that he had a destination in mind.

"To a special place," he told her.

Gremlin flew on and came to a wide flat area, jutting out from the side of a mountain. At the back of this expanse, in the middle was a large opening. The dragon made for the entrance and entered with Teagan still on his back. He walked through the large and evenly dug out cave, she noted shadows that moved on the walls, but when she tried to look at them directly, they seemed to disappear. Finally, they arrived at a huge tiered cavern. It stretched out before them, stepping down to a glowing bottom. Without hesitation, Gremlin launched himself from the edge and circled to the bottom, landing before a low wall which surrounded the cause of the glow, a pit of molten liquid. The heat coming from it was ferocious and she could feel it start to burn at her exposed skin. Teagan slipped from the saddle, keeping Gremlin between her and the pool. The sound of the bubbling rock was loud in the area and the smell of sulfur stung her nose. Teagan leaned against Gremlin as she felt the heat start to suck all the energy out of her.

"We have to go—" she said weakly, trying to get back in the saddle. Her hands were drenched with sweat, and she found she could not grip the leather seat.

"Dig deep, Teagan, Child of Dragons." Gremlin commanded. "Dig deep past your human form, to the dragon within. Your first test is today. Prove to me that you are who I have created." Gremlin flared his wings high above his body.

"I don't understand, what do you want to do?" she asked, collapsing to the hot rock.

"Stand before the fiery pit. Face your fear and grow into who you were meant to be." His voice boomed not only in her mind but echoed off the circular cavern.

"I'll die," she whimpered.

"No, you will not. Now stand," he commanded.

Slowly she got to her feet. Sweat dripped from her body in rivulets, stinging her eyes as she wiped her face on her sleeve to clear it. As she did, Gremlin moved and the full heat from the lava hit her. She stumbled back, but he supported her with his neck, holding her up. The fiery liquid turned her skin first red, then it started to blister. Teagan screamed at the pain and with fumbling fingers began to tear at the remaining clothes she had on. Now standing nude, her body shook as the outer skin burned away. It melted from her body, slipping, and exposing raw flesh underneath. A scream she so desperately wanted to release caught in her throat.

"Into the lake." Gremlin commanded.

Each step she took was labored, she tried to stop herself, but found her body would not respond. Her mind screamed at the thought of the agony and death that she was sure awaited if she obeyed the Dragon King. But she went. Standing on the precipice, in a gap of the wall, the scream at last escaped her lips as she stepped down into the rock from the center of the world. She felt it burn, but no more than a hot bath would. Further in she stepped, turned to the dragon, and then lay back, sinking beneath the surface of the lava. It covered her face, invaded her nostrils and finally her mouth. She drank in the fiery liquid rock, felt it invade her completely. Her veins now burned with it, and there was something else. The awareness.

The world opened to her. She felt every living thing, be it animal or plant, insect or human. All were connected with her. She felt the power the very world was imparting to her. The magic that the first dragons had before being consumed. It flowed through her.

With a great gasp she rose from the lava. Stepped with purpose and without pain from the glowing pond. Standing on the edge the remains of the lava dripped from her renewed body. Teagan looked down at her skin, it glowed in the light a slight rainbow hue, which appeared as if small soft scales covered her. She looked up and blinked at Gremlin. Her eyes now a full gold, the silver now gone and replaced with the sign of a true dragon. She was now fully the Child of Dragons. Master of the magic that had been lost. Commander of Dragons.

Across the world she heard the dragons roar. The celebration of her coming fully into her own. They called out with one voice in their collective mind as well as individual voices. She saw all humans stop and stare, listening to the call. It frightened some, it filled others with awe. Their own awakening happened as the dragon blood took hold.

The world stopped for a moment as it celebrated the coming of Child of Dragons.

Declaration

The air felt so cool on her skin as Gremlin flew her high over the mountains. Their sharp pinnacle tops glided past underneath them at amazing speed, but Teagan failed to notice any of the splendor of the scenery. Her mind was still on the call of the world that had reached out and celebrated with her. It was only a small world, even smaller than Earth, but it was full of life. Gremlin's true name had come to her the moment of her awakening.

Gremlin swooped and dove over the ground getting closer and closer to it. Skirting around the border Rostra and the Riders of the Realm that were stationed there, giving them a wide berth to keep them out of sight. At length, he came to rest on a finger of rock that thrust its way up out of the mountain. Standing strong and proud, resilient to the weather that scoured its sides.

Gremlin adjusted his grip on the rock and looked far below them. His deep emerald scales blending in well with the surrounding faces of the cliffs.

"Teagan," he said gently to her.

"Yes, Gremlin?" she replied.

"Time to concentrate," he reminded her.

Teagan gazed around her at where they had landed. Down far below them was a small valley. Once probably good farming land, but now it was covered in tents, wagons, horses, and moving between all of these were figures. Small, ant-like figures going about life in a military camp. They were garbed in different colors and those colors matched the many flags that fluttered in the wind that was funneled through the valley. The water source of a stream glistened at the base of the mountain on the other side, she could see that where it entered the camp it was clean and clear, but by the time it exited at the other end, to carry on its journey, it was brown and sluggish. This pollution of such a pristine area made her mad.

"This is the army we are to face?" she asked.

"No, this is only one part. They have been camped here for a while. This valley cannot be seen by the Riders and their scouting flights have become sluggish and lax," Gremlin told her.

"Urmond must be made aware of this. How many more camps like this are there?" she asked leaning forward so she could get a better look.

"There are eight more disgusting camps like this, and an area is being prepared for one more," a small red dragon said beside them, as he crept from a hole in the cliff face. "This one is made up of mercenaries, many bands. Some others have bands such as these and a regular army. The Convocation has been very busy and spending a great deal of coin it seems," he told her, as he picked something from his teeth with a claw from his very human-like hand.

"Thank you, Squirt," she said instantly knowing the name he preferred.

"It has been my pleasure, Child of Dragons, to be of service to you." Squirt gave her a flamboyant bow; his head almost touched the ground it was so deep. Then he continued with his report. "I believe that the last lot will be the new group I observed coming through the secret pass. I took a little peek into the lands of the Convocation and I could see no more marshalling or marching towards the border. I believe that The Dragon Realm needs to act soon. These groups are spread wide in valleys such as these. We can neutralize them easily enough. But if we wait until they march in full, then it will be too late." He delivered his opinion carefully.

"I believe you are correct. But it will still be up to the King. He is still the ruler of these lands. I am just a commander."

"I will leave it up to you, my lady." Squirt bowed again.

"Keep an eye on the border, Audel. If it looks like they are on the move let us know." Gremlin instructed.

"It shall be as you command, oh Great Ones," he said with a little smirk.

Muniath stood on the practice platform staring out looking both up and down the valley but could see no sign of Gremlin and Teagan. He was becoming worried. He then sent out a thought to connect with either of them, but it seemed to be blocked, deliberately. He knew something momentous had happened as he had heard the dragon calls earlier. It was a joyous sound and felt at a loss as to what had happened.

"You worry too much," Fleet said, slipping under his hand and stepping forward. His hand slid over her slick scales and rested on the back of her long neck; her head now raised higher than he stood.

"But she is not used to this world, and besides," he said looking up at his bonded dragon. "It is my job to worry."

"She is with my brother; he will make sure she does not come to any harm." Fleet reassured him.

"I agree with the youngling," a male voice said behind them. Muniath turned and saw Scetis standing at the entrance.

"How did you get in here?" Muniath demanded.

"There's a back door. I'll show you if you like, but I don't think the dragons will be happy that I have given their long-held secret away."

"Muniath is one of us and should know," Fleet said dismissively.

"My apologies, youngling," Scetis smiled and bowed to the dragon.

"I am a youngling no more. I am flying," she said with a sniff.

"I had heard of your exploits from last night," Scetis grinned.

"I hope my sister was well when you left her last night." Muniath tried to make the tone of his voice light, but there was still a slight edge to it. Ide was his sister after all, and he did feel protective over her.

"Ide was well and happy, I believe, when I left her. Though I feel the coming events are weighing her down a little. Can we do something about Orcades at all, soon?" he asked, the worry was there and Muniath warmed to him a little. He knew instinctively that this man loved his sister deeply, more so than he first thought.

"Believe me, it would give me no greater pleasure than to drop that traitor from a great height." Muniath growled, then turned at the sound of a roar that echoed around the lake valley.

From the south the dragon came, the great emerald green, with a wingspan larger than any other, but flying as if he were a graceful soaring eagle. He roared again and from beside him Fleet raised her head and roared along with her brother. From deep within the mountain more calls came.

"Rejoice!" they all called. It was the same as just a few hours before.

Gremlin circled around the practice platform and landed gently. The claws on his feet scraping on the small rock. *"Rejoice!"* he called again.

From his back slipped a figure. Her bright flaming hair covered her face for a moment and as she moved it away with a gloved hand, the sun burst through the high cloud that had gathered throughout the day. The shimmering rainbow played over her face and her eyes burned gold with a ring of her normal green showing at the edges.

"Behold, the Child of Dragons!" Fleet called out to the world. Her wings spread and her head bowed low, so it touched the rock.

"Teagan?" Muniath asked as she stepped before him. "What...?" he asked, lost for words.

"We have a lot to talk about and a lot I have to explain. But first I need to see the King. Will you both accompany us?" she asked, taking Muniath's hand and looking at Scetis, then back to Muniath. He raised a finger to touch her face. Now that she was closer, he could see the delicate lacy scales that covered her skin. They shimmered as she moved and were mesmerizing.

"Muniath, I think we had better do as she asks." Scetis said, staring at this woman just as Muniath was.

"We'll go now," Muniath replied quietly, coming to himself and starting to head inside. Teagan let his hand go.

"I shall meet you at the palace. Gremlin needs to be in this conversation." She launched herself onto the back of the dragon and he took off.

"See you there." Scetis called out, grabbing Muniath's arm and pulling him inside.

"Did you see?" he asked Scetis.

"I did." Scetis grinned at him.

The white doors opened and Urmond stood on the other side. He started to speak but stopped and stared at Teagan a moment, as a rainbow flash flickered over her face. He regained his composure and stepped aside for the three people standing before him.

"We can't talk here, my Lord King," Teagan started, with only a minor hesitation, her true self took over. The Child of Dragons was not meek and hesitant.

"And why would that be Lady Teagan?" Urmond asked confused and almost slightly amused at this change in her.

"Gremlin will not fit in your office, so we need to go to the Flyway" Teagan did not wait for any of the men to answer. She turned and headed back the way she had come.

"Lady Teagan?" Urmond called to her, then carried on when she stopped and turned back to him. "Is this something my generals should be here for?"

"General of Riders, yes," she agreed after thinking for a moment. "But not of Foot."

"Wise decision, My Lady." He grinned at her and then looked back into his private office and nodded at someone. From the opening, Muniath's Father stepped out and all four started to follow Teagan.

Making their way out onto the large circular platform on top of one of the towers, the wind caught at the loose strands of hair about Teagan's face. Gremlin stood by the low wall, he appeared to be looking out at the view, but she could tell he was communing with Squirt, gathering all the latest intelligence the small dragon could supply him with.

"He is magnificent," Galanan whispered as they joined her. "I have never seen an Emerald before."

"Now you see what I was talking about," Muniath whispered to his father.

The dragon turned his silver eyes towards the gathered group and came to join them. He moved lightly for one of his size, his footsteps barely making any noise at all. Only the soft clicking of his talons made their rhythmic noise as he walked. He bowed his head to Teagan and Urmond who had come to stand beside her.

"Good afternoon, King of the Dragon Realm," Gremlin acknowledged him.

"Good afternoon, Vojin." Urmond returned the bow.

"We bring you news of your Realm, and it is not good," Gremlin told him, then looked to Teagan to carry on.

"My Lord King, General of Riders, Dragon Master and Heir to the throne," she addressed them. "Things are moving quickly, and we do not have any option but to respond and fast," she told them all. "The Convocation is advancing. There are nine camps already within our borders made up of regulars and mercenaries." She paused a moment and turned to Galanan. "The patrols have become lax on the border Rostra; they must be brought into line and carry out their duties properly."

"How do you know this?" Galanan asked her. "And what has happened to your skin?"

"I know this because I have seen it for myself and," she paused looking at Gremlin who nodded. "Because Gremlin has someone watching them."

"Hello," Squirt said, climbing over the decorated wall. He stood on his hind legs and walked towards them. His movements were more human than dragon, and he bowed to Urmond with his hand over his heart. *"My Lord King, my knowledge is yours, my service is yours, my life is yours. I pledge myself to you and your line til my dying breath. If you would have my council."*

"May I present, Audel," Teagan introduced the diminutive dragon.

"It would be the Crown's honor to have the service of such an advisor. We take you under our wing and our protection shall be yours. Serve us loyally and serve us well. We welcome your council." Urmond said formally.

"I will leave Audel here to advise you and bring you up to speed. I must go now to take over his role of watcher. I will relay what I find through the Child of Dragons." Gremlin told Urmond then turned to Teagan. "Be wary and watchful, there is some danger here."

"I will Gremlin." Teagan wrapped her arms around his neck and rested her head briefly against him. As she did the colors flashed on her skin, then dulled as she pulled away.

Gremlin carefully stepped into the center of the platform and flared his great wings. As he flapped them, the same shimmer that was on Teagan could clearly be seen on his leather wings. With only a few flaps he was airborne and holding for a moment before soaring away. Teagan watched him go for a moment before a clatter at the door to the tower made her turn.

Stepping out into the bright sunshine in armor that was burnished and highlighted in gold, was the same young man that had stopped them the previous day. His pale blue eyes were suspicious, his whole demeanor screamed at how self-absorbed he was, and his muscles strained the chainmail shirt he wore under his breastplate. If he did not seem to be so vain and self-important, he might be good looking.

"Orcades, what do you want?' Urmond asked. There was no jovial tone for his nephew, there was now an edge to his voice.

"Uncle," Orcades said bowing. "I was informed that there was a gathering of the council. They request your presence urgently." His eyes darted to each face. Lingering on those he did not know.

"So you have been demoted to a page?" Urmond asked with a chuckle.

"No, my Lord King. The notice was given to General Gerarailt while I was with him and I offered to bring you news of it myself." He bowed his head briefly.

"That was very kind of you. Is General Magaoidh, here, also summoned?"

"He is, Uncle." A slight blush and a dart of the eyes gave away the fact he had not expected to see Galanan or even pass on the request.

"Then we had best go. Please join me, all of you." Urmond requested to the gathering.

Orcades did not protest the inclusion of the rest of the group. For the first time he saw Squirt and he made a slight strangling noise in his throat. His eyes bulged and he went to speak, but Squirt hissed at him instead as he passed the overly muscled man, causing him to step back and the words go quiet in his mouth.

The group made their way through the palace and into the citadel with Urmond in the lead, heading purposefully to the Council

Chamber. A large circular room lay before them. Lining the walls under the many high windows were rows and rows of tiered seating, with a rostrum in the center. It seemed to Teagan that the nearer the rostrum a person sat the older they appeared. The clothing they wore were of rich fabric, but all the same style and color, black. The only introduction of color were the cloth caps they wore on their heads. Groups of these colors sat together in blocks and chatted among themselves, occasionally calling out to someone else.

By the central rostrum was a large man of older years. He was the only one in the room that wore a silver cap, and in his hands he held a scroll, tied with a red and black ribbon. He rapped heavily on the rostrum and the room went quiet. The gathered group of men and women all stood and bowed as one when the King entered the room.

"Hail our Lord King!" they all called as one.

Urmond nodded his acknowledgement before stopping and quickly whispering something to Muniath, who turned and headed quickly out of the room. Teagan noticed General Gerarailt hurrying into the room to join the gathered group. She also saw the quick exchange between himself and Orcades. Urmond then moved forward to stand in front of the man with the scroll.

"Councilor Ocuinn, you requested my presence for this meeting?"

"I have, my Lord King. A matter of some urgency has come to our notice this morning and I think it requires your presence to answer the questions that have been raised." Ocuinn said, holding out the rolled parchment.

Urmond unrolled it and scanned the page. Teagan could not see what was written there and sent a message to Muniath. *"Where are you?"*

"Gathering proof for the king. I'll be back shortly," he told her quickly. Teagan turned her attention back to Urmond.

"So, The Convocation wants to know who will reign after me? I do not see it as being The Convocation's business who my heir is." Urmond passed the scroll back.

"They have raised the issue that there are rumors that Princess Orlagh will not take the crown after you pass, and that you have named another heir. They wish to know who that person is, and if I may be so bold, My Lord King, we would also. These rumors have been spreading for some days. Ever since some strangers have been appearing in the halls of the palace." He looked passed the group and stared at Teagan.

Once, such scrutiny would have made her feel shy and inadequate, but not anymore. She stared back at the lean and tall man, never wavering in her stance. Politicians, it seemed to her, were the same no matter what planet you were on.

"My Lord King, you must understand that the matter of succession is a matter that involves the Realm as a whole. The uncertainty of who will reign next can sometimes destabilize the population." Councilor Ocuinn carried on. He had returned his gaze back to Urmond but kept flicking his eyes to Teagan.

"I do well understand, Ocuinn, that this matter must be addressed. I am not getting any younger, but neither am I that infirm, yet." Urmond chuckled a little, hoping to ease the tension that seemed to be rising. "Yes, this matter has been resolved," he finally told them.

This news was like a wildfire to the council and the noise of the murmuring of speculation raged through the chamber. The different sections of colored cloth hats were a sea of movement against their black robes. Some even broke ranks to talk to others in different sections. Teagan noted quite a few who were nodding and looking smug, as if they already knew who that person was.

"That is a relief to hear, King Urmond," Ocuinn's voice rose above all others. The hum of excited voices dropped as a few scurried back to their seats. "Are we permitted to know who this person is?"

"You may," Urmond said, stepping to the rostrum. Teagan could hear the tightness in Urmond's voice, he did not like being questioned by his council. Urmond stood at the rostrum and placed his hands firmly on the carved marble barrier. He stared at the councilors, making eye contact with each of them. Teagan could feel the hesitation of sharing his news; news that could place his newly found son in danger.

"My good and faithful councilor's," he began. "This question has been on my mind for some time. You may ask yourselves why, as everyone presumed my daughter, Princess Orlagh, would take the throne after my eventual demise. However," he paused, leaving it hanging a moment. "The matter of succession is one that comes with certain conditions, as some of you well know."

Again a murmur could be heard and now a few pages could be seen scurrying out of the chamber on urgent errands for some of the departments.

"Those conditions are," Urmond carried on, ignoring the flurry of activity before him. "The person shall be a descendant of the royal line; either directly or indirectly, and I might add, legitimate or illegitimate. Secondly, the heir should contain a certain physical trait."

Behind the small, gathered group by the main door came running footsteps, which calmed to a fast walking. Teagan turned and found Muniath re-enter the chamber. In his hands he held a few books and a scroll tied with a green and black ribbon. He nodded to Urmond who had turned at his entrance.

"That characteristic is to do with the eyes, ladies and gentlemen," Urmond continued, his voice stronger. "Our history is a long one in this Realm. The true name of our lands is The Dragon Realm. It is not because we utilize the strength and power of the dragons. It is because this Realm—the very society we enjoy today—was founded by dragons. At one point we all had a common trait. But with the progression of time and the introduction of other races, that trait has slowly been lost." Urmond paused again and left the rostrum. He began to walk around the chamber as he continued to talk. "That trait is in the eyes," he said softly, but everyone could hear him and were now hanging on his every word. "In some it is very evident and in others it is not there at all. Some of us have silver flecks in our eyes." He stopped beside Ocuinn and turned to face him. "You have that trait, Councilor, can you see it in mine?"

"Indeed, I do sire, but—" he began but was silenced by the hand of his King. Urmond turned back to the seated councilors. "My Lords and Ladies, I can see you each checking the others. This trait—these silver flecks—tell me of your heritage. But they do not make you better than your fellow man. It only tells us who has dragon blood in their veins." His circle of the rostrum was complete, and he mounted the steps slowly to stand before those he had picked to help rule the Realm. "Our history has been forgotten, but thankfully it has come to light once more. It has been researched and studied. You may be asking what does it mean to have dragon blood? It means just that. We are descended from the first dragon-human hybrids, an ancestor created to stop the conflict between the humans who invaded this land, and the dragons who were created and came from the very center of this world."

Urmond turned and beckoned Muniath over to him. With his long stride Muniath was before his King, bowing his head and offering the books and scroll in his hands.

"My thanks to you Captain Magaoidh." He then turned back to the crowd. "It is set in the accords that no one may sit on the throne and rule over The Dragon Realm without the blood of dragons coursing through their veins. My daughter—though I wish it otherwise—does not have a drop of dragon blood. She is aware of this stipulation and has graciously stepped aside so that one who does can rule in her place."

"My Lord King, then who is to take her place as heir?" Ocuinn asked. At that point Teagan realized that the head councilor had already been informed and probably had taken part in the actual study of the situation. He already knew who the heir was.

Urmond started looking down at the scroll in his hands. "Orlagh is not my only child." His declaration stunned the councilors and not one moved in their seats or even spoke one word. "As a young man I was sent as a Rider to a border rostra outpost. There I met the most wonderful and beautiful woman, and we fell in love. As nature is wont to do, a child was conceived from that love. But I did not know this. I was summoned back to the citadel before she even knew. I made her a promise to join me, but when she did make it to the citadel in search of me, it was with a child in her arms. She was sent away. Given a bag of gold and told that I did not love nor want her and our son. This was all done without my knowledge," he said with some anger. "My beloved Aelwen died shortly after, taking her own life, and leaving our son in the slums of the Convocation." Urmond paused once more looking at the bound scroll.

"So he is lost?" A woman spoke from the third tier.

"No. He has found his way here. His history has been confirmed. There is no denying that he is my son." Urmond held up the scroll. "The declaration of his legitimacy to sit on the throne is here. Signed, witnessed, and lodged. This document declares to the world that there is a rightful heir. My son, Scetis." Urmond turned to look at the group.

Teagan watched as Scetis stepped out from behind General Magaoidh. He slowly and with a great sense of occasion, made his way to the rostrum and knelt on one knee before the King, his father. He bowed his head over his crossed hands on his knee.

"I pledge my life to The Dragon Realm," he said in a loud and clear voice, then rose. Urmond handed the scroll to Scetis then embraced him.

"Your pledge is acknowledged and accepted by the crown. Prince Scetis."

Teagan looked around her at the reaction in the room. Most looked happy and stunned, while a few had scowls on their faces. One in particular looked angry. General Domnall Gerarailt of the Foot quickly covered his reaction and gave a warning shake of his head to Orcades. The younger man seemed ready to burst at the seams at this development, like a petulant child. She was not the only one to notice, however. Still out in the hallway stood Squirt and he was watching quite keenly the interaction between the two.

Subterfuge

"Welcome to the family," Orcades said, a smile plastered on his face and hand pushed out towards Scetis.

Scetis gave an equally fixed smile back to the over primped and preened man. The man who still hoped to possess Ide. Scetis thought he needed to be very careful around him. For more reasons than just being a rival in a love triangle. He clasped Orcades hand and was surprised how limp his grip was. Scetis had expected the muscled man to have at least a firm grasp, if not a handshake that could almost break his hand. He could see Orcades measuring him up, trying to assess him and find a way he could insinuate himself into the newly found prince's graces. Scetis had to change his thinking then, remembering who he was related to.

As if Orcades could read his mind he began to speak. "I understand from communications with my family over the border, that you are under the protective arm of the Regulator of the Convocation." He released Scetis hand and hooked his thumb into the belt which held his sword at his side.

"I was his pupil at one point," he said guarding his words and not giving anything away.

"There was a little unpleasantness, I understand?" Orcades asked, still not giving up his line of thought.

"I'm not aware of what you mean," Scetis responded.

"I believe you are—in fact—a wanted man by The Convocation." Orcades looked around the room to see who else was listening to their conversation. "That you are wanted by The Convocation for murder." His voice rose to make sure everyone in the room heard him. He was not disappointed as heads turned their way.

"What is this, my lord?" Ocuinn asked bustling over quickly.

"According to rumors I have heard. Unfounded rumors." Orcades said hastily, trying to appear to smooth over any problems that his words may have deliberately caused.

Scetis stared at him. His blue eyes like ice with hatred for this man. He could feel his anger rising and knowing who he was connected with did not help him.

"councilor Ocuinn," Urmond said, coming to Scetis aid. "Rumors are just that, rumors. But when said and spread can become detrimental to not only the subject of those rumors, but, in this case, the country also. My nephew should already know this." He stared at Orcades who returned the stare unwilling to back down in his stubbornness.

"I am only relaying what my cousin has told me. He is a Physician. I believe Scetis here knows him. Wradech Foghladh?" he inquired from Scetis.

"I do know him, indeed. We do not get along. He was finishing his apprenticeship as I was starting mine," Scetis provided.

"Until such accusations are proved or disproved, my Lord King, should the announcement of Prince Scetis being named heir be delayed?" Ocuinn asked Urmond.

"I think not. A delay of this sort will only destabilize the Realm and could prove to be harmful."

"In any case, my King, I shall write to the Regulator to find the truth of this matter." Ocuinn hurried off and Scetis began to wonder if he was part of the plot. His attention was drawn away by Orcades next words.

"Uncle, I wanted a word as to if we can move our ceremony up. I can't see a reason for any more delays now. Muniath is home and," he flicked a derisive glance at Scetis, "the question of an heir has been settled."

"Now is not the time to be talking of that, nephew. Come see me tomorrow and we can discuss it. I will meet with both you, Ide, and her family to discuss the matter," Urmond dismissed him.

Orcades did not immediately realize that he was expected to leave and stood for a moment like a startled rabbit before giving a curt and almost disrespectful bow before leaving the room.

"My Lord King," Domnall started wandering over to the pair. "The stability of our Realm is paramount to me. If there is the slightest question as to the validity of *Prince* Scetis' right to the throne, the people will not stand for it. As General of the Foot it is my job to keep the peace on the streets. That job will be hard if this ever gets out."

"General Gerarailt," Urmond said a little forcefully and the use of his official title was not lost on anyone in the room who was privy to the vital information of Domnall's treasonous acts so far. "I thank you for your council, but I have made my ruling. I think you have little faith in the great people who make up this Realm. You forget their heritage. You forget the old lore."

"If you persist, there will be blood in the streets of this city and possibly every town and village," Domnall warned.

"Then you best do your job, General, and protect the good citizens of our Realm." The steel in his voice made it quite clear to Domnall that Urmond was not to be argued with.

Domnall stood to attention and unlike his nephew, bowed low and in the proper manner to his King. He left the council room, his boot heels clicking loudly, and he had a hand on the hilt of his sword.

Beside Scetis, Urmond sighed deeply. "It is disappointing to know that a man I trusted—a man I have called my friend for most of my life— could betray me so," he said softly so only Scetis could hear.

"I believe my being here is causing you problems, my Lord King," Scetis said equally quiet.

"Scetis, your being here makes no difference. The plot would have gone ahead regardless. And there is no need to address me so formally."

"How should I address you then?" Scetis stood straight with his hands clasped behind his back.

"It may seem strange to start with, but you could address me as Father. It would reinforce to everyone that you are my son, and Prince of the Realm," Urmond said and Scetis could see the hope in his eyes.

The emotions that raged through him made him hesitate to answer. With each passing second he could see that hope fade and be replaced by hurt. He changed his perception of the man and had the sudden insight of guilt for all these years at the loss of someone he had never met or known existed. Of the depth of feelings this man had had for his mother.

"I think *'father'* is manageable for me," he said a little less formally. His words were rewarded by a large smile from Urmond.

"I understand this all must be difficult for you. I hope in time that it will become easier for you to call me *father*."

Scetis stared out of the large picture window of Urmond's private study. He looked up at the Eyrie and saw a large dragon set forth onto its wings. He reached out to Vojin. *"Where are you off to now my friend?"*

"To inspect the border. I need to know that the orders are being followed." Vojin replied.

"Good flight to you then," he said with a sigh, wishing he could be anywhere but in that room at that moment.

The door opened and Urmond walked in. He smiled at Scetis. "Good morning, you're early."

"I wanted to be here first, to prepare," Scetis said grimly.

"I'm not going to have a problem with you losing your temper, am I?" Urmond asked as he shuffled some papers on his desk. The question, while sounding jovially, still held a hint of seriousness that made Scetis stop.

"No, Father, my emotions will not overwhelm me on that front. I have not lost them at all in my life, that I can remember."

"Good, because this room is not conducive for fighting." Urmond chuckled.

"Orcades will not be in danger from me." Scetis stepped away from the window and came to stand by the desk. "What will you do with him?"

"That is a sticky point. He is the son of my sister, so technically he is a prince of the Realm. My sister also needs to be dealt with." He sighed deeply and sat down heavily. "What would you suggest I do?"

"I don't know. I have not had that sort of education." Scetis said going around the large desk to sit on the opposite side.

"I have a suggestion," Squirt said into the mind of Scetis.

"Father, there is one suggestion I can make. We have at our disposal the council of Audel. I think it is about time that we utilize the dragon. He's very intelligent and knowledgeable."

Urmond considered his words carefully. "Call him in. He is near I take it?" His eyebrows rose.

"I believe he is." Scetis stood and went to the door in the large window, which led out to the small balcony, and opened it wide. From around the corner of the terrace outside came the small red dragon. He walked upright, his hands clasped before him and he bowed low to Urmond.

"I believe you heard my question?" Urmond said, a little bemused by the presence of Squirt.

"My Lord King, the problem of your nephew, his mother, and uncle is a simple one. If you banish them, they will only cross the border and alert our enemies. The course is simple. Incarceration. You still have a prison here, although it has been vacant for some time. Did you also know you have an excellent natural hot spring under this castle?"

"No, I did not know that. You may use it at your will, Audel. Consider it your domain."

"Thank you, you are most generous." He bowed his head at the gift.

"Is this prison still in working order?"

"They are serviceable. I have taken the liberty to place a few new chains in three of the cells, but I have not had the chance to clean them out just yet. I am afraid they are still quite damp and full of rotten straw, not to mention the vermin."

"I don't think we need to bother with that. The new inhabitants may wish to do that themselves." Urmond chuckled at the thought. "The thought of my sister actually having to do some work is very amusing to me. Will you stay during our interview with them? I have invited all parties to attend."

"*It would be my pleasure, my Lord King.*" The corners of Squirt's elongated mouth turned up, giving him an almost comical appearance.

"Please, as we will be working closely together, call me Urmond."

"Of course, thank you. And Urmond, please call me Squirt. My real name grates on my ears."

"Happily will I do so, Squirt." He laughed and held out his hand to his new advisor. The pair shook hands just as a knock came from the door.

Scetis opened it and found Orcades on the other side, along with Domnall and a rather over made-up woman. Her hair showed the grey roots through her obvious newly dyed hair. Some of the extract from the leaves of the lawsonia tree had left marks on the tips of her ears. Her corset was ridged and held in a small bust, while making it look larger. The skirts of her underdress swirled around her calves, shimmering a bright and vivid orange. She stared back at Scetis with undisguised hate in her eyes. He could almost hear her thoughts and could almost see the word 'bastard' on her lips.

Stepping aside he allowed the trio to enter and not one gave him a word of acknowledgement. Just as he was about to close the door, another five people approached. The last to enter after her mother, father and two brothers, was Ide. She looked at him as she passed, and her eyes brightened. Uncharacteristically, Scetis winked at her, remembering their previous night's meeting. The blush that crept over her face let him know she was remembering too.

Closing the door now on the outside world, he turned to see the greetings happening in the room and remained by the door. As he looked about he noticed Squirt was no longer there and wondered where he had gone.

'I'm still here, I only chose not to be so visible for this meeting,' Squirt answered his unasked question.

"Right, shall we get down to why I have called you all here?" Urmond said breaking the low murmur in amongst the groups that were clearly divided.

Orcades went and possessively placed an arm around Ide, who looked at Scetis uncomfortably. Scetis gave her a small smile of encouragement, hoping it would help her, all the while suppressing his instinctive urge to punch Orcades' smug looking face.

"Thank you for calling us all together, Uncle. I formally request that our wedding ceremony be brought forward," Orcades announced with a fixed smile.

"What a wonderful idea!" his mother exclaimed, in a high-pitched voice. "Of course, you two won't want to wait the normal period of betrothal."

"Why wait indeed, Rionach," Urmond said from over by the fireplace. "Is there any particular reason you feel the need to make this a hasty one? After all, weddings such as this joining tend to need a lot of preparation. You are a Prince of the Realm and as such, it is expected to be a very lavish affair." Urmond stared at his nephew waiting for the answer.

"I don't think we need such a state wedding, Uncle. Just family will do. If you would send for a cleric now, we could be wed within the hour." Orcades said puffing out his chest in pride at his suggestion, while looking around the room to gain support.

"No. I would not hear of it. Imagine the shame you would bring to your mother. I know my sister has been planning and waiting for this most important day for a very long time."

Scetis caught the quick and nervous glance shared between the only three who did not know exactly what was truly going on. He walked over to the cabinet and started pouring out drinks for the gathering.

"I have, brother. I have indeed. But, if these two, who are so obviously in love with each other, wish to hasten their union, then who am I to stand in their way. Of course, the decision must be agreed upon by Ide's parents. I would have it no other way," she said automatically taking the goblet that was placed in front of her and taking a large gulp.

"I believe that the decision should be made by Ide," Galanan offered, turning to his daughter. "It has been a long time since we held any sway over her decisions. What are your feelings, Ide?"

Ide looked to her father and then took the goblet from Scetis. She turned her eyes to meet his and drew in a deep breath. "I can see no reason to not bring it forward," she told the room clearly.

"Excellent!" Orcades exclaiming triumphantly. "A toast then, to my wonderful and beautiful wife to be!" he proclaimed, lifting his own goblet to her, before drinking the whole of the goblet full of deep red wine.

A chorus of "Ide," went up around the room and Scetis was pleased to see there was no drink left in the heavy glasses of Domnall, Orcades, and Rionach. Very carefully he went and collected their goblets, depositing them into the fireplace. As the residue dripped into the flames it sizzled and an acrid smell permeated the room.

"What did you do?" Domnall demanded shrilly, realizing that he and his two co-conspirators had been given something.

"Just a simple draught to keep you all calm and pliable. Scetis assured me that it is not lethal, at least not in the dose that he gave you. You did give them the correct dose? I would hate that they died, after all, they are family," the King said.

"I did, Father. One drop each, anymore and they would be in a coma for at least the same number of days," he reassured Urmond casually.

"What is the meaning of this, Urmond?" Rionach demanded. She stood and then immediately sat back down again. Her hand going to her head.

Scetis imagined the symptoms she must already be feeling. Lightheaded, vision swimming, voices sounding muffled and distant. Nothing permanent, but enough so they could be dealt with.

"Sister, dearest. I know of your plans. I know of the troops that your cousin-in-law has let slip into the Realm. I know of your plans to place your son, an unworthy, pompous, over-indulged, egotistical, philanderer, on MY throne," he said with some heat. "Don't worry, Orcades, your seven children will be looked after. It is more than was afforded for my son, and far more than you would have done yourself, having denied they even exist."

A crash from across the room drew the attention of everyone. Galanan was standing over the now prone form of Domnall.

"You traitor!" Galanan said quietly. "You were our friend. How could you?"

Domnall could not answer as he was out cold on the deep red carpet. Blood oozed from his nose, which now had a definite slant to it.

"What are you going to do to us?" Rionach asked timidly, her speech slurring.

"Don't worry, sister. You will not be dying anytime soon. But I cannot have you confined to quarters where anyone can visit you. Open the door please, Scetis." Urmond nodded to his son.

"Yes, Father." Scetis was at the door within a couple of steps and soon two more people were joining them in Urmond's private rooms; Orlagh and Feth.

"I think we can handle this ourselves. There is no need to involve the Foot. Oh, by the way, Captain Aideen Magaoidh, you are now my new General of the Foot. You can promote whom you deem fit to fill your shoes." He smiled at Ide's mother.

"My thanks, My Lord King. Shall we remove these prisoners for you?" Aideen bowed and came to attention.

"Please do." He nodded in reply.

Orcades started to head unsteadily towards the open door. Ide moved quickly and pulled him back by his elaborate scabbard, spun him around and punched him with a loud smack. Orcades stood for a moment in stunned silence, his mouth hung open and a little drool escaped his lips. As he lifted a trembling hand to his already reddening face his eyes glazed over and he fell backwards, his head hitting the floor with a loud thunk that even muffled that of his armor.

"Seven children?" she asked Urmond.

"Yes, aging from six to newborn," he told her gently.

"Here's hoping they don't turn out like their father," she said shaking her hand.

"I intend to see they don't," Urmond promised her. "But they are of no concern to you. I believe that your true intended is waiting for your public acknowledgment," he said softly with a gentle smile.

Ide turned to find Scetis behind her. Her arms were around his neck immediately and his enfolded her close. Their lips met and Scetis felt whole.

Confrontation

"I would suggest, Urmond, that we take the offensive and push the invaders from our lands. The news that Domnall, Orcades, and Rionach have been taken into custody won't have reached them just yet. We need to utilize the surprise element," Squirt told the king as he paced the office. His wings were tucked tightly to his body, so they did not knock anything over, and his clawed hands clasped behind his back.

"This is unbelievable," Aideen marveled at understanding the lithe dragon.

"So you have said many times in the past half hour, my dear, but we need to move past the wonder," Galanan said to his wife with a small chuckle.

Aideen shook her head once more and then focused on what was being said. "Yes, I need to know who in the Foot is loyal to Domnall and this plot of theirs. Now that I know about it, we can investigate how far into the brigade it goes."

"I'm sure a lot of the support will wane now that Domnall has been taken out of the picture. Fair weather friends and all that. It's the ambitious that you need to look for. Those that have been promised too much to give it up." Urmond advised her.

"Be that as it may, we still need to strike while the breath is hot." Squirt responded.

"Your estimate on numbers is worrisome. I don't want to make a push without the Foot to back it up. We need the troops on the ground to harry the invaders out." Galanan said leaning forward in his seat.

"Air support will be no problem." Scetis said quietly. His hand still clasped Ide's and he had not let go since formally asking to marry her from Urmond and her parents. Aideen had at first been skeptical of this new intruder, but after a quiet word with Ide she gave her consent, especially when Ide told her that she would marry Scetis with or without it.

A loud and urgent rap at the door reverberated around the room. All heads turned to see who it was. Urmond opened it and a harassed looking Councilor Ocuinn came bustling in. He was out of breath and in his hand he clasped a scroll that was weather beaten.

"I am sorry for the intrusion, My Lord King, but this cannot wait!" he gasped and thrust the scroll into Urmond's hand. "I think you might find this of the utmost interest." He panted and then turned steely, rheumy eyes to Scetis.

Urmond quickly scanned the scroll then looked up at the expectant faces. "It seems that things have taken a turn. This is from the hand of the Regulator himself. It appears he has been briefed on our situation and has some strong objections to the validity of Scetis being named heir. His language about you is not very flattering I am afraid, son." He passed the paper onto Scetis.

"I didn't think it would be. Their first plan didn't work so now he is trying to flip it to his advantage." His eyes scanned down the very familiar scrawl that stretched across the page.

"They are threatening to invade, my King." Councilor Ocuinn said a little dramatically. "I beg you to call out General Gerarailt to close the border."

"Your advice is sound, Councilor," Urmond told him. "But I am afraid Domnall is otherwise engaged. Aideen will be filling in for him in his absence."

"Absence? Where has he gone?" His words came out as a demand and he checked his obvious confusion. "I'm sorry, but he not being here is greatly inopportune. Can he not be called back, Sire?"

Urmond stared at the High Councilor. *"Well, son,"* Urmond said in Scetis mind. *"What is your evaluation of our Councilor?"*

"Worried. I believe the body is starting to squirm without its head. He knows of the sudden disappearance of probably all three."

"I believe you are correct in your reading of him. It is such a pity." Urmond broke the link with a great sigh. "No, I will not be calling him back. Tell

me Ocuinn, what are your own personal thoughts on the succession matter?"

"My own opinion? Sire, it is not my place to say," he blustered a little.

"We have known each other too long. Come, tell me your thoughts, after all you are the High Councilor and supposedly my highest advisor." Urmond placed a hand on the councilor's shoulder and steered him to a seat opposite Galanan and Aideen.

The old man sat heavily into the cushioned seat. Before him appeared Scetis with a glass of wine and he took it immediately, drinking heavily from it to give himself time to prepare his thoughts.

"Well, my Lord King, I believe that the matter is purely domestic and none of our neighbors' business," Ocuinn said, taking another large gulp of the wine. "These demands are...are purely bluster, designed only to destabilize the throne." He looked up expectantly at Urmond.

"That was very well rehearsed Ocuinn. Scetis what did you put in his drink, was it the same as last time?" Urmond asked, never taking his eyes off Ocuinn.

"This time it was just the powder of a simple root, father. In the correct dose it will loosen the tongue of any man and they will feel the compulsion to tell the truth." He tucked a small vile away into his vest pocket.

"I must thank the Regulator for giving my son such a well-rounded and thorough education. I think he made a mistake there. Who else in my council is involved in this plot?"

"I...I... don't know what you mean, Sire." Ocuinn tried to stand but fell back onto his seat.

"Sorry, a slight side effect. It has always rendered the legs useless I am afraid." Scetis told him, taking the glass from the old man's hand, then checking on the pulse in his thin wrist. "Ask again, Father."

"Do I really need to ask, old friend?" Urmond demanded darkly.

"Only one other that I know of. The Treasurer," Ocuinn said giving up.

"I knew he was greedy." Urmond went to the door and opened it, looked to where he knew his personal page was stationed. "Fetch Councilor Laighin for me please Naiton."

"Yes, Sire." The eager young man turned and ran down the corridor.

"I will have everyone involved in this plot in the dungeons by the end of the day. Aideen and Galanan, I think you should go prepare for an offensive. Scetis, stay here, I have need of your pharmaceutical gifts. I believe there may be more involved than we first thought. You also Ide."

Teagan gripped tightly to the large horns on the back of Gremlin, as they flew close to the mountains. They were not heading towards where the Convocation was marshalling men, but further into the mountains. Great peaks loomed before them, most covered in year long, sparkling snow, while others were bare, craggy rock, poking their peaks above soft voluminous clouds. Valleys far below them zipped past, giving glimpses of wide arable land or steep sided with rushing water carving away at the stubborn rock.

They flew on in the cool morning air, her focus and eyes picking out small details, plants, and animals that lived in this remote and sometimes harsh environment. Her eyesight had changed since her rebirth from the bowels of the earth. It was sharper and more defined. The slightest movement drew her attention and tracked the small animals with ease. So strong was her focus that Teagan missed what was above her.

A loud cry of a dragon turned her head. A great Black was flying above and behind, his wingspan was large and the sound of the wings beating through the air was loud. But he was still not as large as Gremlin. He stared with his red and silver eyes at Teagan and bowed his head. But he did not leave their tail. Before turning back to the front, another soon joined the Black. A large Green of the same dimensions. This time a female. Her cry echoed that of the Black and reverberated from the sides of the large mountains.

Soon they were joined by more. A Red, Gold, a magnificent shimmering White, blues of multiple hues along with pale green and many more, until the sky above, below, and around them seemed to shimmer in a dazzling rainbow. They all followed Gremlin and Teagan, and soon, dropping down with them, circling to lose height, their great wings stretched and hummed with the wind that filled them.

At the bottom of the valley was a large, grassed area. At one end of the enclosed valley sat a large steaming pool. The slight smell of sulfur reached Teagan, but it did not offend her. Instead, it was a welcome smell. The smell of home for her and she wondered at that.

Gremlin landed softly on the long grass. Teagan slipped from his back easily and turned. The multitude of dragons landed behind them, all coming to greet her individually, bowing low then moving to one side to let the next in. Some of the more temperate climate and water dragons moving past her to take advantage of the hot spring. Their manners were very sedated, some of their natural enmity put aside for this meeting.

"Talk to them Teagan. We need their support. We could command them to join us, calling on old ties, but I would rather they joined us and called their own clans," Gremlin whispered to her.

Teagan took in a deep breath; she knew she was being tested. This was a way to show the other dragons she could lead. Teagan let the breath out and looked at the gathered dragons. Some sitting, some standing proudly. She caught the eye of a large pale green female who nodded kindly to her. The beginnings of her nerves left her, then she spoke to the gathered dragons, her kind.

"I thank you for your answering the summons Vojin sent to you. You know already what the reason is for the call. It is time for all dragons to come together, to fight for our home," she started. "The humans are preparing to invade, they have already crossed the borders from our ancient agreement, violating the treaties that were agreed upon. They are no longer content in their lands and have become greedy in their desires."

"We cannot allow this!" a rumble from the black male called out.

"No, we cannot, and we will not." Teagan responded with nods of approval from some of the dragons.

"Then is the ancient decree against eating humans to be dropped?" the Red dragon asked. Teagan could hear the hunger in his voice, and she paused for a moment before answering him.

"For the soldiers in battle, and only our enemies." Gremlin said quietly in her mind.

"That is yet to be decided." Teagan said, the thought of these dragons feasting on human flesh made her own crawl. She heard the snort of disapproval from Gremlin behind her.

"You wish us to follow you into battle? A battle that has not been fought for multiple generations and one that we may never recover from?" a Blue asked, from the hot pool.

"Yes."

"These matters are for men. We have for many generations been hunted by those men, forced from our homes. Our very bones and offspring used in their so-called medicine. Why should we die defending those that have not kept their side of the treaty?" She flicked her tail angrily, sending up sparkling droplets into the air and annoying the Purple beside her.

"Because of the treaty. Vojin is back. I am here. The old treaties will be adhered to, I will make sure of it. It is the time of the dragon again. You created my kind to ensure that peace would reign and that you would be left alone. Let me once more do that for you."

"My clan will follow you!" the Black declared and then scanned the others with steely eyes.

"We will follow." the Red stated getting to his feet.

Soon all were standing including the Blue who had raised an objection. They collectively let out a great roar that reverberated through her whole being. She could feel their calls as they each put out to their clans and the answered replies. The call to wing was universally acknowledged and accepted, and she felt satisfied.

Soon the dragons were leaving the meeting, taking to wing one by one and flying off to their different regions. They had agreed and would be back when called.

Only one remained. The large Red male stepped up and bowed to her. He was a fierce looking creature, strong chest muscles showed he was not a dragon to be trifled with. To Teagan he looked like the drawings of Oriental dragons she had studied when she was back on Earth.

"Child of Dragons. I have a request of you," he growled low.

"If I can grant it, I will," she responded.

"A youngling of ours is missing. Though in truth he would be a youngling no more."

"You speak of Audel?" Gremlin asked coming to stand by Teagan.

"I do."

"He is of no concern of yours anymore." Gremlin told him flatly.

"But he is a deformed and that needs to be rectified," the Red growled angrily.

"He is as I made him!" Gremlin roared at him, looming large. "His destiny is to be with the crown as an advisor and intermediary between the throne and dragons."

"That is the role of the Child of Dragons," the Red retorted.

"In the coming years, the Realm we will need both. When one is absent the other will be there. Right now, Audel is with the current King advising him. He was placed there purposefully. I made his form so that he could be within the chambers of Citadel." Gremlin took a large breath. "He is your son?"

"My offspring is of no matter to me!"

"Then why do you persist in trying to destroy him? The development of his physical form had nothing to do with you. His very spirit is not even from your line, but mine," Gremlin said with a roar, bearing his large fangs at the Red.

"Then warn him never to set foot back in our lands," the Red began to turn away from them both.

"You should be proud of him." Teagan interceded, stepping between the two dragons. "He is intelligent, quick, and already relied upon."

"He is an abomination, just like all halflings, be they interbred or hybrids," Red snorted disdainfully. "To think The Child has come back as one such as you. I will support this battle, my clan will fight beside the other clans, but mark my words Hybrid, humans in whatever form will be fair game." He spread his wings and jumped into the air, flying off, leaving Teagan to stare at his retreating form.

"Why are there always those like him?" Teagan asked in wonder.

"They are small minded and have been separated too long. That clan did not always feel the way he does. It was a Red who first broached the subject of creating a hybrid. He has forgotten his history," Gremlin growled angrily. "Come, we must get back. I have a lot to think on."

Beginning

Scetis stood still, his arms stretched out in the air at his sides as a man dressed in the deepest of red laid a measuring tape around his chest, before making notes in a book which hung from his neck. Not a word did this man speak to Scetis as he took all the measurements he needed. Scetis felt like a scarecrow, and his arms started to ache by the time the man was finished.

"We have nothing fancy, my Lord King," the man addressed Urmond. "But it will protect all his vital bits. I can have a more formal set of armor for him in about six weeks."

"The standard will be fine for now, Master Smith," Urmond told him. "I'll send him to the armory later today to be fitted." He nodded his assent for the smith to leave and waited until he had. "Have you ever lifted a sword?" Urmond asked Scetis

"I have lifted one, but never swung one," Scetis said seriously. "I have been trained in knives though."

"Knives are of no use from the back of a dragon." Urmond said, pouring a cup of taraxacum tea into a porcelain cup. The steam curled up into the room and dissipated, leaving an aroma like a meadow in its wake.

"And only once have I been on the back of one of those." Scetis reminded him.

"That needs to be addressed then, and soon." Urmond blew on his tea, sending the steam flying away from him.

"Have you replied to The Convocation?" Scetis asked curiously as he did the buttons up on his leather vest.

"Not yet, and nor will I. They can object all they wish; we both know that it is only to delay us getting ready. We know their plans and how they have used you. What can you tell me of the Regulator?" Urmond asked sitting at his desk. Scetis sat opposite him.

"A little while ago, I would have said kind and caring. He taught me a lot and was the first to treat me as a human, not a slave. I can see that was part of the plan to break me. It was he who bought me from my mother. I remember it well now. He sought her out, convinced her that he would give me a life that I deserved. Then left me with the slave master." He fell silent staring at his hands before him. He remembered every torment he was subjected to.

"Then you were elevated?" Urmond asked quietly.

"Yes. I was given a level of education that is rare in The Convocation. I am adept in three of the branches."

"There are more?"

"Yes. I thought the last one was nothing more than a myth, but it is very real. I had always heard whispers of a fourth branch, but like other apprentices, I was promised that it was non-existent. An Assassin Guild."

"What use does The Convocation have for such a guild? They are supposed to be for the preservation of life?" Urmond placed his now empty cup down on the desk.

"Medicinal compounds in the correct doses heal. But there are recipes designed to kill. There are some that will make it look accidental and others cannot be detected at all." Scetis shifted in his seat. "My last apprentice was forced upon me. It turned out he was part of this guild. He played his part so well that I was fully convinced. Father," he began quietly. "From now on, any drink you consume, must only be made by my or your own hand." He looked at the cup directly.

"They would not dare!" Urmond said heatedly.

"I am afraid they would. This particular assassin killed his own grandmother."

Urmond stared at the cup before him. "It is a very murky world you grew up in. I am sorry," he said pushing the cup from him. "It's time to close the borders."

"Lady Teagan must be brought into the discussion of planning. You and I may be Dragon-Born, but they will only follow her."

"We shall meet this evening. But first you and I shall go to the Eyrie so you can learn to fly."

As the two men neared the top of the long climb, Squirt stepped out to greet them. Though he was small for a full-grown dragon, he still towered over the men. He bowed low to them both. *"Good morning my Lords,"* he said respectfully.

"Squirt, good morning to you. What brings you here to the Eyrie?" Urmond asked.

"My Lord Scetis is to begin learning how to ride a dragon. As there are none available to bond with him, I humbly offer my services to you," Squirt said with all seriousness.

"I don't mean to sound harsh, Squirt, but are you not just a little on the diminutive side to carry a full-grown man?" Urmond looked a little uncomfortable bringing up this size matter.

"You do not sound harsh, my Lord King. To a normal dragon, carrying someone is as easy as carrying an empty pack on your back. For me it may be a little more difficult, but no less easy. I am strong and my wings have not failed me yet."

"I would be honored to be bonded with you, Squirt, if you so wish. You have been nothing but kind and respectful of me since I have come to know you." Scetis told him, bowing graciously, knowing how much of an honor it was for Squirt to offer.

"Then you must get fitted for a saddle. I don't think the normal ones will fit your frame, so I think we will have the saddler make one specifically for you," Urmond mused.

"I don't think we have time for that, my Lord King," Squirt said respectfully. "From my observations this morning, it appears that the troops of our enemies are readying themselves for something soon. You will just have to learn to hang on, Scetis," Squirt told them with a mischievous glint in his eyes.

"Then we should get started," Scetis replied very seriously, and Squirt laughed out loud as he caught the similar look from Scetis.

"I will go get Screamer then, we shall meet you in the wyvern gate," Urmond said as he started to head away shaking his head.

While they waited for Urmond, Squirt gently explained how he wanted Scetis to sit on his back, where to put his feet and what to hang onto. Their quiet and oftentimes silent conversation lasted until Urmond joined them with Screamer at his side. The two dragons acknowledged each other, but Scetis could discern no particular regard between them. He got the distinct impression that Urmond's mount was not impressed by the smallish dragon and there was some prejudice about his size. On Squirt's part Scetis could feel him ignoring the disdain.

Scetis and Squirt followed Urmond and Screamer to the learning platform. Scetis walked to the edge of the drop off and looked down far below him at the citadel and attached palace that was now his home. The town that was nestled beside the large complex was busy with carts and foot traffic. It was a lot busier than it had been when he first visited but knew that was to do with the coming battle than anything else.

"Are you ready?" Squirt asked him with a note of excitement.

"Have you had any person on your back before, Squirt? Besides me of course" Scetis asked him.

"Nope! But Vojin assures me that I am capable and that it will be a good and necessary bond." Squirt said quietly.

"Well then, the faster we learn how to do this, the better." Scetis said, taking in a deep and nervous breath.

They moved to the center where Urmond and Screamer were waiting for them, Urmond had already climbed on the back of the large Red and Gold dragon, and her head was held high with the obvious pride of carrying the King.

Scetis turned to Squirt.

"Just as I instructed." Squirt muttered.

Going around to his right side, Squirt knelt a little and Scetis climbed up. It was uncomfortable to start with, but soon he found where to place his feet and hands. It felt natural and as if he had been doing it all his life.

"Ready?" Squirt asked, taking in a deep breath.

"I am," Scetis responded with no little trepidation.

Squirt unfolded his wings, stretching them out to their full length. Slowly he began to raise them as far back as they could go, until bringing them down hard. At first there was no movement no matter how hard and fast Squirt would flap. Scetis looked over to Urmond and saw that his father was about to say something. Closing his eyes he sent out an encouraging thought to the dragon under him.

"Lift," he said quietly, encouraging Squirt.

"As you wish," Squirt said back with much amusement.

The ground under them dropped away as Squirt pulled up into the air. The top of the mountain was soon lost to them as they rose through the misty clouds. The air was thinner at this altitude, but it did not seem to influence Squirt. Still higher he climbed, before angling his wings and diving back through the cloud. As they broached the bottom, the pair found Urmond and Screamer waiting, hovering near the practice ledge.

"What do you think?" Urmond called to them.

"Amazing!" Scetis answered back a little breathlessly. Urmond laughed at his reaction.

"Squirt lead the way. I want to see what we are up against." Urmond commanded.

Urmond's office was warm, not only by the crackling fire in the large fireplace, but by the afternoon sun which streamed through the windows. Teagan and Muniath arrived together. Only Scetis saw their hands drop each other's as they entered the room. Making him think of his own love, Ide. His eyes automatically moved to her where she was standing by the window. The streaming light illuminated her dark hair, showing soft highlights of ginger. As if she knew he was watching, Ide turned, and their eyes locked together. He watched as she slowly blushed and he wondered at how this amazing and beautiful woman could have feelings for him. A man who had not felt real love from anyone before.

Urmond began the meeting. Much of what he discussed with the others in the room he had already gone through with Scetis. The plan of attack. His mind wandered as Urmond outlined and discussed his plan with his generals and captains. Scetis wondered at what would happen if they did defeat their enemy and the consequences if they didn't. One thing was for certain, that if they failed then he would die. The secret order of The Convocation would make sure of that.

"No, I will not allow that!" Galanan's heated words woke Scetis from his reverie.

"It will be so," Urmond replied with some determination.

"Father, we cannot risk your life like that. You must be protected at all costs." Orlagh said emphatically.

"I must be seen to be leading our cause. I will not be sitting back here waiting for reports. I was a Rider once before, you know."

"I know, Father. But—"

"I have spoken." Urmond said, cutting his daughter off.

"Don't worry, Orlagh. He will not be leading the charge. That will be my position." Teagan said to pacify her cousin. "The dragons will not follow you, my Lord King. I have already had the assurances of the different sects that they will come to fight for the Dragon Realm, but they will only come when I call. We will only defeat our enemies with the dragons' help. I have seen where we must attack, But I urge that it must be soon."

"The Riders will be ready," Venicones declared, he was a slightly more jovial man than his brother, even though they looked alike. "What about the Foot?"

"Have no worries about us son," his mother, Aideen, told him.

"So we are agreed?" Urmond asked the gathered group.

"We are," the two generals responded together.

"Then let us get to it. Use the cover of darkness to get the troops out Aideen," Urmond instructed.

The night was deep, darker than usual as both moons that usually hung in the sky both hid their faces behind thick clouds. The town below the citadel was well into its slumber, but within the walls of the keep itself, there was movement. Troops filed quietly out of their barracks, their armor and weapons muffled anyway they could, to avoid sound carrying out. They lined up neatly, their orders were already given, and each woman and man knew exactly what was happening and where they were headed.

With a curt nod from General Aideen Magaoidh, the gate was swung open. The hinges had been oiled earlier in the day, to ensure there would be no sound made. The large wooden gates stood wide as the column of Foot soldiers filed through, but they would not be going through the slumbering town. This gate was little used and led to a road past and below the town, running beside the large lake. Runners had already reported that there was no one along it and it was clear to leave. The passing of the troops went unnoticed by the general population.

High up in the citadel it was watched with some nervousness. Urmond stood on the small balcony and watched as his troops headed to battle on his behalf. He had purposefully gone down that afternoon to walk amongst them and give encouragement. He did not know if it helped at all, but it had given him some relief to put faces to those who were willing to put their lives on the line for him, his descendants, and the Realm they called home.

Urmond stayed on that balcony, his hands firmly gripping the balustrade, until the last Footman had left the garrison yard. He watched as the gates came together. As soon as the beam that barred it closed was in place, a guard waved a torch to signal the King that all was secure. He sighed deeply and pushed himself upright. Tugging down his jacket into place, he took in a gulp of the fresh mountain night air.

"All speed to you. May you come home safe and well," Urmond said after the troops, hoping that his wishes would come true but knowing that some of the brave souls would not return.

With one last look he turned and stopped in his tracks. Standing in the open doorway was a figure in black. His stance was tense, ready to move in a second to react to Urmond.

"So The Convocation wishes to try and settle this undiplomatically," Urmond growled quietly.

"You know your fate. I have never missed my mark," the man said in a whisper.

"I would like to look upon the face of my murderer. Remove your mask," he ordered.

"I am not your subject, but I do not mind granting a dying man's wish." The man reached up and pulled off the cloth hood that cast such a deep shadow over his face. A blond head of hair was revealed and the face that smiled at Urmond looked boyish, but the eyes had the haunted look of a man who had killed many times and enjoyed it.

"And your name?" Urmond inquired as if this young man had come before him with a petition.

"Loxa, at your service, King Urmond." He gave a gracious bow, grinning now, enjoying the moment of playing nice with his prey.

"Well, Master Loxa, I think you should get on with what you came here to do." Urmond pulled himself up to his full height.

"You're not going to scream for your guards?" Loxa asked retrieving a long and thin blade from his belt, which glinted in the light that came from the room behind him.

"It would not make a difference. I will be dead before they arrive, your training will see to that. But I would have thought you would try to poison me first."

"Scetis should have you dosed on every known antidote and probably a few that are unknown too."

"You are the boy he thought was his apprentice?"

"I am and now I am the man who shall bring about the end of your life." Loxa stepped forward.

Urmond drew the small ceremonial sword that was strapped to his side, and instantly regretted refusing a more fitting blade for battle. He held it loosely in his hand, feeling the weight of it balanced perfectly. The edge was blunt, but it would still inflict some damage when used in the correct way.

Loxa eyed the sword that was directed at him, and Urmond already assessed the assassin had disregarded it as any sort of threat. The young man flashed a grin at the King as he advanced, ready to strike.

Urmond stepped forward quickly, hoping to put Loxa off guard with the moment. Instead, he moved on cat like feet, deftly spinning out of the way of the King's advance and swinging blade. He turned quickly and the point of his highly honed stiletto dagger pushed through the rich fabric of Urmond's coat. Through the white, crisply pressed shirt beneath and into the skin of his side. Loxa pushed it quickly to the hilt, angling it up to pierce as many vital organs as possible. Urmond reflexively gasped and his hand sought out Lox's shoulder, the small sword in his other dropping to the marble below with a clang, but he did not cry out. The King only groaned at the pain as it seared through him.

"Your kind are an abomination," Loxa hissed. "You are a beast not a man. We shall wipe you all from the face of this world. Then use the mirrors to kill all your kind in every other world."

Urmond stiffened as the blade finally struck his lung. His eyes never left those of his attacker. "The dragons will survive. We always have and always will." He coughed slightly and blood oozed from his mouth.

Loxa pulled the knife from his latest victim and wiped the blade on the fine cloth of the king's jacket. Urmond fell to his knees clasping at the wound, unable to stem the flow of blood that oozed between his faltering fingers.

"You die alone, Urmond, King of abominations." Loxa turned and left through the small room.

Urmond watched him go, then pulled himself up and staggered into the room. Reaching out he pulled down on the bellpull, as he collapsed to the floor. More blood poured from his mouth and through his fingers, pooling on the carpet that cushioned him. He watched as the room dimmed, his vision going black, and coughed as the blood competed with the oxygen in his lungs. The King of the Dragon Realm drew his last breath, before it escaped his lips. His heart faltered with the lack of blood and the new hole that had been ripped through is body. Then it was quiet.

Running steps and shouts woke Teagan. Her new rooms were situated closer to the King's than the ones she had grown up with. She pushed off the covers and made her way to the door which led to the corridor. Placing a hand on the doorknob, she twisted it, tugged at the door, and heard someone running. A page boy, his face fearful and pale, was panting hard as he ran. Teagan stopped him before he could pass her.

"What's happened?" she demanded.

"Assassin," the boy panted, red color started to rise in his cheeks.

"What?"

"The king has been murdered. There's an assassin in the castle," he struggled to say between breaths.

"My god!" she exclaimed letting his arm go. The frightened boy took off at a run, hurrying away to perform whatever duty he had been assigned.

Teagan rushed back into her rooms and dressed. She was just leaving it again when Muniath reached her. Immediately he pulled her into an embrace.

"Do we know any more?" she asked into his chest.

"Nothing more. A search is being conducted, but I doubt we will find the culprit." Muniath let her go and then guided her along the corridor, his hand placed protectively on her back.

"Who found him?" Teagan asked, still struggling with the horrific news.

"Scetis. It was he who recognized the knife. The killer had left it on a table near Urmond's body," he told her quietly. She looked around them at the sudden appearance of the remaining Foot guards, a group largely made up of old veterans and fresh recruits. They positioned themselves along the walls at each doorway.

"Captain Magaoidh," one of the elderly sergeants saluted Muniath.

"Sergeant. Have you seen anything?"

"Nothing, sir." he reported.

"Carry on," Muniath saluted the man and then kept moving.

Muniath guided Teagan through the palace to the King's private office. Standing outside were two guards who were baring the entrance to the small room. Gathered just a short way from the office was Galanan, Venicones, Scetis, and Orlagh, who had his arm around his younger half-sister in comfort. Teagan immediately detected the hardened eyes and anger that was building inside him. While Orlagh was in a flood of tears, he stood dry eyed and almost trembling with wanting to do.

Noise behind Teagan made her turn. A troop of Foot Guard was following close behind Aideen. Teagan watched Muniath's mother as she entered and nodded to her husband. They made for a formidable couple. Technically with the King dead, they were in charge of the Realm. She wondered briefly if they would take advantage of that fact, but that was soon dismissed with Galanan's first words.

"Thankfully, My Lord, the councilors have already acknowledged your right to rule. We just need to have word from the new High Chancellor that the ruling has been enacted," he said to Scetis.

"I would prefer to act than wait. We should be attacking," Scetis said with some heat.

"Not yet, my lord. We need to get the Foot into place as we planned," Aideen said softly. Her tone was patient and motherly. This woman of action was more than a warrior and Teagan could see she was trying to placate any desperate and hasty reaction Scetis might have.

"How long will this take?" Scetis demanded.

"Not long hopefully, a page has been sent to her rooms." Galanan replied.

"Suspicion will be directed towards me. Some may claim that I killed him to become king." Scetis said, worry creased his eyes.

"No, they can't, they wouldn't dare. I won't let them," Orlagh told him fiercely.

The sound of running feet had the group turning. Coming towards them was the same page Teagan had received the news from earlier. In his hand he clutched a roll of parchment, the green ribbons flying as he raced towards them. The boy came to a skidding hold before Scetis and held them out to him.

"My Lord King," he puffed, and he bowed low.

Scetis passed his half-sister to Aideen and took the scroll from the page carefully. He held it in his hand loosely staring at the seals that lay there. The one that held the scroll closed was newly made and still soft to the touch, the other above it was that of his father.

"I will not take up the crown until this conflict is resolved," Scetis said quietly, and looked up to Galanan and Aideen before him. "I'm going to need help with the planning."

"We are in your service," they both said bowing their heads to their new King.

"Teagan, I need you and Vojin up in the air. I need the reports of where the Foot are," he instructed.

"Yes, my Lord King," she replied. "I can relay the locations back through Squirt."

"Very good, and this goes for everyone. No more formal names," he said as he walked purposefully down the hall, away from his father's private office and the body that was still laying there.

Teagan headed to the Dragon Flyway Tower. The sky was starting to lighten as she reached the top. Gremlin was already there and waiting patiently as she mounted his back.

"Another hour and the Foot will be in place." He lifted off the platform and rose high into the sky. "Send the call to our land, Child."

The air was chilly up at this height as Gremlin kept them in place, she gripped him with her knees and raised her arms out.

"The Realm has been threatened. I call upon all who are able to come to our lands' aid and protect the borders. I ask in the ancient name of the Child of Dragons. I ask as one of you." She flung the words far and felt them hear and listen.

The collective roar of acceptance rang through the lands. It echoed in the deep valleys and shook the mountain tops. Teagan felt the thrill and pride of the answer.

"They're coming. Let's go!" she said eagerly, and Gremlin gave a roar as he banked away to head to where the enemy had set up camp.

The pair came to land on an outcrop of rock that loomed large above the enemy camp. The movement down below was erratic, and Teagan felt some satisfaction at the fact that the dragon roar had unsettled these men. She reported back to Squirt who also took some joy.

The morning sun glinted behind the pair as they observed from their perch. The noise of shouted commands and general melee of activity drifted up to them on the fresh breeze. Also with that breeze, which should have been that of sweet mountain air, came the stench of animal and human waste, and of general unwashed bodies.

"Feel like having some fun?" Teagan asked.

"You read my mind." Gremlin chuckled already spreading his long green wings.

Gremlin leapt from the rock, loosening several large boulders to crash down the side of the mountain. Angling up at first high into the air, he then plunged down. His body was as straight as an arrow with Teagan clinging on. Together they raced, picking up enormous speed before levelling out and gliding low over the ground, the wind whipped her loose hair behind her and whistled in her ears. Letting out a great roar, they swept over the camp scattering terrified men and animals alike. Tents were trampled and carts turned up as Tegan and Gremlin made their flight over the enemy. A few braver souls hastily threw spears in their direction, only to bounce off Gremlin's tough hide. One managed to make it past his outstretched wings and came close to Teagan. With a reflex she did not know she had, she managed to flick it away with her forearm.

At the end of the valley, Gremlin pulled up, clawing at the air with his wings beating hard. Just as he reached the peak he banked and turned back. Once more descending fast but levelling out higher than before. He opened his mouth, gave one large roar before a jet of burning hot liquid was released. At first Teagan was horrified at the act but leaning past Gremlin's neck she saw that the liquid burned away quickly and that they were high enough that it did not truly affect anyone. A few remaining tents caught light, but most of the men flung themselves at the ground in order to avoid being burnt. A few more beats of his wings and they were away, soaring up and out of the valley through a ravine.

"Hopefully, that should cause a few desertions," Teagan called to Gremlin.

"That was the intention," he laughed heartily.

"You are enjoying yourself way too much."

"I am," he declared. "Shall we go find our men?"

"Yes," Teagan cried out to the wind. A large smile was plastered over her face and she gave another cry, one of great delight.

Threading through the narrow gullies and valleys they soon found the column, bearing the colors of the Foot. Some were already peeling off under the direction of Ide, who was at the head consulting a map with Scetis. Gremlin landed gently and Teagan slipped from his back.

She watched this couple and saw how much Scetis wanted to touch Ide but held himself out of reach.

"What did you find?" Ide asked her as she came closer.

"A camp in chaos. They know the dragons are coming. We had a little fun creating havoc amongst their ranks," Teagan said as she looked at the map. "They are here." She indicated to a spot that did not seem that far.

"That is only a small part. They are also here and here," Scetis said, indicating some red shaded areas.

"Let the dragons handle some of the smaller pockets. I am sure they can get them to scatter. But these larger ones, we can focus our attention on these with a combination of Foot and Riders," Teagan suggested.

"Sounds like a reasonable plan," Ide said. "I'll send word to General Magaoidh."

"No need, the message will be relayed by mind." Scetis grinned shyly at her.

Teagan could see the link they had and averted her mind and eyes from it. Quietly clearing her throat to gain their attention back to the task at hand. She was just about to speak when a horse came thundering up, skidding to stop, and breathing hard. The rider leapt lightly from the saddle.

"Captain! Ambush!" he declared loudly between panting breaths.

"Where?" Ide demanded.

"Here!" the man pushed a gloved finger into the paper at a narrow gorge.

"We'll go." Teagan said before anyone could speak. She ran to Gremlin and climbed up. He was lifting off the ground before she was truly settled and soaring away. They were soon joined by the red flash of Squirt beside them, Scetis on his back, leaning low to create more of a slip stream. The look of determination on his face in stark contrast with that of Squirt.

You make sure you stay back, Teagan called to them both. She received no response to her command from either, so she urged Gremlin on. She felt the power of his muscles as he edged ahead and were soon over-taking. They rounded the bend to find a battlefield in full melee.

The cries from the men as they clashed and attacked rose to meet them. Gremlin filled his lungs and roared loudly, swooping low over the two armies. Just this simple act was enough to give the Foot the advantage. As their enemy flinched and reacted to the sudden appearance of the two dragons, the Foot pressed in to drive them back. The captains to the rear of the mercenary soldiers were nearly swamped, but their stoic stand brought their forces back to their senses. They reluctantly turned and once more entered the fray, but the damage had been done.

The Foot pressed their advantage further and soon the ground ran red with the blood of both forces. The mutilated bodies of the slain littered the ground and soldiers stumbled over the dead and dying alike. Teagan and Gremlin turned to make another pass, already she could feel the build-up of the fire gathering in his throat. As they straightened it was not this sensation that kept her attention, but the sight of Squirt and Scetis already engaging the captains. Squirt was almost vertical, his wings beating furiously and his talons slashing at their enemy.

With a great roar that sounded as if it should have come from a much larger dragon, Squirt released a great jet of white-hot flame. The Captain he was fighting was engulfed along with his horse in the flesh melting heat. The man didn't have even a chance to cry out as both he and his mount crumpled to the scorched and smoking earth. Black acrid smoke rose off the burning pile of fused together human and horse.

Teagan turned, averting her eyes from the horrific scene. Gremlin was already heading back over the battle. His wings beat hard and she could feel him searching. With another cry he plunged, and his front clawed feet plucked two squirming men from the ground before rising high. Their screams carried to Teagan as she directed Gremlin to the fast-flowing river beside the battle. From a considerable height he opened his claws and the two dropped. They landed in a combined splash that sent a spray of water out and when they surfaced neither were moving, except down river on the current, bobbing along over the hidden rocks.

Gremlin and Teagan worked together to send more and more of the enemy down the river. After the most recent pairing they turned back to find a knot of soldiers surrounded by the Foot. Plumes of dark smoke showed Squirt and Scetis' work and the pair on the ground with the last of the captains pinned under Squirt's hind leg.

Gremlin landed to the sound of the remaining mercenaries dropping their weapons with a clash. In ones and twos, they dropped to their knees, hands raised in the air. Teagan dismounted quickly and met the captain of the Foot who was running towards her.

"My Lady," he called out breathless and bloodied from the battle. "Thank god you arrived when you did."

"That is why we work together, Captain," she replied, and they headed towards Scetis.

"My Lord King," the captain fell to one knee in front of Scetis.

"Rise, Captain, that is not necessary, and I am not King yet." Scetis replied looking a little embarrassed.

"But still our King. What are your orders, Sire?"

"What is your name?"

"Captain Wirguist, Sir."

"Restrain these prisoners and get them away from here. Take this one too, he may have useful information." Scetis instructed, indicating the unconscious man under Squirt's foot.

"Yes, sir," Captain Wirguist readily said and motioned for two men to retrieve the mercenary.

"Once that is done, send some scouts out," Scetis ordered.

"My Lord, would it not be better for me to fly out?" Squirt suggested.

"No, I need you here with me."

"Then we'll do it." Teagan offered.

"Again, you are needed. The horde is coming, and I need you to lead them."

Scetis may not have considered himself King yet, but he had stepped up to the role.

Their orders given, Scetis dismissed Teagan and she was mounting Gremlin once more. Muniath sent out a thought to her.

"Where are you?" he called.

"Heading back to the main column to await the horde," She replied. "I'll see you there."

"He worries about you," Gremlin chuckled to her as his wings pulled them into the air.

"He has no need to," she replied grimly.

Gremlin soared high in the air as they flew back to the Dragon Realm staging area. Circling above the valley Teagan was impressed with the troops formality and discipline. While one group set up tents, another were already forming the defensive ditches around the compound. At one end of the cleared area was a section set out for the Dragon Riders. They landed lightly and as one the dragons acknowledged their presence. Those Riders who had a keenness to the shared awareness looked up at the silent call. Those that had been properly opened up to it also gave their acknowledgment with a bow.

Muniath was not hard to spot amongst the crowd of dragons. His height set him apart. As she approached, she watched as he talked to his apprentice. Teagan could see that Muniath had been an important influence on Wick, he had the same mannerisms as his mentor. She adjusted her thoughts as they were joined by Venicones. Upon a closer look, she noticed that Wick's mannerisms more closely matched Venicones' than Mun's, a detail easily missed unless observing the trio together. As she mused these thoughts, Muniath looked up and caught her eye. She found herself smiling and enjoying the gaze he was giving. Her feet were moving long before she realized, and she was soon standing near the three tall men.

"How did the skirmish go?" Muniath asked, breaking the conversation.

"We prevailed," she replied.

"How far away is the horde?" Muniath asked her.

"Not far." She reached out and could feel the mass migration of the dragons that had responded to her call. "They should be here in about half an hour."

"Where's our King," Venicones asked her, looking about them.

"He's still with the band of Foot that was ambushed. He's overseeing the scouting mission."

"You left him on the front line?" he asked incredulously.

"I didn't have much choice," Teagan retorted. "He gave me an order."

"Order or not, he is our King and needs to be protected at all costs," Venicones left them and was quickly mounted on the back of Scorcher. Just as fast, they were in the air and speeding away.

"Where is he going?" A call behind them made them both turn. Ide was striding towards them, her cloak billowing out behind her.

Teagan had not much to do with Ide before this, but she thought that she was a stunning woman. Very much like her two brothers. She also proved herself to be an amazing tactician and leader. She had the respect of the Foot soldiers under her and they were quick to obey and not argue. Teagan wondered why she had followed her mother into the foot and not into the Riders. She had the dragon blood that was well and truly evident in her eyes.

"After our new King," Muniath told her.

"Scetis?"

"He stayed at the front."

"That idiot!" Ide exploded, but Teagan felt it was more a personal concern than just that of protecting the monarch.

"Squirt is there, they battled well together," Teagan said, trying to mollify Ide.

"They engaged the enemy? Directly?" Ide rounded on her.

"The pair took out their captains, capturing one. He is overseeing the transportation of the prisoners and sending out the scouting party." Teagan reported. "Squirt will make sure no harm will come to him."

Ide looked a little at a loss to say anything.

"Would you like me to take you to him?" Muniath asked gently and so no one near would hear.

"For the last time, I will not get on the back of a dragon. You know I hate heights," she told him just as quietly. "And I can't leave until Mother gets here." Ide then turned to Teagan. "I'm sorry I snapped, Lady Teagan. When this is all over, I would really like to get to know you more."

"I would like that also," Teagan responded.

"But for now I need to make sure we have space for the dragons. Or would they prefer to keep to mountains and open spaces?"

"They are not used to humans, so it might be better that they are not amongst the compound. Speaking of which, I would like to go meet them. If I have permission to leave?"

"Of course, whatever you think is necessary. And I think technically I don't have any sort of rank over you. I'll leave you to prepare," Ide smiled at Teagan and then winked at her brother.

Muniath gave Wick a quick order and the boy went off running. He waited a moment before reaching for Teagan's hand and held it tightly, pulling her closer.

"Not here or now," Teagan protested.

A large leather wing descended over the pair, shielding them from view.

"How about now?" he asked, his eyes twinkling as he leaned down, and their lips met.

Duel

Thundering hoofbeats heralded the approach of a messenger. Scetis had the feeling that the message would be a carefully worded request from Ide for him to retreat back to the encampment. He turned slowly to greet the soldier and his eyes widened as he saw who dismounted the heavily breathing and lathered horse.

"What are you doing here?" he asked once he had collected his thoughts, a small smile played on his lips.

"You!" Ide replied, her voice carefully controlled. Her eyes were brightly flashing with the anger she was barely controlling, and her cheeks were flushed from the hurried ride.

Scetis had a hard time controlling his smile as he thought Ide could look no more beautiful than she was right then. He suddenly found himself eagerly looking forward to their future together.

"Me?" Scetis replied, unable to help himself.

"What the hell do you think you are doing? The King is not supposed to be leading the charge but conducting it!"

"I didn't lead it, Teagan and Gremlin did. All I did was help a little." He looked around him at the still smoking charred remains of the captains and their mounts. The smile which had just been delighting in the sight of Ide, now slipped away. A deep sadness at the waste of life filled him once more. Even more so now knowing he was the cause of it. He was a healer first.

Ide followed his gaze and saw the change in him. Her hand went to his arm and gave it a squeeze of comfort. "It's a horrible necessity," she said gently. Her words quiet and only meant for him.

"No death is necessary."

"They would have killed you, without a second thought. These are mercenaries. They kill who they are told to, who they are paid to." She paused for a moment, when he didn't reply, she carried on. "I need you back at the compound."

"I have work here. There are still wounded who I can care for."

"We have healers who are more than capable of doing that. The Realm needs you. Especially now. The troops need to know you are safe and the line will continue. That there is some continuity in this madness."

"Ide—"

"Scetis, I need to know you are safe," she whispered.

"I am safe," he tried to reassure her.

It started as a low rumble at first, then the earth began to shake. Ide looked past Scetis over his shoulder, deeper into the valley beyond. Her eyes widened at the familiar sound.

"We have to go now!" she cried pulling on his arm, her fingers digging into his flesh.

"No, there are still those that need my care," he objected.

"There is another band attacking, Scetis. I need to get you out of here!"

Scetis turned to see what she was still staring at. From around a bend a great mass emerged. Hundreds of horses galloped at a great speed, from their backs men roared war cries, while brandishing swords. The blades glinted in the sunshine and others beat them against their round shields. Scetis stared for a moment before moving.

"Come on!" Ide called to him, still tugging on his sleeve.

"Too late, Squirt will take us!" he called out looking for the dragon.

"I'm not going on the back of him. He won't carry us both." The anger was now replaced by an irrational fear.

"He'll get us to safety." Scetis stopped her. "I'm not going to risk losing you," he told her adamantly. "Hold onto me. I won't let you fall; I promise."

Ide looked toward the coming battle. Around them were the shouts and cries of those left behind already gathering to face their foe. Her eyes finally rested on Scetis.

"Squirt go slow them down," he ordered the red dragon.

Without hesitation Squirt was in the air, a roar already escaping his jaw. The pair started gathering the men together to protect their injured, both their own and those of their enemy. Too many of the men that stood behind Scetis and Ide were bloodied already, but they were willing to die for their new King.

A great roar that was louder than the small dragon's echoed along the narrow valley. Squirt stretched his neck and a jet of burning liquid shot out. White and hot, it glowed and splashed across the ground between the two armies. A wall of flame rose into the air and the liquid spread over the ground, halting the charge. Scetis could see the front row of horses dancing and starting to panic at the sudden appearance of the flames that barred their path.

Ide was furiously pulling him back behind their front line.

"Protect the King!" she ordered those around her. Ide then grabbed at a man with his head and arm heavily bandaged. "Take my horse and go for reinforcements. I need the Riders!" she ordered, and the man did not hesitate to follow them. After he had left she turned back to Scetis. "Stay behind me."

Squirt was once more making a pass along the enemy lines. Great black billowing smoke heralded the fact that he was now attacking the men behind the curtain of dancing flames. The cries of battle had turned to the screams of dying men. The jets of flame once splashed on the skin did not wash off. Some were throwing themselves into the river, only to find that the burning liquid would not extinguish.

"Form up now!" Ide cried out her orders and the men straightened their lines. "We are going to have to hold until help arrives." Her words and commands brought more courage to the Foot troops and they steeled themselves.

"Arrows!" a guard from the front cried out. Their shields raised immediately to cover the incoming projectiles. Scetis watched a black mass like a great flock of birds sail through the air.

"*Squirt, beware!*" he called out to his friend.

"*I see!*" Squirt called back. The dragon banked away, but not quickly enough. An arrow tore through his left wing and he cried out in pain.

Scetis' vision of Squirt was lost behind a shield someone had hastily pushed over him.

The thuds of the arrows landing around the small band of men and women was unnerving, seemingly going on forever. Some bounced off the shields while others struck and dug deep into the wood and leather.

"Wait!" Ide called out. A moment later another wave of arrows came hurtling in on them.

"Are you hurt?" Scetis called to Squirt.

"A little, don't worry, I'll live," he cried back.

With the last thud of an arrow, Squirt cried out again. Instead of harassing the front, he now aimed his fiery breath at the rear and the archers. The fire that stopped the charge of the enemy was now dying down, as the liquid burnt out. The cavalry did not wait but jumped the final hurdle of flames and continued their charge.

A few of the Foot were archers and they let loose their last precious supply of arrows in reply. They struck their mark with many horses falling, taking their riders with them in a screaming heap, to be trampled under the hooves of those that followed.

Then they were there.

The huddled Foot remained in formation as the horses started to circle them, pushing them further into a tighter pack. The fear and determination were evident in equal parts amongst the men and women. Their weapons held ready to fight to defend their fellow comrades and to fight for their own survival.

The cavalry that surrounded them stopped, their horses dancing with a nervous energy. They were expectant of the battle that would inevitably come, but they did not advance. A commotion at the back of the surrounding troops could be heard and a path soon opened up. A group of three were making their way towards Scetis, Ide, and the small band of Foot. In the lead, a familiar man rode a dappled grey horse and Scetis recognized the rider. From the way Ide gasped beside him, she had also.

Orcades moved with the horse as it approached, seemingly in over exaggeration. The tack on the animal jingled and sparkled in the sunlight. Scetis could see that it was elaborate, just like his cousin's, who followed closely behind. Wradech Foghladh and he locked eyes and was not surprised to see amusement and the same cruel look he always had when he thought he had the upper hand.

The third rider was no surprise to Scetis. The blank stare was almost bordering on boredom and indifference. Loxa sat comfortably in his seat, the reins held loosely in his hand and arms resting on the rich and ornate pommel of the saddle. His eyes did not rest on Scetis, but scanned the situation he found himself in.

The crowd around them was nervous, but quiet as they watched the coming confrontation. Only the occasional cough or sound of weapons against armor or shield could be heard. The intensity of the group heightened as the trio came to a stop.

"Ide, you really should think about who you align yourself with. This idiot doesn't seem to know what he is doing," Orcades gave a chuckle.

"How did you get out?" Ide asked in reply.

"A little help from my family. Did you really think you could round up all those that support me. You missed a couple. They soon had my cousin here to put things straight." He chuckled a little and then turned cruel and dangerous eyes to Scetis. "Just when your reunion with your father was going so well."

Wradech joined in with the cruel laughter of his cousin.

"I was blind. The only person that you could ever love is yourself." Ide spat at his feet and held her sword tighter, ready for whatever may come next, knowing the inevitable outcome.

"I'm still here and have called to Vojin. They will be here shortly. Keep him talking, he thinks that he has the upper hand and is reveling in the fact," Squirt called to Scetis.

Scetis shifted his weight and turned his attention to Wradech. "How is your grandmother? I hope she is alive and well when you last saw her," he asked, trying to keep his tone conversational.

"My dear man, that is why we are here. To arrest you for the murder of our dear, sweet, vulnerable Grandmamma. You took advantage of her good nature, worming your way into her house. And poor, loyal Gant. I understand you cut him down as he was defending her. His last breath when we found him was your name. I did my best to keep him alive, so we had a witness to the terrible tragedy, but alas his wounds were just too great." He exchanged an amused look with Loxa and for a brief second, the assassin's lips curled into a smile. Cruelty was obviously a family trait.

"I will spare you, Ide, if you want to come back to me. For some reason I do actually find you attractive and we would make a good team. I would put you in charge of our armies." Orcades offered.

"I would rather die." She told him.

"Then, so be it.' He growled back at her. He went to turn his horse but Scetis stopped him.

"This could all be settled now. Between you and me. There should be no more waste of lives. If you conquered this way, you would only be seen as a tyrant and most of those who were left would never have your respect."

"Are you seriously suggesting that we duel to see who gets the kingdom?" Orcades scoffed at the idea.

"Yes," Scetis replied.

"You, who have never held a sword or killed anyone. Against me, a seasoned warrior?" he looked around him as he laughed, most of the men joined in.

"That is exactly what I am proposing," Scetis said. *"Where are you?"* he called in his mind to Squirt.

"Close. Don't worry, I'll come to your rescue," Squirt replied.

"Easy for you to say." Scetis sent out the thought. "So, what do you say?" he once more addressed Orcades.

"This will be the easiest fight I've ever won!" Orcades armor creaked as he hauled himself from his saddle.

"Are you sure you want to do this?" Ide asked him in a hushed voice.

"I have to, and don't you interfere. Squirt will be helping me."

"I have only just found you, don't do anything stupid."

"I have a plan," he told her without any bravado or grin. He stepped forward to meet his opponent.

Orcades in the meantime had thrown his reins to Wradech who looked daggers at him for being treated as a servant. He casually dropped the leather straps and nodded his head to Loxa, and the pair moved off to give Orcades and Scetis room.

"Don't take too long, Orc," he said carefully as he left.

Orcades drew his sword with a great flourish, swinging it around as he warmed up his arm. It was not the serviceable type that Ide held in her hands, but one meant more for ceremonial moments. Scetis hoped that the blacksmith who made it did not balance it with a view to it ever being used in battle.

With palms that were starting to sweat at the prospect of facing this seasoned fighter, Scetis stepped forward. He prayed he could hold him off long enough until the horde arrived. He gripped the sword in both hands, hoping the shaking he felt in his limbs was not being transferred to the blade.

The grin that stretched Orcades mouth showed he thought he would win. He raised his sword; the decorative scroll work caught the sun along with the gems that were inlaid in the hilt. It was held loosely in his grip, and he swung it lazily at Scetis, in a broad stroke. He did not aim for any particular part of his opponent, only to scare and put him on edge. But it had no effect on Scetis.

Scetis brought up his own weapon, which was considerably shorter and blocked the swing, with a loud clang the two blades clashed together. The swords moved against each other, screeching as the metals scraped, while Orcades stepped towards him. Scetis pushed him back and Orcades narrowed his eyes, adjusting his thoughts as to the skill of his opponent.

Again, he attacked, this time harder, but still only using one hand with the broad sword. Scetis once more blocked the swing, this time harder and was pleased to see the flinch of pain that the clash transferred to Orcade's wrist. In response his sword was soon held in both hands.

Orcades moved around, his feet crossing over as he stalked his prey. Even Scetis knew that that was poor technique, and he kept an eye on Orcades' pace and when he would be at his most vulnerable to be unbalanced. As soon as he saw the moment coming, he lashed out with his serviceable weapon and caught Orcades off-guard. He stumbled a little as he tried to untangle his feet and meet the blow. This one was harder than Orcades had been swinging and he was left to be pushed back. His foot was caught in a rut in the uneven ground and he stumbled. A titter of laughter from the men behind Scetis could be heard. Most had been abused by Orcades at some point and he was not well liked by any of the men who had once been under his command.

This laughter caused his face to redden and his anger to rise. He attacked Scetis hard. Blow after blow rained down on the man he thought of as the usurper. His anger rose with each blow. His pride and reputation were now on the line, and he had to show who was the greater warrior.

Scetis met each blow with a defensive parry. His feet danced backwards, the movement coming almost instinctively, but not giving up much ground. The sword flashed, reflecting the sun, as it whirled towards him. The shock of each blow absorbed by his loose grip. Scetis watched for the moment when he could return the blows. He quickly pushed the sword to the side, then brought his blade up and slashed at the only space that was unprotected on Orcades' arm. A bright red line appeared as the skin parted under the sharp blade, quickly followed by an oozing bloody flow. Orcades stepped back in shock, glancing down at the new cut in his arm and with growing anger. This was the reaction Scetis hoped for. His anger was going to be Orcades' downfall.

"If you are going to do something Squirt, sooner would be better than later," Scetis cried out to his friend.

"You're doing fine. He has a weakness in his left," Squirt advised.

Scetis studied his opponent as the physician that he was and noticed what his friend could see. Orcades' left shoulder was held lower and there was a slight noticeable difference in the muscle structure when compared with the right.

Taking this new knowledge in hand, he concentrated his next lot of blows on that side. He pressed on with his attack, and once more Scetis managed to trip Orcades up with his own sloppy footwork. Orcades landed heavily on the ground with his armor ringing out. Scetis stepped on the wrist that held the sword, making Orcades cry out and release the heavy sword. His left lashed out at Scetis legs, trying to knock him off his feet. His efforts were pitiful and labored under the weight of his ornate and impractical armor. Scetis placed the tip of his sword to his throat, a small trickle of blood erupted from his skin.

"Submit," Scetis demanded, barely breathing hard.

"You will not get the chance to kill me." Orcades said, his eyes flicking to where his two cousins were still sitting on their horses.

Scetis saw the slight movement in his peripheral vision and acted automatically. The feeling of the sword slipping into the soft flesh of the throat was similar to when he had cut into a patient's flesh for surgery. With that same push he bent down, and his hand went to his boot. From the heel he pulled a small blade, and sent it flying with the same movement. The small leaf shaped blade sped to its intended victim. It slid quickly through the fabric of Loxa's shirt and embedded itself in through the ribs. The tip just missed its mark of the heart, but still released the poison Scetis had carefully rubbed onto the blade that very morning.

Off to the side, Wradech sat on his horse and stared stupidly as two of his family were killed by a man he thought useless in the art of warfare. He only came to his senses as the small band of soldiers raised a cheer at the two deaths. His anger rose at their presumptions and he roared at his men to attack. This roar was lost as it was met by an even louder one of many. The sound of many beating wings soon joined the war cries of the humans as the dragons swooped one by one over the stunned enemy troops. Before they had time to react they were beset.

Large jets of fire scoured through the troops and they finally responded. Their screams were louder than the roars and they pushed at each other in their feeble attempts to get away. The horses reacted as any prey would when a predator was attacking and they bolted, their riders desperately trying to hang on during the stampede.

Scetis watched the mayhem as it unfolded around him. Wradech pulled on the reins of his horse trying to get it under control in order to take him to safety. A large Red dragon landed heavily in front of him and roared loudly. His horse reared and he lost his place in the saddle, slipping over the rear quarters of the horse and landing heavily on the ground, while his steed bolted. The Red roared again, this time letting fly with a jet of fire, which engulfed the men behind the prone figure of Wradech. The wall of flame rose, and the screams of horses mingled with those of men soon petered out as they succumbed to death.

Wradech stood shakily and shook his head. He drew his sword clumsily and rushed at the large Red. Scetis watched the bizarre scene as it unfolded, unable to believe what he was seeing. Slowly Wradech raised his sword with some futility and the dragon opened his jaws. The great maw was filled with teeth and a dripping mixture of saliva and the fire liquid fell to the ground where it sizzled. The dragon extended his neck and bit down on Wradech, sharp fangs piercing easily into his body and biting the man cleanly in half. The legs and what was left of the torso dropped, with a squelching thud, blood spurting out and a muffled scream cut short from the mouth of the dragon. With a few great gulps the top of Wradech disappeared down the Red's throat and he did not pause to finish the rest of the body off.

The great Red turned his huge, spiked head towards Scetis, with eyes burning brightly with blood lust. For a moment Scetis was rooted to the spot, unable to move and react to the large beast before him. He felt no fear.

"More!" the dragon screamed out in a mighty roar, before turning and shambling after the screaming troops.

In one-way Scetis felt complete revulsion at the bloody and messy feeding of a dragon on human flesh, but the dragon side of him understood the need to not waste a perfectly good food source. The dead bodies would just be put in the ground to rot, so why not use them to feed and nourish the dragons who were there. He shook off this feeling, knowing no other human would share his thoughts and feelings on the matter, and turned to find Loxa.

The assassin was nowhere in sight. The melee around him was a confusion of moving bodies, both large and small, the combined mingling of roars and screams of the combatants, and the smell of blood, lots of blood spilling on the ground and pooling around those that had fallen. There was no way he could pick out one man from all others. His mind then turned to the safety and welfare of Ide. His eyes scanned the crowd where she had been at his back only moments before and she was not there. Dragons were on the ground snapping and shooting fire. Above still more flew high, their wings circling over the battlefield. Dragons of all colors and sizes. A thud made Scetis turn, his sword ready for whatever he would face, finding Squirt moving towards him.

"Have you seen Ide?" he demanded with some panic rising.

"She's holding her own. A dragon is with her, so she is protected. I've been sent to get you," Squirt said turning so Scetis could climb on his back.

"I can't leave, I need to get to Loxa." Scetis still searched, more relaxed now knowing Ide was safe.

"He's gone, get on now. There are more troops flanking. Vojin and Teagan are taking the Riders to rout them out. Muniath has given Ide instructions," Squirt called urgently.

"Your wing?" Scetis asked, trying to see where Squirt was wounded.

"It's only minor, stop dilly dallying."

With a moment's hesitation and one last look around him, Scetis climbed aboard. "Let's go then," he called out loud.

Battle

Teagan sat on Gremlin's back, peering down at the mayhem that was occurring below them. The pair were waiting for Muniath to return so they could be on their way to carry out his plan. The noise that drifted up was mainly from the dragons. The mass of enemy troops that once had seemed to have the upper hand were now a mess. No one was in control.

"Let those that manage to escape be," she cried out to the dragons. "They are not our concern,"

A general agreement came back to her, but underneath were a few grumbles. She brushed these off, knowing a few still wanted the old ways to return.

A flash of red rose from the ground and climbed high with a man on its back. Another Red, Gremlin's mother, came swooping in close, hovering beside them, her wings beating in a graceful and smooth movement. On her back was Muniath grinning.

"We can go. Ide has everything under control," he called between them.

"Scetis and Squirt are aloft. Lead the way, Captain," she called out. "By the way, have the generals been informed of this mission?"

"Not yet. But they will understand," he grinned as he guided Screamer off. Teagan could only shake her head and follow.

As they flew she looked back and saw Squirt ducking and swooping. She wondered if she was surrounded by those who thought it was a game and an adventure. Turning back she gathered her thoughts. A necessary evil was how she tried to think of these battles. Trying to keep those from the Realm safe, while defeating those of the enemy with as little casualties as possible. It was not the soldiers' fault this had to happen. They had been drawn in, either by conscription or with the hopes of money that might trickle down to them from their captains.

The sounds of the battle were soon left far behind, as the small band sped through the low valleys and up over the hills and mountains in search of the main band of men. They pulled up and hovered. Muniath sent out the message of how he wanted to attack and there were no arguments about his strategies before they moved off, splitting up into two groups.

Teagan, Gremlin, Muniath, and Screamer stayed as one along with a group of wild dragons and some Riders, while Scetis and Squirt followed Venicones and Scorcher to the opposite end of the valley to drive the enemy to the small narrow entrance where the first group waited.

They were set. The call from Venicones was sent and silently as they could, the group followed Muniath into the bend and entered the valley. The old king's mount held her head high, her glorious golden wings gleamed in the fleeting sunshine, as dark clouds began to roll in over the mountains. Teagan could see she was proud to lead the assault, pleased she could help in some way to avenge her bonded rider's death. Muniath hung low over her neck, a hand resting on her metallic red scales, calming her.

A great cry went up ahead of them. They rounded the last bend and spread out. The roar from the dragons was loud and sustained. Before them seemed to be chaos as the two groups attacked in unison. Lined up across the last narrow part before the valley was a line of carts, all covered in canvas. This canvas was hastily pulled aside to reveal what was hidden beneath. Huge arrows the size of spears, but thicker, were soon lifted into the air, set in large, purpose-built crossbows that were attached to the carts. They were released as one from a command and took to the air, their sharp metal tips not only caught the flash of sunshine but whistled through the air as they flew towards the advancing dragons, spinning on their deadly mission. Teagan watched in fascination as they came closer and closer to the dragons.

"Watch out!" she cried, and the group reacted as one, scattering out of range and reach of this new threat.

The first volley was successfully dodged, but one arrow was late firing. This arrow flew straight and true. Teagan saw that Muniath, and Screamer had not seen it. They were still concentrating on the arrows that had flown past them. She opened her mouth, but she was too late. The arrow found its target and her warning turned to a shout of dismay.

The sharpened metal arrowhead pierced the protective layer of red scales and almost stopped Screamer in mid-flight. She screamed and belched great jets of flames. The burning liquid rained down on the men below. Her front claws gripped the shaft and Teagan could hear Muniath pleading with her to not pull it out, but in her pain and rage she did not listen. The shaft slipped from her body with a huge wrench, leaving a gaping hole that spewed dark blood. She cried out in agony again and fell from the sky as the life left her body. Teagan watched as Muniath clung on the large saddle as she went down. Her wings went limp and folded up above her, hiding him from her view as they dropped fast.

"Muniath!" Teagan called, her face pale and her shock clearly evident. She tried to get Gremlin to follow, she needed to make sure that Muniath was safe, but he resisted her.

"No, we need to destroy the carts first. He will be fine. Duty first," Gremlin spoke harshly, and he carried her away, already spewing a stream of fire and burning the nearest cart.

Thick black smoke bellowed up into the clean mountain air as the carts caught fire. Barrels of pitch that were kept on the decks quickly caught alight and exploded, spraying their contents of the men running for safety. Their screams carried to Teagan where she sat as the great emerald dragon dodged the hastily fired arrows from the ground, their fletching buzzing as they whizzed past.

The Riders on the back of the trained dragons were flying in formation and firing their own in return from their short bows. Their aim was impeccable and their speed amazing. Teagan watched mesmerized for a moment before turning back and trying to spot Muniath.

"There are more of those huge arrow carts ahead." Squirt warned while he sped towards them, ducking and diving, trying to stay out of reach of the enemy's weapons.

"Muniath and Screamer went down." Teagan told them.

"We'll go see if we can find them," Scetis offered, and Teagan watched as they flew past them.

"I can see their command post," Venicones called out from nearby and relayed the position. Gremlin immediately turned to find it.

A group of men stood on a rise above the battle, watching in stunned silence. Some looked mystified as to how to handle the dragons, while others who had clearly more experience with the great flying beasts were barking orders to runners. Only one seemed to be in charge completely. A massive barrel-chested man dressed in the garb of a mercenary. This man did not flinch as Teagan and Gremlin, along with Venicones landed nearby. Both Gremlin and Scorcher roared. The other captains cringed and dropped to their knees in surrender.

Teagan slipped from the back of Gremlin and strode towards the mercenary. He stood his ground and looked Teagan up and down, before turning his attention to Venicones, who he clearly assumed was in charge, due to his uniform.

"Captain, I have my orders and I will obey them. I will only surrender to the usurper and no one, nor beast else," the large man bellowed.

"Captain, you address the wrong person. My Lady Teagan here is in charge of this battle and the dragons in the air," Venicones said, deferring to her.

The mercenary roared with laughter. "Orders from a child, a girl-child at that?

"You have the child part right, but I wouldn't cross The Child of Dragons. If you wish mercy for your men, I suggest you start speaking politely and sweetly to her. Since she has come into her destiny, she has changed a great deal," Venicones advised him.

"Thank you, Ven, I haven't changed that much." Teagan said with a sideways glance at Muniath's brother.

"Child of Dragons? What rubbish is this? You cannot expect me to believe in fairy tales?" the mercenary said staring at her.

Gremlin ambled up behind Teagan and pushed his head between her and Venicones, sniffing the mercenary. *"Place your hand on him and open his mind,"* he instructed her.

Teagan stepped forward and while the man was distracted by the largest dragon he had ever seen, she placed her hand on his arm and soon opened his eyes. The small flecks of silver shone for a moment and he blinked a couple of times, looking dumbly at Teagan at his side.

"Here me and believe," she spoke to him and watched as he shook his head, unable to comprehend that she had just spoken to him without using her mouth. His eyes widened as he began to hear the collective mind of the dragons, hear their calls, and talk as the battle still raged out beyond.

"A living legend!" he whispered, dropping to his knees before her. "My life is yours, my lady. I give up all loyalty and promises made to those who would do you and your Realm harm. I have no other leader from this day forth."

"Stand down children of the Dragon Realm. This battle is over!" Teagan commanded and the dragons all pulled away.

"Tell the men to stand down!" The mercenary yelled at a runner as he rose to his feet. The young boy took off fast, obviously happy to get away from the two dragons who were standing so close.

"What are you doing?" a man in an impeccable uniform hissed at the mercenary.

"Giving up, General Aniel," he said, turning to the man. "I advise you not to counter my orders. You left the running of this battle to me because of my experience. Don't try to start being in command now!" he roared.

"But I have my orders!"

"Your orders are hogwash now. If you feel like fighting dragons as you were ordered, then go ahead and be my guest. I believe any of these magnificent creatures would only be too happy to oblige and have you for lunch," he said, indicating Gremlin and Scorcher. Scorcher stepped forward at the suggestion and the general stepped back, eyes riddled with fright, his whole body now shaking. "Good man. Now if you are good little general you can stay and watch history in the making." He patted the highly ornate shoulder, shaking the man in the process.

A flutter of wings drew Teagan's attention and Squirt was soon landing beside the gathered group. She noted the small holes and tears in his wings, which looked fresh. Scetis nodded to her as he slid off the dragon's back, with a mental thought that he would attend to Squirt's wounds soon. He was grim, but it was not due to the small dragon's wounds. He walked purposefully to her and took an arm.

"Muniath is injured, and I've tended to his wounds as well as I can and have sent him back to the camp. I'm afraid that Screamer did not make it. I'm sorry Vojin," he said to the large dragon.

Gremlin lifted his large head and cried out in grief. Although Teagan had raised him, Screamer was still his mother. The rest of the dragons, including Squirt and Scorcher all joined in his loss. They cried out her accomplishments, praising her grace, beauty, and strength. How she had served her bonded rider well and carried him proudly. They called out the names of her children, the list was only a short one with six names. They bade her spirit to join the ancestors in the shadows and share her wisdom with the collective mind. The lament did not last long and the silence in the world after was deafening.

"So, the Regulator's lap dog has become king." General Aniel said snidely, his voice loud, breaking in the silence that lay like a blanket over the land.

The mercenary swung his fist at the pompous man and dropped him like a stone. "I said, behave!" he spat on the man. "I am Captain Gadbre, and if you are Scetis Mordha, then I am at your service." He went to one knee and laid his hand over his heart, bowing his head.

"I am pleased to hear it, Captain, but my name is now Scetis Cionaoith, as my father wished. Are you able to make sure that none of these other 'gentlemen' escape?" Scetis asked him, indicating that Gadbre should stand.

"It would be my honor to do so, my Lord." He beckoned to a soldier at the entrance to the grand tent that stood in front of the mountain face.

The soldier ran off and was soon back with a few more dressed the same. Within short order the captains and generals of the Convocation were rounded up and led away.

"Is there anything else, my Lord?" Gadbre asked.

"Yes you can show me their plans," Scetis said and followed the captain into the tent.

Teagan followed slowly behind them, her mind wandering as she watched Gadbre and his men take over. The conversation went on without her and then she felt two hands gently on both of her arms.

"You are far away." Muniath said behind her.

Quickly she turned and flung her arms around him, holding onto him tightly. "Why are you here, you were supposed to have gone back to camp?"

"When did I ever follow orders," he whispered deeply into her hair, as he returned her hug. "Do you want to tell me what you were thinking of?"

"Just that it seems a complete waste. Why do men always want what is not theirs and what they have no business having?" A tear escaped her eye, quickly wiped away on his vest.

Muniath pulled away briefly, his hands moving stray locks of hair from her face. "It's the nature of them to feel inadequate. There is something lacking in their souls to be satisfied with what they already have achieved. They feel like the world owes them something. From what Scetis has told us of the Regulator, he seems to be that kind of man. The power is intoxicating, and a little taste can lead to wanting more; by controlling men and their hopes and dreams. He wishes to keep the control so no one can usurp his position or can see what he is sorely lacking. Many men have already fallen by his command even before these battles. Scetis was very lucky to escape when he did. I didn't like him at first, but the more I talk to and am around him, the more I find myself thinking he will make a great ruler. Even better than Urmond was."

"The death and destruction does not sit well with me. I mean, the me before I accepted this mantle of Child of Dragons. I am still the same person I was, but now I have this underlying lust for annihilation. I'm not making much sense am I?"

"You're making perfect sense. I wish there were some other way for this to be resolved. But when we are attacked by an outside force, what are we to do?"

"There may be a way to bring this all to an end without more bloodshed. Gremlin has told me of a development in Fleet. One he didn't even see or meddle with."

"Fleet is not getting involved in this war. She is still too young and with Screamer just dying, she will be even more vulnerable," he said defensively, letting Teagan go.

"It is not a physical development, but a mental one," she told him soothingly. "She can see the dreams of dragons, hybrids, and humans. She can also tell the differences between them."

"So how can that help us?" Muniath asked, clearly confused.

"Gremlin wondered if she could manipulate those dreams." She watched as he pondered her words and saw the moment of understanding as it came to him.

"If she can manipulate the dreams of our enemies, it would put us on a good footing when we face them the next day. It could weaken their resolve."

"If his thoughts are correct, it may mean we will not need to face them at all. I am hoping that their armies desert and we face no one on the battlefield. Those crossbows are too devastating to face again. I thought I had lost you." Teagan did not care who saw them, she pulled him back to her and leaned her head against his chest.

"Screamer died fighting. She felt she could go honorably into the shadows, knowing she had tried to avenge Urmond's death." They stood for a moment in silence, taking comfort from each other.

"I'm going to have Gremlin bring Fleet to the encampment. We need to try this," she said and felt his reaction.

"Can't she do it from the Eyrie?"

"It would work better from being closer to them. She will be able to pick out the groups of men, rather than a full blanket over the country."

"If that is the only way, then it needs to be done," he agreed.

"The call has been sent." Gremlin intruded into their minds and conversation.

"Why does that not surprise me?" Muniath said and chuckled.

Fleet

"Keep going, Sister," Sting called out to Fleet, who was starting to struggle a little. Her wings were flapping madly and beginning to falter between strokes. Her breathing was labored, and she determinedly carried on. There was no way Fleet was going to admit to her sibling that he was better at flying than she was. It already annoyed her that Sting was becoming larger than she was.

The pair flew on and Fleet knew Sting was keeping them low to the ground just in case she needed to land in a hurry. Her muscles worked hard to keep her aloft as she scanned the area, trying to see if there were any men in their immediate area. So far they had been lucky and the only humans that had been seen were being transported in the wagons of the wounded, heading back to the citadel.

A red flash up ahead made Fleet forget her aching wings and tiredness. She took in a deep breath and ploughed on through the air. She sent out her thought again and recognized the pattern that returned. For some reason, the little red dragon fascinated her. It was not Squirt's stature that made her curious, but his mind. It was fast and just as inquisitive as hers. Also his dreams had given her an insight into some of what he had gone through. The pain of rejection was still so strong in his mind and heart, and she could not imagine going through that herself. Even her own pain that she was experiencing in losing her mother was not a match for his. Her mother was dead, but she could still be able to see her in the shadows. Squirt's mother was still alive and did not want to ever see him.

Another flash caught her attention and she now saw him flapping towards them. Squirt looked tired and his normal fast flight was just as labored as her own. There were also small, ragged holes in his wing membranes. 'They should be looked at before they become permanent,' she thought with concern welling up for him.

"There you are. I have been looking for you all morning. I thought you would have come further than this," Squirt said and landed on the rich green grass.

"We would have been faster if my sister had not been so lazy," Sting said landing nearby.

"Not lazy, tired," Fleet gasped. *"You would be too if you got no rest night after night."* She stretched out the cramped muscles by extending her wings to their fullest.

"The dreams?" Squirt asked with some concern.

Fleet only nodded her response and sank into the cool soft grass, enjoying the comfort of cushioning it gave her.

"Rest for a moment then, Sister, then we need to be on our way," Sting said as he peered around them, trying to appear as if he was protecting her.

Squirt gazed at Fleet for a moment and felt her frustration at not being as fast as her brother. "The more you fly the stronger you will get. You will soon be outflying both of your brothers," he told her. "But, I must echo Sting's urging. I don't want to see you exhausted later."

"Just a moment or two is all I need," Fleet said as she rested her head on her fore feet. Her eyes closed against the brightness of the day and she was soon softly breathing. The sun moved far in the sky and proclaimed the lateness of the afternoon. Shadows stretched out below the trees nearby and Fleet awoke to a soft nudging to her side.

"It is time to wake, Sister," Sting said.

"But I have only just closed my eyes," Fleet protested.

"I'm afraid the day has been marching on without you," Squirt informed her as her eyes opened, blinking at the brightness as it stabbed at her eyes.

"I suppose it's best we go then." She quickly rose to her feet and ruffled here weary wings, moving the blood through them.

Sting and Squirt followed as Fleet lifted into the air and she headed off with a sigh.

The trio flew for another couple of hours and the smoke from the fires of men drifted in the air before them. It was the first time she had seen so many dragons in one place before. The field where they were placed was vast. Many lifted their heads in greeting to Screamer's children, calling out their regret at her passing and wishing the two youngsters well. To Squirt there was no greeting, only an oblivion of his presence.

"I'm sorry, Squirt," Fleet said softly, speaking only to him.

"There is nothing for you to be sorry for, Fleet. It is not your doing what they choose to think and believe," Squirt replied and then banked away to go find Scetis.

"He is right, Sister. They will believe what they will. We can only show him our own friendship and acceptance," Sting told her.

"You have changed your mind, then?"

"Since I have gotten to know him, it has changed. As his renown grows, more will change their minds also. As our brother says, they have forgotten that there were once small dragons who walked the halls of the citadel, and there will be again."

"I hope so, Brother," she said wearily as they landed and furled their wings. Wick was soon at their side checking both dragons carefully and to care for their needs.

Stars sparkled in the clear night sky, gems shining brightly beside the thin crescents of the blue and green moons that hung on opposite horizons in the evening darkness. A breeze moved the flames that burned brightly in the ash filled hearth, setting the bright orange tongues dancing over the charred logs. A call from an owl pierced the hushed ground of the camp and barely went recognized by those that slumbered under canvas and sky.

Only a few sentries were awake along with five dragons and seven humans. The fire they were gathered around was set outside the confines of the defenses of the large encampment. All eyes now turned towards Fleet expectantly, and she felt like hiding behind Vojin.

"It is time, Sister," he told her, gently encouraging.

"I will try," she said, uncertainly.

Since he had come to her with this idea, Fleet had tried to convince herself that she could do what he wanted. Her need to be needed, and in some way, part of this offensive was great. Now faced with actually doing what Vojin wished, doubt was setting in.

Lifting her head high she sought out the enemy camps. She could feel them out there, or rather, she could feel their dreams. She pulled them into her, breathed them in deeply, feeling her inner fire building in her gullet. Drawing more and more in, feeding her heat before she felt she could take in no more. With a roar that was deep and loud, she pushed them back out, releasing the fire within. It burst from her throat, rising high into the night sky, so bright it briefly obliterated the glittering stars. The hot jet climbed higher and higher, the leading edge spreading out towards the west. A blanket of flame surged out and away from the Realm's soldiers and dragons.

Her heat spent for now, she waited, watching the spread of the flames on the wind carry new dreams back to the men and women who slept and for a brief moment had stopped dreaming. The dreams it now carried turned and darkened, designed to seek out the fears of each and capture them in a strong hold they could not wake from, until the first light of the new morning.

Fleet shuddered at the thought but continued. Finding the next enemy camp and repeating the process. The night sky was soon littered with flames, seeking out their intended victims. Another two times she sent those dark nightmares out. At the end of the last, she collapsed, breathing deeply, and feeling her throat hot. Muniath approached her with a bucket of cool spring water for her to drink. It slipped down her throat with a sizzle and a few wisps of steam escaping her mouth.

Muniath placed a caring hand on the side of her face. *"Thank you, Fleet. You have done well tonight."*

"I just hope that the plan works," she replied feeling more tired than she had ever before.

"Rest, I will go see if your efforts have had their desired effect," Squirt said, gently resting his forepaw on her head before taking to wing and heading out into the deepening night sky. The blue moon, the brighter of the two, had fallen below the horizon, the green now rose to preside over the land.

Fleet watched him go, staying with him long after he had gone from sight. The murmur of those around her no more than a hum and unheard as she waited to hear if their plan and her actions had worked.

"My sister, you have done well," Vojin broke through her thoughts.

"Do not thank me yet, Brother," she told him.

"I am sure it has worked," he said meaning to reassure her.

"You put too much on Squirt."

"I put nothing on him that he does not offer himself. He has resources of strength and endurance far greater than the normal dragon. He is special. I created him that way."

"Just as you gave me this gift of dream manipulation?" she asked him.

"I did not give you this gift. Just like the hybrids have changed, so have the dragons. Many of what was once common among our kind has been lost. But that seems to be changing now that I am back."

With her sight still with Squirt, Fleet saw the fire of an enemy camp and with his ears she heard the shouts, calls, and screams of those dreaming the nightmares she had created for them. At first she tensed her muscles, contrite about the deed, but her brother's caring wing hovered over her smaller body in comfort. He could hear them too.

"It has worked, Sister, just as I knew it would. Thank you for your service. You did very well, Aisling," he said, citing the name their mother had given her.

"I have not come to adulthood yet, brother." she said angrily.

"I beg to differ, Aisling. Your actions and deeds show me you have come of age already. Being who I am it is my right to declare you an adult." Gremlin released the declaration before she could protest. Once made it could not be taken back and all acknowledged her name.

"What about our brother, Vojin?" she asked.

"He will prove himself soon," Gremlin replied enigmatically. "Now rest and sleep. You have earned it."

Healing

"The reports are coming in now. The dragon scouts are saying that the camps are in disarray. Some of their soldiers are trying to desert and are being rounded up. It appears that the nightmares only affected some. The contingent who was not affected, are in charge, and they are not being gentle with those that have been either," Gadbre told the group gathered the next morning.

"It was worth a shot," Scetis said leaning on the table before him which was littered with maps and reports. "It seems that an all-out battle is our only choice. But to face so many on three fronts is a daunting effort."

"I have a few suggestions, my Lord, if you would hear them?" Gadbre offered.

"I bend to your knowledge, Captain."

"We send in scouts again after dark. If the dragon Fleet could lock the enemy in sleep again, then we could take out the carts with the cross bows. That will give us back the initial advantage of the dragons, then we send them in at first light with the Foot close behind. We may not have the initial numbers on our side, but with the element of surprise attack, we will win."

"Aideen, Galanan, what do you think?" Scetis asked, turning to his generals.

"It is sound, my lord," Aideen replied.

"Good, I will leave it to you all to discuss the details," Scetis said pushing himself off the table. "Get organized to act tonight," he told them, the group bowed as he left the tent.

Scetis stood outside in the fresh air and breathed in deeply. He wandered away into the camp, not really knowing where he was going, until his feet led him to the Rider's camp. For once he wished he were invisible as the Riders came to attention at the sight of him. He waved them all to sit, not enjoying the infamy and being so well known. Scetis had gone from total obscurity even among his peers, to being thrust into such acknowledgement. It did not sit well. He would have been more comfortable if he could just live out his days in peace and unacknowledged with Ide.

Ide. Just the thought of her made his heart race. Her whole being made him tongue-tied around her. But she seemed just as quiet as he was. Scetis laughed to himself at that thought. The story of how they met will go down in the annals of history.

A path had been opened by some Foot soldiers who thought they were being helpful to him. It amused Scetis that this young man knew where he was going, when he himself had no clue. But his feet soon found the one person left of his family, Orlagh.

The tents were now left behind, and the dragons lay slumbering on the flattened and now churned up grass. Their breathing was deep with the occasional odd rustle of a wing as he passed. Amongst all those giant mounds of gleaming scales, he found his half-sister, tending her own mount. A tear was very evident in the large wing and Orlagh was trying to get the thin membrane to knit together, with little success.

"Can I help?" he offered, already unshouldering the satchel that seemed to be permanently adhered to his side.

"I've left it too long I think," Orlagh replied, looking up from her work.

"Maybe not. Before I left the Convocation, I was working on a method of closing wounds without using a needle and thread. My hypothesis was that it would leave a cleaner scar, rather than the puckering that stitching makes." He peered at the wound in Storm's wing.

"But their wings are different from human skin," she protested.

"Not really so different. Still skin, still blood vessels and a tiny bit of flesh," he said rummaging now around in his bag. He pulled out a long, debarked stick and a pot of clear gel looking substance. Unscrewing the lid he placed it down with his bag and then looked at the wound again. The edges were jagged, as if it had been caught on a branch.

"Shall I hold the wing?" Orlagh offered.

"Please. There is a component of this that will sting, just a little," he told them both. Dipping the stick into the jar he then lifted it to dab just a small amount on the lower part of the tear. Dropping the stick, he moved the two parts together, holding them in place for a moment. Storm, to her credit, only let out a small moan and stood steady so Scetis could do his work, instinctively trusting him.

"I wouldn't fly for a few hours, let it set it properly, otherwise it will tear, and I won't be able to mend it," he instructed.

"Thank you," Orlagh said inspecting the mend in the wing. "So what are you doing here?"

"I felt the need to be here. Are there other dragons who need tending to?" he asked looking around.

"Many, but you might be standing on some toes, in the form of Muniath and Wick. They are very particular about treating the dragons," she informed him.

"Will you take me to them, I'd like to help, after all that was my first calling." He smiled shyly at her.

"The second, being King?" she teased as the pair began to walk further into the field of dragons.

"No, that was chemistry, then trading. This King thing has been forced upon me."

"You know our father never wanted to be King. He wanted to follow his passion and be General of Riders," Orlagh told him. "But his older sister died, and so he was elevated. That's why he was called back from the border."

"And away from my mother," he said somberly. "I didn't know this, he never told me."

"He probably would have at some point got around to telling you. He was quick to act when it was necessary, but things like that he felt could wait. The Realm came first,"

"And you second?" Scetis asked, getting some insight into the life of his half-sister.

"It felt that way sometimes, but not always." Orlagh gave him a small smile. "Some advice for you, Scetis. When you marry Ide, make her your equal. Our father made that mistake with my mother. She did not appreciate playing second to a whole country. I feel she became very lonely towards the end of her life. In many ways, I believe that is what started her illness. There really was nothing any of the healers could do. She didn't have the will to keep living."

"She loved our father?"

"Deeply. But we now know that his feelings for her did not run so deep," she said sadly.

"I'm sorry," Scetis said quietly.

"What for? It wasn't your fault, or even father's. Ultimately, it was Grandfather's. It was he who did not want Father to marry your mother."

The pair remained quiet for a while as they thread their way through the dragons until they found Muniath and Wick working together, looking at Squirt's wings. Scetis felt a stab of guilt at the thought he had neglected his friend and mount.

"I've brought help," Orlagh called to the pair before Scetis could say anything.

The two men turned from their work, Muniath greeted them with a smile, but in Wick's eyes there was clearly still some suspicion. Scetis could not blame the boy, after all it had been him who had stolen the eggs and started this whole mess in the first place.

"He brings with him an amazing compound that will close all those holes." Orlagh reached out and stroked Squirt's neck, the dragon almost seemed to melt at her touch.

"I would very much like to see it work." Muniath told him as he and Wick stepped back to let Scetis get to work.

"Ow! You could have warned me that it would hurt!" Squirt cried out as Scetis applied the setting glue on the edge of a tear.

"Sorry my friend," Scetis told him, but carried on working, nervous under the scrutiny of the Dragon Master.

Muniath and Wick were suitably impressed with how it had worked.

"What is it made up of?" Wick asked eagerly.

"A bit of this and that. I'll write up a list and how to make it for you if you like?" Scetis offered, pleased the young man was taking an interest.

"Yes please. Have you anything else we can treat dragons with?"

"A few that might help larger wounds. Would you like to carry on with Squirt's injuries?" Scetis held out the pot to the boy.

Eagerly Wick took it and a new clean stick that Scetis retrieved from his bag. After a little more instruction, while watching Wick, Scetis stepped back and Muniath placed a friendly hand on his shoulder.

"I do believe you have won him over," Muniath told him.

"I could see that. Now if we could only convince the rest of the Dragon Realm."

"They'll come around. Already the stories of your actions on the field are being circulated. And now this." Mun indicated Wick and Squirt. "A man who can care for a dragon is also an indication that he will care for the Realm. And his wife," he said pointedly.

"Orlagh advised I make Ide my equal in the Realm, that we rule together."

"Sound advice, especially where Ide is concerned. My sister would start to take over anyway, it's in her nature. She's too much like our mother," he chuckled.

Teagan lay asleep on the rough blanket laid out on the ground. In her dreams she could hear the dragons around her. The connections were wide-spread and far reaching, but they did not disturb her, they only seemed to smooth her growing fears. Since Screamer's death she had become uneasy. She did not like losing one of the dragons, especially one so close to her. She took it as a personal insult that she could not protect her or her rider.

Muniath claimed that he had not been badly hurt from the fall, but Teagan knew better. She had seen him wince when he moved and instinctively his hand reached for his ribs. When she had confronted him about it, he had denied all injuries and refused to go see the healer. She was soon learning that he was incredibly stubborn.

The dream now shifted to Muniath. Here in this private part of her mind she gave her imagination free reign. Muniath stood before her, shirtless and the top button of his breeches undone. She could feel her breath catch in her throat as she saw the beauty of his masculine body walking towards her. His hair was down and damp, like he had just returned from a swim. Playing across his lips was that small smile, and mischief and desire twinkled in his eyes. He opened his mouth to say something, as a great roar coursed through her.

In horror she watched as Muniath melted away. The image engulfed in flames. Teagan could see he was seeing the same on his side of the dream, the sound of her name could be heard as he sought to protect her from whatever was disturbing their connection.

The roar raged still as she tried to drag herself from her dreams. Her eyes fluttered open and the roar still continued, only multiple voices joined it. She struggled from the blanket she was twisted in and out of the tent she shared with Orlagh and two other female Riders. Standing just outside she searched frantically for the cause. Bellows of fire now flared up into the sky. Rolling, boiling flames from multiple jets of dragons' breath. The heat from the flames washing over the camp.

Voices now sounded from the Riders running to their mounts and Teagan joined them. A heavy weight landed on her heart and she called out into the night with her mind as well as her voice.

"Gremlin!"

She threaded her way through the mayhem until she found him. Gremlin lay on the ground, his eyes closed as if he were asleep. He still breathed, but it was labored and loud. Teagan reached his side and knelt by his head, a hand going to his cheek.

"Who? What?" she stammered.

Gremlin opened his eye just a crack, his silver dull under the lid.

"*Loxa,*" he sighed before sinking into unconsciousness.

"Teagan!" Muniath called reaching her.

"Get Scetis, Mun, now!" she called, still stroking Gremlin's cheek. She turned to him, her eyes wide with fright and fear for her friend.

Muniath stared for a moment before running away. He was back shortly after with Scetis and Ide in tow. The other Riders were out with their mounts trying to calm them down. While she waited for them to reach her, she had moved her hands over Gremlin's great body to see if the injury was external or there was another cause. Just under his wing she found a few scales missing and a gaping wound, pouring with blood. In the flickering light of the fireballs, she could see the dragon's blood pooling on the ground.

Scetis was at her side and trying to speak above the sound of all the roars.

"Peace my dragons. Let us help him," Teagan called out to the collective mind.

Scetis ran a hand over the wound. "There's something in there, just under the surface." He wiped his hand on his shirt, leaving a dark smear on the white fabric. "I need light!" he called out as he opened his bag.

A bobbing light appeared quickly after his call and was held so it would shine its light on the wound. Quickly he pulled out a sharpened blade and set to work. Carefully he opened the wound more, exposing the end of a spear. The metal tip visible where it wrapped around the hardened wood. Gremlin moaned a little but did not stir.

"If I pull on that it might do him more damage. It's deep." Scetis told them.

"What do you need?" Wick asked transferring the torch to his other hand.

"Your help for one, Wick. I also need a few things that might be in the stores here, but one that is in my rooms at the castle."

"I'll go get that." Teagan volunteered.

"I'll take you." Squirt added, coming up quickly.

"Your wings are still healing Squirt," Scetis said.

"They'll be fine. You need speed and I'm fast," Squirt told him.

"What am I looking for?" Teagan asked, eager to be gone.

"A case. It looks like a book, but it holds all my more dangerous compounds."

"I know the one," Squirt said confidently.

"We'll be back soon." Teagan said to Gremlin with a final pat and then climbed onto the back of Squirt.

They were soon in the air. As they sped along they were joined soon after by a multitude of flapping wings. Teagan looked around at the night sky and found they had an escort. A large white was to her left and an equally large Red to the right. Behind were one of each of the Dragon clans, all eager to help and protect Squirt and Teagan.

"Mother," Squirt acknowledged the large Red.

"Son. Fly true," she bade him with some pride in her voice. Teagan could feel him double his efforts as he realized his mother was proud of him.

The ground sped away underneath them. The rivers, valleys, and mountains left behind as they reached the largest valley holding the citadel and castle. As they neared the town, they saw flames burst from a building and in the flare of the light, men swarming the streets. Cries of the people reached them.

"Help them!" Teagan cried out to the dragons in their wake and watched as they peeled off to head to the streets. Only the Red and White now were with them. Roars from the dragons and screams from the invading soldiers were soon dominant in the night.

Squirt landed on the flyway on the topmost tower and Teagan was soon slipping from his back. Quickly the pair entered the tower as the White and Red landed behind them. Racing through the halls many people were about as the attack became more known. Squirt led her to Scetis' rooms, and she tried to open it. The door would not budge as the lock held in place. Squirt placed all his might to the door, and it burst open. Inside they quickly located the box and headed out to the tower and launch pad.

A group of foreign soldiers with an old man dressed in black robes stepped out from a side corridor and barred their way.

"Where is Scetis?" the old man demanded.

"Not here," Squirt said, stepping in front of Teagan.

"Who are you?" Teagan cried out, clutching the box to her chest, trying to keep it from being moved too much.

"I am he who would have this realm and all others under one roof," he replied, his arrogance evident in his smirk.

"You're him. Tavae Stiobhard. The Regulator!" Teagan said steely.

"I am. And I can see Scetis has learned to send others to do his work. I had counted on him being arrogant enough to come himself," Tavae said. "Tell him, he has lost, and he is once more a no-one."

Squirt roared and sent a jet of flame towards the four soldiers. They screamed and fell over themselves to get to cover. Tavae turned and fled down the corridor and mounted the steps to the flyway tower. Squirt and Teagan gave chase.

Just as the pair burst through the doorway onto the strip, they watched Tavae reach the center of the landing pad. There was no way out, nowhere else to go. He turned on the spot, finally seeing the two large dragons that now flanked him.

The White was quicker than the Red, and lunged at The Regulator, his great jaws showing the rows of sharp teeth. He snapped but landed on air as the old man moved quickly out of the way. The Red tried next, her dark eyes never leaving the man in black, but she missed too. Tavae backed up his head turning between the two, already as white as a sheet as he faced the beasts he so detested. The pair stalked him, moving slowly as he tried to move away from them, until he hit the stone wall that edged the flyway.

With a roar that could only come from an adult dragon, Sting rose up from the drop off and lunged at the Regulator. His large mouth open wide he bit down on his head, freeing it easily from the body, and crunching it between his teeth. Blood spurted from his jagged neck, as the body collapsed onto the stone, spreading out in a pool of red. The White and Red advanced, each taking up a half, and pulling, devouring what was left.

Teagan was not horrified but accepted the Dragon's actions. *"Only this one time,"* she told the three of them, to which they agreed.

The group were soon winging their way back to the camp after checking the dragons had the invasion under control. They landed and gave Scetis the box. Around him he had carefully prepared all that he would need, including a roaring fire. With great care he opened it, inspecting each item until he found what he needed. Pulling on thick leather gloves, he slowly stoppered the vial and dipped in a stick. On the end when it was pulled out, was a black oily looking substance. Scetis indicated for more light to Wick, and he hesitantly started to lubricate the wound with the stick. Working at the wound until it was coated in the substance, he threw the stick immediately into the fire nearby, where it sizzled and threw up thick black smoke.

Still with his gloves on, Scetis picked up a pair of tongs that was sitting in hot water beside the fire. He plunged the ends into the flesh and latched onto the end of the broken off spear. He began to pull on the tip, but it would not budge. He pulled harder, bracing his foot against the side of the dying dragon.

"I'm sorry my friend," he muttered to Gremlin.

Taking a deep breath, he pulled again, using all his weight. It began to slide out, with a sickening squelch it released from the side of the dragon, bringing with it more scales. Blood poured from the wound. Scetis dropped the spear head and immediately began packing the wound with a gauze from another bowl, with a greenish tinge to the water.

"Don't touch that spear!" Scetis shouted, as he pushed more of the wadding into the wound.

By the time he was finished, the oily black substance had disappeared, and the bleeding had stopped. Muniath beside him, handed him another bowl filled to the brim with a white paste. Scetis picked up handfuls of it and smeared it over the gauze and wound, encasing it all. The plaster soon started to harden and once he had inspected it for any gaps, Scetis pulled off his gloves and tossed them into the fire.

"I will have to change the dressing in a few hours, but that should hold for now. The herbs should counter whatever poison was placed on that spear, I can only hope that Loxa underestimated Vojin's weight and didn't put enough on," Scetis said gently to Teagan.

"I'll sit with him overnight," she told no one in particular as she sat by Gremlin's head stroking him.

"So will I," Muniath told her, dropping to the ground beside her.

"My Lord King," Squirt started, stepping closer now. "I have news. The Regulator is dead. He tried a sneaky attack on the citadel and town, but we arrived shortly after they did. I am very happy to announce that The Regulator is now no more thanks to Sting."

"That is good news," Scetis sighed as he packed up his things. "Hopefully, things can settle down now and there will be peace."

Morning broke over the valley with bird song and warmth. Tendrils of steam lifted off the river, creeping over the banks and through the camp. There was a hushed tone to the stirring of the men and dragons, all aware by now of the fate of Gremlin. Fires were stirred as breakfasts were made and soon the news that the war was over filtered through the camp. It was met with smiles and handshakes between the troops, and orders were given to break camp. Slowly tents were struck, gear packed away, and carts loaded with the supplies. By mid-morning, the camp was ready to move out. All except for two.

Teagan refused to leave the side of the dragon and Muniath stayed with her, bringing her food and drink. He left her for a moment as he organized Wick, gave him instructions, and helped a group of Riders move a tent nearer to the dragon. He made his farewells to his family who had come to see them, finally taking instruction from Scetis about the dose and application of the antidote to the poison. All this done without Teagan really taking in what was happening around her.

Her mind was fully linked with Gremlin's, her energy taken up with keeping his spirit alive while the poison raged through his blood, chased quickly by the medicine that was applied on the gauze. She gave all she could spare and more, feeling her own life force diminish as she helped her friend.

'Fight,' she pleaded with him. 'You have so much more to do, Gremlin.'

By nightfall, his breathing was easier and the help she had given him was bolstering his strength. His eyes opened briefly, and he moved slightly to get more comfortable. Muniath applied the next lot of antidote to the wound and noted to Teagan that it seemed to be working. For the first time since it happened, Teagan sat back from the dragon and sighed. She went to stand and found her legs would not hold her. Muniath caught her as she dropped and picked her up, carefully carrying her into the tent and the bed that had been made for her. He laid her down and pulled a blanket over her.

"Sleep and rest, my love," he whispered and kissed her forehead gently.

The list seemed to be never-ending. Scetis reviewed the paper in front of him as he walked to his quarters. The Chamberlain had tried to move him into his father's old quarters, but he felt that it was too soon, especially as they still had to lay Urmond to rest. He opened his door, noting that the damage Squirt had done breaking it in, was now repaired, and shut it behind him. Inside, all was in order, there had been little that needed to be moved and it had all been put back into place by the staff of the castle shortly after he had given the command.

He glanced at the papers in his hands again, noting with satisfaction that a group had already been sent out of the realm to help Farmer Uen and his son Pont with their harvest. Also that rooms were being made ready for the father and son in the palace so Pont's leg could be seen to. The next in the pile was a letter from Rozenn and Elpin, agreeing to visit as honored guests at the upcoming celebrations. He smiled and wondered what some of the lords and ladies of the court would make of this pair.

Another thought invaded his mind. The questions of what to do with Domnall and Princess Rionach. The pair were still being held in the dungeons far below the citadel. When Orcades had been broken free it appeared that he had happily left them behind. When Scetis had interviewed Rionach she only had nasty things to say about her son. They would need to be dealt with soon.

Scetis placed the list of things to do the next day on the table by the fire, which was already lit and dancing merrily, sending out much needed warmth into the cold room. He turned to the side table and began to pour himself a drink from the carafe of wine which sat there. Picking up the glass he studied the contents within and noted that there was a swirl that should not be there. He placed it back down on the table and sighed.

"Come out, Loxa," his voice was loud in the quiet room.

"I don't have your adeptness in poisons, yet," Loxa spoke behind him.

Turning slowly, he was ready to react to anything that the man could do.

"There is no such thing as a poison, only a wrong dose. I thought I taught you that," he said conversationally. "I see you've learned enough to keep you alive."

"I took precautions before even going to that meeting. You were a bit predictable in your choice." Loxa reached into his jacket and pulled out the knife that Scetis had thrown at him. "Nice blade, well balanced and highly honed. You know it didn't really hurt as it entered me."

"I'm pleased it meets your approval."

"You killed my whole family," Loxa accused him quietly, flipping the blade in his hand.

"Not your whole family. I believe your grandmother died by your cousin's hand. And as for your father—he didn't have a lot of experience with dragons. And while we are throwing accusations around, there is the matter of my whole life that '*family*' took away from me!"

Loxa was quick but not quick enough for Scetis. He had been waiting for the throw and it came just when he thought it would. The blade sped through the air without a sound, just as it had been designed to do and missed his ear as he ducked down. Scetis' hand went to his boot and the replacement knife he had placed there only that morning. It was out of its hidden sheath in the heel of his boot and spun through the air. It was a move that Loxa had not foreseen, he had thought that now peace was assured, Scetis would have become complacent. He looked down in shock at the handle protruding from his chest. Blood began to seep out and spread quickly through the fabric of his shirt, a dark red stain that dripped down. He grabbed the handle and pulled the knife out, bringing a splatter of red droplets with it, spraying the carpet in front of him. The color in his face drained quickly to a pallid white and he looked up at Scetis with wide eyes. A gurgle escaped his lips and foaming blood dribbled from his mouth.

Scetis stood and watched this man, the boy he had taken under his wing and thought he could trust. The knife tumbled from his failing grip and he sank to his knees, toppling over onto his side. Loxa's lips started changing to a shade of purple, a symptom of the poison that now coursed through his dying body. Scetis waited only a moment more, waiting for the last tell-tale sign of the poison, a yellowing of the eyes as the life left them. As soon as he saw it, he reached for the bell pull to call someone to his rooms. Stepping quickly over to the door, he opened it and waited for the page who was assigned to him, that same boy who served his father.

"Fetch a guard would you, Naiton? I seem to have a problem. Also could you send one of the cleaners, preferable someone with a strong constitution. I'm afraid there is a little bit of a mess," he said calmly. Naiton looked passed Scetis at the prone body of his would-be assassin.

"Yes, sire. I can see you have a bit of a problem," he replied and went to do his king's bidding.

"That boy will go far," Scetis said to himself and went back into his room.

Using the cloth that sat by his basin, he picked up the small knife and placed it in the basin. He poured the water in the matching jug over the knife and then opened the drawer underneath. He pulled out a vial and tipped the contents into the water, turning it blue on contact.

A rush of feet heralded the approach of guards and when he turned it was to find Venicones and Ide both rushing in. They stopped and stared at the prone lifeless body of Loxa.

"Well, that solves that little problem," Venicones said as he knelt down beside the man.

"Don't touch any of his blood, it's contaminated by a very nasty poison," Scetis warned him.

"I presumed it would be. I sent Naiton to fetch an undertaker as well," he said standing again.

"Are you alright?" Ide asked, coming to his side.

"I'm fine. He didn't touch me." Automatically he placed his arms around Ide and pulled her close, feeling the need of her comfort and touch.

"The sooner we get you crowned and married off, the better," Venicones said and left them alone for a moment.

Conclusion

High above the citadel a large emerald dragon circled stiffly and the riders on his back willed him on to the Eyrie. Gremlin landed heavily after passing through the sky windows into the long gallery and Teagan and Muniath slipped from his back quickly. They walked slowly, his strength still not quite returned and sapped from the long flight back to the valley of the Dragon Realm's seat. He turned and headed into a chamber, with the inside already lit and a bed made for his comfort. Wick stood and went to his side as Gremlin lay down, checking on the wound which was still unhealed.

"Rest, Gremlin," Teagan said as she kissed the dragon's head.

"King Scetis has already taught me what to do next with his wound. If you want to leave him with me, I can start," Wick spoke softly to Muniath.

"Do you need a hand?"

"I can manage. You see to Lady Teagan," he suggested. Muniath nodded his assent and put an arm around Teagan, walking her out of the chamber.

"If there is anything, you call me," Teagan instructed the young man.

"I will, my Lady," he promised, already turning to the task at hand.

It had been four days since Gremlin had been injured and Teagan had been awake for most of it. She now stumbled on the smoothed rock under her feet and Muniath caught her, lifting her up into his arms. His own steps were labored with his increasing tiredness as he carried her to the entrance of the Eyrie.

"Muniath," a call came from behind him, and he stopped. Fleet came bustling up out of the shadows along with Sting. *"Can we help?"* she asked with a loud whisper.

"I can carry her down for you, if you want?" Sting asked confidently.

"And I can carry you, I've been practicing, and I am stronger," Fleet added.

"Your help would be most gratefully received," he told the two dragons. There had been a change in the pair since the battle. Now both deemed adults they still had more growing to do until they would reach their full size.

Gently, he lifted Teagan on the back of Sting. "Be careful," he needlessly instructed the young dragon.

The pair, now burdened with their charges, lifted into the air and Muniath had to agree that Fleet was indeed stronger. She flew more confidently as they made their way down to the castle and the wyvern gate. As Muniath was helping Teagan off the back of Sting, Squirt came to meet them.

"Let me help," he asked, his arms already outstretched to take Teagan from Muniath.

"Thank you, Squirt." Muniath handed her into the safe arms of the small dragon and followed behind him. "Thank you two, also," he said to the brother and sister, who nodded back to him and flew off, back to the Eyrie to check on their brother.

Teagan was soon put to bed, after a long bath. She lay back on the soft pillows and was soon asleep. Muniath stayed at her side for a moment to make sure she was resting and then headed to his own quarters. After bathing himself he sat in his chair, his head back with his eyes closed. The events of the last week seemed to roll into one as he finally allowed himself to think about it. In fact, they seemed to be one long event since being woken from his drunken stupor by his brother. It seemed so long ago.

A soft tap at the door brought him back and his eyes opened. He rushed to the door and flung it open, expecting to see Wick or someone summoning him back up to the Eyrie. Standing before him was his brother, Venicones.

"Welcome back," he said with a smile and seeing the concern on his younger brother's face, it slipped. "Don't worry, Wick is looking after Gremlin, I checked on him before I came down."

"Thank god." Muniath sighed and stepped back into his room, with Venicones following.

"How's Teagan?"

"Sleeping, hopefully." Muniath collapsed back into his chair and ran weary hands over his face.

"It looks like you should be too." Venicones studied his brother and sat on the edge of his bed.

"I will, soon. Is this a social call?"

"Of sorts. I came to check on you and to let you know that father wants to see you when you have recovered. He said that there was no rush."

"I'll see him in the morning."

"That would be a good idea. Also, I came to get a bit of advice from you," Venicones said slowly.

"From me? This is a strange occurrence."

"Yes, and probably won't happen again, so make the most of it." Venicones gave a chuckle.

"What's the problem?"

"I want to ask Meara for her hand. But I'm afraid she will say no."

"You're asking the wrong person, shouldn't you be talking to her father, or her son?" Muniath gave his brother a wink.

"I already have, but they both laughed at me."

"And said what after?"

"That I should."

"There's your answer then, you don't really need me to tell you what to do. You've loved her for a long time, since we were all kids together. You stood back and watched as she was courted and wed Nabarus. You never tried to get between them once, instead you let her follow her heart." Muniath paused a moment. "When I was in my drunken state at her place, she would come and tidy a little, when she thought I was asleep. She would prattle on to me, not just how I was wasting my life, but about her hopes and dreams. She may think I have forgotten some of our conversations when I did respond, but I remember it all. We would always wind up talking about you. She holds a flame that has been ignited about as long as yours has been for her. Go see her, Ven. Go be happy."

"Really?" Venicones asked skeptical at first.

"Really. In this matter I would not tease or lie to you," Muniath said solemnly.

Venicones stood and headed straight for the door, it opened quickly, and he stopped on the threshold. "Thank you, Mun."

"You're welcome." Muniath watched him go and then stood himself. Taking the short steps to the bed seemed to take a lifetime and he collapsed on top of it, asleep as his head touched the pillow.

The sound of many horns filled the air around the citadel and echoed around the valley. The music swelled and seemed to travel through the many halls, following the pair as they walked hand in hand. Ide squeezed Scetis' hand gently and with some encouragement as they made their way to the grand throne room. The doors opened wide and the sound of the crowd inside died down as they stood at the entrance, then took their first steps onto the red carpet that led to the matching thrones at the other end. The mighty white columns that supported the high vaulted roof were decorated with garlands of flowers wound around them and large golden sheets of cloth were draped over the balustrade of the two platforms on either side.

Scetis did not see any of these decorations as he and Ide walked side by side towards the Chief Councilor at the other end. Councilor Conghaile was not dressed in her normal black of office, but in red with a white trim. As Scetis walked, he could feel Ide holding him back, and he checked his stride, aware suddenly of how eager he was to get this all done with. The events of the day before, and now today were beginning to take their toll on him.

The state funeral for Urmond had been delayed, not only for dignitaries from other realms to travel to the Dragon Realm, but also for Lady Teagan and Muniath to recover. Gremlin was still gaining strength and Scetis himself went up once a day to check on his progress. He was very impressed with Wick's work and care of the dragon. The boy had a real talent for herbs. He made a mental note to himself to make sure he spent more time with the young man to instruct him properly. His mind wandered further as he thought about it and decided that the Realm needed its own college of medicine rather than relying on the Convocation.

A tug on his hand brought his mind back to what he was supposed to be doing. The couple had reached the steps to the thrones and they began the short climb up to them. Reaching the matching chairs, which he had hastily changed the night before, because the previous was only a single chair, they turned and faced the room full of people. Their many hues of colors in their robes and dress swam before him in an almost undulating sea. 'Like one of my hallucinations when I was sick,' he thought.

The Chief Councilor stood before them now. She smiled at them both and began the ceremony. The words she spoke washed over Scetis and he wasn't sure if Ide took much in either. He answered her questions when prompted, hoping that he did so clearly and carefully, as they had rehearsed, and then she declared them married. The cheer that went up from the crowd was a large one and a fanfare of horns sounded the news to the waiting crowd outside who added to the din of celebration.

Once it was all over, Chief Councilor Conghaile faced them once more. This time flanked by two pages, dressed in the traditional ceremonial garb of white breeches, with an emerald-green stripe up the right leg. A tight-fitting vest of the same color was worn over a gold linen shirt, each having been highly starched and pressed that very morning for the pages to wear. The pair held a cushion each before them and a crown sat on top of each. They were matching, a circlet of thin gold, with the only decoration an etching of a dragon around it. The pages took their roles very seriously and felt the great honor of being chosen. One was Naiton, his own page, and the other one Naiton had suggested to be Ide's page. A boy of similar age and obviously his best friend.

Conghaile turned and spoke to the crowd, informing them now of Scetis' decision for both himself and Ide to rule jointly. Many nodded their agreement, while a few others frowned slightly. This did not surprise him, some just did not like change.

The promises made to serve the Realm above their own wants and wishes, the crowns gently bestowed on each head, Scetis finally relinquished his bride's hand. Before they took up their thrones for the first time, Scetis pulled out of his jacket a necklace. With trembling hands he placed the pendant he had purchased from Elpin around Ide's neck. The emerald stone seemed to glow as it touched her skin and he kissed her gently. As the new ruling couple sat, a fanfare blared around them and the noise of cheering crowds from both outside and in rose to the rafters, filling the halls with jubilation and celebration. Scetis let out a final breath.

'The hard work is just beginning,' he thought to himself.

"I can't believe they let that beast in here," an overweight man of some middle years said loudly, then downed a goblet of the finest wine. A plate with the scattered remains of the feast sat before him, showing how much he had partaken in the festivities.

Muniath paused for a moment and looked over to where Squirt was seated, in a place of honor at the head table and talking with Conghaile. He bent down between this man and the woman he had made the comment to and spoke quietly to him. "My good sir, I mean no disrespect when I say, that you in turn are disrespecting our new monarchs. Councilor Audel has the King and the Queen's good favor and ear. I suggest you get used to seeing him in the halls from this time on, and I dare say, many more like him. This is the DRAGON Realm after all." He did not wait for the reaction of either of the guests but left quickly, heading back to his seat at the main table, beside Teagan.

The Lady Teagan Loinsigh was dressed in the deepest of green, which set off her flaming hair beautifully. She had recovered in the last couple of days and now in the flickering light of candles on the table, he could see the iridescent colors playing over her skin. They were mesmerizing and intoxicating to him. As he sat he picked up her hand and kissed it. Their discussion the previous night came back to them both and she blushed. He had asked and she had accepted. The love for this woman burst through his heart and set it on fire. The sudden need to sing it to the rooftops and shout about it all over town suddenly came over him, escaping in the form of a grin.

Venicones had come to him the day after they had spoken with news that Meara had agreed to marry him. They sat together now, holding hands, and talking quietly to each other. His sister was now married to Scetis and he could see that it was definitely meant to be. He could not be happier for her. And now his own happiness was complete. Tharain, who had been recalled from his exile by Scetis, had readily agreed to the match when Muniath had approached him.

Tharain himself was also happy. In amongst the papers left on Urmond's desk, Scetis had found a formal pardon for the once General of Riders. He had set about sending for Tharain without anyone knowing and presented the document to him formally, with Teagan at his side. The old man wept. He had grown stronger on the farm holding, preferring to tend to it himself rather than sit back and let someone else do the work. He was stronger, healthier, and better for it. When he was offered rooms back in the castle again, he turned it down, preferring his little home in the valley.

Muniath glanced over at the man who was to be his father-in-law and saw him talking with his own father and mother. Their friendship was still sound, and it gladdened his heart that it would continue.

"Mun?" Teagan said quietly, gaining his attention.

"Yes, my love?" he replied, still holding her hand.

"I asked you if you wanted to go for a ride tonight. Gremlin wants to stretch his wings."

"I like the idea," he agreed readily.

"We can sneak out soon." She smiled radiantly, the colors shifting over her skin.

"Why not now?" Muniath whispered. "We won't be missed."

Teagan nodded and was already rising from her seat, pulling him along with her. They headed out into the garden by the Throne room, the moons' light brightening the paths between the formal beds.

"Do you remember when we first met?" Muniath asked her, his arm going around her shoulder.

"It was here. Father was seeing the King about the dragon eggs. I was sent out here with you to keep an eye on me," she replied.

"Who would have thought that we would be here now." He stopped and turned her towards him, his arms holding her close.

"Who would have thought." Teagan echoed.

475

L.C. Conn grew up on the outskirts of Upper Hutt, New Zealand. Her backyard encompassed the surrounding farmland, river, hills and mountains which she wandered with her brothers and fed her imagination. After discovering a love for writing in English class at the age of eight, she continued to write in secret. It was not until much later in life that L.C. turned what she thought was a hobby and something fun to do, into her first completed novel. Now married, L.C. moved from New Zealand to Perth, Western Australia, and became a stay-at-home mum. While caring for her family and after battling breast cancer, a story was born from the kernel of a dream. The first book of The One True Child Series was begun, and just kept blooming into seven completed stories.

Connect with LC:

Facebook: https://www.facebook.com/LCConn

Instagram: l.c.conn

Twitter: https://twitter.com/ConnLoraine